BEHIND THE IRON

BEHIND THE IRON

A HANK FALLON WESTERN

William W. Johnstone

with J. A. Johnstone

PINNACLE BOOKS
Kensington Publishing Corp.
www.kensingtonbooks.com

PINNACLE BOOKS are published by

Kensington Publishing Corp.
119 West 40th Street
New York, NY 10018

PUBLISHER'S NOTE
Following the death of William W. Johnstone, the Johnstone family is working with a carefully selected writer to organize and complete Mr. Johnstone's outlines and many unfinished manuscripts to create additional novels in all of his series like The Last Gunfighter, Mountain Man, and Eagles, among others. This novel was inspired by Mr. Johnstone's superb storytelling.

ISBN-13: 978-0-7860-4211-1
ISBN-10: 0-7860-4211-7

First printing: November 2018

10 9 8 7 6 5 4 3 2 1

Printed in the United States of America

First electronic edition: November 2018

ISBN-13: 978-0-7860-4212-8
ISBN-10: 0-7860-4212-5

Chapter One

The little man in the extremely large—and very brown—office opened a drawer. He pulled out a file.

"This," the small man said, "might interest you."

What interested Harry Fallon right then was this thought about killing the man, and the little man's son, in the Chicago office, but Fallon didn't. Fallon would have to get past the other men outside the office doors, and out of Chicago. And then what? Besides, Harry Fallon still needed that pathetic, tiny man.

"It's right up your line of work, Fallon," the small man with the big head and big ideas said. "I've found your niche."

Fallon walked back to the large desk and the small man.

"And what," Fallon said, "is my niche?"

The small man grinned over his foul-smelling cigar. "Going to prison. And getting out."

Harry Fallon felt older than his thirty-three years.

With a heavy sigh, Fallon found the chair in front

of the sprawling desk and sat. Grinning, the small man held the folder of papers in his little left hand.

The small man slid the folder across the massive desk.

Fallon opened the folder.

"Tired?" the small man asked.

Fallon felt no need to answer. Tired? Who wouldn't be exhausted? Just a short time ago, Harry Fallon had been at the Illinois State Penitentiary in Joliet, saving the lives of a few guards during a bloody riot, and that act of bravery, kindness, humanity—just a spur-of-the-moment decision, truthfully—had led to a parole for Harry Fallon, former deputy United States marshal for Judge Isaac Parker's court in Fort Smith, Arkansas. Fallon had been given a job at Werner's Wheelwright in Chicago and a place to live at Missus Ketchum's Boarding House near Lake Michigan. And then this small man had changed Fallon's life.

The small man was Sean MacGregor, president of this American Detective Agency, a man with dead, green eyes, and thinning orange hair streaked with silver. Sean MacGregor had a job he wanted Harry Fallon to handle, just a minor little bit of work. All Fallon had to do was break his parole—but MacGregor could make sure the authorities thought the ex-convict was living up to his agreement with the state of Illinois and the solicitor for the United States court. Go to Arizona Territory. Get arrested and sentenced to prison at Yuma Territorial Prison, also known as The Hellhole. Somehow make friends with Monk Quinn, a notorious felon and murderer who, six years earlier, had robbed a Southern Pacific train of some $200,000 in gold bullion. Escape from The Hellhole with Quinn. Cross the border into Mexico. And bring back Quinn, and any of his associates, dead or alive—preferably dead—and return the gold. So that Sean MacGregor and his American Detective Agency could reap the glory and the rewards.

Somehow, Fallon had managed to do most of that, although the gold bullion wound up being recovered by MacGregor's rival, the Pinkerton National Detective Agency.

Somehow, Harry Fallon had managed to live through it all. When he had left Chicago for Arizona Territory he was an inch over six feet tall and weighed ten pounds shy of two hundred. Big man. Leathery. Rock hard. You had to be big and tough to get out of Joliet in one piece. After that short while in Arizona and Mexico, Fallon had returned with a few more scars, some premature gray hair in his brown hair, and about twenty pounds lighter. It had not been the easiest assignment in Fallon's life—and Harry Fallon had pulled some rough jobs riding for Judge Parker all those years ago. His eyes remained brown. His eyes rarely missed anything.

"Remember our little agreement, Fallon," Sean MacGregor said in his thick Scottish accent.

You didn't forget a little agreement like that.

The little man reminded Fallon, one more damned time. "You want the man who framed you? You want the man who's responsible for the death of your family? You want that . . . you do this job for me." He put the big cigar between his thin lips. "Savvy?"

The American Detective Agency's offices could be found on the top floor of the building in Chicago. Harry Fallon didn't know exactly what part of Chicago. He had scarcely had time to even see much of the city—just the depot and Lake Michigan (and the American Detective Agency's offices, of course) before he had been waylaid and brought to see the small little man in the massive but Spartan office of brown paneling, brown rugs, brown tables, and brown filing cabinets, with one window where the brown drapes were pulled tightly shut.

There was some color to MacGregor's office, of course. The lamp on his desk and the others on the walls had green domes. And the ashtray on MacGregor's desk was silver. The color of the folder was tan, which Fallon figured was as close to brown or green as MacGregor could find.

Fallon looked at the top sheet of paper. His stomach and intestines twisted into knots, but he showed no emotion. He merely wet his lips and turned to the next page. "You're sending me back," Fallon said dryly.

"Closer to home," MacGregor said. "Your old home. It's not like I'm returning you to Joliet to finish the rest of your sentence. Which I could do." He blew a thick cloud of smoke toward the ceiling, leaned back in his green leather chair, and chuckled. "I could even have you killed. I've had lots of people killed. And nobody would mourn the loss of a rogue deputy marshal, a paroled convict. Would they?"

No, Fallon thought sadly. The two people who would have mourned Harry Fallon were dead and buried. His wife and daughter. Murdered. While Harry Fallon was sweating and hardening behind the walls of Joliet.

"Dan," MacGregor called out to his larger, more handsome son. "Fetch Marshal Fallon a slice of cherry pie, would you?"

"Yes, sir," MacGregor's son said. Fallon kept looking

at the pages. He heard the door open, saw some light filter into the dark brown room, before the door shut out the light and the fresh air. He went through the third sheet of paper and read the final page.

Carefully, he gathered the papers, tapped them on the big desk until they were even, and laid them back inside the folder, which he closed and left on the desk.

"Jefferson City," Fallon said.

"You've been there, I assume," MacGregor said.

"Just in passing."

"Well, you lived through Joliet and you survived Yuma. How hard could a little prison in a backwoods state like Missouri be compared to those two pens?"

Fallon stared. "The chances of someone recognizing me as a lawman or even a convict in Yuma were remote," he said. "But someone did recognize me in The Hellhole. Even though I'd never been in Arizona Territory till you sent me."

He tapped the folder. "I rode for Judge Parker's court in Arkansas and the Indian Nations. Missouri's just north of Arkansas. I arrested quite a few men who hailed from Missouri. I was born in Missouri. There's a pretty good chance that someone locked up there will know me."

"So what?" The small man dropped the cigar in the ashtray. "You're not the first badge-wearer to find himself behind bars. You can even use your own name this time. I don't think any warden or guard in Missouri will have enough brains or investigating skills to figure out that you're supposed to be on parole in the state of Illinois. And even if they do, they wouldn't be likely to give up a warm body and ship you back here to finish the completion of your original sentence. Be yourself, just another jailbird doing time."

The door opened. Light reappeared. The door shut. Darkness prevailed except for the lamps on the sprawling desk and the match that Sean MacGregor struck to light another one of his cheap, repugnant cigars.

Dan MacGregor slid a plate in front of Fallon.

"You like cherry pie?" Sean MacGregor said over his cigar.

"I prefer pecan," said Fallon, who hadn't tasted any dessert in years.

"Thaddeus Gripewater likes cherry pie," Dan MacGregor said. He spoke, unlike his father, without a trace of the Scottish Highlands. In the short time Fallon had met up with the MacGregors, he found few similarities between the two men.

Except this: A man would be wise not to trust either one of them. Fallon did not even think father and son trusted one another.

The younger man repeated the name: "Thaddeus Gripewater."

Fallon turned to look at the younger man. There had been no mention of any Thaddeus Gripewater in the four pages Fallon had just finished reading.

"Prison doctor at Jefferson City," Dan MacGregor explained casually but informatively. "You manage to get him a cherry pie, and he'll be putty in your hands, do anything for you, even get you to help him out in the prison."

He found the spoon and cut into the pie. He brought up some of the pie and smelled it.

"It's not poison, Fallon," Sean MacGregor said.

"There is some gin in it, though," Dan MacGregor

said. "Thaddeus Gripewater likes gin, too. Probably better than cherry pie. You use gin to make your pie, and you'll rule the infirmary ward at Jefferson City."

After all those years in prison, Fallon found sweets unpalatable, and he didn't trust himself with alcohol, even if it had likely burned off while baking. He set the spoon on the side of the plate. "Thaddeus," he said. "Gripewater."

"It's his real name," Sean MacGregor said. "As far as we've been able to ascertain."

"His parents should be the ones in prison," Dan MacGregor said.

"So I'm supposed to get gin and cherries in prison and somehow bake the good doctor a pie, and get it from my cell—I assume I'll be a prisoner, again, right?"

"Well," Dan MacGregor said, "it never occurred to us to try to get you in as a guard." He smiled.

"They don't hire parole violators or disgraced federal lawmen," the elder MacGregor said. He did not smile.

Harry Fallon did not smile, either. He glanced at the plate and realized why Dan MacGregor had brought a spoon, and not a fork, with the dessert. A man who had spent ten years in Joliet could use a fork like an Indian could use a knife. Fallon envisioned the fork being pulled out of Sean MacGregor's neck, with blood spraying the dark room from the dying man's jugular vein, then slamming the fork between Dan MacGregor's ribs and into his heart.

"You still owe me something for the Yuma job," Fallon said.

"I told you already," Sean MacGregor said. "I didn't collect enough money, thanks to those damned Pinkertons. And whoever tipped them off that we had the gold bullion." He stared hard at Fallon, but Fallon gave nothing away. "Your payment is that I don't send you back to Joliet . . ."

Fallon finished the sentence. Hell, he had heard it enough: ". . . or another facility for completion of my original sentence."

The small man flicked ash from his cigar and smiled. "That's right."

"It's not enough," Fallon said.

"Dan will tell you something on your way to the train depot," Sean MacGregor said. "When you're finished with this assignment, we'll get you out of Jefferson City and get you across the border and back to your lovely boardinghouse near Lake Michigan. It's beautiful in the fall. Colder than a witch's teat, but beautiful. You should be back by October."

"I see."

"Cold will feel mighty good, Fallon," the small man said, "after spending a few months in hell."

"Yeah."

"Finish your pie."

"The cherries are too tart. I'll find a better recipe."

"You won't find it at Missus Ketchum's Boarding House," Sean MacGregor said. "Her meals are like sawdust."

"I wouldn't know," Fallon said. Which was true. He had yet to see the place where the warden at the Illinois State Penitentiary thought he was living. Likewise, he had yet to meet his alleged employer, Werner. Fallon didn't even know the wheelwright's first name.

"Dan will fill you in on the particulars," Sean MacGregor said as he set the foul cigar on the gaudy ashtray. "Do we have an agreement?"

"It depends on what Dan tells me," Fallon said.

"Fair enough. Aaron Holderman will be delighted to escort you to Joliet . . ."

Aaron Holderman worked for the American Detective Agency, but Fallon had known him in Arkansas and the Indian Nations, where he had run whiskey to the Indians, drunk what he couldn't sell, and used his fists on men, women, and children. He had spent time in Joliet, in Cañon City, Colorado; in Angola, Louisiana. He was exactly the kind of investigator a corrupt operation like the American Detective Agency needed.

"Yeah," Fallon said, "for violation of my parole, to finish the completion of my original sentence."

"No." MacGregor picked up his cigar. "You will face a new judge. The Almighty. Holderman will just be sending your dead body back to confirm that it is indeed Harry Fallon."

CHAPTER TWO

Out in the hallway, Dan MacGregor waited for a few other operatives of the American Detective Agency to head into other rooms. When the hallway was empty, he turned to Fallon and said, "The warden's name is Harold Underwood. He's the only one who should know you're working for us. You'll want to keep it that way. If an inmate finds out you're a detective, you're dead."

Fallon waited. "Is that it?"

The tall, handsome man glanced at Aaron Holderman before his eyes fell back onto Fallon. "No. There's another reason we picked you for this job."

Fallon let out a chuckle that held no humor. "I thought it was because I know how to rot behind bars."

"Mr. MacGregor's a man of his word," Aaron Holderman said. "He said he'd help you find out who killed your family, who framed you, and got you sent to Joliet. You listen to him. He'll help you out."

Now Fallon turned to the brute wearing the bowler. The city hat was brown, as was the big man's ill-fitting suit. He probably wore brown to please the corrupt president of the American Detective Agency. The suit did not fit Holderman well, but even Chicago's best tailor would find it hard to outfit this mass of muscles.

Fallon studied Holderman, his mustache and beard, too brown it seemed to Fallon. The monster likely dyed his hair with shoe polish. The brass shield on his chest that identified him as a private detective was tarnished. The bulge underneath his left shoulder indicated a revolver. A Chicago billy club protruded from his brown boot. It would be hard for Holderman to run with a nightstick in his left boot. From the size of Holderman, though, it would be hard for him to run anyway.

Dan MacGregor, on the other hand, looked like he could run alongside a thoroughbred for six furlongs.

You're thinking of trying to escape, Fallon thought. *Stop it. You've a job to do. Just remember this is all for Renee. For Rachel. For justice.*

No, he was fooling himself. Ten years inside Joliet had changed him. He no longer wore a badge. Even the American Detective Agency had not pinned a shield on him. He was just being used. But Fallon kept figuring a way that he could use Sean MacGregor and his minions. But not for justice.

Revenge.

"What's the reason?" Fallon asked MacGregor.

"I'll tell you," the young detective said, "when I'm sure the walls aren't listening."

Holderman snorted.

Doors opened down the hallway, and voices became louder. Fallon could hear the footsteps behind him.

"All right," Fallon said.

MacGregor pointed. "Let's go."

They walked to the elevator. Aaron Holderman rang the button, and two awkwardly quiet minutes later the carriage arrived, the door opened, and the elderly black man said, "Headin' down, folks. Climb in."

Holderman moved in first, and Fallon started but felt something pull on the back of his vest.

"After you, Christina," Dan MacGregor said pleasantly, and gave a tall, attractive blonde woman his most handsome smile.

"Thank you, Dan," she said, and studied Fallon. "Who's your friend?"

"A lawman from way back," MacGregor said. "Working on a case with us."

She was already in the elevator. So were two other men. MacGregor let the last man, a thin man with huge spectacles, step inside, too, before he smiled at the black elevator man.

"You look crowded enough, Carlton," MacGregor told the black man. "And Holderman weighs more than three men and takes up the space of four. Run these good people down and come back up for us, will you?"

"Yes, suh."

"Aaron," MacGregor called out to the big detective. "Go on. Meet us at the depot. Make sure everything's ready."

"But . . ."

"Just do it," MacGregor said as the door closed.

He turned toward Fallon but said nothing until the creaking and clanging of the elevator revealed that it was at least two stories below them.

"There's one thing my father did not tell me to tell you, Hank," the handsome man said.

Hank, Fallon thought. *It's Hank now. Only my friends call me Hank.*

"Just one?" Fallon shot back.

MacGregor let out a genuine laugh. "One that I'm willing to share."

Fallon waited.

"Judge Parker sentenced you to fifteen years," MacGregor said.

Still, Fallon waited. He could hear the elevator begin its ascent to the top floor of the brownstone building.

"Parker was a federal judge." MacGregor's face showed no emotion. "So why were you sent to the Illinois State Penitentiary in Joliet and not the Detroit House of Corrections? Ever consider that?"

Fallon did not part his lips to respond.

"How many men did you send to Joliet? Other than Holderman, but if I remember right, you made that arrest in Illinois, after Holderman crossed the Mississippi around Cape Girardeau, and Illinois wanted him worse than Parker did."

That much was true. Fallon had arrested Holderman twice in the Indian Territory—another deputy had arrested him, too—but none of the charges ever stuck. So when Fallon had gone after Holderman all those years ago, across Arkansas, into Missouri, even into Kentucky briefly before back into Missouri, and finally into Illinois and made the arrest, he had found himself surrounded by some Illinois badge-wearers who wanted Holderman for stealing a horse, beating a blacksmith half to death, and robbing a Mason of three double eagles he had been taking to an orphanage.

MacGregor went on. "You were arrested for robbery

in the Creek Nation. They couldn't make the murder charge of that federal deputy against you, though the solicitor tried his hardest. That's a federal charge. Federal prisoners in that part of the country get shipped up to Detroit, Michigan. But you wound up in Joliet."

"So did Joey Kurth," Fallon said. Fallon had run into Kurth in Joliet.

"Yeah, but that was different," MacGregor said. "Kurth was arrested for running spirits and resisting arrest. But he was also wanted for a string of robberies in Beardstown, so Parker sent him to Illinois to be tried there, sentenced, and upon completion, returned to Fort Smith to get sentenced again. Just didn't happen."

Thanks to Kurth's untimely demise during the riots at Joliet.

"All right," Fallon said. "The way it was explained to me was that because I was a onetime lawman, with many, many men I had sent to prison serving their time—some of those sentences were for life—in Detroit, I was being sent to Joliet for my own safety." He shook his head, felt the gall rising again, and said again, his voice acid now: "Safety."

"Parker threw the book at you. You think he cared about your safety? He figured you betrayed him. From what I've read, Parker got you that job as a deputy marshal. He even talked you into reading for the bar. When you were accused of robbing that stagecoach, he felt like he'd been stabbed in the back."

The elevator arrived. The mechanical sounds echoed across the hallway.

"Did it matter where I wound up?" Fallon said. "Detroit. Joliet. Neither one is quite the Drovers Cottage."

The doors began opening. "Chris Ehrlander was your lawyer, wasn't he?"

Fallon nodded.

The black man in the red jacket reappeared. "You ready, suh?" he asked MacGregor.

"Interesting," MacGregor said, keeping his eyes on Fallon, before he turned around. "Yes, Carlton. My friend here has a train to catch."

On the loud, grease-smelling elevator ride to the ground floor, visions of Judge Isaac Parker . . . of Renee DeSmet Fallon . . . of attorney Chris Ehrlander . . . of faces of men he had known as a lawman and as an inmate . . . all flashed through Fallon's mind.

MacGregor stared at the black elevator man in the red jacket. Fallon studied the back of Dan MacGregor's head. He remembered the man from some university in Illinois who had stopped in at the marshal's office in Fort Smith. The man talked to the marshal, the federal prosecutor, and the deputies who happened to be in town about how the shape of a man's skull could determine if that man were a criminal or a decent person. Fallon and everyone else in that room had figured the man was no better than the confidence men with their shell games, marked decks, and rigged faro layouts, but now as he stared at Dan MacGregor's head, he tried to remember exactly what shapes the Illinois professor had said meant a man was a criminal.

The elevator came to an abrupt stop, and the jolt seemed to return Fallon's faculties.

He thanked the black man as he followed Dan MacGregor to the front door of the brownstone building. They stepped onto the sidewalk.

Chicago was crowded at this time of day. Fallon walked alongside Dan MacGregor. Neither man spoke, they simply bent into the wind and moved along with the herd of people.

This city wasn't for him. Too many people. No sense of order. No guard telling him where he needed to go or when he could hit the privy to relieve his bladder. No rolling hills and clear water of the Indian Nations. No wife. No daughter. And after spending what seemed like an eternity in that Hellhole called Yuma Territorial Penitentiary, after enduring the Snake Den, and some of the most ruthless cutthroats Fallon had ever seen—after escaping to Mexico and witnessing more carnage and destruction—Fallon just did not fit in with women in their bloomers and fine hats, men in their Prince Albert coats and shiny black leather shoes carrying grips and cases or umbrellas—even though the skies seemed clear.

"Here," MacGregor said, and he turned down another street, not as crowded, but far from deserted.

Why doesn't he hail a hack? Fallon thought. *It is a damned long walk from here to the depot.*

Another turn. Another. And then one more that led them down a narrow alley. A cat screamed, leaped out of a stinking can of trash, and bolted between Fallon and MacGregor.

MacGregor smiled, but the smile faded instantly.

The cat wasn't alone in the alley.

Four men came from behind a mountain of trash. Two carried baseball bats. Brass knuckles reflected off the tallest man. The fourth wielded a knife.

Fallon glanced behind him. Two other men, armed with revolvers, approached from the side street.

Chapter Three

"You carrying a gun?" MacGregor whispered.

"I don't have one of your brass shields," Fallon said. "And it's illegal to carry a weapon in Chicago, especially for a hard-timer out on parole."

The four men coming down the alley began to spread out.

"You have a gun," Fallon said, adding, hopefully, "Don't you?"

"Not to see you off at the station, Hank."

Fallon's mouth began to dry up like spit in the Arizona desert. "My friends call me Hank," Fallon said. He stepped away from the detective and began easing his way to the approaching four men. "You take the ones coming up the alley," he told the detective.

"There are only two of them," MacGregor said.

"Yeah," Fallon said. "But I have experience in this kind of fighting." He glanced back and gave the young man a slight smile. "Besides, chances are, one of those two has a gun."

A cat screeched, stopping Fallon's advance—and the approach of the four toughs—and the feral animal bolted off a box of garbage, started toward Fallon, hissed, its hair rising like spines on a cactus, spun around, and raced toward the four men.

The one with the brass knuckles laughed as the cat ran between him and one of the men with a baseball bat. He laughed because the man yelped and dropped the bat.

"Yer as yeller as a petticoat," said the one with the knuckles.

"Shut up!" The big brute bent to pick up the rolling bat.

The one with the knife said something in some rough language, not German, but something European.

"Let's get to it," said the tallest of the four, and he stopped slapping the thick part of the bat with his meaty left palm, and gripped the narrow end, just above the knob, with both of his ham-sized hands.

Behind Fallon came the noise of a curse, shriek, and glass breaking, then flesh meeting flesh. MacGregor had started the row with those two other men, but Fallon dared not look behind him. He spread his legs wider, controlled his breathing, made sure he did not blink, and waited for the four men to get closer.

They spread out as far as they could, which wasn't that much considering how narrow the alley was, and how many piles of reeking trash had been started along the brick walls.

That feral cat had stopped Fallon at the narrowest passage in the alley, where only three men could get through at a time. So, Fallon figured, this seemed as good as any place to wait. Three-against-one was better than four-against-one. He studied the trash near and all around him. He listened to the commotion behind him. He thought that maybe, just maybe, a Chicago copper might hear the ruckus and start blowing his whistle, or, even better, firing his revolver. But in this part of town, he figured, peace officers made themselves scarce.

The four men reached the mountain of refuse. The man wearing the Irish woolen cap and carrying a baseball bat stopped, nodded at the one with the brown corduroy coat who sported the brass knuckles. These two stepped down the narrow pathway. The Pole with the knife and the skinniest one with the baseball bat let the first two come about halfway through the garbage, maybe three feet, before they started in behind them.

That's when Fallon's left hand brought up the rusty horseshoe that was lying atop a busted wooden crate standing longways up, and let it fly. The horseshoe slammed into the center of the face of the man with the brass knuckles. He cried out, and spit out blood and bits of teeth, as more blood ran over the tarnished knuckledusters and his stumps of gnarled fingers.

Someone—Fallon didn't know which one, and he didn't give a damn which one—cursed. The man with the busted face slammed against the trash heap on his left. His work boots flew out in front of him, tripping the first of the baseball-bat slingers, and toppled over to his side, still covering his face.

By that time, Fallon had grabbed the busted crate. He thought he read a label proclaiming PEACHES, but he wasn't sure. After he brought the crate down on the head of the man who was trying to push himself to his feet and grab the bat he had dropped, Fallon would never know what the crate originally carried.

The wood splintered, sending chunks of wood back toward the remaining two thugs. The soft cap did nothing to lessen the blow, and the man fell back over the first brute's legs. He lay unconscious. The one with the busted face sobbed, cursed, and kept spitting out blood, teeth and maybe a piece of his tongue.

The fellow with the second baseball bat tried to charge through the passage but tripped as the first baseball-bat slinger crashed in front of him.

His bat disappeared in the heap of two-bit muggers, and as he came toward Fallon, Fallon brought his right knee up. It caught the wailing, waving fool in his chin. From the sound of the crunch, Fallon figured he had broken the man's jaw. Still, just to make sure, he slammed two more punches into the man's head just as he crashed against more trash, sending old cans and bottles empty of everything but rainwater and urine spilling onto the mud, dirt, and grime.

This wasn't the first time Fallon had gone into a fight outnumbered. Before he had pinned on a deputy marshal's badge, he had cowboyed on herds heading to Kansas, and many a waddie always enjoyed a good round of fisticuffs to help celebrate a long trail drive of eating dust and smelling cow dung for months on end. Fallon couldn't remember the number of saloons he had busted to pieces, or the eyes he had blackened or lips he had split wide open.

As a deputy marshal, there had been more fights. Some Fallon had won. More than he would care to remember he had lost. Fort Smith, Arkansas, wasn't populated by Quakers, after all, and the Indian Nations were home to some buckets of blood and inns that were worse than some of those joints Fallon had visited in Kansas as a kid.

Those had seasoned Harry Fallon. Ten years in Joliet, on the other hand, had finished his education in the ways to use one's fists, knees, elbows, fingers, head, teeth and turn anything from a pencil or a spoon to a pillow or a piece of paper into the deadliest of weapons.

A knife? Hell, nobody at Joliet was scared of a knife. Fallon didn't even need a weapon to meet the last of the four goons who had challenged him.

He picked up the bigger of the two bats, however. It wasn't like their original owners had use for them anymore.

As soon as he realized that Fallon had the baseball bat, the giant with the knife backed up. Harry Fallon hurdled over the mass of moaning or unconscious men, slipped on the wet ground, but slammed against the trash, sending old newspapers, magazines, and who could tell what, bouncing off the surface. Somehow, Fallon managed to keep his feet, and he sucked in his gut as the knife swept past his stomach.

The thug had taken a desperate swipe upon realizing that Fallon had stumbled. He muttered something in his native tongue as the momentum of his desperate swing took him spinning toward some rotting woolen blankets.

Fallon started toward the last of the men, but something grabbed his foot, twisted it, and down went Fallon. He rolled over and saw the one who had eaten the rusted horseshoe had stopped whimpering. Despite his contorted, bloody, ugly and ruined face, the man had found enough strength to climb beneath his two unconscious colleagues. He spit red saliva. Hatred filled his eyes. His knuckledusters remained on his right hand. His left, however, gripped a derringer.

The angry villain brought the little pocket pistol up.

Lying on his back, hearing the goon with the knife scrambling to his feet, Fallon brought his left leg up, bending it at the knee, and sent his bootheel smashing into the face of the man with the knuckledusters and the derringer. That blow caught the vermin in his forehead, sparing Fallon's footwear most of the blood, and letting that pathetic criminal join three of his pals in unconsciousness.

Fallon thought about scrambling for the derringer. But he knew he didn't have that much time. In fact, he had no time.

He rolled over, saw the flash of the blade, and this time brought both of his legs up. His hands shot up and somehow managed to grab the rock-hard wrist just below the big knife. His knees, calves, and boots stopped the rest of the giant's body from crushing his chest. Fallon rocked backward and sent his legs—and the big man—over his head. His hands let go of the man with the knife. He watched the big man somersault and land on his back on the heaping pile of his three comrades.

Instantly, the big man rolled over. Fallon was rolling, too. He saw that the man still gripped the knife. Fallon sucked in a deep breath, let it out, and grabbed the baseball bat as he backed out of the narrow passageway. His chest heaved again, and with more room to operate, he used the bat to help push himself back to his feet.

Still in the six-foot-long canyon of trash and other foul matter, the tough came at him, crouching, slashing the knife left to right, then right to left. The man grinned, but Fallon knew the criminal was hurting.

On the other hand, Fallon wasn't feeling all that good himself.

The big man straightened when he had cleared the trash piles. Fallon looked up into the man's pale eyes. He had to look way up. This giant had to be at least six-foot-six, and his shoes were flat.

"Hell," Fallon said, and would have added—*What do you need a knife for?*—had it not hurt so much when all he had said was *Hell.*

He shot a quick glance behind him, but found no policemen coming to his rescue and few passersby on the street at the other end. He looked beyond the goon and the trash and could barely make out Dan MacGregor still tangling with one or two of the remaining thugs. His eyes rapidly came back to the grinning behemoth.

Fallon brought the bat up, made a feint with it at the man's belly. The man did not flinch.

The blade slashed. Fallon jumped back and almost dropped the bat.

The giant laughed.

Fallon recovered, but did not wait a moment longer. He charged, swinging the bat, causing the big brute—shocked by the unexpected attack—to stumble back toward the trash. But Fallon stepped on a bottle, and that sent him sailing toward the ground. He had to drop the bat and send his hands out to break his fall.

He hit hard, rolled over, saw the man coming at him again. Desperately, he reached out for the bat, but couldn't find it. He thought about trying to bring his legs up again. Instead, he rolled to his left, over the bat, and saw the attacker stumble past him. The brute must have been expecting Fallon to try to flip him over his head again with his legs.

Whatever the reason, the few seconds Fallon had were all he needed to pick up the bat.

The man spun around, shifted the knife to his left hand, and stopped. He was sweating, too, and breathing hard. He grinned and spread his legs.

That's what gave Fallon the idea.

He brought the bat down to his right side and used his left hand to wipe his brow. He breathed in deeply and as he exhaled, he brought the baseball bat up hard, savagely, and caught the fool right between the legs.

The man's face went white. The knife clattered on the ground as the giant's hands reached for his groin, and as the man sank to his knees, Fallon brought the baseball bat up, lifted it above his head, and started to bring it down on the head of the big man, who now leaned over and vomited.

Chapter Four

He couldn't do it.

Harry Fallon had buffaloed men with the barrels or handles of revolvers before. It was a good method to knock a man out, or at least get a fellow's attention. But he had known a few lawmen who had clubbed a drunk too hard with the pistol and left those men dead—or wishing they were dead—instead of just knocked out. A baseball bat? Even considering the size of the big Pole, Fallon thought the bat might kill the leviathan.

Joliet and Yuma had hardened Fallon—but not that much.

He brought the bat up, leaned the top half across his shoulder, and was starting to turn toward MacGregor and his muggers.

That's when the bullet splintered the bat and sent Fallon to the ground.

He lay there trying to shake the feeling back into his right hand. And Fallon realized that he had been right when he had told Dan MacGregor that one or both of the criminals coming up the alley might be carrying a pistol.

Seeing the splintered bat, Fallon realized that by not clubbing the giant with the bat, and instead bringing it down, well, that might have saved his life. Otherwise that bullet might have hit Fallon in the neck, throat, or head.

The big tough was on all fours, still out of the fight—for now, at least—so Fallon rolled over toward the towering, sprawling trash heap. He heard footsteps as the two men ran toward him. No, Fallon figured out a moment later. Not two. Just one.

He stopped rolling and stopped near the trash heap, rising no more than to his knees and hands. The feet kept pounding. Yes, one man.

Fallon started for the entrance to the passageway. One thought almost made him stop.

Could the man running toward him be Dan MacGregor?

Another thought followed:

Had this been some kind of setup to get me killed?

No. That made no sense. And even if that were true, it did not matter.

A running man was maybe twenty feet from Fallon, and that man certainly meant to kill Fallon.

Then, Fallon remembered the derringer.

He crawled rapidly and dived to the entranceway through the trash heaps. The derringer lay on the ground amid the tangled mess of flesh, clothing, trash, and blood. Fallon dived again. His right hand gripped the cold pearl handles of the silver-plated belly gun. He brought the weapon up just as one of the other two brutes appeared in the opposite entrance through the canyon of garbage.

Fallon heard a little pop, and his fingers and palm

warmed suddenly. The man screamed. Something whined. Glass shattered.

Fallon came up, squeezed the trigger again, sending lead from both barrels at the other assassin. The man was on his knees, gripping his stomach and muttering for his mother. Harry didn't see any blood seeping between the mugger's fingers. The little pistol the thug was carrying lay on the ground, next to the other baseball bat.

"Gawd a'mighty," the man said, as he started to straighten.

Fallon stepped over the mounds of men who remained unconscious, bent to pick up the pistol—it was a small Smith & Wesson hideaway gun—lifted it over his head, and when the man stopped clutching his belly and looked up, Fallon brought the weapon down.

Not hard enough to kill the idiot. At least, Fallon hoped he didn't. The man groaned and slid against the trash heap briefly before he joined his colleagues. Fallon noticed the big brass buckle on a belt that held a holster for the little Smith & Wesson and a pouch, probably for ammunition, on the other hip. The buckle was dented. Apparently, one or both bullets from that derringer Fallon had picked up had struck this one in his midsection.

"Lucky," Fallon told him, though the man couldn't hear anything right now. "Otherwise you'd be gutshot and dying real slow."

Fallon looked down the alley. Dan MacGregor lay spread-eagled between a makeshift tent of newspapers, petticoats, and an old, rat-chewed yellow rain slicker, and the other one of the criminals. He hoped MacGregor was just unconscious. At this point, he really didn't give a damn about the fellow on the ground next to the detective.

That reminded Fallon about the big cuss, so he waded across the other men, cleared the canyon, and saw the brute crawling his way toward the opposite street. Fallon caught up with him and cracked the barrel of the Smith & Wesson against the back of the giant's skull. He had to do it again before the man groaned and fell onto his face.

He was, Fallon was reassured to see, still breathing.

As he walked back through the trash canyon, he broke open the Smith & Wesson and looked at the cylinder.

"Hell," he said in disgust. Only three shells—though the .32-caliber popgun could hold six—and all three had been fired. He snapped the cylinder shut, glanced at MacGregor and the other unconscious thug several yards down the alley, and stopped beside the one who had been carrying the pistol.

Fallon squatted, pushed back the linen duster, and opened the pouch on the unconscious man's left hip. He swore again. The pouch did not carry .32-caliber cartridges for a Smith & Wesson hideaway gun.

Thinking that he might find or even buy bullets to fit the .32, Fallon shoved the pistol into his waistband and looked and felt again inside the pouch. He came out with a cigar, tossed it on the ground, and reached in again. This time he brought out a double eagle. He found another twenty-dollar gold coin in the pouch, too.

These, he pocketed, and as he stood, he glanced at the cigar. He stopped, bent down, and picked up the cigar. A bum, or a brute like this, Fallon expected to be keeping a well-used, soggy cigar, but this one still had the wrapper around it and had not yet been clipped—not that a mugger would have known to clip a good cigar first.

As he rose, Fallon brought the cigar under his nose. It smelled strong. He walked toward MacGregor but first stopped at the unconscious man lying near the detective. Fallon again smelled the cigar and looked at the name on the band. He cussed himself for not paying enough attention and squatted by the man Dan MacGregor had managed to knock out. He was just unconscious, with his face already purpling with bruises. Dan MacGregor must have known a thing or two about boxing, for he had managed pretty well. He probably could have taken both of these goons had the one with the pistol not used the walnut butt to club MacGregor from behind.

Fallon found another cigar of the same brand in this gent's vest pocket. It was unsmoked, too, and Fallon tossed it to the side. He also found some matches, so he bit off the end of the cigar he had kept, struck the match on a piece of iron, and held it to the cigar until it was glowing red and Fallon could feel the smoke in his mouth.

After withdrawing the cigar for a moment, Fallon spit and went through the other man's pockets. He found no identification, no .32-caliber cartridges, and only a penknife, three copper pennies, and two double eagles. He let the man keep the pennies and the knife, but Fallon slipped the gold pieces into his pocket. He glanced down the alley, and thought he would likely find a cigar and some forty dollars in gold in the pockets of those hired muggers, too.

But he didn't have that much time, or inclination, to rob thieves.

The cigar returned to Fallon's mouth, and he sucked on it, as he moved closer to the out-cold American Detective Agency's operative.

He gently slapped MacGregor's face. "Dan," he said, after removing the cigar. "Dan," he said louder, and slapped the face harder. "MacGregor."

The man moaned, but that was all. He smoked more of the cigar, studied the label again, and took a few more puffs, then brought the dark cigar past his nose, breathing in deeply. He tossed the cigar across the alley, spit onto the ground, and swore softly.

He might not have gotten a good look at the label, but Harry Fallon would remember that smell. A strong cigar. No, not strong, but damned near potent.

Fallon moved back to the cigar he had not smoked, and decided to keep it, just to show MacGregor. Maybe. And maybe Fallon would show MacGregor the gold coins, too. This cigar smelled just like those Sean MacGregor, the detective's father, smoked.

So . . . had Sean MacGregor hired these six goons to beat up, and maybe even kill, Fallon? And had Dan MacGregor let himself get knocked out?

Or had ten years in Joliet and not that long but too damned long in Yuma just made Fallon as paranoid as a trusty?

He slapped MacGregor's cheeks again.

The goon must have hit MacGregor pretty hard. So Fallon decided that this had not been the younger MacGregor's idea.

He looked down the alley toward the street. The wind must have picked up, because the few people who passed by had their heads bent and their collars pulled up. Somewhere a church bell began to chime, and a few carriages rumbled down the street. No one bothered to look into the alley. For a moment, Fallon considered heading for the street to get some help.

But he quickly dismissed that idea and opted for a better plan.

He pulled open MacGregor's coat. The man must have been confident. Wearing a coat like this, most men would have taken it off before engaging in a brawl down some disgusting Chicago alley. He saw the watch chain and fob, and a cigar sticking inside the top pocket. Fallon withdrew it, saw the band—Knights of Pythias, not one of the imported Havanas his father smoked—and returned it to the pocket. He saw no shoulder holster, no hideaway pistol. Dan MacGregor hadn't lied; he wasn't heeled.

The inside coat pocket showed some bulk. Fallon reached inside. No pistol, but an envelope—no, two envelopes—and a wallet. He didn't care about the wallet, so he withdrew the envelopes. One held paper currency in mostly twenties and fives, by Fallon's rough estimate, around two hundred dollars. The other was a letter. Fallon read the name and address, which made Fallon curious—but not enough to open the sealed letter. The envelope wasn't one of those he had seen at the American Detective Agency. In fact, there was the address for the sender in the corner.

Open the letter, and MacGregor would know it had been read. And the only person who could have read it was Harry Fallon. He cursed his luck, read the name and address again, and returned the letter and the envelope with the money back to the coat pocket. He let the wallet be.

He was pulling his hand away from the coat when he felt the cold steel of a gun barrel press behind his left earlobe. A second later, Harry Fallon heard a sound a lawman never forgets.

The metallic clicking of a hammer on a revolver being pulled to full cock.

CHAPTER FIVE

"An' wha' d'ye think ye be doing, laddie?"

The Irish brogue was thick. The barrel of the pistol did not move.

"I'm just helping this man," Fallon said.

"Aye. Ye be helping him by taking his money, or so it appears to me and my tired ol' eyes."

"Trying to find out who he is." Fallon raised his hands and slowly, very carefully, began to turn his head.

The Chicago cop was a big man, with a bulbous, rose-colored nose and watery eyes. He sported a massive mustache, the handles curled up and stretching toward his flapjack-sized ears. The policeman used his free hand to wipe the bit of nose one could see behind the red mustache. Finally, he took a step back and motioned with the revolver's barrel for Fallon to stand. It felt a whole lot better not to have that cold steel against his ear and skull.

Fallon obeyed the command, and the burly policeman took a step back, kept the gun trained on Fallon's chest.

"Stop!" the copper shouted. The finger tightened on the trigger.

Fallon froze.

"Ye be carrying a toy, I see," the policeman said. "Would ye mind pulling that toy from ye pants, but not too fast as I wouldna wan' to get excited and blow a hole in ye middle."

Fallon removed the Smith & Wesson .32 and held it, butt forward, toward the policeman.

The copper took it and sniffed the barrel.

"Ye be taking target practice, laddie, within the city limits."

"I took it off a thief," Fallon said. "They were robbing this gent." He motioned at MacGregor.

The police officer took a quick glance at Dan MacGregor's long body. Next, he looked at the one MacGregor had managed to knock out.

"Would that be ye partner?" the policeman asked.

Fallon shook his head. "No. This one was trying to rob this one." He nodded at the respective bodies.

The copper chuckled.

Maybe, Fallon thought, he should have said that MacGregor was his partner, but that would not have explained why Fallon had been going through the detective's pockets.

"An'," the copper said with a surly grin, "ye, being the upright and outstanding citizen that ye are . . . ye decided to pitch in and help a total stranger." He still had not lowered the hammer on the big Schofield .45. "We dunna find that many Good Samaritans in Chicago, laddie. Especially in this part of our fine city."

While he was talking, the Irishman fiddled with his pocket until he got it unopened and shoved the empty .32 into the opening.

"Six-to-one," Fallon said, "just didn't look like a fair

fight to me, sir." Maybe the *sir* would help, Fallon thought.

It didn't. But the *six-to-one* got the big police officer's attention.

"Six-to-one d'ye say?"

Fallon nodded toward the mountain of trash down the narrow alley.

The copper looked. His eyes grew even wider. He took a couple of steps back and shot another quick look at Dan MacGregor and the thug beside him, and finally stared hard into Harry Fallon's eyes.

"Move," the cop said, and motioned again with that still-cocked cannon of a .45. "An' be quick about it. But not too quick, laddie. Ye resemble a fine pacer we used to race north of Dublin, and I'm jes an old plow horse. In other words, ye look like ye can run, and ye are a few inches taller and thirty pounds lighter than me, but I dunna think ye can outrun a bullet. On. Toward those feet and hands I see amongst the garbage that stinks to high heaven."

Fallon turned and moved hurriedly, but not too fast, to the pile of men in the canyon through the mountains of garbage. He had to hurry. Neither the muggers nor Dan MacGregor would stay unconscious for long. In fact, one of the baseball bat–wielders appeared to be stirring.

Once they reached the tallest trash heap, the copper again motioned with his pistol, and Harry Fallon backed up till he felt the bricks of the tenement building against his back. The Irish policeman turned. His mouth opened. He wiped his nose with the sleeve of his uniform coat.

"Bloody hell," the copper said, and looked back at

Fallon. He shot a quick glance again at the carnage, before repeating, "Bloody hell," and then he added, "Jesus, Mary, and Joseph." He crossed himself with his free hand. "D'ye mean to tell me, laddie, that these four blokes were in on this wee little set-to?"

Fallon gestured. "There's another over the mountains and through the woods."

The one who had been wielding one of the baseball bats started to rise. The copper pulled the billy club from his belt and slammed it against the man's head. Fallon couldn't see the stick strike the criminal, but the sound made him cringe.

"Six?" The copper returned the stick, bent, kept the Schofield aimed in Fallon's general direction, and his left hand disappeared into the canyon cut through the garbage. The hand came back into view. The little derringer looked even smaller in the policeman's huge hand.

"An' this wouldna be yer's either, I be guessing?"

"No."

The copper tried to drop the derringer into the pocket with the Smith & Wesson, but realized there was no room, so he stuck it beneath the belt around his ample midsection. Again, he looked at the bodies, and then motioned Fallon to walk back toward him.

Fallon moved carefully.

"Four here, one, ye say, beyond this dung heap, and one back with our sleeping beauty. This would be what we woulda called, in me days with the Irish Brigade many years ago back during the late war, a running fight."

"I would have preferred just running," Fallon said, "but they had us boxed in."

"Us?"

Fallon nodded. "After I stepped off the street and called out for these thugs to stop, they kind of circled around us." He figured to tell the rest of the story close to the truth. "The man in the nice clothes took two of them. I went after four others."

The free hand pointed inside the canyon.

"And wha' did ye use on this one's face? Or, perhaps I should say, what be left of his face."

"Whatever I had handy," Fallon answered. "And that included a horseshoe. And the heel of my boot."

"Bloody hell," the copper said. "Jesus, Mary, and Joseph."

"I didn't ask their names," Fallon said. "They didn't give them."

The face turned blank. The copper's mouth opened underneath the mustache. Finally, he understood the joke and grinned, but the smile did not last more than a second. "Dunna get smart with the sergeant back at our fine little station, me boy. He isn't as nice as I am. And ye most definitely dunna want to get smart, or funny, with Judge Killian when ye go before him."

He pointed toward MacGregor.

Fallon started walking.

The copper kept talking.

"Seven arrests. That'll make Judge Killian happy. And seeing how bad these blokes are, it shall please Doctor Ishee, too. The city has to pay him, ye see, for treating unfortunate thieves."

"How are you getting all of these men to your jail?" Fallon asked. "Or the nearest hospital?"

"I dunna have enough manacles for all these blokes, laddie, so when we reach the street, I shall send someone to the precinct for a wagon." He chuckled. "And maybe an ambulance or three."

They walked.

"Stop," the Irishman said suddenly when Fallon reached the bodies. MacGregor's head was turning left and right, right and left, and his eyeballs were fluttering beneath the eyelids.

"It appears that ye friend might have his faculties returning," the policeman said, and he took a few steps past Fallon. He looked at the detective, and something caught his eye.

"Bend down," the policeman said. "Pull back that coat a wee bit."

Fallon obeyed. The Irishman's pale eyes widened. "Now, be so kind as to read the words engraved on that piece of brass."

Fallon stared at the shield pinned to the lapel of MacGregor's vest. He looked again at the copper, and a thought struck him. Maybe the policeman could not read.

"It says," Fallon started, and he lied: "Pinkerton National Detective Agency."

The copper took a step back. "Ye dunna say?"

Fallon shrugged. MacGregor's eyes opened, closed, and the head shook.

"Mac?" Fallon said softly. "Are you coming around, Mac? It's all right. We have a Chicago police officer here. And those six curs that tried to mug you, and then beat the hell out of both of us, are out of the game. Mac? Mac?"

"That'll be enough of yer gabbing, laddie," the copper said.

Fallon looked up, and then past the policeman, and felt his stomach begin to sour.

"Officer," Fallon said in a hoarse whisper. "There's a big man coming up behind you. And he's really soft on his feet for a man that size."

The police officer chuckled. "Ye must think I was raised by a couple of dunces, laddie." He waved the big .45. "If that lad comes to, good for him. But I think ye, the fine hero that ye claim to be, and I need to make our way to the street so we can get some assistance. On ye feet, me lad. On . . ."

He must have felt the presence, or maybe he at last heard the sounds of Aaron Holderman's big feet as the bearded giant crept down the alley.

The copper whirled, but Aaron Holderman's huge fist flashed. The mugger, Fallon realized, was not the only person donning some brass knuckles on this fine day. Fallon grimaced as the heavy weapon connected against the Irishman's forehead, just above the corner of his right eye. The sound was sickening. The pistol discharged, and Fallon felt the bullet slice just inches over his head and whine as it ricocheted off a stone and again off the bricks of the nearest building.

Down crashed the cop with a moan, and a groan, and a thud.

"What the hell happened?" Holderman sang out. "What did you do to Dan?"

"Hell," Fallon said. He pointed down the alley, and Holderman turned on his heels and began waving his big hand at the crowd that had gathered. "Get out of here, you mugs!" he shouted. "Mind your own damned business."

The man in the sack suit, the priest and the nun, and

the woman with the parasol turned and disappeared. But Fallon could hear their screams.

"Help! Help! Police! Police!"

"They're murdering some poor men down that alley!"

Holderman spun back. His face showed panic as he realized what was happening. "Mr. MacGregor will have my head on a stick," he said.

"Help me get Dan to his feet." Fallon struggled. Consciousness was slowly returning to the addled Dan MacGregor. Once Dan was standing, but only with the support of Fallon and Holderman, Fallon shoved him over Holderman's shoulder.

"Follow me," Fallon shouted, and he took off down the alley. He could hear the whistles now from down the street, and more voices began crying out for help, for mercy, for the police.

They made it to the canyon between the mounds of garbage. They did not try to avoid the unconscious vermin that blocked their way, but only tried not to trip over the bodies. They came through and moved toward the other street. Those whistles grew louder. Fallon turned abruptly to his left. He saw the rickety door that led inside one of the dirty brick buildings. He stopped just long enough to kick it open, breaking the lock and knocking the rotting wood off one of its hinges.

He ran through the building, pushing cobwebs past him, breathing in the rank and musty smell of the abandoned, darkened building. The light from the opening was all he had, but it was enough. They rounded a corner, and Fallon spotted more light a few yards down a littered hallway. The light was at the floor, with a little more creeping down the side. Fallon kicked that door open, too, but this one was solid. It took two more kicks. Then they were out in the street.

He could still hear the whistles and shouts. But he saw one chance. He stepped into the street and waved his hands over his head.

The driver of the hack managed to stop before the dun horse ran over Hank Fallon.

Chapter Six

The driver stood in the box of the wagon, still pulling tightly on the reins. "What is . . . ?" he started, but Fallon had already stepped back to the sidewalk.

"We've got a hurt man here," he said. He jerked the door to the cab open. A handsome woman in a fine evening dress gasped.

"I'm sorry, ma'am," Fallon said, as he held out his hands. "But we have a man who has been seriously injured. We need to get him to a hospital immediately. He's a detective. A Pinkerton man. He was hurt stopping a brutal beating."

Fallon helped the woman out. He could hear footsteps from inside the tenement.

"Get him in the hack!" Fallon bellowed at Holderman. The big fool moved to the door as Fallon helped the lady, who smelled of lilacs and rouge, to the sidewalk. He pulled one of the double eagles from his pocket and placed it in the woman's tiny left hand.

"For your troubles, ma'am."

The woman's eyes sparkled.

Fallon fished out another coin. "And this one," he said, as Holderman climbed into the cab and managed to pull Dan MacGregor's feet into the wagon. "This one, too," Fallon said. "If you'd be so kind as to tell the police that we went"—he indicated the opposite direction—"that way."

He smiled his most charming smile, and turned, planted a boot on the hub of the front wheel, and pulled himself into the box beside the driver.

"Hey, now," the hack started, "just a danged minute. We don't allow riders . . ."

"Shut up." Fallon sat. "Move, damn your hide!" he yelled. "We're carrying a hurt man inside. Gravely injured. A Pinkerton detective. Hurry."

The wagon was already moving, picking up speed. The driver slashed out with a whip. The coach turned right at the corner, just as Fallon looked back to see the handsome woman turning toward a squad of Chicago's finest spilling out of the abandoned building.

"Turn left," Fallon said, "at the next street."

The coachman obeyed. Fallon caught his breath.

"What hospital?" the hack called out.

Fallon turned around and leaned toward the door and windows.

"Hey!" he shouted above the rattle of the wheels and hooves as the coach rolled along. "How is he doing?"

"Comin' around!" Holderman yelled back. "What the hell was . . ."

"Shut up!"

Fallon pulled himself back around. Damn, he could use a strong shot of whiskey right about now.

"Mac," the coachman said, "what hospital you want me to take your detective to?"

Fallon found another gold piece. He set it on the seat between the driver and himself. The driver saw it, his eyes widened, and he looked back toward backside of his horse and the road.

"What hospital?" the man asked again.

"Forget the hospital, friend," Fallon said. "Just find us a saloon. A quiet one. But not too far away. And then, why don't you take a nice ride to Lake Michigan."

"Anything you say, capt'n." The coachman eased back on the reins, and let his right hand pick up the gold coin and slide it inside his pants pocket.

They sat at a corner table in a dark little saloon that smelled of pipe smoke, beer. and strong liquor.

The driver had told Fallon that they would be fine inside the little hole in the wall. "Just tell them that Franciszek Nowakowski says to take good care of you."

Fallon wasn't sure he pronounced the name right to the bartender or even if the bartender understood English, but they had a good view of the street, and no one bothered them.

Dan MacGregor kept rubbing his head and sipping the clear, potent whiskey in front of him. Aaron Holderman was on his fourth stein of porter. Fallon was only halfway through the black, bitter coffee that would put hair on a bald man's head and likely float an ironclad.

"They were waiting for us," MacGregor said at last.

"Who was waiting for you?" Holderman asked. "That copper? I took care of him."

"Shut up," Fallon told him.

Holderman glared.

MacGregor stopped rubbing his head. Now he turned toward the big mass of muscle.

"I told you to wait for us at the depot," MacGregor said.

"I was. And when you didn't come . . ."

"We weren't that late," MacGregor said.

Holderman set his stein down, but not until he had finished it.

"I don't think we were late at all," Fallon said. "In fact, from what I remember of the train station, you barely had time to get there yourself."

"That ain't true, Dan," Holderman said. "He's tryin' to play you ag'in me, Dan. You was out cold. And don't forget that I stopped that mick from cartin' the both of you to the calaboose."

MacGregor stared hard at Holderman, then shot Fallon a cold stare. He sipped the liquor again and looked out the window. No policemen. Just the typical bustle of hardworking immigrants heading home or to saloons or to work.

"What time is it?" MacGregor asked.

Holderman told him.

"When's the next train to St. Louis?"

"I don't know."

"Why don't you find out? Now."

"Dan," Holderman said, "you ought to see a doctor. You taken a nasty lump, and that knot on your head ain't gettin' no smaller."

"Get out," MacGregor said. "Get to the station, get tickets on the last train tonight, and then get back here in time to make sure we get to the station safely."

"I'm not sure I can find this place again."

"Some detective you are."

Holderman started to lean forward, whispering, "Now, Dan, you need to listen . . ."

"And don't stop to talk to my father on your way to the station. If I think you've said one word or sent one word to my old man, you'll disappear. The lake's pretty deep this time of year. And I know where my father likes to drop the bodies so they never rise to the surface."

Holderman rose. His hands were shaking. "All right." He started for the door but stopped and turned back. "But what if there ain't no more trains to St. Louis tonight?"

"Then get us on the first train tomorrow."

He made it a few feet this time before MacGregor stopped him by calling out his name.

Once Holderman turned, MacGregor said, "If you're not back here in a half hour, with tickets, we'll be heading to the docks to take a trip across the lake."

The nod was barely perceptible in the smoky haze before Aaron Holderman rushed out of the door.

MacGregor picked up his glass, sipped the liquor, and rubbed his head again. "I suppose I need to thank you."

Fallon shrugged. "For what?"

"You took four of them?" MacGregor let a mirthless smile cross his face. "I couldn't even handle two."

Fallon gave the detective another shrug. "Four men against one? They have a tendency to be extremely overconfident. Two against one? Well, those know that in a brawl, in a saloon or an alley or anywhere, anything is possible. Besides, you were in the open. I had those four where I wanted them. No, not where I wanted them. Just where I needed them to be. Worked in my favor. But I was lucky. Damned lucky."

"I still don't know how you managed it. And then you took the one who knocked me out, too."

The coffee was cold and seemed even stronger now. "I've had experience at these sorts of things."

"Yeah."

Fallon grinned. "I don't always win."

MacGregor's laugh sounded genuine. "I am a detective. I detect things. I investigate things. Fighting"—he gestured with his glass of whiskey toward the front door to the groggery—"that I leave to men like Aaron Holderman."

"Holderman's no man," Fallon said.

This time, MacGregor polished off the whiskey in a savage gulp. "He set us up."

Fallon shrugged. "Maybe."

"You called it." MacGregor's eyes had started to water, most likely from the shot of what might have been two hundred-proof, Polish rotgut whiskey. Or maybe from that big bump on his head. "You called him on the distance to the train depot."

"Dan," Fallon said softly, "I don't even know where the station is. From here. Or from that alley. I haven't been in Chicago long enough to know where anything is. Hell, I don't even know where I'm supposed to live."

MacGregor laughed again. "Trust me. You probably don't want to find out." He raised his hand as though to signal the bartender for another drink, but immediately thought better of that. The hand fell onto the table. He stared at Fallon.

"Well, you were right."

"A lucky guess."

"Are you always this lucky?"

"I'm alive."

The young man leaned forward, sighed, and propped his elbows on the table and folded his hands around his face. His head shook. "It was my father, you know."

Fallon remained quiet.

"He arranged our little greeting party."

"Not Holderman?" Fallon was testing the detective.

"You're not stupid, Hank."

"I've already told you. My friends call me Hank."

"I'm trying to be your friend. And you know as well as anyone that Aaron Holderman couldn't arrange that kind of ambush. That was Father's doing."

Fallon knew not to interrupt. He would let the still-reeling Dan MacGregor keep talking until he wised up and realized whom he was talking to. Only MacGregor stopped talking. He merely stared across the table at Fallon.

"Your father," Fallon said, "wanted you, or me, to get beaten to hell."

"Me beaten to hell. You killed."

Fallon leaned back. "He's sending me to Jefferson City. Why would he want me dead here, when I can easily get buried in that dungeon?"

"He's not sending you to the Missouri pen. I am."

Fallon shot a glance at the bar, but now was not the time to start drinking. MacGregor whispered. "I told you that I'm your friend."

Now, it was Fallon's time to chuckle. "My friends have sent me to nicer places than those bloody acres along the Missouri River."

Leaning back in his chair, Dan MacGregor studied the lawman. He wasn't smiling at Fallon's joke. Instead, he said, "My father promised you something. But you know he doesn't aim for you to get what you want."

"And what is it that I want?"

"Revenge. Maybe justice. That's what I thought at first, when Father first came up with this idea. Justice. You were a lawman. But I think Joliet changed you."

"I wouldn't be the first."

MacGregor sighed. "I guess you wouldn't." Two minutes passed before MacGregor spoke again. "I asked you before: Why did you get sent to Joliet, a state prison in Illinois, and not Detroit, where federal prisoners typically go?"

"I don't know."

"You might think about that. If you get out of this job alive." He leaned forward, came close to the table, and leaned across it. "Father can help you get that revenge, or justice, or whatever you decide you want."

What about you? Fallon considered asking but thought that might shut up the kid whose head had to be pounding. Or maybe it was guilt, or something else, that had the youngster talking.

"Look. Father needed your help for that job you did in Yuma. But he knows you double-crossed him by letting the Pinkertons take all that glory." Now, MacGregor straightened and laughed. Again he leaned back in his chair. "That was beautiful, Hank. Beautiful. Not many men I know can pull something like that against the great Sean MacGregor."

Fallon kept quiet. His face revealed nothing. Certainly, Fallon did not trust Sean MacGregor. He wasn't sure he could trust the conniving Scot's son, either.

"Father promised you things, things he can deliver, but things he won't deliver. He realized he had made a mistake. So he's sending you to prison to get killed. And then, as a joke, he thought it might be better if he got rid of you in Chicago and let me take a beating to put me in my place."

"There are easier ways to kill a man," Fallon said.

"And a million ways to die in prison. Especially in a place like Jeff City. That place makes the Bastille look like the best hotel in New Orleans."

Fallon leaned closer to MacGregor. "But I believe you just said that it was your idea to send me to Missouri."

"It was. It is. Because you can get some valuable information, something that might help you find out who got you put in Joliet for ten years, who got your wife and daughter butchered."

Fallon felt his face flushing. He saw his fists clenched. He tried to control his breathing.

"Do the names Kemp Carver and Ford Wagner mean anything to you?" MacGregor asked.

Fallon pushed away from the detective.

They most certainly did.

Leaning back in his chair, he remembered.

Chapter Seven

Fifteen years earlier

The wagon was white, except for the iron bars that had been painted black, the board along one side that was painted red with gold trim, and the gold letters on the red-and-white side that proclaimed:

U. S.
COURT

You could also find a few spots of brown staining the white paint. That came from blood of some of the prisoners the wagon had hauled out of the Indian Nations and into Arkansas over the past few years.

Folks called it a "tumbleweed wagon," and it—and others like it—transported prisoners to the dungeon known as a jail in Fort Smith. This one had twelve men inside, sweating, cursing, and their shackles rattling. The air and sun felt murderously hot, drenching the prisoners in sweat. Harry Fallon was sweating, too, but at least he had the comfort of the roof over his head and the coolness of the air as it blew across the driver's seat. He also had a canteen of water at his side, and the six-point star of a deputy U.S. marshal pinned to the front pocket of his shirt.

He had everything a lawman needed—except a gun.

Judge Isaac Parker and the supervising marshal over the Western District of Arkansas and the Indian Nations had made it clear that drivers of tumbleweed wagons were not to carry weapons. No pistols, no rifles, no shotguns, no knives, nothing that a prisoner might be able to get his hands on and turn against the lawmen accompanying the wagon.

Two deputy marshals, Jim Beckett and Caleb Holloway, were accompanying this one, and had made the arrest of the dozen sweating men caged behind Fallon. Fallon was wondering where those marshals were, but he knew to follow orders. He kept the wagon moving slowly down the road that ran to the Arkansas River. He could take the ferry across the muddy, deep river, and keep right on down the road until he came to the old fort, which now held Judge Parker's office, the district court, and the hellish jail where federal prisoners waited and rotted and, sometimes, died.

Fallon had been wearing this star for three months. When the federal marshal and Judge Parker had first given him the badge, Fallon, youngster and former wild-roving cowboy, had expected nothing but adventures like something out of a dime novel. He had dreamed of wild gunfights and becoming some kind of hero like Kit Carson, Wild Bill Hickok, or Buffalo Bill Cody. Instead, here he sat, on the hard, uncomfortable seat of the tumbleweed wagon, sweating, bored out of his mind. The closest thing to gunfire he had heard had been when one or both of the mules farted.

Being a deputy United States marshal had turned out to be about as exciting as riding drag on a herd of two thousand cattle from Texas to Kansas for three or four months.

The prison wagon rounded a bend in the road, and Fallon looked up, felt his heart leap in his chest, and he quickly pulled back on the leather and brought the mules to a stop. The cursing and griping from the prisoners stopped.

Fallon's throat turned dry. Two men stood in the center of the road. The one in the black hat had a sawed-off scattergun pointed at Fallon's chest. The one in the linen duster held a Winchester rifle. Behind that dangerous pair, a third man sat in a saddle on a paint horse. He held no guns, but the reins to four horses with empty saddles. Fallon's eyes shot toward the woods, trying to find two other men with guns pointed in his direction. Seeing none, he focused on the man with the shotgun.

"Shuck yer iron, boy," the man said.

His face was pockmarked, he had not shaved in a few days, and his left ear looked as though it had been bitten in half by a bear or coyote or some other kind of wild animal.

After swallowing down the bile, Fallon said, "I'm unarmed." He stumbled with that twice before he could get the words out freely.

"The hell you say," the shotgun-loaded man said. He was short, probably just a few inches over five feet, and his right boot—of an old cavalry style—was split down the side and sported a big hole in the foot so that Fallon could see the man's big toe. He wore no socks.

"That's true, Shorty," said the one on the horse. "The lawdogs don't let the driver carry no weapons."

The shotgun lowered, and the ugly runt in the black hat laughed. "Well, hell, that makes this a whole lot easier."

The man with the rifle waved the barrel, but did not lower it, and said, "Open the back, boy. And then get the chains off your passengers."

One thought raced through Fallon's mind: *Marshals Beckett and Holloway will kill me for letting all these prisoners loose.*

The man on horseback gave Fallon something else to think about. "If you don't hurry, boy, we'll shoot you dead and leave you for the crows. Get moving."

After setting the brake and wrapping the heavy leather lines around the handle, Fallon climbed out of the driver's box. The men in the jail-on-wheels began talking excitedly, softly at first, and then began cheering and hissing when they realized they were being freed.

The runt in the black hat followed Fallon, and, upon seeing the prisoners, he turned toward the other two and said, "Maybe we should just let Kemp and Carver go."

The one on horseback shook his head. Fallon began to realize that this one was the leader.

"No," the man said. "This'll give the lawdogs more trails they'll have to follow. Give us a better chance to clear the territory, maybe get back down to Texas."

He was looking at Fallon when he was talking. Fallon figured the man was lying, hoping that Fallon would send the posse south. That thought gave Fallon some hope, though, for if that was the plan of the outlaws, it meant that they did not plan to shoot Fallon dead.

"Open it up." The man rammed the shotgun against Fallon's spine.

He flinched, bit his lip, and rammed the key into the hole. Once the padlock released, Fallon swung open the door, and stepped back. The dozen prisoners immediately bolted for the opening, at least as fast as their shackled feet could take them, and Fallon's instincts took over.

He grabbed the door and swung it hard, the iron bars slamming against the first felon's head, and sending him down. "One at a time!" Fallon yelled, and realized what he had done. A bullet would likely split his spine at any moment. Instead, above the jangling of chains and curses and shouts from inside, the man on the horse chuckled.

"I ought to cut him down!" said the one with the shotgun.

"Let him be," the one on the horse said. "He's just stalling, hoping his pards come along to stop us."

The man on the ground with the Winchester chuckled. "Your fellow star-packers are on another trail, boy. Next time you meet up with them will be on the road to hell."

"Shut up," snapped the one holding the reins, and he said, softer, but firmly to Fallon. "Open the door again, kid." His voice rose to a commanding shout: "But you heard the marshal. One at a time. You first, Kemp."

The blond-headed kid with the rosy cheeks stepped to the door, eased it open, and jumped to the ground.

"Get the irons off him," the one on horseback

ordered, and Fallon found the keys to the ankle and wrist manacles. The kid, Kemp Carver, was no older than Fallon, but several inches shorter and many pounds heavier.

"Ford," the leader of the outlaws said, "you're next."

The others in the tumbleweed wagon began grumbling. The man holding the Winchester sent a bullet over the roof of the wagon. "Easy. Easy. You'll get your turn. But you don't do like we say, and you'll either stay in that wagon or stay here on the ground, till you get buried."

Fallon unshackled the second prisoner out of the wagon, a redheaded kid named Ford Wagner. Both had been caught with a wagonload of rotgut whiskey they had been selling in the Cherokee Nation.

Wagner and Carver hurried to the one holding the reins. "What's takin' you so long?" Carver asked.

Wagner climbed into the saddle of a dun horse and took off down the road at a gallop.

Carver called after his whiskey-running partner: "Where you off to, Ford?"

"Maudie's!" the redhead shouted.

The man who had been holding the reins chuckled while Kemp Carver shook his head.

A burly man who had stomped a man half to death on Garrison Avenue in Fort Smith climbed out of the wagon but didn't wait for Fallon to unlock his manacles. He hurried toward the man on horseback. Fallon noticed that the one with the Winchester had mounted his horse, and the shotgun-toting runt in the black hat was walking away from the wagon and toward the horses.

Apparently, they only wanted Kemp Carver and Ford Wagner.

"Danny!" the burly man said. "Wait, Danny. Let me come with . . ."

He stopped and brought up his shackled hands. "Don't, Danny, for—"

Fallon never saw the leader draw the Colt, and the gunshot startled him. It sent the next man coming out of the wagon back inside, while the old drunk with the silver braids began singing a spiritual in a mixture of English and Creek.

"They're gonna kill us!" yelled another whiskey runner. "They're gonna shoot us dead."

Fallon just watched as the man kicked his horse and walked the animal over to the man wanted for assault and illegal flight.

"Why don't you call me by my full name?" the leader said as he reined his horse to a stop by the burly man, who lay on his back, groaning, coughing, trying to keep the blood from rushing out of his belly, and spitting up more blood. The leader thumbed back the hammer, aimed the Colt, and squeezed the trigger.

By then, the whiskey runner named Carver and the man holding the Winchester were galloping after the youngster named Wagner. The man with the shotgun had to chase down his startled horse and dropped the scattergun as he caught a rein and the horn and somehow managed to bring himself off the ground into the saddle—like an old Pony Express rider.

The leader did not look at either Fallon or the man he had just shot down in cold blood. He holstered his Colt, spun the horse around, and put the gelding into a gallop after the trailing dust.

Chapter Eight

Fallon blinked, and suddenly realized that two more prisoners had leaped out of the wagon and were stumbling toward the woods, still wearing their leg and arm bracelets. Another leaped out, and the next one was hurrying for the door.

Fallon grabbed the bars and swung the door shut. He heard the crunch of bone and felt the spray of blood as the escaped murderer clutched his nose and fell onto his knees inside the wagon.

"Don't any of you jackals even blink!" Fallon shouted and was surprised when the remaining prisoners stopped. They stared in disbelief or shock as Fallon found the padlock.

"Wait," said a half-breed Choctaw who had broken a federal deputy's arms and ankle. "He got no gun."

By then, however, as a white-haired man bound for the gallows gripped the iron bars, the door was locked again, and Fallon was stepping away from the tumble-weed wagon.

* * *

He caught up with those who had left, still in chains, fairly quickly. One had resisted, noting that Fallon had no pistol, but Fallon knocked him out with the branch of a cedar. He made another one of the locked-up prisoners carry the unconscious man back to the wagon, making the others wait as they walked up the road to where the bloody body lay.

Fallon leaned over the body and checked for a pulse that he knew he would not find. Next, he walked up the road and picked up the shotgun the man in the black hat had been carrying. Opening the breech, he saw two shells, and he pulled one out. Buckshot. The second shell was the same.

"That'll do," he said aloud, and went back to the tumbleweed wagon. *That'll do?* he thought. *It'll have to do.*

The shotgun silenced the prisoners.

He made the same prisoner as before follow Fallon to the body of the murdered prisoner. Fallon wrapped the corpse in a rain slicker, but made the prisoner carry the dead man back to the wagon.

Fallon opened the door and let the others return to the jail, one at a time. The man Fallon had knocked out and the prisoner the butcher named Danny had murdered were loaded inside, too. The door closed and was locked behind them, and when one of the men complained about his broken nose, Fallon ignored him.

When another grumbled, "It ain't right, making us ride with a stinkin' dead man."

Fallon brought the scattergun halfway up. "I can make this tumbleweed wagon a hearse. Is that what you want?"

The men fell silent.

So Fallon climbed back into the driver's box, released

the brake, and rode toward Fort Smith—trying to figure out how he could explain everything to Judge Parker, the U.S. attorney, and the U.S. marshal. He hoped Jim Beckett and Caleb Holloway, his fellow lawmen, would catch up with him before he made it to the ferry. He prayed that the outlaws who had sprung Kemp Carver and Ford Wagner had been running a bluff, making Fallon think that his two colleagues had been murdered.

Two miles up the road, Fallon felt sick.

The bodies of deputy marshals Beckett and Holloway lay in the ditch on the side of the road, Beckett's dapple gelding grazing about two hundred yards down the road, Holloway's black nowhere to be found.

Fallon jumped off the wagon as soon as he jerked back the brake and slid into the ditch. Water and leaves and muck seeped into his boots as he started to turn over the body of Beckett, the closest. He stopped and looked at the pattern of holes that riddled the deputy's leather vest.

"Shot in the back," Fallon seethed. He glanced up at the wagon, and he cursed bitterly. "With that twelve-gauge."

Once he had pulled the corpse out of the ditch, Fallon moved down the road about twenty-five yards. Only Holloway's left leg was in the ditch, and he had not been shot in the back. From the size of the hole in the lawman's back, Fallon figured the man with the Winchester had shot him—from a good distance. That was the exit wound, though, and when Fallon turned the dead man over, he saw where the bullet had first struck the deputy just underneath the six-point badge.

Closing his eyes, Fallon cursed again. He remembered just the other night, when they had been sitting around the campfire—after Fallon had fed and watered all the prisoners. Fallon had been sitting by the fire, polishing that nickel-plated badge he wore. Finally, Deputy Holloway had chuckled and said, "Hank, don't you know no better than to make that star shiny?" Fallon had stopped and looked up. "Why?" he asked innocently. Holloway had laughed harder this time and said, "Kid, that'll just make it easier for some fella ridin' the owlhoot train to draw a bead on your chest."

So, if Harry Fallon were a detective—and he most certainly did not consider himself anywhere near that—he would have said that Holloway was shot first, with a long gun at a good distance—and likely died instantly. Beckett had then turned around and was reaching for his Remington .44 when he caught two barrels of buckshot in the back.

Satisfied, the man named Danny then led his men and two horses to catch up with the tumbleweed wagon.

Well, Fallon thought, they had not killed him. For a moment, he vaguely wished they had. He had met Beckett's wife. She was supposed to have a baby around Christmas.

As he dragged the bodies to the wagon one at a time, he kept thinking about the one called Danny. That outlaw had let Fallon live. Why? So a green kid fit for nothing but feeding and hauling prisoners and emptying the wagon's slop bucket would tell the marshals that the killers were riding toward Texas.

Fallon stopped. He stared at the gun rig buckled around Holloway's waist. The killers had not even bothered taking the dead men's guns. Fallon started thinking. Suddenly, he had unbuckled the belt and put it around his own waist. He drew the pistol, pulled the hammer to half cock, opened the loading gate, and checked the cylinder. Five bullets, unfired. You always kept the chamber underneath the hammer empty—"lessen you want to cripple yourself by blowing a hole in your leg or your damned foot off," Holloway had advised Fallon a few months back.

Fallon thumbed a .45 cartridge from a loop in the belt and filled the empty chamber with the brass casing. He lowered the hammer and shoved the pistol back in the holster.

When he had Beckett's body by the wagon, Fallon found the Remington and shoved it into his waistband. He cautiously approached Beckett's dapple, took the reins, rubbed the gelding's neck, and walked the horse back to the hoodlum wagon. Fallon drew the Winchester from the scabbard and walked to the back of the jail-on-wheels. He looked at the men and finally chose one of the whiskey runners. A man running illegal spirits in the Indian Nations knew practically every gambling parlor, brothel, trading post, and whiskey outfit in all of the territory.

Fallon waited for the old man to look up. When he did, Fallon said, "I'm going to ask you once, and just once, and you better answer without thinking. Where's Maudie's?"

The old man blinked. "What the hell—"

The rifle roared, and the old man fell onto one of the unconscious men's legs, screaming, soiling his britches, and clutching the bloody part in his scalp with his shackled hands.

Fallon jacked the hammer, sent a smoking brass casing into the sky, and drew a bead on the half-breed with the silver braids.

"Your turn," Fallon snapped. "Only my aim might not be as good now. Where's Maudie's?"

Smoke wafted from the chimney over the dugout that had been cut into the hill not too far from where the creek bent and turned southeast. From the creek bottoms, where he did not think he could be seen from inside that rank-looking shack, Fallon studied the place run by a woman named Maudie. Maudie, one of the prisoners had told him, was a good spot to sell or trade your stolen horses for other stolen horses. Get drunk. Or just have a little hot food before taking back to the owlhoot trail. Or, if you had enough money, you might be able to occupy yourself for a while with whatever girl Maudie had working for her this week.

Wood was stacked next to the front door, the only door, to the dugout cut into the hillside. Piles of trash surrounded the stacks of rough-chopped wood, except for a path that led from the door to the pile. A man leaned against the wall, smoking a cheroot. The Winchester rifle leaned against the wall. Fallon recognized the man as the one with the rifle who rode in with the man named Danny. This may have been the man who had killed Holloway.

A lean-to stood a few yards away near the corral. Fallon counted more than a dozen horses in the big round pen, but none of those horses belonged to the murderers of deputy marshals Beckett and Holloway or to the punk kids called Kemp Carver and Ford Wagner. Their horses were tied to the hitching rail on the side of the hill.

Fallon wasn't certain, but he guessed that although

the dugout had no windows, a few of those dark spots in the hill were actually gun ports.

So, Fallon wondered, *how to I get from here to that front door?*

The door opened, and a woman walked out. Fallon watched. She was young, black-haired, wearing a camisole, apron, bloomers and beaded moccasins. She carried two buckets, ignored the killer with the Winchester, and headed toward the well between the lean-to and the gate to the corral. The man with the Winchester tossed away his smoke and said something.

The girl kept walking.

Maudie? Fallon thought. No, she was too young. She was probably Maudie's new girl.

That would explain why the man took off his hat, laid it on a water barrel next to the door, and walked after the woman. His rifle remained against the dugout's wall. Fallon watched as the man caught up to the woman, helped her with the buckets as far as the well, then took her by a hand and led her to the mountain of hay next to the corral.

When they disappeared on the other side, Fallon hobbled the dapple and climbed out of the bottoms. He glanced at the dugout, the gun ports, and wet his lips before he started running, crouched, across the flats toward the hay.

His hat flew off about a quarter of the way across.

He did not slow down until he rounded the mountain, and as the man who had murdered Holloway pushed himself off the girl and reached for his belly gun, Fallon smashed his face with the butt of the rifle. Bones cracked, blood spurted, and the man let out a whimper as he slammed hard against the ground. The woman—an Indian girl, probably still in her middle teens—simply looked up, wiped the killer's blood off her cheek, and yawned.

"Stay here," Fallon said. He grabbed the pistol the murderer had dropped and stuck that in one of the deep pockets of his trousers. He noticed that the killer's shirt was the same color as Fallon's. Fallon loosened his own bandanna, which was beige, and exchanged it with the man whose face he had just smashed. That bandanna was scarlet with yellow polka dots. He also picked up the man's hat, a dingy white, and shoved it on his head.

It was too big, so Fallon pushed it back a little.

He sucked in a breath, repeated to the uncaring Indian girl to stay put, and he walked toward the dugout.

When he reached the door—surprised to still be standing, to still be among the living—Fallon stopped to catch his breath. He looked back at the hay but saw nothing of the girl or the man who likely would not be waking up for a good long while, and maybe never.

Fallon saw the man's Winchester, and thought about grabbing it, too.

Then he laughed a dry laugh.

You have three six-shooters already, plus a rifle. You only have two hands, Hank, and . . . if my math's right—there are only four men you're after inside there. If Maudie wants to pitch in to help them, then five.

Five . . . against . . . one . . .

He tried to spit, only to realize he had nothing in his mouth or throat even remotely wet.

"Hell," Fallon said aloud, "you can't live forever."

And he kicked open the door.

Chapter Nine

When he looked back on it, he saw everything as he had seen it that afternoon. It had felt like he was moving in a waltz, so slow, so easy to see. The inside of the dugout had been dark, with the only light coming in from the doorway he had just kicked open, turning him into some monster of a silhouette. Two candles provided the only light inside.

It was, Kemp Carver later testified, "so damned dark I couldn't tell the suits of the cards I was holdin'."

Yet to Harry Fallon, it was bright as noon in the middle of Kansas.

The man with the black hat—Talbot Kidder was his name, or at least it had been the one he was going by, and the one the undertaker had carved onto the headboard back in Fort Smith after no one claimed his body—was smiling, reaching for the latch to the door when it had been kicked open and Harry Fallon had filled the opening.

The smile vanished. Talbot Kidder spit out the cigar he was smoking and clawed for the gun in his waistband.

In the trial at Fort Smith, Ford Wagner had cursed,

spit, and declared, "Had Kidder had his scattergun, that lawdog would've been the one whose guts got sprayed across Maudie's parlor."

Parlor. Hell, there was no parlor.

But Talbot Kidder had dropped his shotgun while trying to get aboard his horse. That shotgun was in the scabbard of the dapple down in the creek bottoms. Kidder managed to get the pistol up, but the front sight snagged on the coarse wool. The murderer had already cocked the hammer, and his finger was on the trigger, so that when the barrel got caught, the .44 went off, and Kidder's dark face turned white. The front of his trousers smoldered and burst into flames.

The .44 fell onto the dirt floor.

Talbot Kidder stood there, weaving, and he whispered above the deafening echo inside the cramped quarters: "Mother Mary, I am kilt."

Yet he still stood there, pants afire, his face growing whiter with each passing moment, until Fallon slammed the Winchester's barrel against his neck. Talbot Kidder let out a meek groan and toppled onto a round table, overturning the tin dishes and heavy whiskey glasses, as well as a stool and a high-backed chair, and he landed facedown in the dirt.

Five seconds, if that, had passed since Harry Fallon had kicked his way inside the dugout.

To Fallon's right, Kemp Carver sat at a table against the wall, playing blackjack with Ford Wagner. Fallon saw them, but he also caught movement from the back of the darkened room, and that's where he swung the barrel of the Winchester. Although, again, the room had little light, Fallon remembered seeing Daniel K. Huntington so clearly as the killer leaned against the bar, holding a wineglass toward a buxom blonde woman in a low-cut blouse, men's denim jeans, and high-heeled stovepipe cowboy boots with spurs. The man set the glass down casually on the makeshift bar and palmed a pistol in his right hand. Fallon saw the flash of the muzzle, felt the bullet zip past his left ear, heard it slam into the wall, and felt the splatter of bits of stone and dirt bounce off his shoulder and neck.

He pulled the trigger. The Winchester slammed against his shoulder. The candle on the bar went out. Both men fired again. Both men would have been killed, or at least desperately wounded, had they not been moving after firing their first shots.

Fallon's rifle bullet smashed the glass on the bar.

Huntington's round flew through the open doorway.

Then Huntington was grabbing Maudie, and both of them went over the bar, toppling into a heap. They disappeared in darkness and dirt.

By that time, Kemp Carver was standing and pulling his pistol off to Fallon's left.

Fallon felt as though he had no time to lever another round into the Winchester's magazine. For some reason—he never quite figured out what his reasoning had been—he brought the rifle out as far as he could with his right hand still in the lever, and slung it forward, releasing it and sending it like one of those wild boomerangs he had read about in *Frank Leslie's Illustrated Newspaper.* It zipped across the room and somehow, by luck or God's guidance, slammed into Ford Wagner's head as he was drawing his pistol. Ford Wagner crashed against the wall, cried out in pain, clutched his bleeding head, and toppled to the floor. That spoiled Kemp Carver's aim, and by the time

Carver had recocked his pistol, Harry Fallon was diving onto the floor.

Carver's second shot showered Fallon's head with dirt from the wall. The Winchester-shooting outlaw's hat had fallen off Fallon's head when he had leaped into the dugout after kicking open the door.

Fallon rolled onto his side and pulled Beckett's .44-caliber Remington from his waistband. His left hand reached for the other pistol he had shoved into his pocket, only to realize he must have dropped that one at some point during all this ruckus.

He eared back the hammer, brought the barrel up, squeezed the trigger without aiming, and felt the heat, the kick of the big pistol, while the flash of the muzzle made him cringe. Another bullet singed his back. That one had come from Huntington from the ruins of the bar. Fallon ignored him, for Carver was closer. He saw the young punk come up on a knee, trying to hold his pistol steady. He rushed his shot and jerked the trigger. Fallon took his time and slowly squeezed his finger. The Remington roared, and almost instantly Fallon heard the boy wailing for his mother, and, "God, my arm, my arm, my arm, you damned low-down dirty son of a whore."

His ears rang from the roars of the weapons. His eyes burned from the gunsmoke and burning woolen pants. His mouth still held no spit. But he could taste the fear, he could hear the commotion from the destroyed bar at the end of the dugout, and he could see Huntington begin to stand out of the rubble.

Fallon rolled onto his back, cocked the Remington with his right thumb while his left hand reached across his belly and pulled out the Colt in his holster.

He saw Daniel K. Huntington step closer. Fallon almost touched the trigger when he realized that his barrel was aimed not at the murdering thug but a blond-headed woman wearing a low-cut shirt.

His finger relaxed against the trigger.

Danny Huntington's voice, two octaves higher than it had been down the road about a million lifetimes ago, wailed: "Don't you move, lawdog. You move, and I'll blow this girl's head clean off. You hear me? You don't move. Don't move. You move, and I swear to God, I'll kill her. And that'll be on your conscience, you damned dog."

Fallon did not lower the .44. He kept the barrel pointed at Maudie, whom Daniel Huntington, coward that he was, kept tight against his body. Huntington's pistol was aimed not at Fallon but jammed into the big blonde's ear.

"Don't move. I'll kill her. God as my witness, I'll blow her head clean off."

Fallon did not blink, although his eyes burned even harder from the smoke and dust.

The Remington kept trained on its mark. Huntington practically dragged Maudie through broken glass, busted chair legs. He turned, keeping the woman rustler's body in front of his own, in front of Fallon's gunsights.

Behind Fallon, Kemp Carver sobbed.

Fallon also heard the killer in the black hat, whose burning pants had slowly burned out, as the dying man muttered a prayer in some soft, foreign language.

"Shut up, damn you!" Huntington bellowed.

Fallon did not know whom the killer was yelling at, but it could not have been Fallon. Harry Fallon had not, to the best of his memory, uttered one word since he had kicked the front door off one of its hinges.

"Now you listen to me, you damned lawdog." Huntington kept his gun against Maudie's head. Fallon thought the man might try to gun Fallon down, but perhaps the addlebrained fool thought Fallon might be willing to shoot Maudie and hope the .44 slug would go through her body and into Huntington's. Which, Fallon later realized, was fairly likely.

"I'll kill her. Swear to God, I'll shoot her dead."

He kicked the dying man in the black hat's head, silencing him, and stepped over his body and dragged Maudie with him.

"God, my arm," Kemp Carver sobbed. "My arm. God. It hurts. It hurts so bad. So bad. Oh, Mama, Mama, Mama please make me feel better. Please, God. I don't wanna die."

"You." Fallon could see how clear, how wide and how blue, Daniel K. Huntington's eyes shone. He had stepped into the light shining through the doorway.

Fallon lay on his side, arm outstretched, but never wavering. The heavy .44 in his hand felt like a quill pen. The killer had reached the doorway and was about to go through it and into the outside.

"You don't do nothing, lawdog," Daniel K. Huntington said. "I'll blow her damned head off. Clean off. I'll kill her and anybody else who gets in my way."

"Mama," Kemp Carver sobbed. "Mama. Mama. Mama."

"Shut up," Huntington said.

Fallon wondered if all outlaws were like this. Brave when you had a man by surprise. Scared as a frightened kitten when you realized how close death was.

"Shut up!" Huntington barked again. "Don't you try nothing. So help me, I'll kill her. I'll kill everyone."

He glanced through the doorway.

"Danny," Fallon said softly. At that time, that was the only name he knew the killer by.

Daniel K. Huntington's head swung around. His eyes landed on Fallon.

And Harry Fallon touched the trigger of the Remington .44 in his right hand.

Chapter Ten

Chicago

Dan MacGregor grinned. "I see those names do ring a bell," he said.

Fallon let his head nod slightly. Leaning back, he said, "First arrests I ever made." It had been his first gunfight, too, and he frowned at the memory of Daniel K. Huntington, the first man Fallon had ever killed. Sure, Fallon might have been responsible for the agonizing death of Talbot Kidder, but that black-hearted scoundrel had shot himself. The solicitor in Fort Smith had said he had not enough evidence to convict John Smith, which was the original handle the man with the Winchester had given the court, of murdering a deputy marshal, but he did get fifteen years in the Detroit House of Corrections for accessory to the murders of two lawmen and for his role in the unlawful release of federal prisoners Kemp Carver and Ford Wagner.

"And Kemp Carver and Ford Wagner hate your

guts," MacGregor said. "After fifteen years, they still hate your guts."

Fallon let a wry smile cross his face. "They're not alone, you know. I arrested many men since who likely hate me more."

"Maybe not," MacGregor said.

Fallon shrugged. "Perhaps. The man I killed when I arrested those two and another, Danny Huntington, he was an uncle of those two. More like a father, to hear the way they talked in court."

"Not the kind of father most of us . . ." MacGregor did not finish but frowned.

Fallon looked away, thinking that Daniel Huntington probably, as a father figure, was not much worse than Sean MacGregor. At least Huntington never claimed to be fighting for justice. He was just, as most criminals would never actually admit, too damned lazy to try an honest day's work.

The door opened, and both men looked, but it was not Aaron Holderman returning to the saloon from the train depot, but a couple of stooped, dusty workers who made quickly for the seedy little bar and ordered whiskeys.

Fallon leaned in toward the detective. "So how did you know all about those two boys and me?"

"Court records," the young man said.

"I happen to know those records burned in a courthouse fire some years back."

"Newspaper accounts."

"I was there. I could read. And, young lawman that I was back then, I read those newspapers."

"Then let's just say I'm a pretty good detective."

"All right." Fallon thought: *And once I was a pretty good lawman.*

Maybe not on that little episode. That had been the luck of a dumb green kid's sheer audacity. He remembered bringing the tumbleweed wagon with the horses carrying the dead bodies tethered behind. He could picture the faces of the citizens of Fort Smith as he led that cargo toward the district courthouse, and he remembered Judge Isaac Parker himself running down the steps with several attorneys and the district marshal, gawking like some of the women and old codgers that Fallon had noticed outside the general stores, grocery stores, and saloons.

After that, Deputy U.S. Marshal Harry Fallon was never assigned the job as driver of a prison wagon. After that, Fallon usually had a driver for the tumbleweed wagon and sometimes as many as six deputy marshals serving under him. He was the officer who had avenged the murders of two of his own. He was the lawman who had ended Daniel K. Huntington's reign of terror in the Indian Nations, Missouri, Kansas, Arkansas, and Texas.

He would become one of Parker's favorite lawman—until the disgrace and shame and conviction some five years later.

"They're in prison, you know," MacGregor said.

Looking back at the detective, Fallon brought himself out of the past and back to the present. "Judge Parker gave them three years. They might have gotten out early for good behavior. I don't know. That was a long time ago, and I never ran into those two again."

"You will," MacGregor said. "They're in Jefferson City."

Fallon shrugged. "Can't say I'm surprised. What are they in for?"

"They were riding with Linc Harper's gang when Linc robbed a train near Glendale."

"Glendale?" Fallon chuckled. "Like the James boys."

"Well, if you know Linc Harper, you'll know he's trying to top anything and everything that Jesse James ever did." MacGregor pulled an envelope from an inside pocket on his coat. "Both of them wound up in St. Louis, drunk as a skunk and spending money like it was candy and displaying a fine gold watch known to have been taken from a citizen on that train. They both got twenty years."

"That's a hard sentence," Fallon said.

"Even harder if you know Jeff City. But your buddy Isaac Parker isn't the only tough judge in the West."

Fallon leaned forward. "You were supposed to fill me in on the particulars of why I'm going to Jefferson City."

MacGregor grinned and rubbed the back of his head. "Seems we got a little distracted and interrupted in that alley. I do thank you for your help."

"If you really wanted to thank me, you could send someone else to prison."

The young man laughed. "You read the four pages back in Father's office. I think you have an idea of what we want from you."

Fallon leaned closer, lowered his voice, and spoke from memory.

"Young Jess Harper had been sentenced to the Missouri State Penitentiary as an accessory to a bank robbery committed by the notorious Harper Gang in Plattsburg. According to the bank president, Linc Harper's gang made off with $42,927.32. A posse caught up with the outlaws, killing two, but Linc Harper—as usual—somehow managed to escape with a couple of the other bandits. When the trail went cold, the posse moved to St. Charles, where a Pinkerton agent—and this must have really angered Sean MacGregor—learned that a woman living in a rented house near the river was not Mrs. Jessica Taylor, wife of a traveling drummer of farm implements, but actually Jess Harper, the young wife of the bank- and train-robbing scourge of Missouri."

"You have a good memory," MacGregor said.

Fallon shrugged.

"So you know the details of the case and the crime. What do you know about Jess Harper?"

Fallon grinned. "I've never met her, to the best of my knowledge."

"From the reports you read," MacGregor said, but he was smiling, too.

Fallon started to wonder if he liked this detective, or if maybe the detective even liked him. But liking a person and trusting a person, Fallon knew, weren't one and the same.

He exhaled, thought, and remembered what he had read in the American Detective Agency office.

"About five-foot-four, a little over a hundred pounds, brunette, no visible scars, hazel eyes. Both parents dead. How they died weren't on the sheets of paper. She grew up in Ray County. Parents were dirt poor, but they lived across from where Linc Harper's folks farmed. Age listed on the prison sheet as twenty-two."

To that, MacGregor snorted.

Fallon kept talking. "Parents were named Benton. No surviving brothers or sisters for Jessica. She left Ray County two years ago and was thought at that time to have been seeing Linc Harper. Disappeared until one of your rival detective company's operatives located her in St. Charles, put two and two together, and poor Missus Harper wound up in prison."

"She might have put on some weight," MacGregor said.

"In prison?"

MacGregor grinned. "Could you recognize her?"

Fallon shrugged. "I won't have to. Most of the inmates will know who she is."

"And you know what we want."

Fallon said: "You figure Linc's young bride knows where the money might be, or where you might be able to find Linc."

"The railroad and the governor have put up a substantial reward for either," MacGregor said.

"So I'm to get in good with the woman, find out what your father needs to know, and get out."

"Not Father," MacGregor said. "This is *my* case. My idea to send you there. You do know that the state pen houses women along with men."

Fallon's head nodded. "Indeed. As long as I can remember."

"That's right." MacGregor waved for the bartender to bring another drink. "You want something other than coffee, Hank?"

"No," Fallon said. "And I've had enough coffee."

"Just one more for me, pal," MacGregor said. He looked back at Fallon. "Since eighteen forty-two," MacGregor said, always the detective. "If the pen's hell on men, imagine how hard it is on a woman. Especially a refined, young woman like Jess Harper."

The bartender passed by and hurriedly slid a glass of rotgut toward the detective.

Fallon said: "And you know that, unlike in the ancient days when the prison first opened, they have a separate building for the women inmates."

"Yes, since 1876. Seventy-eight cells, although they have never had that many women prisoners. Separated from the men's cells by a wall of stone, and that wall is at least twenty feet high."

"I don't believe they allow much socializing between women prisoners and men convicts."

"Hardly."

Fallon nodded. "Thaddeus Gripewater."

"Of course. You will get yourself to the prison infirmary as an assistant to our lovely, drunken sawbones."

His head bobbed once more. "Cherry pie and gin."

"However you do it is fine by me. But you can't wait too long."

Fallon waited.

"Jess Harper's pregnant."

Fallon sat back. MacGregor sipped his drink.

"How far along?"

"She's showing," MacGregor replied. "Our sources seem to guess six months, maybe seven. That gives you two, three months."

"Unless the baby decides to be premature," Fallon said. "Or the girl has a miscarriage."

MacGregor set the glass down and gave Fallon a curious look before snapping his finger and nodding his head. "Of course, of course, you were married yourself. And had a girl. You know of those . . ." He must have seen the look on Fallon's face because he stopped, bowed his head, and mumbled, "Sorry, Hank. Didn't mean to bring up bad memories."

Damn, Fallon thought, *if the son of a bitch doesn't sound sincere.*

"There's another possibility," Fallon said.

"No." MacGregor cut him off. "Not her. She loves her man. Wants to mother a cutthroat's son. Women are so damned strange."

"There has to be easier ways to do this, don't you think?"

MacGregor finished his drink. "I'm sure there is. Now, my father, and our dear, fine, upstanding warden in Jefferson City, they would likely prefer to bring the young woman—I don't think she's out of her teens—into a basement and pull out her fingernails and toenails and maybe even put her on the rack. That's their methods. I kind of prefer something closer to human decency. And something tells me that you're the same. No matter how hard those years wearing a badge, and those ten long bitter years in prison turned you."

"And don't forget my recent little sojourn to Yuma Territorial Prison and the Sonoran Desert in Arizona and Mexico," Fallon pointed out.

"But that was Father's doing. This is mine."

"Jeff City isn't any better than Yuma." Fallon had never been inside those walls, but, as a kid growing up down in Gads Hill, he had gotten to the state capital a few times and remembered staring in awe at those brutal, haunting walls and hearing the noises that sounded behind the tall stones and barbed wire.

He would send men to prisons, but he never had thought much of what it might be like—until he had to learn for himself, first in the dungeon of Fort Smith, then in Joliet, and just a short while back, in the hell-hole down in Yuma.

"Agreed."

The door to the dingy saloon opened again, and this time it was Aaron Holderman, who waved two train tickets in his left hand as he pushed his way toward the table.

"We'll finish our talk," Dan MacGregor said, "on the train."

CHAPTER ELEVEN

His face damp with sweat and his lungs heaving, Aaron Holderman dropped into the vacant chair at the table and tried to catch his breath as he slid a handful of paper tickets across the table toward Dan MacGregor. The big brute's sweat stank so much that the young detective almost gagged, and that made Fallon almost smile.

Yeah, the big man good for nothing except brute force smelled awful, but nothing compared to some of the smells Harry Fallon had endured in the federal jail in Fort Smith and later in Joliet and Yuma. Dan MacGregor might have been a good-enough detective, but Fallon wasn't sure how he could handle fieldwork—especially the kind of assignments MacGregor was sending Harry Fallon to work.

As MacGregor picked up the tickets, Holderman found a silk wild rag in his back pocket and brought it up to his face, wiping his flushed cheeks and thick beard relentlessly.

"Seven-fifteen," MacGregor said and slid some of the tickets to Fallon. "Ever been to Peoria?"

Fallon's head shook. "Big slaughterhouse or something like here, I've heard."

Holderman had recovered enough to laugh. "If you think Peoria's got a slaughterhouse, wait till you get to Jefferson City."

MacGregor said, "Aaron, why don't you just shut the hell up?"

Fallon studied the tickets.

It seemed pretty straightforward. Fallon looked over the tickets again before lifting them off the table, folding them neatly, and sticking them in his vest pocket. "Seven-fifteen departure to Peoria. One hour there, then another train to St. Louis, and from there the westbound to Jefferson City."

"Here's your tickets, Aaron." MacGregor held out the papers, which Holderman took, crumpled, and shoved into his pants pocket.

There were still tickets on the table. MacGregor took his and slipped them into his coat pocket.

"You sure you want him to come with us?" Fallon said.

The big man turned and glared at Fallon, who ignored him.

"It'll keep him from bending Father's ear," MacGregor said.

The bartender brought a mug of foaming beer and set in front of Holderman, who smiled and lifted the beer and took a quick swallow.

MacGregor was already standing. "Let's go," he said.

Fallon rose.

The big man's eyes widened. "But . . . I just got my . . ."

"We don't want to miss the train." MacGregor was already heading for the door.

"But we got plenty of time." Holderman must have realized he was talking to himself because Fallon was only a few steps behind Dan MacGregor.

"Pay the bartender," Fallon said as he went through the front door behind MacGregor.

They grabbed supper, the three of them, at a café a couple of blocks from the train station, walked to the station, where MacGregor bought two newspapers and a sack of peanuts from a vendor and moved inside to wait for the train to be announced. They had an hour-long wait, and Holderman looked bored half that time, angry the rest of the time. Fallon had to figure that MacGregor was refusing to let the big oaf out of his sight—just in case Holderman tried to get word to Sean MacGregor.

There had not been enough time, Dan MacGregor must have thought, for Holderman to send any information back to the detective agency's offices during his quick trip to the train station to get the tickets. That seemed to be what Dan MacGregor thought. Maybe he was right. On the other hand, Fallon did not think Aaron Holderman was as worthless as he appeared, especially when it came to double-crossing someone for money.

Fallon filed that theory to the back of his mind. He was still trying to figure out the dynamics of the American Detective Agency. It seemed to go something like this:

Sean MacGregor doesn't care much for his son . . . Dan MacGregor doesn't care much for his father . . . Aaron Holderman knows his paycheck is signed by Sean MacGregor . . . Aaron Holderman is not a man to be trusted.

So what did that mean? Fallon knew he didn't trust Holderman. He certainly didn't trust Sean MacGregor. He wanted to trust Dan MacGregor—but he didn't. Those years behind the walls in Joliet made it hard for Harry Fallon to trust anyone.

MacGregor poured a handful of peanuts into Fallon's hand, took a couple for himself, and tossed the bag to Holderman. The young detective handed Fallon one of the papers and opened up the *Evening Chicago Herald* for himself.

The peanuts were roasted and heavily salted. Fallon cracked the shells, popped the nuts into his mouth, brushed the shells onto the depot's floor, and opened the *Chicago Weekly Journal.* Aaron Holderman ate his peanuts, shells and all.

There was no conversation on the train. The rocking, rhythmic motion of the coaches made it easy to sleep, and after all Fallon had been through in that Chicago alley, he needed some sleep. Six hours later, he woke as the train pulled into Peoria. They found a little place across from the depot that proclaimed it had not closed in four years, three months, seventeen days. The coffee tasted that old, too, but the hash browns were filling and the ham and eggs tasted fresh, although neither food nor coffee could diminish the stench from the stockyards nearby.

Back at the depot, they waited another hour and then departed for St. Louis. Ten hours later, they sat inside the bustling station in St. Louis on benches as hard as rocks and twice as uncomfortable. Again, Dan MacGregor walked to a vendor and returned with newspapers and more peanuts to keep Holderman's attention.

MacGregor had the *St. Louis Chieftain*. Fallon read the *Citizen Standard of Eastern Missouri*.

Fallon skimmed the headlines but noticed two men in linen dusters sitting across from him. They were dressed in nice suits, blue and gray, wore new bowler hats and, from all appearances, were just a couple of young businessmen on their way west.

Each of the men had a newspaper, too. Discreetly, Fallon memorized their faces.

A porter came by and announced that the train to Jefferson City and Independence would be boarding on Track Four. Fallon rose, folded his paper, and stuck it in his coat pocket. Dan MacGregor tossed his newspaper on the bench. Aaron Holderman tried to pick some peanut shells between his teeth.

"Aaron," MacGregor said in a whisper. "Keep your eye on those two men." His pointer finger waved at the two men in the dusters, by now a good fifteen yards ahead of the three men.

Fallon said, "My guess is they'll be in the smoking car."

MacGregor said, "We're in Car Three."

"What am I looking at 'em fer?" Holderman asked.

Fallon and MacGregor exchanged looks.

MacGregor said, "How many men have you seen wearing dusters?"

"Plenty," Holderman said. He looked happy. He had finally gotten the shells from between his teeth.

"On horseback," MacGregor said. "Not taking a train."

The big man scratched his beard.

"Nice hats," MacGregor said. "Nice suits. And worn boots."

"Coffeyville boots," Fallon said. "Popular in Kansas among cowboys."

"Popular with the men who ride with Linc Harper, too," MacGregor said.

Holderman nodded and hurried after the two men in dusters.

MacGregor looked at Fallon. "You noticed them, too, I see."

"The newspapers," Fallon said.

"Newspapers?"

"Last week's."

"It would be unbelievable," MacGregor said, "if Linc Harper tried to rob this train and we got him."

"It would keep me out of prison," Fallon said.

MacGregor laughed, and they walked to the tracks.

More than halfway into the last leg of their journey, MacGregor had decided that those men in their Coffeyville boots were likely just cowboys who had splurged on new duds.

"All right," MacGregor announced.

Fallon yawned, pushed his hat back, and pulled his feet off the seat next to MacGregor.

"No pardon for you this time, Hank."

Fallon shrugged.

"Big Ears and Mouth isn't here, so we might as well get down to the nitty-gritty."

Big Ears and Mouth had to be Aaron Holderman. Fallon waited.

"You remember the warden's name at Jefferson City?" MacGregor asked.

Fallon nodded. "Underwood," he said. "Harold Underwood."

"Very good. Remember, he knows you're working for us. He knows you were in Joliet. But he's not going to make things easy on you."

"Of course," Fallon said.

Ignoring the sarcasm in Fallon's voice, MacGregor said, "And the prison doctor is . . . ?"

"Gripewater. Thaddeus Gripewater."

"Right. So Aaron and I will get you to the warden's office. The way it will look to the guards, trusties, and inmates is that we are delivering you from Springfield for your sentence. You are Hank Fallon, and you beat a man half to death over a card game in Springfield."

MacGregor pulled a clipping from a newspaper, which he handed to Fallon. It was worn and ragged, but still legible. Fallon was impressed.

"I just happen to be carrying a newspaper article of that fight I got convicted for."

"You take pride in your work."

Fallon grinned. "How did you manage to get this printed?"

"That's easy. Anyway, it should convince the prisoners that you're for real. And Kemp Carver and Ford Wagner will know your past career as a federal marshal. And they'd have to know that you got sent to Joliet ten years ago."

"All right."

"Underwood knows you're working for us. Nobody

else. Once you get in, you'll have to get friendly with the prison doctor. Gripewater. Thaddeus Gripewater."

Fallon nodded, but he said, "You've told me all this before."

"And you know that you don't have much time to get what we want out of Jess Harper."

"I understand."

"And how do you get in good with Doc Gripewater?"

Fallon felt like he was back at that subscription school in Gads Hill again.

"Cherry pie," Fallon said dryly. "And gin. Or any way possible."

"You're likely wondering why the warden can't just put you in as Gripewater's assistant," MacGregor said.

"No," Fallon said. "That's obvious."

"It is?"

"It's not the warden I have to convince," Fallon said. "I have to convince the inmates that I'm not a spy."

"And then you have to get Jess Harper to trust you."

"In a very short time."

MacGregor frowned. "Maybe you think you could figure out a better idea?"

Fallon chuckled and shook his head. His mind raced: A better idea than sending a former federal lawman, known to some of the inmates in the hellhole on the Missouri River, into prison as a spy? With an assignment to find a way to get a trusty's position in the prison hospital? To meet, befriend, and possibly woo or even seduce a teenage girl who happened to marry an outlaw named Linc Harper and was now pregnant with the killer's child? Have her somehow tell him where Linc Harper stashed all the loot he managed to take in a train robbery?

"I know it's a hard task," MacGregor said.

"It's damned near impossible, Dan," Fallon shot back. "You're assuming Linc Harper told his wife all his secrets or at least the secret he probably would keep closest to his vest: where he stashes his stolen booty. You're assuming Linc Harper didn't just spend that forty-two grand on horses, cards, dice, loose women, and fancy clothes. You're assuming that the convicts in that dark and bloody ground, once they find out that I'm a lawman—*was* a lawman—won't stick a knife between my ribs two nights into my sentence. This is what you call a good idea?"

MacGregor sighed. "You got out of Yuma. You can get out of this."

By that time, however, Harry Fallon had stopped listening. The door opened, but it wasn't the conductor coming through. It was one of those men wearing a new suit, new bowler hat, well-traveled linen duster, and black-leather, tall-heeled Coffeyville cowboy boots with red tops inlaid with Lone Stars.

The man stopped by the stove and lighted a cigarette, straightened, and slowly reached up and grabbed the cord above his head.

"Hell," Fallon said, and braced himself.

The stranger pulled the cord, sending a signal to the engineer to make an emergency stop.

Chapter Twelve

As the wheels screeched and groaned against the steel rails, sending sparks rising past the window, Harry Fallon kept his seat as the train ground to a stop. Dan MacGregor flew from his seat to Fallon's, but managed to extend his arms. His hands, fingers extended, pressed hard against the hard wood, his elbows bent, and he shoved himself back into his seat.

A few passengers screamed.

"We've derailed!" a woman shrieked.

A baby began bawling. An old man swallowed his chewing tobacco and began gagging.

"Wreck!" a boy shouted with enthusiasm. "We've wrecked."

Dan MacGregor's instincts took over. He reached underneath his coat toward his shoulder holster.

"No," Fallon whispered. "There are women and children to consider."

The man who had pulled the emergency cord had already drawn a big Colt with a long, long barrel. The massive .45 he held in his right hand. His left had pulled a big grain sack that had been folded and crammed under the left side of his jacket.

"Folks!" he drawled. "Kind folks, if you please. Stay put. We ain't derailed, ain't hit no cow on the tracks, and collided with no eastbound choo-choo. Just relax and hush up." He fired his gun to get their attention.

The baby cried harder. The old man threw up into a spittoon. A woman screamed. Another fainted.

From beyond the passenger coach, Fallon made out the reports of other guns being fired. Some sounded as though they were being fired in other coaches, and more than one came from the outside. There was no way, he realized, to figure out how many bandits were involved in this robbery.

Smoke from the outlaw's Colt had that acrid smell.

The man stepped from the side of the coach into the aisle and began shaking the coarse grain sack.

Fallon memorized the face.

He was not one of the two men Fallon and MacGregor had spotted at the train station in St. Louis, although he, too, wore a pair of Coffeyville boots, although his appeared much worn, patched, and the spur ridges on the sides of his boots were scarred. In fact, the spot just above the heels had been worn so roughly that the leather had ripped. He did not wear spurs, but Fallon figured a pair was likely stuck in the saddlebags on the horse waiting somewhere nearby.

Without those high-stacked heels, the man was likely an inch or two shorter than Fallon. He wore woolen trousers of black-and-gray stripes, suspenders, a solid blue shirt, tan canvas trail jacket with dark brown corduroy cuffs and collar, and a plain red bandanna. The hat was gray, nondescript. A gunbelt was buckled across his waist, and Fallon thought, from the bulge in the canvas jacket, that maybe he packed another pistol on his left hip. The face was round. His sandy hair was thin, and Fallon thought the man might be bald underneath that hat. The eyes were light, but Fallon would have to wait till the man came closer to figure out the color. He wore a handlebar mustache, and the rest of his face was covered with a day or two of beard stubble. His accent had an Ozarks twang.

"Folks," the man said as he stopped by the first occupied seat in the coach. He grinned as he shook the sack in front of the woman with her gray hair in a bun and wearing a proper dress of black-and-gray wool. The big Colt remained trained down the coach, moving from male passenger to male passenger. "On this fine mornin' you good folks has gots the privilege of bein' robbed by Linc Harper and his pals." He grinned, revealing buckteeth, a bottom incisor missing, and a gold filling in the center of one of those huge, top beaver teeth. "And we gots the honor of takin' any money, watches, rings, and jew'lry. Partin' is such sweet sorrow, but think of all them stories you'll be able to tell yer kids, grandkids." He glanced at the woman. "And yer great-grandkids, ol' lady, sweetie pie, ma'am."

The gun's barrel moved toward the woman's chest. She gasped. The barrel waved a few times and then returned and stopped in the general direction of Fallon and MacGregor. MacGregor had to crane his neck. Fallon could look straight at the gunman.

"Lady, I don't reckon I did say broaches in particular, but that would fall underneath that department of jew'lry, which I'm plumb sure I did say. In the bag, or I'll deliver somethin' else you'll be able to tell your great-grand-young'uns—once yer busted jaw be healed up good."

The woman started sobbing, begging that the broach had belonged to her mother's mother.

The old-timer a few rows behind her and across the aisle stopped vomiting long enough to lift his head, spit—missing the spittoon—and say, "Give him the thing, lady, else he'll kill us all."

"Please!" shrieked the mother of the screaming infant.

MacGregor turned away and looked out the window.

The woman began removing the broach pinned over her heart.

"Two men," MacGregor said in a soft whisper. "Outside the express car."

Fallon nodded.

"That's all I can see."

"Three passenger cars, right?" Fallon's voice was barely audible.

"I don't wanna hear no talkin', folks!" the bandit yelled. "So y'all shut up so I can hears what's happenin' in this here train *and* what's happenin' outside."

MacGregor nodded to answer Fallon's question. "No Pullmans," he mouthed.

"But a smoking car," MacGregor's lips moved.

"Two with the engineer and brakeman," Fallon whispered.

"One to hold the horses," MacGregor mouthed. "No, most likely two."

Fallon held up both hands close to his chest, spreading out all five fingers on his right hand but folding his thumb on his left. "Ten," he mouthed.

MacGregor let out a sigh. "At least," he said softly.

"Hell." Fallon exhaled.

"Holderman." MacGregor's lips moved deliberately. "Smoking car."

Fallon did not blink, did not answer, and just let his cynical stare tell the detective his thoughts.

"Yeah," MacGregor whispered. "I know."

"No talkin'. Not even whisperin'. Ever'body needs to shut up. Unless I start talkin' to you. Like I'm a-doin' right now."

The bandit had made his way to the woman with the baby. He grinned. "Boy'r gal, ma'am?" he asked.

"Boy," the mother sobbed.

"Where's the runt's papa?"

"Dead," the woman said.

"That's a shame. Your watch, lady. An' that ring. I mean, yer a widder woman now, not married no more, so you don't need that ring."

The items fell into the sack. Seating across the aisle, a man in a black broadcloth suit and flat-brimmed gray hat leaned forward and said, "How can you be so cruel? This woman and her child—"

The long barrel of the Colt slammed across the man's skull. The hat flew off, and the man crumpled to the floor, unconscious.

"I gots to eat like ever'body else," the man said. "He thinks he's outsmartin' me. Boy!" He trained the Colt on a kid, about eight years old, traveling with his parents. The Colt moved from the kid to the man and wife. "Don't worry. He won't get kilt, but I ain't got no reservations 'bout makin' him an orphan if you get smart." The gun's aim turned back toward the boy. "Get down and go through that gent's pockets. I know he's got a mouth on him, so I reckon he's got some greenbacks and gold."

The boy seemed excited for the chance to take part

in a robbery. The father pulled his sobbing wife closer. A few more gunshots outside made the passengers inside this coach shudder, and the baby cried harder no matter how much the frightened mother rocked him and patted his back.

A wallet, a few silver dollars, a gold watch were retrieved by the youngster. The boy dropped those in the sack and then showed the bandit a Remington over-under derringer he had taken off the coldcocked Good Samaritan.

"That's nice," the man said. "No, sonny. That don't go in the bag. Put that li'l lady's popgun in my jacket pocket." He nodded at his right side, and there the youngster slipped the derringer inside.

Smiling, the outlaw held the bag out toward the kid.

"Boy," he said, "take one of the coins outa this here sack fer yer troubles." The man grinned again, the gold filling reflecting sunlight from the nearest window. "Yer now an honorary member of Linc Harper's gang. But don't get no gold coin. Make sure it's just a Morgan dollar."

The father started to object, but the massive barrel of the outlaw's Colt stopped him. The boy grinned, held up the coin for the outlaw's inspection, and then slid into the seat behind his parents.

The outlaw took two watches, a purse and a billfold from the boy's parents.

"Don't throw up yer breakfast on my boots," the outlaw said as he came to the man who had swallowed his chewing tobacco. "You might not think much of my boots, but they cost me fifteen dollars twenty-one years ago. When I was perty much as honest as most of you folks."

The pickings from that man seemed mighty slim,

but the next couple gave the outlaw a string of pearls, a diamond pin from the gentleman's tie, a fine gold watch, a checkbook, coin purse, and wallet.

Outside, someone began shouting. The robber waved the Colt at Fallon. "Open that winder," he said.

Fallon obeyed.

"Fuse is lit! Fuse is lit! Fuse is lit!"

The man and wife currently being relieved of all their valuables sucked in a deep breath. The man sat down opposite them, swearing softly, and started to say, "Folks, best brace—"

The explosion roared, shaking the entire train, and the concussion jarred four more windows open. It sounded like hailstones pelting the roof of the coach, but Fallon understood it had to be debris from the express car.

He could already smell smoke from the explosion.

"I hates dynamite," the robber said as he pushed himself back to his feet. "And I shore don't care much for an expressman who won't open the door when he knows what's a-gonna happen if he don't. Linc Harper ain't one to trifle with, folks. I bet he used an extra stick of dynamite just to teach that damned fool of an expressman a lesson."

The man chuckled as he stopped at the seats occupied by Harry Fallon and Dan MacGregor.

"That damned fool of an expressman is likely scattered all across that express car, and maybe all the way to I-oh-way and down to Arkansas. Don't you reckon?"

The barrel waved at Fallon, who slowly spread open his coat. "Nothing," Fallon said. "No watch. No wallet. Nothing."

"I call that horse apples," the outlaw said, and his finger touched the trigger slightly.

"Don't be a damned fool!" said someone sitting behind Fallon.

MacGregor cleared his throat. "It's true, mister." MacGregor slowly pulled back his coat, revealing the brass shield of the American Detective Agency.

The outlaw's eyes—they were green, Fallon decided—widened. "You're a law dog?"

MacGregor shrugged. The Colt now was aimed directly at the bridge of MacGregor's nose.

The outlaw laughed. "He takin' you to Jeff City?"

Fallon nodded.

"And you think maybe I'll just take you instead of this gent's watch and wallet?"

Fallon shrugged. He wasn't sure if riding with Linc Harper was a better option than being slammed behind the iron and stone of the Missouri State Penitentiary.

"Well, that ain't happenin'. The split us boys get from Linc ain't gettin' no smaller."

"But . . ." Fallon sang out desperately. "Listen . . ."

The man's head whipped around to Fallon. "Shut up!" he bellowed and brought the Colt toward Fallon's chest.

Then he saw the movement and swung the Colt back at MacGregor.

Two gunshots roared. Fallon felt the muzzle blast as the big .45 blew out the glass of the window. He couldn't hear the baby bawling anymore. All he heard was a deafening ringing in his ears, and Fallon wondered if his eardrums had ruptured.

CHAPTER THIRTEEN

Fallon realized he was standing, holding the arm of the gunman. He felt the heat of the Colt's barrel, as he ripped the heavy revolver from the train robber's hand. The man offered no resistance, and Fallon pushed him away, but used his free hand to pull the derringer from the outlaw's pocket.

The bandit fell between the seats across the aisle. His eyes remained open, staring at the ceiling of the coach. They did not blink. The man did not breathe. Fallon saw the smoldering hole in the center of the outlaw's chest, the shirt blackened by the powder flash, and just a little splotch of blood.

All of this had happened in mere seconds. Fallon's right ear still rang, but he heard someone's voice, sounding like a bad echo, in his left. He saw Dan MacGregor brushing past Fallon. The detective held a smoking Smith & Wesson in his right hand—Fallon wondered where he'd gotten it—and he knelt in the aisle and reached for the corpse. His left hand jerked the trail jacket, revealing, as Fallon had suspected, another holster. This one also held a .45-caliber Colt, which MacGregor drew from the holster.

Somehow, Harry Fallon heard something else. He turned toward the door that led to the front of the train. A man wearing a duster and Coffeyville boots—one of the two Fallon and MacGregor had noticed back in St. Louis—had kicked open the door. He stopped, cursed, and raised the heavy revolver he had carried with the barrel pointed toward the floor.

Fallon and MacGregor fired, their shots sounding just like one, and dust puffed off the robber's black coat as he slammed through the open doorway, hit the railing, and fell into a heap.

It sounded like everyone in the coach had started screaming now, almost sounding even louder than the roaring echoes of gunshots.

Holding two guns—his own and the dead man's across the aisle—Dan MacGregor started toward the door and the second dead robber.

As he ran past the white-faced, stunned people at the front of the coach, MacGregor turned around. "I'll take the front!" he yelled. "You take the back. This is our best chance!"

Fallon did not know what the young man meant by best chance. Best chance at taking Linc Harper alive? Best chance at getting themselves killed? The latter seemed a more likely scenario.

But Fallon was running toward the next coach. This was the last coach, after which there would be a baggage car and the caboose. Dan MacGregor was running toward two more passenger coaches and the express car, and Fallon figured, most of the robbers would now be at that express car. Or from the sounds of the gunfire in the third passenger car, those killers might be heading this way.

He had no time to contemplate. He pushed through the door and stepped into the platform between the coach and the smoking car. He didn't know what time it was. Perhaps mid-afternoon, but the air did not feel fresh. He smelled the thick smoke, and he saw it, too, burning his eyes worse than the pistol shots in the close confines of the coach he had just left. But Fallon was not outside long.

Lowering his shoulder, he slammed through the door, passed the closets on his left and right, and dived to his left in the smoking car.

A bullet punched through the hard wooden seat, sending splinters into Fallon's cheek and right hand and thudding into the paneled closet behind Fallon.

"Sumbitch!" the outlaw swore.

Fallon came up, above the seat, started to aim, and quickly dropped to the floor as another bullet slammed into the closet's exterior wall.

"Everybody!" Fallon shouted. "Everybody get down! Get down on the floor!"

That's why he had not chanced a shot at the second man with the duster and Coffeyville boots. A bullet might have blown the head off a spinster, a rabbi, a kid, or a couple of poker players. He thumbed back the hammer on the dead outlaw's Colt.

Another bullet clipped the top of the seat above Fallon's head.

A crazy thought flashed through his head:

What are a kid, an old widow, and a rabbi doing in the smoking car of a train?

He thumbed up the loading gate of the Colt and

spun the cylinder on his arm. Another shot dug into the rug in the aisle.

The dead outlaw had boarded the train prepared. He had filled every cylinder with a .45-caliber shell. Two of those had been fired. Four shots. That's all Fallon had left, plus the two rounds in the derringer—if the little Remington were loaded. He heard gunfire from the front of the train.

Somewhere, likely hiding on the floor, groveling, perhaps even soiling his britches, Aaron Holderman was inside this smoking car. Aaron Holderman also had a pistol, and maybe more than one. The big, fat slob could help.

More gunfire. Curses. Fallon thought he heard horses whinnying loudly out on the northern side of the tracks, but he still couldn't be sure because of the pealing in one of his ears.

He knew that he would get no help from Aaron Holderman. Fallon adjusted the cylinder on the big .45, snapped the loading gate shut, and pulled the Colt to full cock. He brought the pistol up, and, without raising his head to look, squeezed the trigger.

It snapped on a spent cartridge.

Swearing vilely, Fallon pulled back the hammer and pressed the trigger again. He got the same result. He couldn't hear the loud click as the hammer again landed on a cartridge that had already been fired. His right hand had not bucked, and he had felt no heat, smelled no smoke.

Fallon cursed again, and quickly eared the hammer back to full cock.

Now he heard everything clearly. The man in the

linen duster and fancy hat shouted, "You're empty." Boot steps then sounded on the aisle.

Fallon dived, landing hard on the filthy carpet near the door, the .45 at about the level of the seat bottoms, and tilted upward. He squeezed the trigger, and this time, as Fallon knew, the hammer struck a live bullet.

His hand was jerked upward, and he had already cocked the Colt and brought it down. Fallon held his fire. He was counting his shots. Three rounds left, and there was no need to put a bullet into a dead man.

The bullet had smashed into the outlaw's throat, and he lay in the center of the aisle, about six seats up from Fallon, blood spurting toward the ceiling as the man clawed desperately at the red spray. The old woman fainted in her seat. Fallon saw that the kid was limp, like a rag doll, and held by a man in a sack suit.

The rabbi—indeed, he was a rabbi, or maybe a thespian dressed like one—bent over and picked up the revolver the gunman had dropped.

Fallon looked behind him at the door, still open, and glanced out the windows on both sides as he hurried toward the bearded Jewish man and the dying—no, he was dead now—train robber.

Fallon stopped by the rabbi, and extended his left hand.

"I'll take his gun, sir," Fallon said.

The old man looked up with dark, sad eyes. "It is empty, my son."

Fallon swore, but did not question the old rabbi. Instead, Fallon stepped over the dead man, and imagined he heard his boots making a squishing sound on the lake of blood soaking into the carpet.

Once he was past the dead man and the Jewish man, Fallon stopped.

He bellowed, "Holderman! Where the hell are you?"

A hand appeared atop a seat, followed by another big, hairy hand with swollen knuckles. Aaron Holderman's dark hair came up next, and finally those eyes widened as he saw Harry Fallon coming down the aisle, a smoking Colt in his right hand and a derringer—Fallon had pulled that from his coat pocket—in his left.

Holderman's appearance seemed to say that he thought Harry Fallon had come to the smoking car to kill him.

Which, Fallon later conceded, would not have been that bad of a plan.

"Get up," Fallon snapped.

"But . . ."

Fallon was already past the big coward. "Up. Get your gun."

More gunfire sounded toward the front of the train. "Head toward the engine. MacGregor's up that way, and he needs your help."

"Where are you going?" Holderman was coming right behind Fallon. They passed more frightened men: gamblers, drummers, and businessmen. Fallon kicked open the door. He stared across the platform. A baggage car. There could be outlaws inside. Fallon and MacGregor had not considered that possibility when they had counted the number of cutthroats Linc Harper had with him.

No. No, had there been men back here, they would have come inside the smoking car by now. More gunfire appeared to confirm that thought.

Fallon moved to the side of the platform. Carefully, he peered around the corner, but only for a split second. He came back, breathed in deeply, and turned quickly to the brute beside him.

"That way!" Fallon motioned with the pistol's barrel. "Looks like everybody's outside right now."

"What do I do?" Holderman stammered.

"What you're paid to do!" Fallon snapped.

He stepped over the railing, switched the Colt to his left hand, and gripped the metal bars that made a ladder to the roof. "You take the ground. I'm coming across the top."

Holderman nodded, though his face showed ashen with fear, and moved through the gate and jumped onto the embankment on the south side of the tracks. He fell onto his side, rolled down the small slope, but came up heaving and weaving, and at the pace of a sloth, started past the smoking car and toward the three passenger coaches, the express car, the tender, and the locomotive.

Gripping the bars above his head with his right hand, Fallon pulled himself over the railing. His left hand hung down, still holding the warm Colt, and his boots managed to find a hold on lower rails.

Thick smoke still clouded the sky, and more shots and loud curses came toward the express car—or what was left of the express car after Linc Harper had used dynamite to blow open the door and blow the express agent to hell and gone.

Fallon braced the Colt against the railing for some measure of support, and started to raise his free hand toward the railing above his head.

Then a bullet burned his right forearm, and Fallon swore, lost his hold, and crashed against the rocks alongside the graded track.

CHAPTER FOURTEEN

Fallon landed hard, but somehow could still breathe. He could also hear.

"Charley!" a voice screamed from the southern side of the tracks. "He's on yer side! Kill him. I'll get that fat chuck o' lard headin' toward the engine."

Fallon rolled over. He saw a man in brown pants, brown coat, brown boots—not Coffeyville boots, either, and brown hat—pulling a string of horses alongside the caboose.

Of course, Fallon thought. The horse holders!

He expected those horses to be closer to the express car by now. The man let go of the lead rope and clawed for the old Navy Colt stuck in his waistband. Realizing that he still held the Colt, Fallon brought the barrel up, cocked the .45, and punched the trigger.

He missed, but the gunshot had frightened the horses. Two buckskins at the head of the pack, squealed, reared, and jerked the rope from the stunned horse-holder's gloved left hand. He turned toward the horses, which now tumbled into a heap. The robber realized his error and turned back toward

Fallon. The bandit cursed. He pulled the trigger again, and the bullet ricocheted off one of the smoking car's heavy iron wheels, sending sparks flying onto the stones and grass as Fallon rolled underneath the car.

"Son of a gun!" Fallon heard. "The horses. Linc, Linc! The kid has lost the horses!"

Fallon rolled over the crossties and stone, over the iron rail, and down the embankment on the southern side of the tracks.

The man who had shot at Fallon, the other one of Harper's gang left in charge of the horses, stopped running after Aaron Holderman. He must have heard shouts and the gunshots. Now, seeing Fallon lying on his back in the grass, the man cursed, and began sprinting back toward Fallon.

Holderman kept running.

Fallon brought the pistol up and started to squeeze the trigger.

The running man pulled a trigger. Fallon saw that the slim man in farm duds and a straw hat carried a repeating rifle. Fallon held his fire.

Let him come, Fallon told himself. Another bullet made a whanging sound as it hit the rail above Fallon's head. He felt the sparks land on his hair and face and heard the deadly ricochet of the bullet. The horse holder on the northern side of the tracks cursed again.

For the time being, Fallon ignored that outlaw. The one coming at him on this side of the railroad line worked the lever as he ran. He brought the rifle up again, fired from his hip, sending the bullet well down the tracks—not even close to Fallon.

Still, Fallon told himself, not yet. Not yet.

He was sweating profusely. Maybe even more than

Holderman had back in Chicago, what seemed like an eternity ago.

The man jacked the hammer. This time he stopped and brought the rifle to his shoulder. Fallon had no choice.

He squeezed the trigger. The Colt roared, and the punk spun onto his side, pitching the rifle to the ground near the front of the smoking car. Fallon came up, cocked the Colt. If his math was right, he had one shot left. He started for the Winchester the wounded robber had dropped. Then a bullet creased his left calf, and Fallon felt himself stumbling. The Colt fell from his grip, hit the wet grass in front of him, bounced up, and was lost in the grass.

Fallon dropped hard into the thick grass, knew blood had begun leaking from his leg, felt the fire of pain. He gritted his teeth.

"I got him, Forrest!" called the horse holder, the one called Charley, from the other side of the tracks, the one who had lost the string of horses. "Finish him, Forrest! Finish him!"

Forrest could not answer. He was too busy trying to keep the blood from pumping out of the hole in his middle.

Forgetting the horses, the outlaw named Charley was scrambling. A sharp glance underneath the car showed the man's boots disappearing as he pulled himself onto the platform between the smoking car and the baggage car. Fallon also glimpsed the pounding hooves of the horses as they bolted for the trees about a hundred yards north of the tracks. A few outlaws appeared to be running after their mounts.

He didn't have time to check on Forrest, whom Fallon figured, or at least prayed, was mortally wounded. Nor could Fallon try to grab the Winchester rifle Forrest had dropped. Fallon reached inside his jacket and hurriedly pulled the Remington .41-caliber derringer out. He brought it up in his left hand and tossed it to his right. He wished he hadn't lost that big .45. Even with only one round left, Fallon felt more comfortable with a long-barreled pistol of a heavy caliber than a two-shot derringer with minimal range.

Charley came over the platform in a hurry, a move that Fallon had not expected. The gunman fired a shot that scattered rocks in an explosion of sand and pebbles that stung Fallon's cheek near the splinters he had received inside the smoking car.

Fallon swung the derringer up. Charley came up to his knees. His Navy popped. The outlaw cursed. He was using an old relic from even before the Civil War, a weapon many poor gunfighters still used, but most of those had converted those weapons so that they could take modern cartridges. Charley's gun still used percussion caps and leaden balls.

"Darn it!" Charley snapped. He pulled back the hammer and aimed again.

The over-and-under derringer popped in Fallon's hand.

Fallon saw a red dot appear on Charley's left forearm.

"Darn it," Charley said again and spun to his left, but only briefly. The Navy Colt spoke this time, but the ball hit the wood near the smoking car's flooring. Fallon pulled the trigger again as Charley straightened and cocked the Navy one more time.

This time, Fallon's slug tore off Charley's right ear, and Charley spun to his right, touching off a round that dug up the grass just a few yards in front of the bloodied robber.

Yet Charley was far from finished, and Fallon knew he was out of bullets, and out of luck.

Still, as Charley somehow managed to bring back the Navy's hammer to full cock, Fallon threw the derringer at the gunman. Charley just tilted his head and the little Remington sailed past the man's bloodied head and was lost in the brambles behind the robber.

The hammer dropped. The pistol snapped.

Not a misfire. No, Fallon knew that Charley's .36-caliber relic was empty.

Charley swore harder than his usual "Darn it." He rose, started to charge Fallon and brain him with the butt of the revolver, but stopped after no more than three or four steps. The man straightened, lowered the pistol, and laughed.

Feeling the shadow behind him, Fallon turned, and dived toward the train tracks. He rolled over, and saw Forrest, bleeding from his stomach, but standing now, his face pale, both of his hands holding the Colt .45. The lucky bastard had somehow found the handgun in the grass.

Behind Fallon, Charley laughed.

Fallon dived to his right. He heard the roar of the .45 and felt something crease his neck. Not a bullet. His ears were ringing again, but he seemed to recognize a new sound. Fallon came up, blinked, spit out dust, and saw the outlaw named Forrest holding both hands to his face. Blood poured between the fingers—or, rather, the remnants of fingers on his left hand—and out of the man's ears. His stomach was also bleeding from the bullet hole Fallon had put there.

The Colt was gone. The barrel must have been

packed with mud and sand, and the .45 had blown up in the robber's hand. Fallon didn't care about that. He saw the Winchester, the weapon the dying Forrest probably wished he had picked up instead of the dirt-clogged Colt.

Fallon slid through the grass, gripped the stock of the Winchester, and brought it up. He could not recall if Forrest had chambered a fresh round after firing a shot, so Fallon hurriedly worked the lever. A casing flew up and over Fallon's shoulder, but Fallon didn't notice if he had ejected a spent brass cartridge or a good one. It didn't matter. He had a Winchester and Charley was coming at him with a knife.

Another noise sounded, a loud screeching of metal against metal, and the rattling of chains.

"Stop!" Fallon yelled at Charley.

Charley, running with the knife, did not obey Fallon's order.

So Fallon stopped him.

The Winchester roared, a bigger hole appeared in the center of Charley's face, and backward he flew about six feet before he crashed on the ground and rolled down the embankment. He was dead. They were both dead.

Fallon felt pretty certain of that.

He sucked in a deep breath and spun around, looking through the opening between two of the railroad cars. He tried to spot the rest of Linc Harper's men. Then he wasn't looking at the running horses or the patch of woods a hundred yards on the other side of the track. He was looking at the smoking car, its windows, not a glimpse of any passenger—they were likely still huddled on the floor.

Fallon swallowed. Another opening gave him a

quick glimpse of the woods and landscape, only to be replaced by the red-painted wood and the yellow gold yellowing:

Hannibal – Saint Louis – Jefferson City
RAILROAD COMPANY
Missouri's Most Trusted Line
Since 1888

"Damn," Fallon said and followed that curse with: "What the hell."

The train. The damned train was moving. Backing up. Heading toward St. Louis.

Still holding the smoking rifle, Fallon ran down the tracks toward the platform between the third passenger coach and the smoking car. He gritted his teeth against the pain all over. His lips tasted blood. Sweat stung his eyes. His calf hurt like hell from the crease a bullet had made, and he could tell that wound still bled. It felt like it was bleeding a lot. He could even feel blood in his boots, damping his socks.

He needed attention. But first he needed to get back on that train.

Fallon came up the embankment. Briefly, he considered pitching the rifle, but that was the only weapon he had. He shifted it to his right hand, raised his left. He swiped at the iron railing. Missed. Tried again. He stumbled but righted himself and pushed his legs harder. Once he caught up to the platform, he ran a little past it. The train was picking up steam and speed. Fallon grabbed the railing with his left hand. His fingers clenched tightly, and he threw the Winchester over the top rail. The barrel hit the flooring; the long gun bounced up and landed near the open doorway. With his right hand free now, Fallon grabbed a firm hold on the iron bars. His feet started dragging along the gravel near the bed. The wheels screeched. He remembered those times as a kid, and once as an adult, when he had seen the remains of men and a couple of kids who had gotten caught beneath a train's iron wheels.

Fallon pulled himself up, bent his legs, and climbed.

His left hand slipped free, came up immediately, and found a higher spot to hold. With a grunt that matched his effort, Fallon pulled himself up, and over onto the platform. He landed, rolled over, and tried to catch his breath. The train kept moving, faster, faster, faster.

Fallon looked at his boots, saw the ripped leather that revealed his socks. Indeed, one was stained red with fresh blood.

But he was on the train. He was still alive.

Then a man appeared galloping on a sorrel mare alongside the tracks. The man seemed shocked as much by Fallon's appearance as Fallon was by his. But the man had the reins in his teeth, and Remington .44s in both of his hands.

The dark revolver in the man's right hand pointed at Fallon.

CHAPTER FIFTEEN

The gun in the man's right hand exploded as Fallon dived toward the Winchester. The blast clipped Fallon's hair and whined off a metal rail. Fallon landed on his knees but did not stop. His right hand grabbed the rifle's barrel and he kept his momentum carrying him forward as the horseman's second shot tugged at Fallon's jacket.

A moment later, Fallon found himself back inside the smoking car.

The rabbi was looking up and starting to stand.

"Get down!" Fallon tried to say. He wasn't sure if the rabbi, or if anyone had heard him. Fallon couldn't be certain that he had even said anything, though he knew his lips and jaw had moved.

A bullet shattered a window in the back—no, actually the front—of the coach.

The rabbi dropped back out of sight.

All the other heads remained below the windows.

He tried to figure out who was driving the locomotive. Or who was making the engineer and fireman keep the train speeding east. Certainly not Aaron

Holderman. Dan MacGregor, perhaps? Or Linc Harper or one of his henchmen? MacGregor and Holderman would be doing this to get the train, and the passengers, away from the murdering outlaws. Linc Harper would be doing it because his planned method of a getaway, his horses, were across the flats and into the woods by now—except the one the gunman was riding alongside the smoking car right now.

Fallon looked out of the windows, but the rider would be down the embankment now. The windows just revealed the countryside as it flew past. How fast were they going? Fallon wondered. Ten miles an hour? Fifteen? Not as fast as a horse could gallop. But as long as the fireman fed the boiler, the train could outrun the man on horseback.

Fallon glanced through the glass at the back of the coach but saw only the countryside. A sudden fear made him sweep his head around and look to the south. The rider couldn't have been on that side of the tracks, but there might be another horseman. Nothing. Just trees and blue sky.

Biting his lip, Fallon crouched and moved back onto the platform. He eased his head around and saw the country. Clear. For now. Fallon went out, toward the passenger car where he had been talking to MacGregor when the ruckus began. He leaped over onto the next car and saw the rider, but barely.

Fallon swore. The gunman had ridden up closer to the train now, and was leaning in his saddle, trying to grab hold of the metal bars that formed a ladder, trying to pull himself onto the train.

Fallon moved back toward the smoking car when a bullet shattered the doorknob he was reaching for. Fallon dropped to his knee, spun, and saw another man on horseback. This one rode a dun. The front brim of his hat was pushed up against the crown as he galloped. Unlike the first horseman, he didn't keep his reins by his teeth, but held them in his left hand. His right hand trained the revolver. It was a self-cocker, and the man squeezed the trigger twice more.

Both bullets slammed into the wooden panels on Fallon's left. He fired the Winchester. The bullet missed the rider but hit the horse—Fallon hated for that to have happened. Down went the horse, sending the gunman sailing over the horse's head and landing hard on the ground. The man bounced twice before the dead dun rolled over him, driving the broken man deeper into the ground.

The lever jacked. Fallon moved to the side of the platform on the back of the passenger car. Leaning over the side, he brought the rifle to his shoulder and took careful aim.

Fallon swore. The horse held no rider and was slowing to a trot, drifting away from the roaring train, the reins dragging in the grass and tangle of briars. The rider had made it onto the train.

Fallon moved back through the open entrance to the smoking car, his rifle ready. He saw nothing.

Where was the gunman? Waiting? Fallon swallowed and dropped to a knee behind the bullet-riddled wooden seats where he had first taken shelter when he had entered the car.

He held his breath and glanced at the bloodied calf. A smart man would have taken this time to wrap a rag around the wound and try to stop the bleeding. But Fallon was not about to let go of the Winchester.

The wheels made that clicking and clacking sound, and the cries of the baby in the coach behind Fallon reached his ears. That's when Fallon realized that his ears were no longer ringing. He could hear, almost clearly.

He heard something then.

Fallon looked up at the ceiling and raised the rifle.

The gunman was on the roof, maybe halfway down the coach. Fallon aimed, put his finger against the trigger, but quickly let off the pressure. He had no idea how many bullets remained in the rifle.

He looked down the aisle and he stood. The killer would be heading toward the front of the train. Fallon could hurry through the coach, come out on the platform between the smoking car and the baggage car, climb to the roof.

And then what? Fallon thought. *Shoot the man in the back?*

He blinked and answered his question out loud.

"Hell, yes."

But Fallon did not move. He could hear the man on the roof. Even with the wind rushing past his ears, the man on the roof might be able to hear him. And no matter which side Fallon came up on the killer, front or behind, Fallon would have to raise his head to get a clear shot at the man on the roof. That meant the man on the roof would have a clear shot at Fallon's head.

He backed toward the door and kept the rifle pointed at the ceiling.

The ceiling creaked. Fallon pressed his lips tightly together.

The rabbi started a prayer.

"The hell with this," Fallon said, and pressed the trigger. The stock slammed against Fallon's shoulder, and he rapidly worked the lever. Through the white smoke he saw the round hole in the ceiling. The Winchester spoke three more times, punching more holes in the ceiling. His ears were ringing again, but he saw a mass drop off the roof on the southern side of the tracks.

Fallon raced outside, moved to the side, and looked down the tracks. A body lay on the gravel halfway down the embankment as the train kept backing up. Fallon sucked in a deep breath, exhaled, and stepped toward the center of the platform.

A shadow crossed his face. Instinctively, Fallon dropped to his knees as a bullet whined off the metal railing. The Winchester blasted. Fallon saw the man standing on the roof of the passenger coach spin around, dropping the shiny pistol he had just fired at Fallon. But the man did not fall over the side. He landed on the roof. Immediately, Fallon gripped the metal bars that formed a ladder and climbed toward the roof. He paused only long enough to extend the rifle away from the wood and iron and flicked his wrist and sent the stock forward while gripping the lever for life. A spent shell was ejected, and Fallon jerked his wrist and arm the other way. The Winchester returned to his hand, barrel upward, hammer cocked, ready to fire.

Fallon came up the ladder, laid the rifle on the roof, and saw the man as he clawed for a pistol with his right hand. His left hand hung bloody and useless at his side.

Fallon squeezed the trigger. The gun did not buck, and he realized he was mistaken. The Winchester had been cocked, but it was empty now.

The man laughed, and Fallon came up the rest of

the way, screaming something like a charging bear and a mad dog.

The man's gun cleared his pants, and he pulled the trigger as Fallon swung the rifle at the gunman's legs while diving toward the center of the roof.

Both men dropped onto the roof, Fallon rolling toward the south and the gunman rolling toward the north. The Winchester fell over the edge. Fallon came up and dropped back as the man hurled the pistol—which was also empty—at Fallon's head. It missed completely.

Both men stood, cautiously, getting their sea legs.

Fallon recognized the man before him. Maybe in his thirties, blond hair, cold eyes, a mustache and underlip beard. Linc Harper in the flesh.

Harper tried to pull a knife from the top of his Coffeyville boot, but Fallon came at him with a flying kick. Both men landed hard, and Harper rolled toward the rooftop's edge. Fallon came up, saw the knife Harper had dropped, and grabbed it with his left hand.

Both legs throbbed now, but the wind from the rushing train cooled his sweat. Harper somehow managed to roll back toward the center of the roof. He sat up, sprang up, and stared at Fallon, who pushed himself to his feet. Fallon showed the outlaw leader the knife, made a feint with the blade. Harper wet his lips.

Fallon hated knives. He wasn't good in a knife fight, and he wasn't sure how much longer that leg of his, still bleeding from the calf, and bruised from so many falls, would support him.

After spitting out blood that the wind took away to the west, Harper pulled his wounded arm toward his stomach. Next, the most wanted man in Missouri turned and ran.

Fallon tried to shake some clarity into his head, and ran, or wobbled, on the rooftop as fast as he could. He watched the wounded man leap across the narrow abyss and somehow manage to keep his feet and not fall off either side on the next passenger coach. Fallon did not slow and let out a wild yell as he jumped. Harper's landing had been anything but graceful, but the bandit had managed to keep his feet. Fallon fell onto the roof, his jaw slamming hard, slamming his teeth together. He sat up and looked at his right hand. That fist no longer held a knife.

Desperately, Fallon felt his stomach, and shook off that fear. He hadn't stabbed himself with Linc Harper's hideaway knife. He had dropped it during his hard fall. He looked left, right, behind him. The damned weapon must have gone over the side. He looked up and saw Linc Harper leaping to the first passenger coach.

Fallon came up, and moved, weaving, this way and that, his leg burning, his teeth aching, his head pounding, and now—as the two men made their way toward the engine—smoke stung his eyes. Just ahead of the first passenger car was the smoking express car. The wheels were miraculously intact.

Linc Harper was on top of the express car now.

But the killer had nowhere to go.

Fallon leaped across the opening. His leg gave way, and he fell to his right, just as Linc Harper's Coffeyville boot clipped his left ear. Had Fallon fallen in the other direction, the heel of the boot would have caught him dead center in the face and likely sent him off the train. But Harper's kick sent him falling, too.

Fallon swore and came up in a crouch. Harper made rolling toward the edge look almost graceful. He bounced onto his feet and moved toward the smoke.

Fallon came toward him. The black smoke was blowing away from Fallon, in the wind, toward the train's tender and locomotive. He could see the hole in the center of the coach, near the doorway of the express car. It looked to be maybe ten feet wide. There was a narrow ridge on the southern side of the roof, but not enough room for a grown man to traverse. Fallon stared at Harper, who moved to the edge of the rim.

The men said nothing. They just stared at each other.

Suddenly, Harry Fallon roared, gritted his teeth, and lowered his shoulder. He hit Harper in the side as the killer turned to try to avoid the onetime federal marshal. And the next thing Harry Fallon knew was that they were falling through the hole in the roof Linc Harper had caused with dynamite.

They were falling into the smoke. Into the abyss. And probably, Harry Fallon thought, all the way to hell.

Chapter Sixteen

Coughing, blinded by the thick smoke and the awful smell, Fallon pushed himself to his feet. He blinked and moved to the opening in the side of the coach. He rubbed his eyes with his fist, coughed again, and looked into the decimated ruins of the express car. There was no sign of Linc Harper, and Fallon slowly grasped that the outlaw had rolled through the opening he had blown into the car. Linc Harper had fallen off the train.

The train still sped east. Fallon now took time to pull a bandanna from his pocket and tie it tightly above the bullet wound in his calf. He had to get this train stopped, but he still didn't know who was running the engine. Or how he could make it to the engine.

Pull the emergency cord? Yeah, like the petrified engineer would obey that command. That's what had pretty much started the robbery attempt.

Fallon saw shelves along the side of the car, filled with letters, some burned, some not, and other boxes and sacks. He practically fell against the shelves, but pulled himself up toward the roof, turning the wooden holes into a makeshift ladder. The wind felt good once his head cleared the ceiling. He could breathe again. Grunting, he managed to drag his body onto the other side of the express car's roof.

He dragged himself a few more feet, came up onto his legs, and wobbled painfully toward the tender. He dived onto the pile of wood and felt thankful that this cheap-ass railroad still used wood and not coal. If the engine wasn't being commanded by Dan MacGregor, a chunk of pine would be a hell of a better weapon than a handful of coal.

He crossed over the wood, and the engine came into view. Holding the piece of firewood over his head, Fallon crept closer. He saw a familiar face, and Fallon let out a sigh of relief.

Aaron Holderman, the big galoot, never looked so good.

"Hey!" Fallon called out through cupped hands. He shouted Holderman's name.

There was no response, so Fallon yelled again. Still nothing. He even waved his hands. Holderman scratched his beard, so Fallon pitched a chunk of wood at the big fool's feet.

Jumping back, Holderman looked up while reaching for the revolver in his shoulder holster, but then recognized Fallon, and turned to yell something inside the engine's cab. Wearily, Harry Fallon started climbing from the wood and into the engine. He couldn't hear Holderman, and could barely recall climbing down, but the next thing he understood was that Dan MacGregor was easing Fallon into a seated position.

Fallon saw the engineer and the fireman staring at him.

He cleared his throat and told the detective. "Stop this damned train. Right now."

MacGregor nodded at the big engineer, who reached for the controls.

"I got the robbers in the passenger car," MacGregor said, "saw Aaron running alongside the train, so I joined him. Somehow . . ." MacGregor shook his head, which was bleeding from a scratch near his cowlick. "Somehow Linc Harper didn't see us as we moved to the engine. And the two men keeping a drop on Mr. Schultz and Mr. Doolittle . . ." MacGregor waved in the general direction of the engineer and the fireman.

"We killed them deader than dirt," Holderman proclaimed.

"*I* killed them," MacGregor corrected as he wrapped Fallon's calf with a long piece of silk.

"But I drew their fire." Holderman pouted.

"When the dynamite went off, and then when I glanced from the window and saw the horses scattering, I thought the best thing to do was to get the train out of here." He pointed toward the locomotive's cowcatcher. "They had barricaded the tracks with ties and an old buckboard, so the best thing I could come up with was putting it into reverse. Going east."

"We saw most of those boys hightailing it after the horses," Holderman announced.

MacGregor's chuckle sounded bitter. "Father will

want our heads when he learns we let Linc Harper get away. It would have saved you a stint in the Missouri pen."

"Maybe not." Fallon waved at the back of the train. The fireman handed him a canteen, and Fallon drank thirstily, wiped his mouth, and told them about his rooftop fight with Linc Harper. Fallon kept drinking until the canteen was empty.

"Thanks." He smiled at the fireman and shook his hand.

MacGregor straightened. He quickly turned to the engineer. "We need to get this train going back. West. Now."

Fallon cleared his throat. "First," he said, "we need to make sure none of that bunch is still with us. And check on the passengers."

"And we must see about Major Mosby," the engineer said.

"Who's Major Mosby?" MacGregor asked.

"The conductor," the engineer replied.

"But Linc Harper might get away," Holderman said.

"No," MacGregor said. "Hank's right. And if Harper's on the run, he's afoot." He looked at the engineer. "Would you happen to have an emergency telegraph kit aboard?"

The engineer shook his head but said in a German accent: "One mile or two west of the barricade there is a relay station."

"Let's hurry," MacGregor said.

Werner Schultz, however, was not going anywhere, west or east, until he had inspected his train. He had

Holderman and Mr. Doolittle, the fireman, removing the barricade the bandits had put up to stop the train, while he, Fallon, and MacGregor walked down the rails.

"Where is Mr. Whitaker?" the engineer asked.

"Who?" MacGregor asked impatiently.

"The express agent," the German replied. He did not like the smoke still coming out of the ruins of the express car, so MacGregor was sent to round up some able-bodied men to come help put out the fire. While they were seeing to that task, Fallon had to climb back inside the car and see about the express agent.

He found an arm in one of the cubbyholes atop blood- and soot-smeared letters bound for Jefferson City. A brogan, luckily with just some blood and yarn from a sock, against the engine-facing wall, and some substance that looked like brain matter and cartilage on a parcel heading to Fort Larned, Kansas. Fallon stuck the arm in an empty sack and set it gently on the floor of what was about to become a morgue.

"If there's anything else left of him," Fallon told the engineer, "I expect that Harper and his bunch tossed it out."

Fallon's ruined boot toed at a mass of blood on the floor near an opened strongbox that spread to the blown-apart doorway. That, he figured, was also all that was left of the expressman.

The engineer frowned, but MacGregor and Holderman were back with the rabbi, two gamblers, a cowhand, and a drummer. They shoveled dirt onto the smoking heaps and pounded out the few flames remaining with canvas mail sacks while the detective, Fallon, and the engineer gathered the dead bodies of outlaws still aboard the train. These carcasses were deposited, unceremoniously, in the ruins of the express car.

By the time the fire was out to Mr. Schultz's satisfaction, Holderman and Doolittle reported that the rails were now clear.

The passengers returned to their respective cars, and MacGregor glared at Mr. Schultz. "So," he said, "you think we can go looking for Linc Harper now? Before he's in Iowa or Canada?" MacGregor spat, and offered this enticement: "There is, you might remember, a price on his head for four thousand bucks."

Mr. Schultz didn't appear to be listening. He kept looking down the train, past the passenger coaches, the smoking car, all the way to the caboose.

"Major Mosby," the German said softly. "It is not good that he is not here."

"Maybe," MacGregor said, "they tied him up. We should have checked on him sooner, sir. Let's go find him."

They found him, but he wasn't tied up. He wasn't alive, either.

Major Mosby lay on the caboose's floor, the coffee he had spilled when he dropped his tin cup all but dried or drained through the cracks in the flooring. The blood underneath his navy blue woolen coat had stained the floor. Fallon placed two fingers on the conductor's throat but knew he would feel no faint beat. His left hand reached up and closed the dead man's eyes.

"They give him no chance," Mr. Schultz said. "He did not even have a gun on his person."

"Truly," Dan MacGregor said, "I am sorry for this

good man's passing, but he must be glad that we have avenged his death by cutting down all of his killers."

Nodding slightly, Schultz pulled himself to his feet. Fallon rose too, found a blanket, and covered the dead man with it.

"We'll leave him here," MacGregor said. "I can have my man Holderman ride back here, sir, if you feel that necessary."

"There is no need," the engineer said.

"Very well," MacGregor said and headed out the back door they had left open. "Then let's get moving. Now. We need to find Linc Harper."

Werner Schultz kept the locomotive at a slow speed, as Fallon leaned out on the northern side of the rails and Holderman studied the terrain to the south. Atop the tender, Dan MacGregor used a pair of binoculars to study the distant woods on both sides of the track.

"Mr. Schultz," Fallon called out.

"I see it," the big German said, and the wheels began that screech as the train slowed to a stop. MacGregor must have seen the body, too, for he climbed down before the train began to slow and turned to Holderman.

"Get to the passenger cars. Tell them to keep their heads down and stay on the floor. Tell them Linc Harper's gang could be anywhere and we don't want them to get hurt. Now."

Holderman's face was blank with confusion.

"Do like I say, damn you," MacGregor snapped.

Harry Fallon wasn't sure what to think, either, but when the train stopped, MacGregor practically kicked

Holderman out of the cab and shouted, "Now. Now. I don't want anyone to see this. Get to it, man. Hurry."

As the big man hurried to the first passenger coach, he issued the warning, "Stay down. Get on the floor. It's for your own good."

MacGregor was running in the opposite direction, toward the body on the gravel, near the rails, lying in a pool of blood.

Limping, Harry Fallon slowly followed. The German engineer and the fireman came right behind him. They stopped as Dan MacGregor struggled to overturn the body.

"Linc Harper," Werner Schultz said, "rob no more of my trains."

That, Fallon thought, *was a damned understatement if ever I'd heard one.*

When Fallon and Harper had fallen through the hole in the roof of the express car, Fallon had hit nothing but floor, ash, and scattered sacks and papers. Linc Harper landed on a piece of ragged timber that likely had been propped up by a strongbox. The jagged edge had torn through Harper's stomach, punched through his back, and Harper had rolled out of the doorway blown open by the dynamite charge. If he had not been killed outright, he had bled out quickly.

The blood Fallon had seen on the floor of the express car, it turned out, was not from the blown-to-oblivion express agent. It was Linc Harper's.

"Damn!" MacGregor said. "Damn it all to hell." He turned from the corpse and glared at Fallon. "Why couldn't you have taken him alive?"

Fallon studied the detective. This reaction came as a surprise. Linc Harper, the most wanted train robber in Missouri, was at last out of commission. Dan MacGregor, and the American Detective Agency, could claim not only wiping out Linc Harper's gang—but killing the leader, too, and stopping another train robbery.

"Boss," Doolittle, the fireman said in a consoling voice, "y'all just killed ol' Linc Harper. You folks gonna be heroes across the whole United States of America."

MacGregor swore. He spit the bile out of his mouth. "Four thousand dollars," he said, and spat again. "That's all the state of Missouri has put up for Harper. I don't care about four thousand dollars. His last robbery netted him forty-two thousand, nine hundred and twenty-seven dollars and thirty-two cents in cash, coin, and bearer bonds. That's not including watches, jewelry, and trinkets and the cash they took off the passengers. Which is probably all the survivors of the robbery got, anyhow. That's what I'm after."

So, Harry Fallon had just learned something about Dan MacGregor. The apple doesn't fall far from the tree. Isn't that how the saying went? For all his nice talk, Dan MacGregor was turning out to be just as corrupt as his old man.

Chapter Seventeen

Harry Fallon waited until Aaron Holderman managed to turn MacGregor's wrath away from Fallon and back on that worthless tough, which did not take that long.

"I reckon we should just cut our losses," Holderman offered. "Four thousand bucks is better than nothing."

"Shut up, you fool!" MacGregor snapped. He looked back at the passenger coaches and suddenly grinned. "Wait a minute." He rose and faced the engineer.

"What time will we be at Mount Van Zandt?"

The engineer stared as if the detective had lost his mind. "This train does not stop at Mount Van Zandt," he said.

The fireman added, "Lessen the bridge over the Gasconade be washed out."

"This train is stopping there today," MacGregor said.

"But we are late already," Mr. Schultz said.

MacGregor pulled greenbacks from his wallet. "This train is stopping there today."

Mr. Schultz wet his lips with his tongue. The fireman shoved his big hands into his deep pockets and stared at his filthy boots.

MacGregor turned toward Fallon and explained: "There's an icehouse in Mount Van Zandt. I went to college with the owner's son." He quickly looked back at Mr. Schultz. "That icehouse is still there, isn't it?"

The engineer shrugged. "I do not know. I guess. Maybe. I have not stopped there since, as Doolittle said, the last time the bridge was washed out during a spring flood. Last year."

"It was there a month or two back," Doolittle said. "Ain't much to that town, though, so I don't know how long it can stay in business."

"It supplies ice to Rolla, and also ships to towns along the Rock Island line," MacGregor said. "That's how it stays in business. And the fact that there's hardly anybody left in that town makes this even better."

He peeled off a few bills and handed them to Mr. Schultz, then took two more bills and gave them to Doolittle, who reluctantly pocketed the bribe.

"We take Harper's body off the train," MacGregor told Fallon. "Dump his carcass and let's find the location of the money from Harper's last robbery."

Fallon nodded. No, the apple does not fall far from the tree.

"You said there's a relay station near the spot where the train was first stopped?" MacGregor again turned his attention to the engineer, whose head nodded.

"*Ja*. One mile. Maybe two."

"We'll stop there," MacGregor ordered. "Wire the

stations ahead, tell them that we've just been held up by Linc Harper's gang, but that we have wounded men and are screaming our way to Jefferson City. They should hold all eastbound trains till we arrive. We'll tell them that we've also got practically all of Linc Harper's men. Dead. Except we did not get Linc Harper."

The engineer stared at Fallon, who just looked dumbly back at the German.

"Get Harper's body loaded into the express car," MacGregor ordered.

"With that stick still in him?" Holderman asked.

"Unless you want to pull it out," MacGregor said.

It took all five men to lift the body and toss it through the wide opening. Holderman and Doolittle then climbed into the ruins of the car and dragged the body out of sight.

"What do you think?" MacGregor asked Fallon.

Fallon just stared, thinking: *You really don't want to know the answer to that question.* So he just shrugged.

"What about the other bodies?"

Holderman's question from the blown-open door to the express car turned MacGregor's attention away from Fallon.

The fireman had leaped down, but Holderman remained in the car.

It was a question, apparently, that Dan MacGregor had not considered. His mouth opened, closed, and he pressed his lips together and thought.

"You should leave them," the engineer said. "We need to get to that relay station quickly. I do not know when the next train will be leaving Jefferson City, but finding a side track can be hard on short notice. And a train robbery, a destroyed express car, one dead express agent, and a murdered conductor are enough for one trip. We do not wish to add a head-on collision to our tally."

"We're not leaving any bodies for wolves or bounty hunters once the word of the robbery hits Jefferson City," MacGregor said at length. "We stop. Throw the bodies aboard this same coach." His head nodded as though he were convincing himself that this plan was indeed the best option.

"Makes sense to me." Holderman climbed out of the baggage car and dusted off his hands on his thighs once he was back on solid ground. "That way we can at least get any reward the men we killed have on them. And maybe this cheapskate railroad company will pay us a few dollars for saving their hide."

Mr. Schultz grunted as though any money from "Missouri's most trusted line since 1888," the Hannibal-Saint Louis-Jefferson City Railroad Company, would not amount to much. "This line," the engineer said, "does not even have porters on its trains."

MacGregor did not seem to hear or care.

"You two head back to the engine, get this train moving west," MacGregor said. "Slow, though. You'll see the bodies, and when you do, make sure you stop the train. We'll get off, like the conductor. When the body or bodies have been loaded, I'll wave at you, and you start riding again. We'll keep that up till we get to where this damned old ball first started."

Fallon cleared his throat. "All the dead men should be right where they started the ball. The only one I know that got killed after you started backtracking east was Linc Harper."

"You're right." MacGregor beamed at that thought. "Excellent. Excellent. Let's get moving."

Fallon began thinking: *Forty-two thousand, nine hundred and twenty-seven dollars and thirty-two cents minus . . .*

The train moved down the rails east until the first dead outlaws appeared, and then Werner Schultz eased the train to a stop.

"Everybody in the coaches!" MacGregor yelled after stepping off the train and walking down the tracks. "Stay with your heads down. There still might be some bandits lurking about."

As Fallon grabbed a dead man's legs and MacGregor picked up the corpse by the arms, Fallon asked, "You think so?"

"Not really, but maybe." Holderman and the fireman were walking away from the tracks. MacGregor's head tilted toward them. "Two of the bunch ran after the horses. I dropped both of them as we started the train reversing down the tracks. That's who Holderman and that big black cuss are picking up now. A couple more were also running for their mounts, but when they realized what was happening with the train, they quickly returned to try to get aboard." MacGregor grinned. "I set their sun, too."

"You were busy," Fallon said.

"So were you. You must have had your hands full with Harper."

Fallon shrugged.

By the time the last corpse had been tossed into the express car, the dead cargo numbered twelve—two more than Fallon and MacGregor had estimated. The body count did not include the express agent, since there really wasn't any body to speak of. Nor did it include the conductor, since he was stiffening in the caboose.

Eleven train robbers, plus Linc Harper, should make for a substantial reward, Fallon thought, but certainly not forty-two thousand dollars. Still, Fallon could not figure something out. Did Dan MacGregor want to turn in the money for a reward? Or did he want that forty thousand bucks for himself?

When the train reached the relay station, MacGregor leaped off and sprinted to the little wooden shack with the pitched roof on the north side of the tracks. Fallon limped over, his calf throbbing and his leg beginning to stiffen from the crease of that bullet. The engineer withdrew a key, stuck in the big, shiny chunk of brass, and released the padlock. MacGregor pulled open the door and smiled at the sight of the telegraph machine.

But the smile died instantly. "Who knows Morse code?" he said in a panic.

Werner Schultz answered: "Major Mosby."

"Hell's fire!" the young detective snapped. "Who still alive knows Morse code?"

With a heavy sigh, Fallon slid past MacGregor and found the dusty stool. "You'll need to connect the wires," he said casually. "And keep in mind I haven't done this in sixteen years, and my training on the Katy line was pretty much nothing. And don't expect me to go very fast."

Once the wires were connected, Fallon tapped out a signal and waited. The reply came quickly enough, so Fallon drew in a deep breath, looked up at Dan

MacGregor, and asked, "What exactly is it you want me to tell them in Jefferson City?"

Before MacGregor could answer, Aaron Holderman shoved his way into the shack. "How can you be dead certain this hombre will send the right message? He might try to be smart, say something else maybe. I wouldn't trust this convict, Danny boy."

Fallon shook his head. "Yeah," he said sarcastically. "That's exactly what I'm going to do. I'll tap out a message and maybe have a passenger or freight train, or a combination, come screaming down the tracks to meet us at twenty miles an hour and send every mother's son of us—not to mention every innocent passenger in those coaches—straight to hell."

Fifteen minutes later, the telegrapher working for the Hannibal-Saint Louis-Jefferson City Railroad Company in Jefferson City had assured Fallon that the track would be empty and that law enforcement and some of the best doctors in Missouri's state capital would be waiting for the arrival of the westbound train from St. Louis.

Fallon signed off with a thanks and disconnected the machine. He slid back in the stool and looked at Dan MacGregor and Aaron Holderman.

"Then everything's working out perfectly," MacGregor said. "Just perfectly." The handsome detective spun around and nodded at Werner Schultz. "Mister Engineer, you can take us straight to Mount Van Zandt. Finally, things are starting to look a bit brighter."

Fallon cleared his throat. He waited until the detective was giving him complete attention.

"We're what, two hours from the station at Mount Van Zandt, right?"

Werner Schultz nodded.

"You're going to have a hard time getting Linc Harper's body off this train without some of our passengers noticing," Fallon said.

Holderman sang out: "We'll just tell them that Linc Harper's bunch is hiding in the woods. That'll keep their cowardly hides on the floor, hugging the carpet and praying for God's mercy."

A lengthy silence followed before MacGregor sighed, cursed, and spit on the shack's filthy floor. "I think Fallon's right. Our passengers are mighty sick at lying on the floor. Curiosity gets the better of even the most yellow coward."

"So how do you get around this?" Werner Schultz asked.

Chapter Eighteen

The young detective grinned, revealing his perfect and perfectly white teeth.

"We leave them behind," Dan MacGregor said. He smiled up at the engineer. "You'll have to tell them, Mr. Schultz."

"No," the big German said, "I not get shot. No matter how much gold you offer."

The passengers aboard one of "Missouri's most trusted line since 1888" appeared to be on the verge of riot, and, perhaps, murder.

"Ladies," Dan MacGregor pleaded, waving his arms and trying, but not coming close to succeeding, to quiet the raucous mob. "Gentlemen. This is for your own protection."

Aaron Holderman tried to help. "Do you folks want to get shot down like dogs?"

The rabbi shook his head, and when the crowd, Holderman, and MacGregor also paused, the elderly Jewish man said: "You abandon us in the middle of these thick woods, so thick it feels as though we are in a cave. There is no telling what beasts, what hoodlums, live in this unholy forest."

"And," said an erudite woman, "what happens if another train roars down these tracks, east or west?"

MacGregor gestured. "You will be safe on the siding. It will be more dangerous for us to take this train the last few miles to Jefferson City."

Voices sang out. "My brother is sick and maybe dying." . . . "We have been through enough torment already." . . . "My lawyer is Jason James Johnathan the Third of Columbia, Missouri, and he will be suing your railroad for ten thousand dollars if you leave us here." . . . "We got no food on this train, no liquor neither, and half the women aboard are older than my grandma, so what the hell is it we're supposed to do till an engine comes from Jeff City to pull us in?" . . . "You folks just want to leave us so all the newspapers will give your side of the story, print your names in the paper. That just ain't right."

"Ladies and gentlemen," Dan MacGregor said, waving his hands down to quieten the raucous passengers. "You have just endured one of the bloodiest holdups in the annals of our young, noble country."

The engineer leaned close to Fallon and whispered, "Is he running for office?"

He's running for something, Fallon thought.

"And you also," the detective went on, "have just become part of American history. That robbery attempt, which left a longtime employee of the Hamilton Express Company and a loyal and immensely dedicated servant to the Hannibal-Saint Louis-Jefferson City Railroad Company dead—killed defending your lives and the property of decent, hardworking citizens in this fine state and elsewhere . . . this robbery was perpetrated by Linc Harper."

That did manage to silence some of the passengers.

"All of the bandits are dead," MacGregor said, and he reached over and put his left arm around Fallon's shoulder. "And this brave lad, a criminal just like those who took part in the assault on this train, whom we are bringing to the prison in Jefferson City . . . he risked his life to save you good, kind folks. And he was seriously injured by a bullet from one of those two-bit assassins."

He turned away from the crowd to shake Fallon's hand.

"It hurts like hell," Fallon said, "but I don't think that bullet wound is serious."

"But this speech will make it more believable if you get paroled in three, four, five months." With a wink, MacGregor turned back to face the throng.

He's more polished than his father, Fallon thought. *That could make him more dangerous.*

"So," MacGregor went on, "ladies and gentlemen, I beg of you, I plead with you, to wait here. On the siding. Out of harm's way. It would not be out of the question that Linc Harper, deceitful, despicable, dastardly criminal that he is, has more men in the woods and waiting for the chance to rob this train again, perhaps on the Gasconade River, in an attempt to exact revenge on what I, our brave conductor, engineer, and fireman, this felon with a bullet in his body, and my trusted comrade with the American Detective Agency have done to his reputation and his pride."

The people fell silent again. Fallon shifted on his legs and grimaced. He didn't do that for MacGregor's sake or to help the crowd change its thinking. The wound in his calf throbbed, and he could still feel some blood leaking out. Likely, he needed a few stitches.

"Colonel Schultz," MacGregor said, "our esteemed and dedicated engineer, will get us to Jefferson City as quickly as possible. Then an H, SL, and JC engine will return here quickly, to bring you fine citizens to Jefferson City." MacGregor wet his lips. "And I am absolutely certain that a number of Jefferson City reporters will be traveling with the peace officers, a doctor, and the train's crew. Staying here," MacGregor concluded, "will give you time to think about the robbery, your experiences, your bravery, before you face the members of the Missouri press."

He stopped, shook Schultz's hand, and quickly turned again to the people. "Besides, surely the H, SL, and JC will refund you for your tickets, after all the hardships you've endured, and even give you a pass for a future trip on the fine Hannibal-Saint Louis-Jefferson City Railroad Company."

MacGregor shook Doolittle's hand, clapped Holderman's back, and put his arm around Fallon as he led him to the engine. "The rabble bought it," MacGregor whispered.

"You sold it," Fallon said.

"Unhook the coaches," Schultz told the fireman. "We're keeping the express car." He shook his head. "Or what's left of it."

On the far side of the Gasconade, the much shorter train pulled to a creaking halt next to what might have passed for a depot. It was late afternoon, and the sun was almost ready to dip behind the tall trees on the rolling hilltops.

"Stay here," MacGregor ordered. "Get that stick out of Harper's body and throw it into the river. I'll find my pal Mickey, see what all this is going to cost me, and then we'll get that body into the icehouse."

"You should hurry," Schultz told the detective. "They will wonder what took us longer."

"They'll have to wait," MacGregor said and he crossed the tracks in front of the humble little railroad station and made his way down a narrow road toward an even shabbier little town.

The biggest structure, closer to the river and against one of the hills, had to be the icehouse, Fallon thought. There was an inn, a corral, and livery, and a handful of scattered houses, more shacks than homes. The icehouse, though, looked substantial, made of rocks, which probably could hold in the cold like a deep cave. Another building stood next to the big warehouse of ice, which might have housed one of those contraptions being used to help make ice these days.

Fallon saw a few mules, two horses, a donkey, and a dog. Nobody came out of the homes or businesses to see why a train had stopped today.

"You're helping me," Holderman said. It wasn't a question.

"Yeah," Fallon answered dryly, and he turned and headed for the ruins of the express car.

As a young deputy marshal in the Creek Nation, Fallon had pulled an arrow out of another deputy. Eli Walking Horse had gotten drunk, robbed a Methodist missionary and busted the sky pilot's jaw, and then announced he was returning to the old ways. He was going to fight a one-man war against the white eyes. The war didn't last long. He shot a quiver of arrows at the marshals assigned to bring him in to Fort Smith, but quickly sobered up when a few Winchester bullets struck the cabin in which he had holed up. One of those arrows, though, had sliced into Deputy Marshal Johnny Powell's shoulder, and Harry Fallon was given the job of doctoring the deputy. He had to push the arrow through, then cut off the barbed point with his knife, and then, after laying Johnny Powell on his back, he had braced his right foot on the lawman's arm, gripped the shaft of the arrow with both hands, and pulled as hard as he could while Powell had screamed his head off before passing out.

Getting a chunk of two-by-four pine out of Linc Harper's body was a bit more difficult.

Fallon held the stiffened corpse under both shoulders and locked his wrists together while Aaron Holderman jerked and twisted and finally heaved the piece of wood out. Holderman fell against the wall, and almost went through it, as he pitched the bloody pine onto the body of one of the other killers.

Both men spit onto the floor and took the body of the bandit to the hole in the wall. Fallon returned to pick up the wood that had killed Harper and brought it back, handing it to Holderman.

"Do what the man says," Fallon said. "Drop it into the river."

The big oaf frowned, but took the wood, stepped out of the car, and headed down the railroad tracks to the bridge that spanned the Gasconade. By the time he had returned, Fallon had retightened the makeshift bandage around his calf. Ten minutes later, while Holderman chewed tobacco and Fallon rested in the shade of the express car, Dan MacGregor returned. The smile on his face told him that everything was in order.

"Mickey's at the icehouse, getting the door opened. Let's hurry."

They brought the body—Holderman and Fallon—walking behind MacGregor down the path, through the woods so fewer citizens might see what they were doing and quickly moved into the cold, dark icehouse. Mickey, the owner, had laid a tarp down on the ground. This they used to wrap the dead outlaw's body, and then again, Fallon and Holderman lifted the corpse and took it into the deepest reaches of the cavernous building, moving from blocks of ice to buckets of ice, and finally laying the covered body atop a mountain of ice.

"He should keep," Mickey joked.

"I always thought Hell was hot." MacGregor handed some bills to his friend, and they returned to the train, where they climbed inside the engine's cab.

Without speaking, the engineer and fireman went to work, and the train pulled away from Mount Van Zandt. MacGregor seemed happy. Holderman just looked like Holderman.

As the train began picking up speed, Fallon leaned over closer to the engineer and called out over the noise and rattle and pounding of the steam engine.

"How long before we reach Jefferson City?" he asked.

Mr. Schultz answered.

Nodding, Fallon came back to the back of the cab.

"You in a hurry?" MacGregor grinned and offered Fallon a cigar, which he politely declined. "Not many men I know are in a hurry to go to prison. Especially behind the iron of where you're going."

He and Holderman chuckled.

A wry grin stretched across Fallon's face.

"Prison," he said, "can't be any worse than what I've just been through."

But from all his experiences in Joliet and Yuma, Harry Fallon knew that would not be the case. Not by a damned sight.

Chapter Nineteen

Werner Schultz slowed the engine as it approached the bridge that spanned the Missouri River. Jefferson City lay across the Big Muddy. The city was green with trees, unlike Yuma down in Arizona Territory. Jeff City wasn't what you might call hilly, but it was far from the flats and bleakness of Yuma. Yuma was a raw, frontier town in the middle of the desert in a territory that looked more like Mexico than the United States. In fact, most of the residents in the town spoke Spanish.

Jefferson City? Well, this was different. It was the Missouri capital and had been since the 1820s, although every once in a while, folks from St. Charles or Sedalia might try to stir up some support to claim the capital. Fallon could make out the dome to the state Capitol building. The city was spread out, with buildings crammed along the central business district and at least a dozen steamboats docked along the levees. It wasn't Chicago, but it was a whole lot different from Fort Smith. As the train neared the city, Fallon looked to his left and saw the one thing Yuma, Arizona Territory, had in common with Jefferson City, Missouri.

The prison stood on a hill that rose above the Missouri River. The stone walls looked haunting. Yuma Territorial Prison was called "The Hellhole," and Fallon had firsthand experience to know that nickname was well deserved. A lot of folks called the Missouri State Penitentiary "The Walls," because of those towering, foreboding blocks that had been quarried by some of the first prisoners housed there. Yet the prison had another name, too.

The bloodiest forty-seven acres in the United States of America.

As the train eased toward the depot, Fallon spotted at least two cameras on tripods, with the photographers ready to hold up their flash and try to record a historic moment in the annals of Missouri law enforcement. Several newspaper reporters huddled about, maybe two dozen police officers, soldiers from the Army, and Fallon figured that among the masses had to be officials from the state pen.

"Hell," Dan MacGregor breathed.

"What did you expect?" the engineer said as he eased down on the throttle.

"I know," MacGregor relented, and he twisted in the sweltering cab of the Baldwin locomotive to face Aaron Holderman.

"Take the reporters to the express car. But don't tell them anything. Just let them see the bodies and tell them that I will answer all questions but only after I have delivered a prisoner to the warden."

He wiped sweat from his brow and looked at the engineer and firemen. "They'll want to hear from you. Tell them the truth. Up to where Fallon joined us in the cab and we stopped the train. You can tell them about your brave conductor. But anything about Linc

Harper—and don't mention him at all." He tilted his head toward Fallon. "You don't even know his name."

MacGregor twisted some more to stare at Fallon. "And you're mute till we get to see the warden. And you don't tell him a damned thing about the train robbery."

Fallon said nothing.

The train screeched, hissed, and vented as it lurched to a stop. One of the cameras flashed, sending a cloud of smoke toward the blue sky, and men in sack suits with pencils and pads of paper stampeded toward the engine.

"Remember what I told you," MacGregor said. "All of you. Don't slip, or you'll catch hell." He nudged Fallon's shoulder.

"Let's go," he said.

But no one could go too far. Fallon and MacGregor were surrounded by a mass of men who shouted questions that no one could understand. MacGregor kept both hands on Fallon's shoulders, trying to use him to push through the horde, but that wall remained as solid as those a few blocks away that kept thousands of prisoners penned away from society.

"Gentlemen . . . gentlemen . . . gentlemen . . ." MacGregor begged.

The reporters tried to crush them more. Another camera flashed, filling the platform with the scent of sulfur.

"Is this one of the robbers?" . . . "What happened to Linc Harper?" . . . "Is the money safe?" . . . "How many bandits?" . . . "How did you manage to stop them?" . . . "How many passengers and crew were wounded or killed?" . . . "Who are you?" . . . "What's your name?"

Fallon's ears began to hurt again, this time from

the shouting reporters. He could smell the stench of cigar and cigarette smoke on their breath, and some were so close he could breathe in their sweat and feel the saliva as it sprayed across his neck, cheeks, and clothes as they shouted their questions.

Eventually, Dan MacGregor stopped trying to get through the barricade of bodies.

He stood behind Fallon, his hands still gripping Fallon's shoulders, and waited, not answering the questions, probably not even looking at any of the reporters. Another camera flashed. Fallon wondered if Aaron Holderman, Mr. Schultz, and Doolittle, the fireman, were fending off another herd of news-crazed inkslingers.

"Shut the hell up!" MacGregor's words came at the split second of silence when every reporter seemed to be sucking in a breath before firing off another question. It almost deafened Fallon, but it managed to leave the reporters speechless for a moment.

MacGregor took advantage of what had to pass for silence on the noisy platform of the railroad station.

"Gentlemen of the press," MacGregor said—and, to Fallon's surprise, no one interrupted. "I will be glad to answer as many of your questions as I can. But right now, people, I have to get this man to the state penitentiary."

"Is he one of Linc Harper's owlhoots?" someone cried out.

Before MacGregor could answer, about a half dozen more questions were hurled in the faces of Fallon and the detective.

MacGregor waited until there was another pause.

"No. This man has already been sentenced and I and another employee of the American Detective

Agency were transporting him to prison to serve his sentence."

"Who is he?" someone shouted.

"What's his name?"

"He looks beaten all to hell. Mister, did Linc Harper do all of that to you?"

"What's he in for?"

"His name," MacGregor answered, "is not important. My name is Daniel J. MacGregor." He spelled out his name. "I am vice president and chief of detectives for the American Detective Agency out of Chicago, Illinois."

"You're a Pinkerton man?" someone in the back sang out.

Fallon had to hide his grin over that question.

"The American Detective Agency," MacGregor said through tight lips. And he deliberately spelled out those words as well.

A million other questions fired out. MacGregor managed to catch his breath and lift his hands off Fallon's shoulders to wave down the excited band of newspapermen.

"Gentlemen," MacGregor said. "Please. Just give me time to take this man to where he belongs, and then I shall return and give you as much information as I can that will not jeopardize our search for the wounded Linc Harper."

"Harper's still alive?" . . . "Did he get away with any money?" . . . "How many men did he kill?" . . . "Was it Harper who beat up your prisoner?" . . . "Was Harper wounded?" . . . "Did you see Linc Harper in person?" . . . "How did Harper stop the train?" . . . "How many men were riding with Harper?" . . . "Did you Pinkerton men set up a trap to lure Harper to this robbery?"

"We are not Pinkertons," MacGregor seethed.

"What about you?" A bearded reporter with a toothpick moving around his teeth nudged closer to Fallon. "You sure you weren't part of Harper's gang? Or are you a stoolie for the Pinkertons? Is that why Linc Harper beat you all to hell?"

Fallon wet his lips. He said, "You know, boys, there are about ten dead outlaws in the express car back yonder. Harper's men blew the hell out of that car, too."

"Criminy!" . . . "I'll be damned." . . . "Hell, that's something I can get a good glass-plate negative of." . . . "Dead outlaws!" . . . "Holy hell!" . . . "Gawd a'mighty, I bet that *Harper's Weekly* contributor is already over yonder." . . . "Let me through, boys! Let me through."

Most of the crowd parted. MacGregor's hands returned to Fallon's shoulders, and both men managed to suck in air that did not stink of scribblers of newspaper articles or damned lies.

A couple of men, and one woman, remained.

One started to open his mouth, but MacGregor said, "If you say the word Pinkerton I'll knock your teeth down your throat."

The woman, a handsome blonde in a plain brown dress, laughed. "American Detective Agency," she said, and spelled out Dan MacGregor's name perfectly.

"Meet me here, ma'am. In thirty minutes. That's all I should need to get my prisoner delivered. You gents can meet me here, too."

"Maybe," the woman said, "we can accompany you to see the warden."

"No," MacGregor said firmly. "Back here. In thirty minutes. You fill your time taking in the sights of the express car and talking to the engineer and the fireman."

"What about the conductor?" the thinner of the two male reporters asked.

"He's dead."

"What was his name?"

"Ask the engineer."

"How much dynamite did they use?" said the potbellied newspaperman with a bushy graying mustache and goatee.

"Enough to blow the express agent to pieces."

"Gawd!" roared the younger, thinner reporter, who shoved his pencil and pad into the pocket of his sack coat and raced down the depot.

The fat man started toward the train, too, but stopped and looked back.

"Thirty minutes?" he asked.

MacGregor nodded. "Maybe a little longer, but I'll be here. I always have time for the working press. It's the policy of the American Detective Agency to support the free press."

That left the woman, who smiled.

"You sure I can't show you the way to the prison?" she asked.

MacGregor smiled. "You'd miss the big story back there."

"Something tells me the bigger story is right here."

That caused the young detective to laugh.

"I'll see you here in a half hour. If I see you before then, I'll forget the American Detective Agency's policy and you'll be out of luck."

She grinned. "Very well." She looked at Fallon. "And maybe I can talk to you."

Fallon said: "I don't know much, ma'am."

"How long will you be behind 'The Walls'?"

"Four years is his sentence," MacGregor answered.

"But with luck he will realize the error of his ways, reform himself so that he is fit to return to society and be a credit to the Missouri State Penitentiary's rehabilitation."

The woman laughed. "Mister," she said, "you don't know anything about 'The Walls.'"

"A half hour," MacGregor said.

"Very well. I look forward to talking to you, Daniel J. MacGregor, American Detective Agency, Chicago, Illinois."

"Thank you."

"And you as well."

Fallon was already walking.

She called out to them as they began their way down the steps off the platform. "I'm Julie Jernigan. *Kansas City Enterprise.* That's Kansas City, Kansas. Not Missouri."

"Thirty minutes," MacGregor said. "Or better yet, why don't you meet me at the saloon at the Hotel Missouri on Jackson Street."

"They don't allow women inside the hotel's bar, Mr. MacGregor. Not in Missouri."

"Then maybe my room," he said.

"I'm staying in that very hotel," she said.

"Then . . ." Dan MacGregor looked hopeful.

"But I think it would be better if I just meet you here," Julie Jernigan said. "In thirty minutes."

Laughing, MacGregor turned Fallon's shoulders down Water Street, and they headed toward those towering walls.

Chapter Twenty

MacGregor released his hold on Fallon as they crossed the street to the boardwalk on the other side. At the first corner, the detective told Fallon to stop. Fallon obeyed and saw MacGregor looking back toward the depot.

"Nobody's following us," he said after a moment. "At least as far as I can tell."

He waited another full minute before he appeared satisfied. "Let's go," he said, and they crossed the street.

The buildings were a mix of wood and frame, some two stories, a few one, all overshadowed by those dark towering walls of the prison. "The Walls," people had called it in Jefferson City. The name seemed fitting, especially as Fallon and MacGregor approached the massive prison and its towering walls. Fallon spotted the guard towers, the barbed wire. They crossed over to Main Street and kept walking.

Fallon's leg throbbed. He wished MacGregor would have hailed one of the cabs or hopped aboard an omnibus.

He didn't. He took Fallon down an alley, then back

to Water Street—and none of this made sense to Fallon. The detective had told all of the reporters that he was escorting Fallon to the state penitentiary. They didn't have to follow the two. They could easily walk or ride to the prison's gates and wait for them there.

When they turned onto Lafayette Street, they remained on the other side of the street from the massive building of graying rock walls. They passed the entrance and now Fallon understood why MacGregor wanted no snooping inkslinger to follow them. The young detective did not take Fallon inside the prison. Instead, they stopped at a home across from the foreboding structure, a home that looked comfortable, inviting, new—unlike the prison across the street.

The building was a wooden frame, though the foundation appeared to be limestone. The walls were painted red with white trim along the windows, below the roofline, and on the wooden columns, balustrades, and handrails. The roof pitched like waves, one chimney of brick rose above the shingles, and a rounded tower jutted out on the opposite end. There were two porches on either side of the house. First MacGregor checked up and down the streets, and even across the street at the prison. Feeling clear, he nodded at the path to the porch farthest away. Fallon walked ahead of him, came to the door, and stepped aside, enjoying the shade.

Most of the houses and buildings Fallon had passed in the city were old, the paint beginning to chip or the stones or bricks showing their age. This one couldn't be more than five years old, Fallon guessed. Maybe ten, but that seemed unlikely. It sat on the corner, a nice lot with plenty of shade trees along both sides of the house. The lot next to it was vacant, as was the one beyond it.

Daniel MacGregor found the blackened brass hammer and knocked several times on the door.

Footsteps sounded inside, and the front door opened. An elderly black man dressed in the gray uniform of a prisoner studied MacGregor and looked at Fallon twice.

"Yes, suh?" the old man said.

"Daniel MacGregor," the detective announced. "We are expected."

"Yes, suh," said the Negro, and he stepped aside and motioned both men inside.

Once the door closed, the man locked the door at the knob and slid a bolt for extra security.

Fallon looked at the walls, finding no photographs or paintings. No samplers. Just wallpaper. A grandfather clock stood in the corner.

"If you gentlemen will jus' follow me, sirs. You all can hangs your hats there." He nodded at the corner across from the grandfather clock.

The coatrack was empty, but this was a rather warm day, and the humidity from the Missouri River didn't make things any cooler. Fallon hung his hat, turned, accepted MacGregor's and placed it on the other side. The old man was already moving toward the staircase, and Fallon and MacGregor followed.

There were no hangings on the walls of the second story, either, and the old Negro stopped at an office. It would be the one with the balcony, Fallon knew, over the first porch. Fallon had noticed the door and windows. A man sitting up there would have a good view of the state penitentiary.

"Yes," came an authoritative voice from behind the thick, dark door.

"They's here, suh," said the old butler in a convict's uniform.

"Show them in, Homer."

The old convict nodded at the men and opened the door. He held it open as Fallon and MacGregor walked inside, their boots softening as they left the hardwood floors and stepped onto a Persian rug.

"That'll be all, Homer," said the man sitting behind a big desk. It wasn't as big as Sean MacGregor's monstrosity in his office in that flatiron building in Chicago, but it was not small. The door closed, and the man, still sitting—not offering his hand or greeting—nodded at two wooden chairs with padded seats of red leather in front of the desk.

"Have a seat," the man said.

He was a grave-looking man, his thinning hair a mixture of gray and gold, with long Dundreary whiskers that had not started to gray falling off his face and onto his shoulders. He wore a green jacket and red silk tie over a white shirt. He removed his silver spectacles and dropped them on a tray.

Fallon settled into his chair and stretched out his wounded leg. It felt good to be off his feet again. That had been a long, hot walk.

"Some excitement on the train, I hear," the man said. He still had not offered his hand or any acknowledgment. Nor had he offered either of his visitors any of the water in a pitcher to his right. Or any of the Scotch or brandy from the bottles on his left.

"Yes," MacGregor said.

"Too bad you didn't kill that scoundrel Linc Harper," the man said.

"Well . . ." MacGregor grinned at the joke he must have just come up with. "The American Detective Agency did not wish to deprive you of enjoying Linc Harper's company, warden, for the rest of his natural life."

This was the home of Harold Underwood, warden of the Missouri State Penitentiary. Of course, Harry Fallon had made that assumption when they first walked up to the house. Who else would live this close to one of the worst prisons in the United States? Fallon figured even the warden did not like living here.

"I prefer director instead of warden," Underwood said.

MacGregor nodded. "My apologies, Mister Director."

Underwood picked up some papers on his desk, looked at them without help from his eyeglasses, glanced over the tops at Fallon, then let the papers slip back to the top of his desk.

"This is the man you wish for us to accommodate," he said to MacGregor but kept his eyes on Fallon.

"Yes, sir. I've explained everything to him. He knows what he has to do. And he knows that he'll have to do it alone. With no help from you."

The warden—that is, director—frowned and turned to study MacGregor.

"You make it sound, Mister Detective, that my guards have no control over the inmates."

"Not at all, Mister Director . . ."

The man turned in his chair and pointed at a framed certificate on the paneled wall behind him. Unlike the rest of the house, the penitentiary's director's office was covered with paintings and certificates or diplomas and even a couple of clippings from newspapers and even *Harper's Weekly*.

"This has been presented to us. We ran the most efficient prison in our United States. Housing these criminals, keeping them healthy. Making them work. Feeding them. And we do it for eleven cents a day, per inmate."

"Impressive," MacGregor said.

"Damned right," said the warden. Fallon decided he didn't care much for the title director. He wasn't sure that Harold Underwood even deserved being called warden.

Eleven cents a day. For bed and grub. He could hardly wait to step inside his new home.

"How long will we have"—Underwood glanced at the papers on his desk—"the pleasure of Harry Fallon's company?"

"Just as long as it takes him to get what we need. Two months. No longer than four. With luck, much less than two months."

"And you think you can find out information about that last payroll and train heist that Harper's bunch managed to pull?"

"That's our objective."

The warden's eyes returned to Fallon. "And *this* is the man you think can get this job done?"

"He's a good man," MacGregor said.

"Well, if you don't mind me saying so, Mr. MacGregor, he looks like we just dragged him out of the dungeon underneath A-Hall. I sure hope, sir, that you are not bleeding on my rug."

"I'm trying not to," Fallon said. Maybe Harold Underwood deserved neither *warden* nor *director*. He certainly didn't rate a *sir*.

Underwood returned his attention to MacGregor. "So what do you need from us?"

"Just let Hank do his job. I've told him that he'll have to figure out a way to become one of Doctor Gripewater's trusties himself, although the beating he took during Harper's attempted train robbery, and that cut a bullet carved across the calf, that should, at the very least, get him inside to see the good doctor."

"All of our prisoners are first examined by Doctor Gripewater," the warden said.

"Right. But we don't want to make things look too convenient."

"You didn't have any women detectives you could send in?" Underwood said. "That would have made things a hell of a lot easier."

MacGregor shook his head. "We have no female operatives in the American Detective Agency."

"Pinkerton has some."

MacGregor bit his lip and shoved his fingers underneath his thighs. "Well, I don't think Hank will pass as a woman, so we'll have to let him do his job."

"He barely passes for a man, the shape he's in."

"Yes, sir. But Hank mends fast. Really fast." MacGregor leaned forward in his chair and pointed in the general direction of the papers on the warden's desk. "There are two men, you'll notice in our report, that we'd like to keep away from our operative, Mr. Fallon."

The warden nodded. "Kemp Carver and Ford Wagner. I've read your report." His gray eyes turned back onto Fallon. "They have some problems with this former deputy marshal, I see."

"Yes. It's just for Fallon's own protection. So he can

focus on his job of finding out what we think Missus Harper might know."

"I'd say your man Fallon needs all the protection he can get." The warden laughed at his own joke, but quickly turned serious. "And what, if you don't mind my asking, is in this for us?"

"If we get the money," MacGregor said, "as soon as the express agency and the other companies who lost money pay that reward, you will get fifteen percent of what we earn."

"Just fifteen?"

"It's rent, Mister Director. You're renting out space for Fallon. Fallon puts his life on the line, and the American Detective Agency has spent a lot of money trying to set this all up. As you well know."

The warden smiled, and then chuckled. "And we thank you for your donation." The smile and laugh died quickly, however, and Underwood said: "And if you don't get the money from the robbery, or you don't capture Linc Harper alive? Or dead, for that matter?"

Fallon held out his hands and shrugged. "Then you, sir, are out eleven cents a day for a few months."

The warden nodded. "And if Hank Fallon here gets killed?"

"Surely, you won't allow that to happen."

"As long as both of you know the risks." Underwood waved toward the French doors that led to the balcony. "And there are many, many risks once you step into 'The Walls.'"

"We understand," MacGregor answered for Fallon and himself.

"Good. Then you won't mind signing this little slip of paper my attorney prepared."

They both signed the waiver, and after that the warden poured a snifter of brandy for MacGregor, and himself, and grinned at Fallon. "It wouldn't seem right, you see, if Doc Gripewater or some of the inmates smelled liquor on your breath, Hank."

Fallon thought: *Only my friends call me Hank.*

"All right." Underwood was taller than Fallon had expected. His long legs carried him quickly across the Persian rug to the door. He opened it and called downstairs for the prison trusty who served as the warden's valet, butler, or something.

"Homer will see you out the side entrance, and take you to the deputy warden, who will oversee Hank's introduction to the prison. The deputy warden, Mr. Fowlson, will be waiting outside the main entrance with two guards."

The warden started back inside but was stopped by Dan MacGregor.

"Any questions, Hank?" At least Dan MacGregor offered his hand.

Fallon shook. "If I need to get out in a hurry?"

MacGregor looked to Underwood for an answer.

The warden shrugged. Footsteps sounded on the stairs. "The guards can't know. I'm the only one who knows. You'll just have to think of a way to get to the hospital, where you can get word to me. That's the best I can do. You're dealing with a woman, a young kid, basically, but this is going to be quite the dangerous assignment."

Harold Underwood seemed to enjoy the look on both faces. He turned back outside, and gave his instructions to the trusty, and held the door open as Fallon and MacGregor stepped out.

CHAPTER TWENTY-ONE

The closer they got, the higher the walls to the prison grew. The deputy warden, Mr. Fowlson, and two men in black coats, pants, and hats stood outside the main entryway along Lafayette Street.

That high wall down the side seemed to run forever.

"My word," MacGregor said, "this place must cover five or six city blocks."

"It's not the jailhouse in Dodge City," Fallon said.

"Forty-seven acres, right? Isn't that what they said? Forty-seven bloody acres."

They stopped at the front steps, and the deputy warden and the men in black came down from the heavy doors. Fallon looked at the ivy growing up the column to the left of the main entrance. He didn't think a prisoner would try to climb down on ivy. It wasn't that thick. And, well, the prisoner would have to cut through the iron bars over the long, narrow windows first.

"MacGregor?" the deputy warden said. Fowlson was smaller than Underwood, a good deal younger, with dark hair, darker eyes and a thick mustache and beard. He shook the detective's hand and looked at Fallon. "This is your delivery?"

"Yes, sir."

"You have all the paperwork?"

MacGregor pulled several folded sheets of paper and passed them to Fowlson, who glanced at the first few pages, smiled, withdrew a few greenbacks, and slipped those inside his pocket.

"Sentenced to Joliet instead of Detroit and now put here." The deputy warden handed the papers, but not the money, to the nearest man in black.

"The judges had some sympathy," MacGregor explained. "Before he became a bad apple, he was a good federal deputy for Judge Parker."

"Yeah. Well . . ." Fowlson spit between his teeth. "I don't like apples, sweet, sour, crisp or rotten. And I sure don't like lawmen who cross the trail."

"He's yours for the duration of his sentence or he is paroled."

"Yeah. That's usually the case."

"And," MacGregor said, "we know he has sour relationships with two of your guests, Kemp Carver and Ford Wagner."

Fowlson's dark head bobbed up and down. "A lot of us have sour relationships with those two. But they are harmless compared to most of our *guests.*" He spit again.

"There might be others who hold a grudge against Fallon," MacGregor said.

"He should have thought of that before he soured." He nodded, and two of the guards went to Fallon's sides. They grabbed his arms and squeezed so tightly

Fallon felt as though their fingers and thumbs dented the bones in his arms.

"He did," MacGregor tried, "help us out when Linc Harper's gang hit the train we were on."

"So if Linc Harper ever shows up here, Mr. Fallon will have another friend to help him enjoy his stay."

MacGregor must have realized he was getting nowhere, and he likely also remembered he had promised the newspaper scribes an interview. More than likely, he recalled how attractive Julie Jernigan was.

"He's all yours, Fowlson. Good day."

The guards turned Fallon around and led him up the steps. The deputy warden followed, and once they were inside, the light vanished for a moment, and the heavy doors slammed shut.

That was the noise that almost rocked Harry Fallon to his very core. It was the sound of solitude, of permanence, a sound that could make the toughest man go weak in the knees or wet his britches or break down and cry—or all of the above.

Harry Fallon just blinked.

They moved through this part of the prison quickly, and came out on the other side, stepping out of the towering building and into the light outside.

Fallon saw the cell houses.

He saw signs with arrows pointing. He read the board quickly, saw *prison*, and heard the guard who did not have a viselike grip on his arms say casually, "A-Hall." So the men carried him over the grass and in the opposite direction from the prison.

A cat crossed their path, but the guards did not stop. One of them even kicked at the cat, which screeched and jumped aside, turning to hiss, its tail straight up, and every hair prickled. The guards laughed, and the cat turned and sprinted off toward another building of cold, foreboding limestone.

Naturally, Fallon thought to himself, *the cat had to be black.*

They moved quickly toward a gloomy building of four stories of more of that hard, cold rock, barred windows, and ivy crawling up the nearest corner. The guards led Fallon to the center door and waited for the free guard to open the door and lead the way.

The thought about asking to see Doctor Gripewater did not last long. Fallon had spent enough time in Joliet to know fresh fish asked guards nothing. Even his short stay in Yuma had reminded him that the best way to survive a prison sentence was to keep your mouth shut and your eyes and ears closed.

Inside, A-Hall reeked of every foul odor Fallon had ever had the misfortune to breathe in. The long, wide hallway ran the length of the building, with doors to cells lining against the walls. The doors were dark, heavy, and short. The way the closed doors were spread apart, Fallon knew the cells were small.

The cellblock wasn't sweltering, though. The air did not circulate, and Fallon saw no fans. Nor did he see any way that the prison could have been heated. Not that he wanted heat right now, but in the winter, this place would be colder than the Arctic.

The guards stopped in front of Cell Number Seven.

They released their pinching grip on Fallon's forearms and wrists, and he took the time to try to rub circulation back into his hands while the guard who was in command found a key, stuck the big chunk of iron into the lock, and opened the door.

Fallon saw no prisoner inside, just stacks and stacks of gray wool and black patent leather.

"How tall is he?" the guard leader asked.

"I'm six-even and he's taller than me," said the big cuss on Fallon's left.

"You're six foot tall my arse," said the leader. "What are you, Fallon? Six-two? Six-one?"

"Six-one," Fallon answered. He thought: *According to Joliet, Illinois.*

"Hold these up." The guard tossed out a pair of gray woolen trousers. Fallon caught them, shook them loose and held them to his waist. Although they were a couple of inches too short, the guard said, "Perfect fit."

The guard moved to the other side of the cell. "His feet are smaller than yours, O'Malley, but an elephant has smaller feet than yours." A moment later a pair of ugly, tough work boots pounded over the stone floor and stopped a few feet in front of Fallon. "And here are some socks."

They landed in a puddle of water. At least, Fallon hoped it was water.

"Put them on," said the guard with the big feet.

"Socks go on first," said the other guard.

So Fallon undressed and bent to pick up the pants he had laid on the floor before he started to disrobe.

"Gawd," said the smallest of the guards. "What the hell happened to your leg?"

"Bullet crease." Fallon tightened the makeshift bandanna, although the blood had dried and moving the cloth tore hairs from his leg.

"Hell," said the big guard. "You need stitches."

Maybe, Fallon thought, they would take him to see Doctor Gripewater.

But he still pulled on the coarse, itching prison

pants, the wet sock and the dry one, and the pair of boots, which he laced up.

The shirt came next, poorly made muslin, along with a coat, also gray, also of wool that felt like iron cactus needles. And at length, they tossed him a hat. He pulled that over his head. It was like a baseball cap, only with gray and white stripes.

"A-teeeen-shun!" the guard bellowed from inside Cell Number Seven.

Fallon stood straight, knowing that he looked like a clown. His hat was too big, his pants too short, his boots pinched so that they might cripple him, and his jacket made for a man who weighed three hundred pounds.

"What do you think, O'Malley?" said the leader, Mr. Fowlson.

The big man grunted. "Make a fine addition to a dime museum in New York City."

"Yeah. You'll get your soap, towels, and some long johns and another pair of socks when you're settled in, Fallon. Let's go."

At least the guards did not try to rip his arms out of their sockets. They walked toward the far end of the building, and then went down the depths to the basement.

Fallon saw eight doors to other cells. He wondered which one he'd have.

The guard named O'Malley quickly grabbed Fallon from behind, his giant arms pinning Fallon's arms at his side, while squeezing most of the oxygen out of Fallon's lungs. Fallon's hat toppled onto the filthy floor as O'Malley swung around so that Fallon now faced the leader of the threesome.

He caught only a glimpse of the fist, and the flash

of brass, as a pair of knuckledusters crashed against his jaw.

Immediately, Fallon tasted blood. He saw a flash of wild colors in strange geometric shapes. His head rang.

The remaining guard grabbed Fallon's hair and jerked, pulling his head up.

"So why are you here, you damned sneak detective?" Mr. Fowlson asked.

Fallon braced for another blow to his jaw.

Only this one buried itself in Fallon's stomach.

"You think Underwood's a fool?" the guard said. And kneed Fallon in his groin.

He felt vomit in his throat, then knew he was sending it onto the floor.

"What do you know, mister?" Another punch wrenched Fallon's neck. "Huh? And who the hell told you about our sweet little deal?"

Two more punches landed, but Fallon could not tell where he had been hit. His lips were mashed into a mangled mess. He felt blood leaking from other wounds, and for all he knew, his insides might be filling his body with blood.

His hair was jerked back, and he felt himself looking at the ceiling. Or was it the floor? Or had they pulled his head completely off?

"There's no damned way you're here to talk to some little hussy who got herself in the family way by some cut-rate train robber?" He must have been hit again, but every part of his body throbbed, groaned, and bled by now.

"Why . . ." Another punch. "Are . . ." Hit. "You . . ." Kick. "Here?" Three quick uppercuts. "Answer us!" And a haymaker to his ear.

He smelled the foulness coming from his body. He thought he was lying on the cold, hard floor of the basement. Fallon couldn't be certain.

"Don't kick him, O'Malley," the leader said. "He won't be able to talk for a week."

"What do we do with him?"

The smallest of the guards chuckled.

"Why don't we feed him to The Mole?"

Chapter Twenty-two

When Fallon opened his eyes, or got them open as far as he could manage, he saw nothing but the blackness of eternity.

He couldn't be dead. Dead men did not feel this much pain. He wasn't in Hell. In this midnight void, he shivered in the cold dampness. He could not see his hands, but he wiggled his fingers, but that might not mean anything. He remembered people who had arms or legs amputated and still sometimes reached to scratch an itch from a limb long since sawed off. Fallon balled his fists tightly and carved his fingernails into his palms. He could feel that slight pain, so at least he still had his arms and hands. Next he tried lifting his legs and dropped them down.

Fallon cursed. He felt that, too. Pain shot through his calf where the bullet had torn, but despite the stinging, he did not feel any blood seeping from the wound. And although he could not see and lacked the strength to reach down and check for himself, it felt as if the rag that had served as a bandage had been removed. After all, he did not feel any hairs being ripped from his leg by the bloodstained bandage.

"So . . ." an ancient voice called from somewhere in the deep blackness. "You are awake. And alive."

The sound bounced off rock walls that Fallon could not see.

"Who's there?" he asked.

The voice answered: "They call me 'The Mole.'"

Fallon twisted his head. He smelled straw, and slowly realized that he must be lying atop a mattress covered with straw.

Words tugged at Fallon's memory—*feed him to The Mole*—and he thought those had been said by one of the laughing guards of "The Walls" who had beat the bitter hell out of him.

"The name's Fallon. Hank Fallon." He decided to let The Mole become his friend in a hurry.

"Welcome, Hank Fal- . . . Did you say Fal-lon?"

"Yeah." Fallon thought: *I think that's my name.*

He tried to sit up but couldn't manage it. His eyes sought for some glimmer of hope, a sliver of light. There was nothing but pitch black.

"Fallon," the voice in the midnight said in a heavy sigh. "Do you need anything, Fallon?"

Fallon tried to clear his throat. "You wouldn't happen to have some water, would you? My throat is parched."

"About your waist. Right side."

Fallon wanted to ask about a match, but he worked up the nerve, the energy, and fought back to searing pain as he pushed himself into a sitting position. Two or three minutes passed before the dizziness stopped and the nausea passed. His lungs heaved, the pain became searing, but he kept sitting. Eventually, his right hand fumbled into the darkness until he found the wet rim of a wooden bucket. His fingers groped for a ladle, even a spoon, but when nothing could be found, he cupped his hands into the cold water, leaned forward, and brought the water to his mouth.

Water had never tasted so good.

"Or was that my slop bucket?" The Mole said.

Fallon lowered his hand. A moment later, he laughed just enough to hurt his ribs.

In the darkness, The Mole chuckled, too. "Laughter means you are mending, Hank Fallon. And that you are alive. I am glad you came to visit."

Fallon drank another handful of water.

"Not too much," The Mole warned.

"I know."

"You have been injured before?"

Fallon rubbed his face with his wet hand. "I have been prone to accidents."

"Such as the bullet crease on the back of your calf?"

"You could say that."

"The warden's guards gave you a good beating," The Mole said. "But they did not shoot your leg."

"No. That came from some train robbers."

"Ah. Then that is why you are here."

"You could say that." Fallon dipped his hand in the bucket and brought it down toward his leg, realizing that his new prison pants had been pulled up to his knee. Again, he had to let the wave of dizziness pass, but as he brought the dripping water onto the wound, he realized something. Again, he looked into the darkness toward the voice of The Mole.

"You stitched this?" Fallon asked incredulously.

"It needed four," The Mole answered. "I could only do three."

"What did you use?"

"My hair."

Fallon leaned back, his face masked in a mixture of pain, shock, and confusion. Over in the Indian Nations, a deputy marshal might have need to stitch some cuts or bullet wounds with whatever he had handy. Fishing line. Horsehair. But . . . ?

"Human hair isn't strong enough to hold a stitch," Fallon tested.

"But The Mole's hair is strong." The voice broke into another soft chuckle. "I had to braid some together. It will hold. But if you are not with me for too long, perhaps whoever is the prison's doctor can remove my stitches and replace with proper ones."

Fallon put his hand into the bucket and drank a bit more water. "Thaddeus Gripewater," he said. "He's the prison doctor."

"Oh. I remember a Doc Wahlstrom."

Fallon shook his head and shrugged.

"How long have you been here?" Fallon asked.

"I was with the first prisoners brought here."

Now Fallon had to scratch his head. He had to be dreaming. Delirious. He must be alone in the solitary cells in the basement of the A-Hall cellblock. Going crazy.

"That was," Fallon said softly, "in the eighteen-thirties."

"Yes," The Mole said eagerly. "Eighteen-thirty-six to be precise. March. While the boys at the Alamo were fighting the Mexicans down in Texas."

"Mister," Fallon said. He stopped. Did it make a person even crazier to continue talking to a figment of his imagination? His head shook. He felt his leg again, but he could not be hallucinating the stitches in his calf. Someone had done that. Someone was in this room, dark as it was, and talking to Fallon. No, he wasn't crazy, but The Mole had to be.

"Mister," Fallon tried again. "That was almost sixty years ago."

"Yes. I have been here a *long* time." His sigh sounded like gas escaping from a busted pipe.

"How old were you when they put you here?" Fallon asked.

"Fourteen," the voice replied. "I stole a man's watch."

Fallon shook his head. "They don't keep a man in prison sixty years for larceny."

The Mole made the sound of a man stretching, getting comfortable, maybe crossing his legs. "There were but few roads in those days," The Mole said. "We arrived by boat. The last prisoner to visit me—who actually talked to me, that is—told me that we built the prison, the first prisoners sent here, but he was mistaken. And young. Much younger than you. No, there were buildings already here when we arrived. A cellblock, a keeper's house, privies, and some outbuildings. And a wall of Missouri limestone."

The voice sighed. "Forty cells. There are more now."

"Yeah," Fallon said, barely audible.

"They shaved my head when I first arrived," The Mole said. "But it has grown back. Long enough to stitch your wound in your leg. Long enough to stitch up many wounds. They did not shave your head."

Fallon shrugged. "I expect they will when they bring me out."

"Will they bring you out?" The Mole asked.

That made him shudder. "I . . . well . . ."

"Some years back, they tossed a man in here to be with me. He was a funny man. At first. They forgot him. They even forgot me. I had to eat him to survive."

Fallon tried to swallow but found his throat and mouth had turned to sand. He reached for the water bucket again but made himself stop. The man was a comedian. So Fallon chuckled. "You have a good wit."

"I do not joke," The Mole said. "His bones are in the corner still. But he was a mean, vile man. I detect that you are . . . not evil."

"I hope I'm not."

"But there is evil in this prison."

Fallon kept quiet.

"We did build this building," The Mole said. "Prisoners, I mean. We cut the stone, hauled the blocks here. It was hard work."

"So," Fallon said, "you haven't been in darkness all this time."

"No. This cell was built . . . I don't know . . . years and years and years ago. There were more and more bad men, evil men, who came here. Too many for forty cells."

Too many for a thousand cells, Fallon thought, remembering the last number he had heard that the Missouri State Penitentiary held, making it something like the second-largest prison in America.

"How about women?" Fallon asked, realized how stupid that must have sounded, and tried again. "Women prisoners? Do you remember them?"

"Yes. We were excited when we first learned that a woman had tried to poison her husband and would be joining us. But, alas, the governor—whoever it was those long years ago—pardoned her. And something like that stopped the next woman from coming. But eventually, maybe after I'd been here six years. No, seven. Yes, in the summer of '43, a woman joined us. They made her work for the warden, as a scullery maid, and then . . ." The Mole broke into a boisterous laugh. "She escaped. She escaped." He must have slapped his hands together or his thighs. "Oh, my, that made us laugh. But she was caught soon enough."

"Where were they confined? After you got more than just one female prisoner?"

"Around the time the big war started, the War Between the States, we—us prisoners again—put up a new cellblock for the women. Before that, they lived in the same facility—but on a different floor."

"And this building?" Fallon asked.

"It went up after the big war had ended. In . . . '68."

"And when were you first sent here? To the basement. To solitary confinement?"

"I was the first. They thought I would die. They tried to kill me. I had tried to escape a few times. They kept a fifteen-pound ball chained to my ankle. After a while, they brought me here. Five days the first time. Thirty the next. Then sixty. Sixty again. One hundred. So at some point—I cannot quite recall exactly when—but I recall there was a big party, something that brought people from all across the world to the city where I was born. Philadelphia."

Fallon did not have to think very long. "The Centennial Exposition?"

"Perhaps. And it was shortly after we heard word that Wild Bill Hickok had been assassinated in the Black Hills."

"My God," Fallon said. "That was back in '76."

"That sounds correct. Yes, 1876. They removed my ball and chain and shoved me back into the cell."

"How often do they let you out?"

The Mole sighed. "They came and said they had jobs I could do for them. And they let me out at night. Always at night. I did not like the jobs."

"What kind of jobs?" Fallon asked. He could imagine. Emptying spittoons, slop buckets.

"We will not talk of those jobs."

The Mole sighed, spit, and sighed again. "One job I did not like at all. I did it. I had to do it. After that, I told them I would never do a job for them again. They were angry. But I have been on no more jobs. They left me here to die. But I have not died."

"For how long?"

"Many years," The Mole said. "You are here for a job?"

"No. They're punishing me."

"But the only time I have visitors is when they put men in here to do jobs. That is why I killed that man. He told me of the job he was to do. I could not allow that job."

Now, Fallon was confused.

"What kind of job?" he asked.

"I am tired. Jobs give me bad dreams. You are not here for a job."

"I'm here," Fallon said, "for punishment."

"I am glad you are here. It makes me happy that I tended your wounds. I am glad you are not going on a job. I am tired of killing. So tired."

Fallon shook his head. He still didn't know what

The Mole was talking about. He tried again: "Sixteen years in darkness. In solitary confinement?"

The Mole laughed. "Not always solitary. You are here. As I have said, there have been others. No women, though. That has always disappointed me. I really liked Martha Castro. She was the first one, the one who escaped, the one who worked for the warden. She was handsome. But after they brought her back, they put her into a cell and allowed no one to see her. Except guards. Some of the guards had their way with poor Martha, and when she became in the family way, she was pardoned. It would not be right to let a baby grow up in prison."

Fallon thought about Jess Harper.

"Some of the men left with me for a day or two were interesting men. They were given interesting jobs. Some jobs needed to be done. Or so I thought. But other jobs . . . And the men to do those jobs." He sighed. "Many were despicable, but they never stayed for long. They only left one, and it angered them that I killed him, but he deserved to die. His bones have come in handy. I will give you a rib. It has been filed down. The guards have line sticks. Prisoners have their own weapons. The late Mr. Sherman's rib might save your life."

His mouth open, Fallon just stared into the darkness.

After a long while, he managed to ask: "How did you see to fix my leg? And my other cuts?"

"I am The Mole. I see in the dark. Only when they open the doors, as when they threw you into my abode, am I blinded. It is the light that blinds me. Even in the mornings, when they open the slot at the bottom of the door to slide in my bread and water, even then—with just that sliver of light—I feel the pain in my eyes and I scream, and squeeze my lids shut, till I am comforted again by the blackness."

Fallon sat with his mouth still open, completely dumbfounded.

"Would you like to eat?" The Mole asked. "I have good jerky."

Fallon hoped the jerky did not come from the late Mr. Sherman.

Chapter Twenty-three

He had always enjoyed sleeping in a dark room with the temperature low, in the fifties or thereabouts, but Harry Fallon could not sleep that night. If it were night. For all Fallon knew, it could have been noon. Somewhere in the darkness, The Mole snored. Yet the rumbling a few feet beyond Fallon's cot was not the reason Fallon lay there, staring up—or was it down—at the ceiling.

He remembered his brief stay in the Snake Den in the territorial prison in Yuma. That had been dark—and here in Jefferson City, there were no rattlesnakes to deal with. But this was beyond dark. This was an eternal darkness. A world without light.

The guards hired by Warden Harold Underwood had done a thorough job of giving Fallon a beating like none he had ever endured. Only now a few bits of conversation began returning to his memories.

So why are you here, you damned sneak detective?

Fallon twisted his head, as though he might hear the guard's words more clearly. Yes, that's what the leader had said, just when the beating started. And then, the question had been repeated, during punches and kicks. *Why . . . are . . . you . . . here?*

He squeezed his ribs again as he sat up, grimacing from the pain, and once breathing did not hurt that much, he checked for the tenth time to make sure none of his ribs had been busted.

Yes, Underwood's guards were very, very good. They could beat a man half to death and not break any bones. When they wanted to.

There was something else, Fallon could just make out the words from one of those men doing most of the beating.

You think . . .

You think . . .

Fallon squeezed his eyes closed. You think . . . ? Think *what*? What was it the guard had said?

You think . . . You think . . . That's about all that Fallon could get. He remembered a trick he had learned years ago, something his mother had maybe told him. If you have trouble remembering something, just try to think of something else. Something not related to what you want to recall. That's all you had to do. Sometimes it had worked for Fallon. Other times he had remained without a clue about what it was he wanted to remember. But Fallon tried. He wet his lips, released the grip on his ribcage, and remembered . . .

"Here." Renee lies on the bed in their home in Van Buren. She looks so fragile, but her smile is radiant, and her eyes are beaming. The midwife stands against the wall, pouring tea from a kettle into a china cup. Fallon stares at the little loaf wrapped in soft cotton blankets.

"What?" Fallon says. His mouth is filled with cotton.

Renee laughs.

"Take your daughter, silly."

"But . . ." Fallon has faced down some of the worst killers in this part of the country. Yet he has never known fear, true fear, until this minute.

"Take her." His wife's voice is stern, but her face shows a playfulness.

"But . . ." Fallon feels the sweat. "What if I drop her?"

"Hon," the midwife calls over her cup of tea. "I've been a-doin' this since afore yer mammie entered this worl'. Ain't never seen a new daddy drop no baby in all my birthin's. Take that girl, Mistuh Hank. Don't make Miss Renee hold her like that. She needs to gets her strength back."

So Fallon takes the swaddled newborn, and Renee lies back onto the bed, still smiling, still so lovely, so wonderful.

Fallon can't help himself. At first he holds the baby far from his body, but gradually, a curiosity commands him to bring the bundle of cloth and flesh and bones closer. He looks at the white-and-blue-and-pink-striped blanket.

"She's beautiful," his wife calls from the bed. "Isn't she?"

Fallon peels back a layer of fabric, and he sees his daughter for the first time. His heart pounds. The baby is so tiny, eyes closed, a little patch of dark hair on her tiny, tiny head.

"She . . ." There must be something in Fallon's eye, but he can't brush it away because he holds the package of a new daughter in his arms. A smile fills his face. And whatever is tormenting his eyes, well, who cares about that bit of nonsense.

Beaming with pride, filled with joy and a love he never thought a deputy United States marshal could feel, he looks down at his wife.

"She looks just like you," he says.

* * *

In the darkness, again Fallon feels that something in his eyes, but the sensation quickly passes, and the memory of those years long passed is replaced by something else.

You think Underwood's a fool?

The guard's voice echoes in the confines of the dark, dark cell. *You think Underwood's a fool . . . Underwood's a fool . . . a fool . . . a fool . . . fool . . . fool . . . fool?*

Fallon whispers the words: "You think Underwood's a fool?"

The rest of the words come back to him quickly, and clear.

. . . who the hell told you about our sweet little deal?

There's no damned way you're here to talk to some little hussy who got herself in the family way by some cut-rate train robber?

Why . . . are . . . you . . . here? Answer us!

Fallon lay back on the straw-stuffed mattress.

Warden Harold Underwood had ordered his men to get some information out of Fallon. The agreement Dan MacGregor had arranged was that nobody except Harold Underwood was to know Fallon's true purpose for being imprisoned. So much for that important secret. The warden with the long whiskers and a beautiful house, probably one of the finest in Jefferson City, thought Fallon was actually here to learn about that sweet little deal.

Whatever the hell what was.

Dan MacGregor had told the warden that Fallon was here to help find money stolen in a train holdup by Linc Harper's gang. And that was the truth. But

Underwood was so damned crazed with suspicion, he thought Fallon was here to find out about him.

So Fallon knew he had two jobs while he was in Jefferson City. He had to get that information from Jess Harper to give to Dan MacGregor so that Fallon could get closer to learning what the MacGregors—or at least Dan MacGregor's father—knew about the murder of Fallon's family. And who had set Fallon up and sent him to that dangerous prison in Joliet. Who had cost Fallon his freedom, his job, ten years of his life . . . and murdered his beautiful wife and daughter.

And somehow, Fallon would learn about this sweet little deal that Mr. Underwood wanted to keep a secret. So maybe Fallon could send Harold Underwood and at least three of his guards to prison.

A man like Underwood would be ripped apart in a matter of weeks in a place like Joliet. Or Yuma. And from everything Fallon had heard, the Missouri State Penitentiary—all forty-seven of those bloody acres—was far worse than The Hellhole in Arizona or that slave shop in Illinois.

He made himself stand and shuffled his feet until he knew he was at the foot of the mattress. Fallon heard the snores in front of him, so he turned to his right. He drew in a deep breath, released it, and took a very short step forward. He had to take short steps. Long steps might wrench his guts out after the beating he had taken.

Reaching out with both hands in front of him, palms forward, Fallon counted as he walked. One . . . two . . . three . . . four . . . five . . . His hands touched the cold hard rocks of the wall to his cell. That would be another step. Eight. Eight feet. He turned around and walked back, counting those eight steps, and he stopped, and moved his left foot, hoping to feel the mattress.

He didn't. He inched forward and tried again. Nothing. One more time, and this time he breathed out with relief after his foot felt the prickly straw stuffing and he heard the crumple of straw beneath the coarse wool covering.

It did not take long for Fallon to reach the other wall. Basically, the mattress ended near the far wall. Fallon guessed twelve feet. Twelve feet deep.

The Mole's snores were to Fallon's left and sounded like the old man was sleeping a few feet across from Fallon's bed. Staying against the wall, Fallon moved carefully, counting his small, baby steps. His boot kicked something, and Fallon heard water. He smelled something foul, and his stomach turned into a rocking ship.

Well, Fallon told himself, when he managed not to throw up the jerky The Mole had given him for supper, or dinner, or maybe breakfast. *Now I know where the slop bucket is.*

He felt ahead and touched the stones, and turned, careful not to kick the bucket again. Keeping his right hand against the far back wall, Fallon moved slowly, still counting his steps, hoping to feel the door or something, but there was nothing but stone. His left hand stretched out forward, and a short walk later, though it took quite a few minutes, Fallon had reached the other corner after his feet managed to kick away sticks or trash or . . . His stomach seesawed again.

Mr. Sherman's bones?

Fallon turned back, counted his paces, turned right, and returned to his bed.

Twelve feet. By eight feet. That was the size of the

cell in the basement. How could a man live in a hole in the ground for days, or months, or in The Mole's case, roughly sixteen years? In complete darkness?

Fallon spit on the floor to get that awful taste out of his mouth.

He wasn't done, though. The Mole snored contentedly, and Fallon counted his steps back to the first wall he had touched. Turning around, he moved toward the side wall, keeping his hands on the stones, but found no door. So he moved back, and this time, his right hand slipped forward and fell against the hard iron door. He kept going. It was a small door. The next wall came to him, no shorter, no longer, at least not by much.

Yes, Fallon was in an eight-by-twelve-foot cell.

Back at the door, Fallon knelt to the floor, feeling along the cold metal until he was at the ground. Yeah, there was a slot, and fairly big. Too big, Fallon thought for just sliding trays of bread and water. Not big enough, however, for a man to squeeze through.

"Hell," Fallon said at last. He was too damned stupid. The slop bucket. The opening had to be able to fit the slop bucket through, too. And maybe toss in a bedroll or a change of clothes.

He rose and leaned against the cold iron of the door. He stared at the far wall but saw nothing. He brought his right hand up and toward his face. It was like there was nothing there. It was like he was God.

Years had passed since Harry Fallon had read his Bible. But Genesis came clearly to him now, as he lowered the hand he could not see.

And the earth was without form, and void; and darkness was upon the face of the deep.

Chapter Twenty-four

He woke.

Fallon did not remember returning to his bedding, or lying down, but he stared up at the nothingness before him, stretched his stiffening limbs, and stopped quickly.

He heard nothing. The small cell was completely quiet.

"You are awake," The Mole said across the room.

Fallon relaxed. "Yes," he said.

"I feared you might be dead, till I heard your breathing," The Mole said.

"I thought the same of you."

"Did I snore?"

"Very loudly," Fallon answered, and The Mole's laugh pleased him.

"They brought us no bread and water," The Mole said. "That is a bad sign . . . for you."

"I am sorry that you must suffer on my account."

The Mole chuckled again. "I have tasted better food."

Grinning hurt Fallon's entire face.

The Mole said: "But if they do bring food tomorrow, pour half of your water into the bucket. And save part of your food. That is how I have managed to live, and keep on living, all this time."

Fallon tried to imagine what The Mole looked like.

"Almost sixty years. The last sixteen in utter darkness."

"I am sorry," The Mole said. "What is that you said?"

Fallon wasn't aware that he had voiced his thoughts verbally. "You could not have been sentenced for all this time just for stealing a watch," he said.

The Mole sighed. "You are young. It was the year eighteen hundred and thirty-six, remember, and things were different all those years ago." Fallon envisioned the long-haired, bearded man shaking his head. "Your laws are much softer now."

That made Fallon straighten. After spending ten years in Joliet and a short stay, for the American Detective Agency, in Yuma, Fallon could not think of the laws of this day and age being soft.

"For sixty years or more," Fallon said, "that must have been a hell of a watch."

"It was," The Mole said. "Or I would not have stolen it. I believe, the gentleman said, it was valued at thirty-four dollars."

At 1836 prices, Fallon thought, that would have been a mighty fine watch.

"Still . . ." Fallon said.

But The Mole waved him off. Fallon blinked. Had he imagined that, envisioned The Mole, leaning his back against the hard, cold stone wall, waving good-naturedly at Fallon and grinning underneath that mass of hair that covered his face and head? Surely, Fallon wasn't becoming a mole himself, able to see in the dark and blinded by the sun. Hell, he had only been in this hellhole for a day or so.

"All these long, dark years later, I do not recall how many years I was sentenced to prison for my lapse in judgment and for forgetting my Christian upbringing," The Mole said. "It was more than two years. Maybe eight months and sixteen days. But such matters are trivial. I broke the law and was sentenced accordingly."

Fallon felt himself frown. Two years, eight months, sixteen days for stealing a watch that wasn't worth over forty bucks. Yes, maybe The Mole was right. Perhaps the law was much softer now than it has been back in the years of The Alamo and whatever else had happened before Harry Fallon had been born.

"I do not remember the man's name," The Mole said. "But even in this eternal midnight, never do I not see his face. He was the man who brought me to the forge. He heated the iron and locked the shackles around my ankle. He was the man who forced me to carry the heavy iron ball. So when the warden decided I had carried the ball and chain long enough, that I surely would have no more urges to run through the woods or to try to swim across the Big Muddy and try to find my freedom, I let the man use his hammer and the . . . what is it called? . . . the tool . . . the tool he set upon the metal rod that kept the iron connected to my ankle. The hammer struck. My leg bled. The shackle parted. I was freed from the weight of the heavy ball. And the blacksmith laughed at me. So I took the shackles and placed them over the front and back of his throat—he was such a tiny man, puny as Ma would have called him. And I squeezed. And I squeezed.

And the smithy no longer laughed. But eventually, mercifully, he died."

Fallon stared at where he imagined his boots might be. His head shook in sympathy. He knew of more than one kid who had been sentenced to the Detroit House of Corrections to do hard time, perhaps, but for only a year, maybe five at the most. And the kid had killed someone in prison.

"They didn't sentence you to hang for murdering that man?" Fallon asked.

The Mole laughed. "Why would they show any mercy on a murderer such as me?"

Fallon nodded. Yes, hanging would have ended The Mole's suffering. But keeping a man in blackness for all this time wasn't humane. His head lifted, and he thought of another question.

"Was that man . . . never mind." Fallon tried to remember all he was taught as a cowboy, before he first pinned on the six-point star for Judge Parker. You didn't stick your nose into another person's business.

"No." The Mole shifted his feet in the dark. "There were others."

"Others?" Fallon asked.

"Others I killed," The Mole said.

"Like Mr. Sherman?" Fallon asked.

"Who? Oh, yes. Well, no."

"Prisoners?" Fallon was curious. "Another guard?"

"No, Hank. These were men I killed outside the walls. And . . . well . . . never mind."

"Outside?" Fallon wet his lips again. "You escaped?"

"I have talked too much. That is why I remain here. I think we should forget about this. These are unpleasant memories. Would you like to play checkers?"

Fallon did not sleep well that night.

* * *

But he woke with The Mole, and after each man took his turn at what passed for a chamber pot, they sat on their beds and stared at the place where the door was. They stared, their stomachs gnawing toward ribs and spine, until they knew the sad truth.

"It is as I thought," The Mole said. "They torture you."

"To break me?" Fallon asked.

"Perhaps. Or kill you. Remember, Mr. Sherman was here for a good, long while."

"But you had no food or water, either," Fallon said.

"Ahhh." Again, Fallon would have sworn he could see The Mole tilting his head back, laughing so hard that his Dundreary chin whiskers bounced across the tattered, filthy prison uniform—likely a uniform from a previous administration. Maybe stripes of black and gold, or gray and white, or perhaps sold blue denim. Fallon feared that his mind was cracking. Perhaps it already had. He closed his eyes and tried to remember what daylight looked like.

"You forget, my friend, Hank," The Mole said. "I had learned. I save my water. I saved some food. And since I did not care much for Mr. Sherman, I shared nothing with him. Perhaps I should have, though. Had I fed him, the meat on his bones might have lasted longer than it did."

"No," Fallon said, and felt his head shaking.

"You are right," The Mole said. "He was in poor condition when he joined me. And the meat was tough and poor already. More of that would have done me little good. In fact, I was sick for two days after I first consumed his flesh."

Fallon shook his head. "No," he said. "I meant that they won't forget me. They don't want me dead."

The Mole chuckled. "They want everyone dead. No matter who is in charge now. I cannot recall the name of the warden who first put me here. It does not matter. But, no, they want us all dead."

Fallon made himself stand. "No. They need me alive. They want to know what they think I know." He shook his head. *And I don't know a damned thing.*

He put his left foot out into the darkness. He breathed in and breathed out. He walked to the wall gingerly, touched the stone, and turned around. Breathing steadily, walking carefully, he crossed the twelve feet to the far wall. After turning, he walked back. Back and forth.

Fifteen minutes later, The Mole asked, "What is it that you do?"

"Stopping myself from rotting away," Fallon replied. "So I won't be a weakling when they come for me."

"Ah. Yes." Again, Fallon felt he saw The Mole's head nodding and the old man's smile trying to make an appearance beneath the massive beard that housed vermin and maybe even rats. "To work your muscles. To keep yourself strong."

Fallon reached the wall, pushed himself away, turned, and came back, always careful to avoid the bucket of extra water that The Mole had been saving for . . . who knew how long . . .

"I am glad that the guards put you in here with me and did not leave you alone," The Mole said happily. "You are no weakling. You have a brain. You want to survive. You remind me of Mr. Sherman."

Fallon had reached the other wall. He turned around, started back again, and stopped. "Why is that?" he asked, and, feeling no lingering effect in his calf or the myriad other injuries the guards had put on him, he moved again to the wall.

"Mr. Sherman," The Mole said. "He had the same idea. For the first week or so. But his resolve did not last through the second week."

Fallon stopped walking, stretching, breathing when his throat turned parched. He found a loose pebble and placed it under his tongue, hoping it would produce saliva.

"Have some water," The Mole said.

"We must save it," Fallon said, and those four words made his throat and tongue as raw as an Arizona creek bed in the dry months.

"Dip your right hand in the bucket," The Mole said. "Let the water run off your fingers, and when the dripping has practically ceased, bring your hand to your lips, lick your palm and fingers with your tongue. Then rest. You must rest."

Fallon stopped. He stared at the floor where he knew the bucket of water had to be. He thought he could see it. An oaken bucket, once red, now brown, condensation on the sides, the handle broken. He closed his eyes and shook his head. Yet he lowered himself to his knees and dipped his right hand into the cold, wonderfully wet water. He obeyed The Mole's instructions down to the letter.

Chapter Twenty-five

"How much food have you saved over these sixteen years?" Fallon asked on the fourth day.

"You save only the jerky," The Mole answered. "Jerky will keep. The bread is not worth saving. It will break your teeth on the day they bring it. Now and then, they will bring beans. The beans are good. The beans can last. Sometimes, there might be a chunk of ham or bacon in the beans. I finger the chunk out, and I use it to catch rats. Rats are amazing animals. There is no place for the rat to enter into my home, but the rat finds a way. The smell of bacon and ham and beans brings him here. And I kill the rat. Fresh meat keeps a man wise. And healthy. Hearty."

Fallon stopped his walking and dipped his fingers in the water bucket.

"Four days," he whispered, hearing the water drip from his fingers and drip into the bucket. He wondered how much more water the bucket held. "Four days," he said again.

"Yes," said The Mole. "Mr. Sherman lasted only three and a half."

"But you didn't share your water with Mr. Sherman," Fallon said.

"Yes." Again, Fallon thought he saw The Mole's hairy head bob in agreement. "He got no rat meat, either."

A tough man, a really tough man, probably more Indian than white man, a man like that could live maybe a week without water. And Fallon had not met many men that tough. And food? Well, three weeks would be pushing a man to his limits. Yet Fallon kept telling himself that the warden could not let Fallon die. The warden had to find out what the warden thought Fallon might know or how much the law beyond The Walls had learned about their sweet deal.

Fallon moved to the corner, held his breath, tried not to gag, and found the rough rope handle to the slop bucket. He brought it up over his head, then lowered it, and lifted it again. Walking was good for one's legs. Walking, even across a dark, damp, stinking cell that measured twelve feet by eight feet, was good at keeping a man's legs from withering to nothing. But a man needed good strength in his arms, too. So Fallon lifted the slop bucket over his head, in the darkness, for thirty minutes three times a day.

Exhausted, he came back, wiped his hands on his trousers, and scrubbed them with the straw from his bed.

He leaned his head against a wall and let his breathing return to something resembling normalcy.

As he rested, his muscles aching, Fallon thought. He wet his cracked lips with his tongue and asked, "Mole?"

"Yes, Hank."

"When I first arrived here, toward the back of the prison, there were a number of buildings."

"There are likely more shops there than I remember," The Mole said.

"There was a smokestack at one. Black smoke pouring out of it. It looked like a thundercloud. That's how much smoke I saw."

The Mole sighed. "There are steamboats beyond The Walls. The Missouri River is right there."

"This was no steamboat. It was on this side of the stone wall."

Fallon imagined The Mole's head nodding. "Aye. Yes. The shops were small when I saw morning, noon, and the sunset. I imagine things have expanded. Progress."

"Prisoners do the labor," Fallon said.

"Such was the case shortly after I arrived. At first, some prisoners were allowed to go to town, to work in shops. But some men of nefarious reputation did unspeakable things once they were beyond these walls. Well, it was soon deemed improper to allow prisoners to work outside of the prison."

Fallon understood.

"So prisoners work like slaves. No pay. The businesses make a hell of a profit."

"They even had the women making uniforms for the male prisoners long before the War Between the States," The Mole said.

"And I'm sure the owners of the businesses pay the warden generously."

"Even The Walls has its limits," The Mole said. "Only a certain number of businesses can operate inside. I wonder if I could have made a broom. It might have been a good trade. Did you ever sweep out your cabin when you were a kid?"

Fallon grinned. "My cabin had a dirt floor."

"So did ours," The Mole said. "Yet Mother always had me or one of my brothers sweep. Then she would yell at us when the cabin became quite dusty."

Fallon remembered that Renee used a homemade broom to sweep up the mud and dirt Fallon had tracked in after a long trip into the Indian Nations. He squeezed his eyes shut. After a moment, he shook his head.

"You are troubled, Hank?" The Mole asked.

"No," Fallon replied. "I thought I had something, but it just doesn't make sense. Most prisons allow convict labor. That wouldn't be a sweet little deal to hide from detectives."

"I would not know," The Mole said. "I was never in prison until I came here."

In 1836, Fallon added, and that fact made him shiver.

Somehow, despite living in a stinking, cramped, wet hole in the ground for days, Fallon still woke when it had to be morning. Maybe living so close to a man he could not see had made him wake with The Mole. If The Mole remembered when breakfast came—if breakfast came—then Fallon wanted to be there.

He sat, staring toward the door, listening but hearing nothing. The Mole sat across from him, and Fallon could picture the ancient convict staring at the door, too. Hell, Fallon could practically see the old man like it was daylight in the Sonoran Desert. He waited. This was . . . what? The fifth day? Despite all his attempts to keep his muscles strong, he felt his life beginning to ebb away. The Mole had little food left, and the water was slowly emptying.

He tried to swallow, but his throat felt as though it had contracted into a minute hole, a syringe. Fallon wanted to wet his lips, but he had no desire to waste any moisture. Or maybe he had no strength to lift his tongue.

So he just looked into the darkness. He heard nothing, but they had heard nothing beyond these walls since he had been thrown in. The blocks the convicts had quarried and hauled and set into the ground were giant, massive, and whatever mortar they had used had not withered in all the decades that had passed.

Just when Fallon started to sigh and think that he had been mistaken that Warden Harold Underwood wanted him to die, to rot, to be forgotten in the depths of A-Hall, he felt an intense pain.

Screaming in bitter agony, he brought both forearms to his head and covered his eyes. Turning from the fires of hell, with the intensity of ten suns, he rolled away, and screamed in pain. He was blinded. Would he ever be able to see again?

He started rolling to one side, but made himself stop, fearing that he would overturn the water bucket. So he rolled back to the bedding, and buried his head into the dark wool covering, smelling the straw, trying to squeeze his eyelids tighter and tighter and tighter. Somewhere in the hellish blackness, he could hear the screams of The Mole, too.

Yet a moment later, he heard the slamming of metal, and he felt the comfort of midnight settle back into the cell he shared with a man he had never seen.

Immediately, The Mole stopped screaming. Fallon bit his lip to make himself stop his horrible, earsplitting shrieks amplified in the grim confines of the cell.

"Are you all right, Hank?"

"Oh, God," Fallon said, after he lifted his head off the straw bed. "That light."

"Yes," The Mole said with sympathy.

"You screamed, too," Fallon said.

"Yes. The guards like it better when you scream."

"Can you see?"

"I see spots now. You will, too. But they shall fade. You will be comforted by the night that lasts forever. Stay, my friend, and rest. I will see what food they brought us."

Fallon waited until he could breathe regularly and finally rolled over. His eyes opened. He saw darkness. He made himself sit and blinked often. The light had been so intense, so sudden, and yet, now that he remembered, he knew that the door had not been opened. The guards had just pulled up the opening at the bottom, and left it open just long enough to slide in a tray. They had not even bothered with the slop bucket, but then that chamber pot was still in the other corner.

"Do you want the bread?"

The Mole was sitting right next to Fallon.

"You said we should not eat it?"

"This is not as hard as it usually is. The bread is . . . it is . . . it . . . I have forgotten," The Mole said sadly.

Fallon reached and felt the bread. It was hard, but not like hardtack or those biscuits that belly-cheater once served on a drive to Kansas. He lifted it to his nose. Not fresh. But no more than two days old.

"Sourdough," Fallon said.

"Yes. Yes. Yes. That is the word. My mother made sourdough biscuits. They were wonderful. I wonder what became of her jar of starter."

Fallon laughed. "Ma had a jar of starter herself. I think it started with her mother's mother."

"Jerky, too. Extra water. A bowl of beans. Is it Christmas?"

Fallon shook his head. "I don't think so."

"But we shall feast. But I will save the jerky. There is not ham or bacon in the beans, or I would have smelled those. So I will not be able to catch a rat. Remember. Half the water shall be emptied into the bucket."

Soon, they began their feast.

"Just half the bread," The Mole said. "It is not that hard, so it will keep another day. Perhaps two. You do not want to eat too much bread because it makes you thirsty. Likewise with the beans. There is salt in the beans. Eat a few spoonfuls, just enough to fill your stomach. But do not eat too much. If you eat too much, after all these days with just what I could give you, then you will turn sick. When you turn sick in this place, you die."

Fallon listened and obeyed. But that taste of beans, the fresh water, and half a piece of day-old sourdough bread was like the best meal Renee ever cooked for Fallon after a long trip into the Indian Nations.

More food came the next day, but this time Fallon and The Mole turned away from the door and stared at the far wall, squeezing their eyelids tightly against the agonizing blaze of light. They still screamed, of course, but that was just to make the guards snigger. They also left the slop bucket to be replaced. And that must have really angered the guards.

Fallon felt himself strengthening from the little nourishment the food brought. He still did his routine of walking and lifting the slop bucket—although since the guards had emptied it, it no longer was that heavy.

The next day was the same. They stored the jerky, poured half the water into the bucket, and tossed the bread aside because the slices served on this morning felt as though they had been cut last week.

"If you could have one wish," The Mole asked that evening. "What would it be?"

Fallon thought. "Anything?"

"Anything that is possible?"

Fallon grinned. "I'd like to get out of here." He sighed. "I don't know. To get my life back in order."

"That is always possible."

Fallon stretched his arms. "And you?" he asked.

"I would like to sit on the banks of the Big Muddy," The Mole said, "far away from The Walls. And I would like to see the moon rise."

"Moonrise?" Fallon asked.

"Yes," said The Mole. "I do not believe I could endure a sunrise or sunset."

Chapter Twenty-six

The next day, the door opened during what The Mole and Fallon figured to be the middle of the day—hours after the daily ration of food had been delivered. The suddenness of it, completely unexpected, sent light that was a thousand times brighter and caused the pain twenty thousand times worse.

Fallon had been doing his walking exercise and was heading straight toward the wall when the iron door opened suddenly, sending light—not even direct sunlight, but light from the inside of the basement—and Fallon squeezed his eyelids shut and turned. He dropped to his knees and shielded his eyes with both arms. Somewhere, he heard The Mole's screaming. Footsteps sounded.

"Nooooooooo!" The Mole screamed.

Hands gripped Fallon's shoulders.

The Mole yelled: "What are you doing? I cannot see!"

"Shut up, you crazy ol' coot!"

Fallon recognized the voice. It belonged to the older, bigger guard who had delivered most of the beating to Fallon just before he was tossed into the basement cell with The Mole.

"Just stay put, old-timer!" That was the voice of the leader of the guards. Fallon remembered his voice, too. "You'll be back in the dark before you know it."

A moment later, Harry Fallon felt a club—one of the guard's line sticks—slam atop his skull, sending him back into the blackness he had known for about one long, dark, terrible week.

Water splashed into Fallon's face, and he blinked, coughed, and felt the pounding in his skull. His eyes opened, but immediately closed for the light, that terrible, blinding light. Slowly, Fallon lifted his left hand to test the knot one of the guards had placed upon his head with the line stick, a metal rod that had been wrapped with leather. Fallon kept his right forearm tight against his eyes, and his eyes remained closed.

"The light is unpleasant, isn't it?" Fallon knew that voice, too. Harold Underwood. Director, warden, the biggest son of a bitch in the Missouri State Penitentiary. "Mr. Fowlson, why don't you close the curtains? I'll turn down my lamp."

So Fowlson, the leader, the deputy warden in the state pen, was here, too. Fallon wondered if the two guards, O'Malley and what's-his-name, were here, too.

He could hear footsteps on a rug, and other steps on hard flooring. There came the sound of a string being pulled and fabric rustling. Fallon felt the light fade and realized the curtains had been closed.

Someone was beside him, on the left. Fallon could sense that, but he did not lower his arm from his eyes.

"The light will take some getting used to, but you'll be fine." That was Warden Underwood, standing beside Fallon. "How was your time with The Mole?"

Fallon just twisted his head and squeezed his eyelids tighter.

"You are one tough bastard," Underwood said. "I'll say that for you."

"Maybe we could use him," Fowlson said.

"No. We could use him, perhaps. But trusting him?" The warden chuckled. "Once The Mole was trusted."

Fallon smelled something under his nose and understood that the warden was holding a snifter of brandy.

"It's very good brandy," Underwood said. "It'll help cure what ails you."

"No, thanks," Fallon said, and the snifter was withdrawn, and the warden walked around the chair to face him. Fallon could feel the man's shadow. He also understood that only the warden and deputy warden were in this office. Outside the door—for the door here was wooden, not iron—feet rustled and a match was lighted. That would be the two other guards, O'Malley and the other hard rock. From outside the window came the sounds of a prison. Inmates walking, but not talking. The only voices came from the guards. Fallon knew all about that. Guards talked. Prisoners kept quiet.

He knew something else, too. All that time, that week in nothing but a place as black as midnight, had heightened Fallon's other senses. He detected the slightest sounds, the briefest movements. His nose caught odors most people would fail to notice. The warden had shaved this morning. Mr. Fowlson smoked cigars and was tapping his line stick against his thigh. The warden was sipping the brandy.

"A telegraph came from your pal MacGregor," the warden said. "Just checking in. Making sure you were all right. He said there was no need to reply. Unless you were dead. You aren't dead. Are you?"

The warden chuckled.

Mr. Fowlson said: "He oughta be."

"I think you can lower your arm now," Underwood said.

Slowly, Fallon did as he was told. Reluctantly, his eyelids opened, closed again, tightly, and he turned his head slightly. He forced the eyes open again, squinted, and kept them open for a moment. After a number of rapid blinks, Fallon twisted in the chair, and made himself look at Harold Underwood.

The warden sniffed his brandy, then killed the liquor and set the fancy crystal on his desktop. They were in the warden's office at the prison. It seemed to be on the second floor from the sound of the voices outside. Fallon wet his lips, blinked again, and glanced at Mr. Fowlson, who had fished a cigar from his coat pocket, ran it underneath his nose, then clipped the end by biting it off and spitting it into a brass cuspidor at the corner of the desk.

"Here are the rules of the prison," Underwood said. "You keep your head down, always. You do not talk. You'll be assigned to one of our factories. You do not talk at work, either, unless you are asked a question by a supervisor or a guard. There is no talking at the Missouri State Penitentiary. Silence is golden. Do you understand?"

Fallon recalled a similar speech when he first stepped inside the gates at Joliet.

"When anyone who is not a prisoner speaks to you, or if you speak to them, your cap is to be removed. Do you understand?"

"Yes, sir."

Chewing the unlighted cigar, Mr. Fowlson moved away from the desk and tossed Fallon his battered old cap.

"I like that *sir*, Fallon. Keep that up. You call guards and officers *mister* and *sir*. But you do not *sir* any inmate, nor do you call any convict here *mister*. Is that understood?"

"Yes, sir."

"Typically, a fresh fish spends his first night alone in a cell." Underwood grinned. "But I think you don't need that treatment. You'll be given a blanket." Underwood frowned. "Mr. Fowlson, before you deliver Fallon to his new home, please outfit him with clothing that fits him better. He looks like a tramp who just jumped off a westbound after a weeklong drunken bender."

"Yes, sir."

Underwood frowned, shook his head, and slowly walked back to the chair. This time, he knelt and put a hand on Fallon's left arm.

"Hank," he said, and Fallon hated the man and his long whiskers right then and there. "I know you think you got a raw deal. Getting a pounding like that, tossed into solitary in that dungeon for a week. Trust me, we did that for your own good."

Fallon stared, waiting.

"This is the worst bunch of scum in America. More than two thousand convicts—men guilty of murder, rapine, robbery, hardened criminals with no hope for redemption and no one to welcome them until

Lucifer shows them Hell. It was you and your associate, Mr. MacGregor, who wanted this to look good to the filth and cold-blooded killers who are incarcerated here. So we gave you rough treatment. But trust me, we had to."

He squeezed Fallon's arm, and grunted as he rose.

"Mr. Fowlson did what he had to do, and he did what I ordered him to do. Because this was the only way the prisoners would accept you. Trust you. You need their trust to do your job. Isn't that right?"

Fallon just stared.

"If you came waltzing in here, just given special treatment and shown a nice cell that you could have all to yourself, well, that would not work. You'd find yourself lying in your bunk with a homemade knife between your ribs after two or three days—and maybe not even that long. This way, your fellow convicts will see you as someone that we, the guards and the other officers here, do not like at all. And well we shouldn't. For you were once one of us, a man of law enforcement. And that's another reason we did what we had to do. Beat you all to hell. Toss you into solitary."

He was back at his desk now, refilling his crystal snifter with more brandy. Mr. Fowlson had found a match and now lighted his cigar. The warden drank a bit, wet his lips, and leaned against the desk, holding the snifter in his left hand and pointing at Fallon with his right.

"You ought to know from your stay in Joliet how convicts treat lawmen who wind up in prison. Most lawmen don't last long behind the iron. You did, though. You got through ten years in Joliet. That's something. And by now the prisoners here know that. They also know that—for appearances, and only for appearances—the guards and I hate your miserable guts."

He finished his second brandy.

"So our beating and your inhumane treatment was a blessing. The men have heard of this, too. So now they trust you. Do you understand?"

Fallon made himself nod.

"Then Mr. Fowlson, O'Malley, and Johnson have been forgiven?"

Johnson. That was the other guard's name. Again, Fallon nodded slightly. His stomach roiled. His mouth tasted like the most bitter piece of gall.

"Good. Good. Good." Turning, the warden found a piece of paper. "The bad news, Hank, is that we could only find room for you in A-Hall." He turned to Fowlson and said the number of the cell, which meant nothing to Fallon. All he knew was that A-Hall had been built in 1868 by the inmates. A-Hall had the basement where The Mole had been kept in solitary—except when he had visitors like Harry Fallon or the late Mr. Sherman—for sixteen years.

"To put you in another cell would have required us to transfer prisoners out of those places," Underwood explained. "And that would have put you back into a state of distrust. The cons here would have decided that you were nothing but a yellow lawdog, and you'd be dead in less than a week."

Fallon wet his lips.

"I understand," he said.

Oh, he understood. He understood everything perfect. He knew that Fowlson and Underwood were lying through their teeth.

"Very well. You want to get in good with Doctor Gripewater, you'll have to figure out a way to see him. He's drunk this morning, so we'll have to forgo the usual examination. But that's for the best, too, Fallon. Because we say we give newcomers complete evaluations from our medical staff, but that's just for show. Our doctor is too busy treating inmates for vicious beatings, knifings, or accidents at the factories where our convicts work. Again . . ." Underwood began refilling his snifter yet again.

"We don't want to have the prisoners thinking you're just some stinking, low-down, miserable spy. We want them to trust you. Like we trust you. Like you trust us."

Mr. Fowlson came over and helped Fallon out of his chair. He pointed his line stick at the door.

"Let's go, fresh fish," Fowlson said.

Harry Fallon turned, muttered a soft, "Yes, sir," and walked to the door.

Why is it, he thought, that every warden he ever met, and probably eighty percent of the prison guards, seemed like they belonged locked up behind bars more than the inmates serving time?

Chapter Twenty-seven

Out of Warden Underwood's office, Mr. Fowlson ordered two guards to take Fallon to his cell, then the deputy warden disappeared down the corridor heading for his office. The two guards, wearing black coats, pants, and hats, escorted the new prisoner down the stairs and out of the building into the main prison yard.

Underwood and Fowlson had both mentioned A-Hall, and Fallon knew that building—especially the damned cells in the cellar—all too well. But the first guard told Fallon to wait, and both guards left him standing on the path. He watched the black cat again as it meandered, sure of itself, down the path that led to A-Hall. Fallon kept his chin against his chest but managed to raise his eyes and study the compound.

The women's cellblock was easy enough to spot, but a twenty-foot-high wall separated it from the rest of the prison's interior. The women had their own cells. That made sense. But would they have their own doctor? He seemed to doubt that. Surely,

Thaddeus Gripewater would have to tend to women as well as men.

The exercise yard was against the walls beyond which, if Fallon's memory hadn't been wiped out during those long, dark eternal days and nights with The Mole, lay Capitol Avenue. Beyond that was another recreation yard, and against the rear walls were plants. More prisoners were being escorted out of one, while others waited to go back inside. The guards spoke. No one else did. Even the cat, which had now disappeared either behind A-Hall or inside it, seemed to know not to make a sound.

Hearing the footsteps of the guards, Fallon lowered his gaze to stare at the path.

"All right, fish," one of the guards said. "Left face, and march."

Once they stepped inside A-Hall, a convict was standing by the storage cell on the ground floor. The man was pale, bearded, with a bulge in his cheek and wild eyes. His face was crevassed with deep lines and wrinkles. For all Fallon knew, this man could've been behind the walls of the Missouri state pen when The Mole entered here, too.

"Get him clothes," said one of the guards. "That fit. And everything else he'll need."

"He'll need a woman," the toothless old coot said. His laugh sounded more like a braying donkey than anything human. "But I's fresh out of wimmin-folks." The donkey hee-hawed one more time before shifting the massive chaw of tobacco in his mouth from one cheek to the other. He started to say something else, but the bigger of the two guards raised his line stick and waved it threateningly over his head.

The old-timer certainly got the message. "All right,

all right, all right," he said, and lowered his head. "C'mon, fish." His voice had dropped to a whisper. "Let's get ya suited up." He waved his bony arm and entered the cramped room. Fallon followed.

Inside, Fallon stripped off his duds and took what the old con gave him. The man stopped laughing, however, when he saw the wound on Fallon's calf.

"You ought to get that ouchie looked at," the crazed man whispered. He did not sound quite as crazy now, and he glanced through the doorway. The two guards busied themselves rolling cigarettes. The ancient convict knelt on the cold, hard floor and studied the wound and its stitches before Fallon pulled up his britches.

"Socks?" Fallon asked softly but making sure he got his point across to the crazy old man. Fallon wanted to get out of here as quickly as possible.

The old man blinked, nodded, spit tobacco juice onto the floor, and moved back to the piles and piles and piles of storage.

Soon, Fallon was dressed. This time, his uniform fit. The old man told Fallon to hold out his arms and began giving Fallon the other items he would need. A thick blanket. A bar of soap. A couple of towels. Extra socks. Extra undergarments. And a coat. He lifted the coat, and Fallon saw the makeshift knife lying atop the socks before the coat's tail was dropped back, covering the weapon.

"Tobacco," the man whispered. He smiled, revealing briefly the well-worn quid in his gums, then shifted the chaw to his left cheek. "Even Change plug be my brand."

"I'll have to owe you," Fallon whispered back.

"Yer good fer it," the inmate said. "Now that I give ya somethin' ya mos' shorely will need."

Fallon nodded, turned, and lowered his head to step out of the small doorway.

One of the guards pointed his line stick toward the stairwell in the corner, and Fallon, keeping his head down and remembering not to look at a guard in the eye, moved in that direction. The two guards followed him, one of them tapping the heavy stick against his meaty palm.

"This one," a guard told him when they had reached the third tier. Fallon stepped onto the grating and obeyed when the other guard ordered him to stop.

The two guards came out and waited beside Fallon. Four guards were escorting a line of prisoners across one of the catwalks that spanned the distance between the two walls of cells. There were three catwalks: one at the far end of the building, one on the side where Fallon stood, and another across the center. The prisoners kept their heads down, and the narrow path swayed as they moved. Fallon looked over the iron railing. That would be a long, hard, fatal fall to the ground floor.

"Just wait here," said one guard.

Fallon understood why. There wasn't much room for traffic going both ways. The floor path looked solid, but the little railing on the edge would do little to keep a man from falling to his death below.

"Or jump," the other guard said and laughed.

Once the inmates had reached this side, they turned and walked down the hard floor, one convict and sometimes two stopping in front of a closed cell door.

When the last man had stopped, the chief guard

barked an order. The convicts opened a door, stepped inside, pulled the door shut, and waited for one of the guards to lock the doors to the individual cells. When the last door was locked, the guards who had escorted the prisoners walked down the path, stopping when they came to Fallon and his two escorts.

Fallon kept his head down. He looked at the jacket that covered the knife.

"Who's this?" one of the newcomers asked.

"Name's Fallon," said the toughest guard.

"What's he in for?"

"The jackasses upstairs didn't bother to tell us," said the guard. "But it's four years or something, so he didn't kill nobody."

There was a lengthy silence, and Fallon felt the new guards considering him, studying him, and even memorizing him.

"I don't know," said one of the escorts. "He has the look of a man who has killed before."

"Hey!" the leader of the escort patrol called. His shout echoed across the third floor.

"Hey," the man said again. "Look up, Fallon. I'm talkin' to you."

Fallon raised his head, briefly made eye contact, and dropped his gaze so that he just looked at the brass buttons on the man's buttoned black coat.

"He's done time before," said another guard with the escorts.

"Most people who visit us have," said another. That caused a few slight chuckles.

"Fallon," said the leader of the escorts. "Look up. There you go. It's not so hard. I don't bite. No, no, no, you just look me in the eye. You won't get rapped hard with this . . ." The man tossed his heavily wrapped line stick up and caught it as it came toward the floor. " . . . Not yet. I mean, not for looking at me. I just want to ask you a question, and I don't want you to think, figure out what I want to hear, or nothin' like that. And you don't blink. You don't breathe. You just look at me the way you're looking at me now. You just look at me and you open your mouth and you tell me the answer. The truth. Not a lie. If you lie to me, Fallon." He tossed the stick up again, snatched it hard, and slammed it against his leg without the slightest flinch. He grinned then and wet his lips.

It was hotter on the third tier than it was below. Not stifling, and nothing like the extreme heat down in Yuma. The heavy blocks of limestone and the spaciousness of the building kept the temperatures cooler. But it was still warm enough for the men to sweat a bit.

Fallon tasted salt on his tongue. He kept staring directly at the boss of the guards.

"You ever killed a man, Fallon?" the guard asked.

Fallon did not blink. He did not avert his eyes. He did not even breathe. He just answered: "Never a prison guard."

It was the kind of answer that could get Fallon thrown over the railing to fall to his death. Probably not, Fallon figured, but it might get him knocked upside the head with one of those line sticks. It certainly wouldn't get any laughs.

It didn't.

"Well," said the guard, "maybe you'll keep it that way. But you ought to remember this, smart aleck. I can't say I've never killed a scum-sucking convict with a smart mouth."

Fallon lowered his gaze and studied his uncomfortable prison boots.

"Where is Full of Himself Fowlson putting this one to work?" the guard asked.

"They didn't tell us that, either." And the tougher of the two guards escorting Fallon cut loose with a string of profanity about both Underwood and Fowlson.

"Which cell does he get?"

The guard answered, but the leader of the escort patrol did not appear to care for that answer.

"No. He can't go in that one."

"It's what Underwood said."

The guard swore. "That can't be right."

Both guards assured the leader that they had their orders.

"Underwood's a damned fool," said the guard.

"Ain't that the livin' truth," said one of Fallon's escorts.

"Well," said the leader of the other group, "I'll have to go straighten things out with that moron."

The guards walked past Fallon, who kept his eyes trained on his bar of soap and the coat and waited for one of the guards to slap him silly. All he felt, though, was the sweat trickling down his cheeks and the throbbing in his stitched-up calf. The guards' footsteps echoed and faded as they turned into the stairwell and climbed down the flights to the ground floor.

"All right, Fallon," said the meaner of the two—but at least he had stopped calling Fallon "fish."

Fallon moved down the path. An oblong window stood in the center of the front and back walls, rising from around the tier Fallon was on to above the fourth. The two windows seemed to provide the only light in A-Hall. Fallon counted the small doors of solid iron that he passed. Not that he needed to, for numbers were chalked onto the black iron.

"Stop," said the lead guard.

Fallon obeyed. None of the inmates the guards had escorted from whatever work detail they had been assigned for the day had entered this cell. It was pretty much in the center of the building. He didn't know how many roommates he would have, or if any would be inside.

He could see the cold floor down on the bottom level. Another group of prisoners was being marched to the far end of the building, turned right, and up the stairs. The black-coated guards shouted at them, cursed at them, and followed them. They disappeared in the well, but Fallon could hear their footsteps.

Fallon's cell was right across from the center catwalk.

The key grated in the lock, the other guard cursed and tried it again, and finally the loud click sounded.

"You got a new bunkie, you son of a dog," said the guard as he pulled the creaking door open and pointed his line stick inside the cell. "Stay put," he told the inmate inside. "And say hello to this fish."

Fallon felt the other guard's line stick poke him in the small of his back.

"All right, Fallon," the guard said. "Go inside and be quick about it."

Keeping his head down, Fallon took a few steps away from the railing, ducked—the doors had been built for circus midgets or to remind inmates of their place—and came inside the cell that reeked of sweat, straw, tobacco, urine, and the foulness of mankind.

As he lifted his head, he realized just how many men had been crammed inside this twelve-by-eight-foot room. Five. Fallon would make six. Only one of the inmates was inside, lying on a straw mattress in the corner, chewing tobacco.

You couldn't smoke in the cell. Matches and prisoners, Fallon knew, were not a healthy combination.

Fallon saw his roommate. The roommate looked up, and his face hardened at the sight.

Fallon was dropping his clothes, blanket, soap, towels and even his knife, as the pale man with blood on his lips and more blood in his eyes shot off his miserable bed and came straight for Fallon.

The man had a knife in his right hand.

Chapter Twenty-eight

Ford Wagner had aged since Fallon had brought him and Kemp Carver in from the Indian Nations to Fort Smith all those years ago. What hair that hadn't been shaved off or fallen out was no longer red but white. The whiteness matched the tone of his skin. And a bloody froth sprayed through his lips. He was rail thin, more skeleton than man. Consumption did that to a person.

But Wagner had a knife—and not one of those homemade contraptions prisoners usually had to put together. Like the one Fallon had dropped with his clothing.

He had no time to try to grab the knife the old man had given him down below. For a sick man, Ford Wagner moved fast. He brought the knife over his head, but Fallon dropped, falling back through the doorway. Luckily, the two guards had not slammed the door shut. There had not been time, this had happened so fast.

Fallon kept his hands out to protect himself, brought his knees up, catching the charging inmate at his waist. He arched backward and flipped the crazed killer through the doorway. Luckily, Ford Wagner was tiny enough after that long lung sickness that he didn't hit either the top of the frame or the sides. He landed on the flooring and skidded toward the edge.

Spinning around, Fallon came to his knees and leaped out.

The meanest of the guards said, "Hell's fire" and backed away.

The other guard started at Wagner, waving his line stick, until the other guard said, "Steve, don't be a damned fool. Can't you see Wagner's got a knife?"

Wagner came up, coughing, waving the knife in a menacing fashion in his right hand and wiping the blood off his lips with his left sleeve.

The knife was a hunting knife, with a crooked, long, and well-worn deer's-foot handle and a curved guard of shiny brass. The blade had to be around seven inches long, dipping from the top and curving from the bottom. Like a bowie. Fallon could tell that the blade was made of very good steel. And sharper than a razor.

Wagner's bloody lips formed a grin as he approached easily, waving the blade left to right. He did not pay any attention to the guards, but Fallon shot a quick glance their way. He also saw the other guards, escorting the prisoners to their cells on the opposite side of A-Hall. Someone blew a whistle.

"What's going on?" came a shout from across the deep chasm.

"The lunger's got a knife!" replied the leader of the two guards who had escorted Fallon. "Showing the fresh fish the law of the land."

"You better hope Wagner wins," said one of the guards across the way.

What was happening came as no surprise to Fallon. The guards on the other side of A-Hall's third floor stepped aside and approached the railing. The prisoners turned, too, but knew to remain in front of their cell doors. Fallon could not see what was going on below him or on the floor above. But the sounds that filled the dark, old building told him this was the main show of the day. Sounds echoed down the stairwell that Fallon had walked up. Out of the corner of his eyes, he saw the first group of guards, those who had escorted the prisoners to this floor, pile out and line up across the flooring near the first cell of the block.

The guards would not break up this fight. A few started placing bets. The prisoners cheered, but it wasn't for Fallon and it wasn't for Wagner. They just wanted to see blood.

Fallon put a hand on the door, wondering if he could use it as a shield. He pulled, then let go and stepped away from the cell. The damned door was too heavy, and Fallon didn't want to be pinned in. Out here, he didn't have much room, but this wasn't his first knife fight.

"I've been waitin' a long time for this, Fallon," Wagner said in a dry, wheezing voice.

Someone yelled from the other side: "What the hell are you doing, Ford?"

Many years had passed since Fallon had heard that voice, but it was one he recognized easily. Kemp Carver.

Well, at least Fallon didn't have to wait forever to figure out when those two hotheaded outlaws would find him. It was better to get things out in the open, and over and done with.

Wagner started to reply to his cousin's encouragement, but he stopped, suppressed a cough, and made a vicious swipe with the blade. Fallon leaped back, sucking in his gut, and found himself against the wall, but as Wagner twisted and tried to jab with the lethal knife, Fallon pushed himself away. He backed up a few feet until he stood in the center of the walkway.

Again, Wagner turned and rushed him, but tripped. He went down to a knee. Fallon tried to kick him in the face with his left foot, but the inmate, more cadaver than man, somehow pushed himself away, rolled over, and came up near the two guards. Fallon found himself back beside his cell. His foot caught something. He glanced down. It was the jacket. He didn't know if the knife was underneath it, but he knew that he could use the jacket. Quickly, his knees bent, his right hand snagged the sleeve and he was up and standing, moving away from the cell, and not even trying to see if his thin little blade with a handle manufactured from pieces of wood was anywhere within reach.

By now the din of cheers, curses, and just screams to blow off steam filled the cellblock. Fallon wrapped the sleeve of the striped coat around his left hand. Ford Wagner looked confused as he came at Fallon again. Fallon popped the jacket like a whip, and the thin man staggered back.

The guards on this side of the cell sniggered.

Enraged, Wagner charged, brought the knife up as Fallon leaped to his right and slapped the side of Wagner's face with the shabbily made coat. A button must have caught Wagner on the cheek, because blood began leaking as Fallon brought the jacket back. This time he rolled it quickly around his right arm.

Wagner coughed slightly and touched his cheek with his free hand.

"Come on, Ford!" Kemp Carver yelled from across the pit. "Get it over with. Kill him."

Did Carver recognize Fallon? Maybe not. He was just like everyone else in this slaughterhouse. He just wanted to see blood spilled.

Fallon started to wrap the jacket around his left arm. Wagner wet his lips. The blade slashed this way, then the other, and Wagner came at him again. But just as quickly as Fallon had wrapped the jacket over his arm, now he slid it up, and tossed it like a lariat at the weak man's stumbling feet.

Fallon jumped out of the way, turned around, and saw Wagner fall. The knife came out of the man's hands. He kicked the coarse woolen jacket from his ankles. Fallon wet his lips, hoping that one of the guards would take advantage of the situation and pick up the knife. End this stupid, senseless fight. Instead, the leader of the duo stepped over and kicked the knife with the toe of his boot—back toward Ford Wagner.

The pale man gripped the hunting knife, keeping his head up, his angry eyes locked on Fallon. Wagner coughed, spit out more blood, and moved on his knees to the walls. He had to grip the cold stones with his left hand and somehow manage to pull himself to his feet. Again, Wagner wiped the blood and staggered toward Fallon.

This time, the deranged, dying man came yelling,

swiping left and right, up and down, blinded by fury. Fallon stepped into the man, which Wagner had not expected. And the longtime prisoner was so blinded by his hate, his desire for revenge, that he barely even saw Fallon.

This wasn't much of a fight. How long had Ford Wagner been incarcerated? How long had he been suffering from the lung ailments? How much longer could a man in his condition live?

Fallon's two hands gripped Wagner's right hand with both of his. He knew he could break the man's wrist, his arm, easily. The man's eyes filled with hatred, and Fallon twisted the hand, shook it, brought it back, and then sent his knee into the man's groin.

The knife dropped and rattled on the floor. Fallon shoved Wagner away, and the rail-thin man staggered blindly, ramming into the younger of the two guards, who angrily, or maybe just reflexively, shoved Wagner away.

"Nooo!" That cry came from the leader of the guards down by the stairwell. The one who had tested Fallon just moments ago. Fallon saw the guard racing down the pathway, while the other two guards turned to look back.

Fallon wasn't looking back, though. Because he was moving toward the railing. He saw that Ford Wagner had no control and staggered to the narrow barrier. Across the pit, Kemp Carver screamed, too. Fallon reached the edge of the walkway just as Wagner hit it. Fallon's right hand grabbed the bony left arm of Wagner as he hit the rail and flipped over.

By no means was Ford Wagner a heavy man, but Fallon felt his ribs pressing against the small round railing that came up to his waist. That was all there was separating Fallon from a long drop to a damned hard landing.

"Ford!" the convict's cousin screamed.

"Help him!" said the guard charging from the stairwell.

Across the pit, convicts or guards—Fallon couldn't tell which—shouted: "Let him fall! Let him fall!"

With a tight grimace, Fallon looked over. Now he could see inmates and guards on the second-level walkways staring up to watch the fight. Below them, a few other guards and prisoners, including the crazy old man who had given Fallon his clothes and knife, tilted their heads so they could watch the excitement.

The sound of Ford Wagner's wrist breaking was barely audible, but Fallon could read the pain in the man's face. He turned, looking at the guards for help, but they seemed frozen. Fallon began pulling the light, limp weight of Ford Wagner up.

"Help him, you damned fools!" the charging guard said, and this time the two men in black snapped out of their daydreams. One grabbed Fallon's free arm. The other went to latch on to Ford Wagner. By the time the leader of the other detail had reached them, it was all over.

Ford Wagner was on the floor, hurting, bleeding, wheezing, spitting up more blood, but alive. The two guards helped pull him up off the floor, gasping for breath. The leader of the other guards had stopped to pick up the lethal knife Ford Wagner had been using.

It was over. Fallon tried to catch his breath.

But across the way, he heard Kemp Carver.

"Fallon! Fallon!"

Fallon turned, gripped the banister, and saw Wagner's cousin, pushing aside one of the guards and stepping onto the center catwalk.

He sprinted across the narrow path. And Harry Fallon stepped over to meet him.

Chapter Twenty-nine

Guards started after both Carver and Fallon, but they stopped at the edge of the catwalk. Nobody had any intention of dropping three stories to the floor of solid rock below. Fallon kept walking, steadily, and in control, but Kemp Carver slowed and stopped.

"I should've killed you at Maudie's back in the Nations," Carver seethed.

"You tried," Fallon reminded him.

"This time my gun won't misfire."

His gun had not misfired back at Maudie's all those years ago, Fallon knew. He nodded and waited. Fallon had always been taller than Carver, and that had not changed. Back in the Indian Nations, though, Carver had outweighed Fallon by quite a few pounds. That had changed with prison along with the fact that Carver didn't have access to all the whiskey and Choctaw beer he had been running. Now, he wasn't slight, but he would be far from a match for Harry Fallon. Fallon had also spent more time in prison. Any time spent in Joliet and Yuma was hard time, too.

And Fallon still had both of his arms. Kemp Carver's

right arm stopped at his elbow. Fallon remembered that gunshot in the darkened cabin of Maudie's. He could still hear Carver's screams: *God, my arm, my arm, you damned low-down dirty . . .*

Halfway across the path, Fallon stopped, too. His eyes were hard. He waited.

Kemp Carver wet his lips with his tongue. His left hand kept clenching, and then unclenching, clenching and unclenching, over and over again. He drew a deep breath, let it out. Behind him came calls from his fellow prisoners.

"Come on, girlie-boy, go after him. He almost threw your cousin to hell and gone."

"Carver. Let's see a good fight. That first one didn't last long enough!"

"Hey, boy, you gonna take care of that fresh fish? Or you gonna come back here and put on your petticoat?"

Carver's face began to flush.

"You men shut up!" snapped a few guards, but their orders resulted in more catcalls and laughter.

Carver started walking again. The prisoners jeered and cheered. The guards started backing away, giving the prisoners room.

"Throw his carcass over the side, Carver. Like Millican done that Mexican four years ago!"

"Two plugs of tobacco says the fresh fish wins this one, boys!"

"You're on. Hell, Carver rid with Linc Harper!"

"You danged, fool. Carver ain't got but one arm."

"Yeah, but that one arm put Munson in the hospital for two weeks last year."

Fallon looked down at the ground floor. He hoped to see one of the guards running outside, to get help.

Fallon had been in Joliet during an incredibly bloody riot. In fact, his actions during that riot had led to his parole. He had saved the lives of some guards. Of course, all that parole got him was working, though not officially, for the American Detective Agency and landing back in prison. Twice. But if a riot broke out here, the only life Fallon wanted to save was his own.

A few feet from Fallon, Kemp Carver stopped. They were closer to Fallon's side of the chamber, but not by very much. The heckles, the catcalls, the curses, and the jeers became louder. When there was finally a bit of quiet, Kemp Carver swallowed and pointed behind Fallon.

"I wanna see my cousin."

Fallon nodded. "Come ahead," and he stepped to the side. There wouldn't be much room for Carver to pass.

"You go first," Carver said.

Fallon shook his head. "And let you come up behind me?"

The one-armed man swallowed. The catcalls, hisses, and obscene gestures started up again.

"What are you doin' here?" Carver asked.

"Come on, Carver," Fallon said. "You've heard about me. I've been behind the iron for years now."

The man's cold eyes brightened and he grinned. "Yeah. Joliet, though. You didn't make it to Detroit. Detroit was the toughest house I ever got sent to. Till Linc Harper sold me out and I come here. You never been to Detroit, buster. You don't know hell."

"I know Joliet," Fallon said.

"Yeah but . . ."

Fallon cut him off. "You want to keep talking,

Carver? My horse can outrun your horse? My pa can whup your pa? Is that your game?"

The jeers echoed now. Fallon thought that some of the guards down below were joining the raucous commotion.

"You want to see Ford, come ahead. But you try something, and you'll lose your other arm."

The big hand turned again into a knot. Carver's lips tightened, and his eyes narrowed into the tiniest slivers. He spit over the side and started toward Fallon, slowing his pace, then moving over toward Fallon's left. Fallon gave him room, gripped the railing with his left hand, turning to his side to give the one-armed man room. Fallon's right hand remained free. And ready.

Now all of A-Hall turned silent. Every convict, every guard seemed to be holding his breath.

As Kemp Carver came nearer, Fallon could see the sweat on the man's face. He smelled sawdust. Maybe Carver was working in the furniture factory. He kept his eyes locked on Carver's face, but he never lost sight of the man's one, strong arm.

Carver stopped, pushed his back against the railing, and slid his feet sideways. Eventually, he looked away from Fallon and concentrated on moving past him. He focused on the distance, on his cousin, on everything but the former deputy marshal he had pulled even with. He looked like all he wanted to do was get around Fallon and to the other side, to see to his sick, dying cousin.

Fallon did not buy that for one second.

So when Kemp Carver brought his left arm up quickly, Fallon was ready. He stepped toward Carver but kept his left hand tight against the railing. His right hand connected against the side of Carver's face, a hard, rocking blow that landed before Carver's swing could slam into Fallon. Only his balance, a good deal of luck, and the handrail that stretched about waist high from one end to the other kept the one-armed man from falling to his death.

The one-armed man grunted but quickly shook his head to clear his vision and mind. His left hand held the railing tightly, and somehow he managed to lift himself off the pathway and kick both legs at Fallon.

Fallon could not have expected that move from a one-armed man, but he was fast enough, experienced enough, to twist his body. One foot missed Fallon completely, and the second just grazed his new, rough prison pants. But even a graze from a man like Kemp Carver was enough to knock Fallon aside.

He turned, jumped aside, and made sure he kept his balance while keeping both eyes on the murderous convict before him. Carver released his hold on the railing and touched his feet down near the side. His momentum carried him into the other railing, but his side and the stub of his right arm took the force of the blow when he struck the round iron bar. His left hand came over and caught the bar, too, and quickly, and very smoothly, Carver pushed himself away from the railing. He found his balance, spread his legs as far apart as he could on the narrow catwalk, and brought his one hand up, balling it into a rock-hard, crushing fist.

Fallon, however, had not just been standing and waiting. He was moving, despite the twisting and shuddering of the walkway. Fallon had stepped toward Carver, and now he put both of his hands on each side of the railing, lifted his feet, and kicked out at the convict. The boots caught Carver in his stomach, and he almost doubled over. Fallon brought his feet down and pushed himself forward as he released his hold on the rails.

Men cheered. Men cursed. Men howled with delight. Even those locked inside the cells, unable to see what was going on, began pounding the floors with their feet. It felt as if all of A-Hall was rocking as though the biggest earthquake since the one at New Madrid was striking Jefferson City.

Carver saw Fallon coming, but he wasn't quick enough to start a counterattack or bring his good hand up in a defensive movement. Fallon swung hard with a right that pounded Carver's stomach, two jabbing lefts to his other side, and another blow just beneath his ribs. When Carver brought his good arm down to defend his midsection, Fallon was ready. He swung wide and hard, and the haymaker caught the whiskey runner, thief, and robber hard.

Carver was hurtled backward by the crushing blow, spinning to one side, landing against the handrail and rolling across the iron bar for perhaps two feet before falling onto the walkway, which shuddered. Fallon stepped away, kept his left hand tight on that rail. Carver rolled more. Fallon's right hand stretched across and grabbed the other railing.

A-Hall became nothing but furious noise. Fallon had been in gunfights that had not seemed so loud.

Now the prisoners across the way erupted into cheers and jeers. Some seemed to be yelling for Carver to roll underneath the railing and drop. Others sang out praises for the fresh fish.

Fallon started toward Carver, who cried out in terror as the edge of the flooring drew nearer, but before Fallon could take another step, the man's left hand reached up and grabbed the railing. The catwalk shuddered again, but Carver stopped himself, and pushed himself away from the edge. He lay there, on his back, breathing in and out deeply. His one hand still gripped the railing, and he used that to pull himself into a seated position.

He glared at Fallon. "I'll kill you for that."

The prisoners jeered.

When something that might have passed for quiet returned, Fallon said softly, "You got three paths, Carver. Go back to the other side. Go see your cousin. Or go down to hell. You try to pull a stunt like you just did, and I guarantee I'll make sure your next stop is three stories down."

Carver spit onto the flooring, wiped his mouth with the stub of his right arm, and used his left to pull himself back to his feet.

"Kill him this time, Carver!" someone across the way shouted. "Don't let no fresh fish knock you on your arse."

"You better hurry, Carver," said another. "Before Under-the-covers Underwood shows up and makes us stop our fun'n'games."

Carver was standing now, the stump and the good arm hanging at his sides. He looked paler, though, and his breath had turned ragged, while his jacket and shirt shook from the pounding of his heart.

The one-armed man knew his fight was over. He knew he could not win. He knew the abuse and beatings he would take because of this, too.

"I want to see Ford," Carver said.

Fallon nodded.

On the other side of the prison, two of the inmates

glanced at each other and raced toward the catwalk. The guards shouted, and one even pointed his line stick in their direction, but none of them dared to move.

Instinctively, Fallon realized what those two convicts, big men, with bulging arms and thick necks, intended to do. He grabbed hold tightly to both bars on the sides of the narrow path.

The railings were attached to the banister and balustrades on both sides of the prison. If the catwalk fell, the rails would still be attached.

"Grab hold, man!" Fallon shouted and nodded behind Carver. "They mean to knock us off."

Carver stopped but did not reach out for the handrails. He didn't trust Fallon and thought this was some kind of trick.

"Damn it, man, grab those bars!" Fallon shouted, as he tightened his grip on the rails and braced his feet tight on the narrow path.

"Good God in heaven above," said the younger guard who stood near the cells behind Fallon.

Too late, Kemp Carver turned just as the two convicts stepped onto the walkway and began jumping up and down.

The path was not the sturdiest bit of construction, and those convicts were big, big men. Carver slipped. The men began trying to rock the path, one pushing toward A-Hall's rear wall, then pulling, while he worked in tandem with his evil, murderous friend. They pushed, the pulled, and the path swayed.

Fallon's muscles tightened. He gritted his teeth and held his breath while watching Kemp Carver roll. The prisoner screamed while he clawed desperately for anything he might grab ahold of to save his life.

But the railing was too high for him to reach. His fingers reached out for the edge of the path, but at that moment, both of the callous big men on the far side of the catwalk began pushing hard toward the back wall. The path seemed to dip. Now, Kemp Carver cried out in terror as he rolled over the edge and dropped.

But not to the ground. Somehow, someway, Carver managed to grab one of the support rails underneath the catwalk. He shouted, the inmates across the way cheered or booed. The prisoners on the bottom floor standing near or under the path quickly scattered, before stopping and looking up. Some pointed. A few hooted. A couple even dropped to their knees, bowed their heads, and prayed.

The two burly men kept jumping on the catwalk, and Fallon had to use both hands to keep from being knocked over the railing or to his knees. Yet many of the inmates now rushed to the catwalk. Fallon held his breath, wondering if they meant to help them. Maybe even knock the whole bridge loose and send it crashing to the floor.

The guards, instead of doing their job, backed farther away.

But the men proved to be a rescue party. They grabbed the two bullies and pulled them off the end of the walkway, forcing them to the floor, where other convicts came and started kicking the bullies, spitting on them, stomping them with their boots, and letting their howls echo across the chambers.

Fallon did not wait for the catwalk to stop shaking. He made a beeline, but not for the safety of the floor behind him.

Chapter Thirty

He did not have to go far. Fallon dropped onto the floor, used his left hand to grip the side of the catwalk, and dropped his right over the other side, toward the dangling, screaming Kemp Carver.

"Grab hold," Fallon said tightly.

Fallon cursed at his own stupidity. *Grab hold? Hell, man, Carver's got only one arm.*

He twisted his body, until he lay crossways on the path, his long legs dangling over the far side. Fallon was tall enough, maybe heavy enough to anchor himself. By now, guards had begun to storm through the door. Fallon heard the barking orders from the warden, Underwood, and the deputy warden, Fowlson. He could see teams of guards heading up both stairwells, and others running down the bottom floor. He even saw Underwood and Fowlson near the entrance. Fowlson pointed up at the third-level center catwalk, at Fallon, but Fallon couldn't look at those men, or anything else, now. He bent his head and shoulders over the edge and grabbed for Kemp Carver.

Maybe the guards would come help.

Whistles shrieked. The pounding of boots on the stairwells seemed to rattle the entire building. Fallon felt the shuddering of the catwalk beneath his chest, his stomach, and around his waist—but the catwalk did not rock nearly as much as it had when those two inmates had tried to knock both Fallon and Carver to their deaths.

Over the shouts of the guards and the curses of the prisoners, Fallon heard Underwood's orders: "Captain Brandt, see to those men. Pronto."

Fallon paid little attention. He held his breath, let it out, and pushed himself a little farther over the edge.

"Help me, Fallon!" Kemp Carver cried out. "For God's sake, help me."

Fallon's arms swept down. But still he wasn't close enough.

"No!" Carver shrieked. "No! Don't leave me. Don't let me die!"

"I'm not leaving you," Fallon said, though he wasn't sure Carver could hear him. Fallon barely heard his own voice. Grunting, sweating now, Fallon nudged himself even farther over the edge.

"I swear to God, Fallon!" Carver was wailing. "I didn't have a damn thing to do with it. I swear to God. It wasn't me. It wasn't me."

What the hell was Kemp Carver talking about?

Fallon felt the footsteps on the catwalk now. He turned his head to see the leader of the guards who had escorted the men from the work detail earlier. The mean brute—but then, weren't most of the guards?—who had asked Fallon, "You ever killed a man, Fallon?" and to whom Fallon had answered, "Never a prison guard." Maybe he was coming to help.

But his face revealed no sympathy, and his pace showed no urgency.

"I'll tell you everything, Fallon! Everything!"

"Shut up," Fallon barked. "Tell me later!"

He didn't need any distractions. Getting this son of a bitch up was going to be hard enough.

Gritting his teeth, Fallon stretched both hands toward Carver's left arm. He cursed as the left hand missed, and tried again as his arms came back, but without any luck. Sweat now covered Carver's face, and the inmate's eyes were wild and wide with fright. The man was trying to scream but could not find any voice. And his fingers were losing their grip on the support beam.

The catwalk began bouncing and twisting again. Fallon could hear footsteps, but these would not have been from Captain Brandt, for they came from the opposite side. And these feet were moving at a desperate pace. The last time Fallon had seen Captain Brandt, he was taking his time, and walking deliberately, as though hoping both Fallon and Carver would drop over the side.

Prison guards usually didn't care much for the idea of dying to save a convict who most likely wouldn't lift a finger to help a guard.

Out of the corner of his eye, though, Fallon saw two guards in their black getups racing across the walkway. Then Fallon could not pay them any attention. He reached out once more, and this time his fingers brushed against the coarse wool sleeve.

He saw Carver's face, the lips moving, and even heard the desperate whisper, "Please."

Above him and to Fallon's right, Captain Brandt

yelled at the two guards, "Stop, you damned fools. This whole bridge might collapse."

The guards did not stop, though. Maybe they couldn't hear. The catwalk trembled.

Fallon's left hand came back, just as Carver lost his grip.

Got him! Fallon's mind rang out.

Somehow, he had managed to snag Carver's wrist. The skin was slick with sweat, and though Carver did not weigh as much as he had fifteen years ago, he was not a slight man. His weight began pulling Fallon over the side.

Let go! Fallon's mind told him.

"No!" Fallon moaned, and saw his right hand swing over and lock onto Carver's good arm.

Yet still he felt the weight pulling him across the path.

Then a crushing blow landed on Fallon's legs, just below his knees. He bit his lips, cut off his curse, and kept a desperate grip on the convict's arm. But Fallon knew one thing. He wasn't sliding over. And somehow, despite the pain and the roaring of the men in A-Hall, Fallon realized what had happened. One of the guards had dived atop his body and stopped Fallon from being pulled over. Easily, the blow could have shocked and hurt Fallon enough that he might have released his grip on Kemp Carver, but Fallon had often been called a bulldog. When he got his mind set on something, it stayed set on that something. And his mind was set—though Fallon couldn't figure out why—to keep Kemp Carver alive.

Yet Fallon felt his calf bleeding again. The guard had reopened that wound, but right now, the blood did not appear to be gushing, just leaking. Hell, Fallon thought, he probably didn't have that much blood left in his body anyway.

"Don't drop me, Fallon!" Kemp Carver had found his voice, though it was hard to hear over the booming voices, curses, pounding feet and hell that had descended into the prison.

"It wasn't me, Fallon!" the dangling man cried out in full panic. "I swear it wasn't me. But I know . . ."

Fallon's neck was pulled up. Someone had grabbed the collar of his shirt. That had to be the other guard.

"I've got him." That had to be one of the two men. Fallon realized he had been wrong about prison guards. Maybe he had spent too much time in Joliet, and Yuma had not changed his views. But maybe all prison guards weren't complete sons of bitches. Maybe some of them cared. Maybe some of them knew a thing or two about what a man behind bars had to live with or deal with.

Fallon found more strength and kept a tight hold on Carver's good arm.

"I don't want to get up," said the other guard, "because he might fall."

"Yeah," said the first guard. "Then we might lose the both of 'em."

Fallon realized something. He had heard the two guards clearly. He heard everything. It felt like he could even hear the sweat dripping over his forehead, into his hair, or falling, falling, falling to the hard, cold floor of stone below.

A-Hall had turned quiet and not just silent. It was an eerie, deafening stillness. All Fallon heard was the clopping of Captain Brandt's boots as he walked toward them.

But the silence did not last long, for almost as soon as Fallon had recognized the stillness, even what could pass for tranquility, the prisoners began cheering. No, not just the convicts. Fallon could see guards raising their hats, their mouths open. Cheering, praising, amazed that something like this could occur behind the iron, behind the stone walls of the Missouri State Penitentiary.

When the roars died down, Fallon said to the two guards, his helpers, "If you two can start pulling me up . . ."

"Fallon," Carver cried out again. "Just tell me what all do you want to know. Just . . ."

He stopped, and his head turned, looking up toward Fallon's right. Fallon realized that the sound of walking boots had ceased, and that the catwalk no longer seemed to be shaking.

"Well, well, well, what have we here?" Captain Brandt said.

"Please, Captain," said one of the guards. "Can you give us a hand?"

"Please, Captain," said the other. "We can't hold them much longer."

The captain chuckled, but Fallon heard the man coming down to his knees, and then lying beside Fallon.

"Yeah," Brandt said.

Fallon could not see the captain of the guards, but smelled his breath, and felt the pressure of his body next to Fallon's. He could see the long black arm dangling to Fallon's right, and the heavy line stick that the captain's right hand held.

"Carver," Captain Brandt said. "Grab hold of the stick and I'll pull you up."

"What the hell . . ." Fallon said tightly.

And then he watched as Brandt pulled his arm back and swung it forward, and Fallon felt the crushing blow of the leather-wrapped and brass-studded stick when it slammed into his wrist.

Chapter Thirty-one

Kemp Carver's mouth hung open, but the scream Fallon heard was his own. He bit it off quickly and despite intense pain in his right hand—Fallon wondered if the captain had broken his wrist—he tried again, in frantic desperation, to grab Carver's arm. The blow to Fallon's right wrist had slammed Fallon's right arm hard against his left hand. The pain, the blow, and the slickness of Carver's one arm were just too much. Fallon had instinctively let go. And his desperate grab for Kemp Carver's arm, or his sleeve, or anything, snagged only the rank, foul air of A-Hall.

He fell in slow motion, or so it seemed. Eyes open. Mouth wide, but Kemp Carver did not scream. Or if he did, Fallon just blacked it out.

Beneath Fallon, a few of the guards turned away. Warden Underwood did not, Fallon noticed. Nor did Fowlson. But Fallon could not hold that against those two men. Fallon knew he could easily have closed his own eyes, but he just could not do it.

Carver's legs hit the walkway that crossed the second floor, and for a brief moment—too short to even consider, actually—Fallon prayed that the man would somehow land there, on the catwalk. Wouldn't that have made a fine story? Prisoners and guards would be talking about that for a hundred years.

But, naturally, it did not happen. It couldn't have happened.

The legs caught the railing, and flipped Carver's body over, twisting him so that now he was falling headfirst, and he spiraled out of control, picking up speed.

Only then, when Kemp Carver could see what was rushing up to stop him, did the one-armed convict scream.

It did not last long.

He landed headfirst on the solid stone, and Fallon could see the spray of blood, as the body cartwheeled, and rolled like a rag doll, just a few feet, and then lay still. Carver's head was tilted at an unholy angle, and his legs and arms were splayed out in ghastly fashion.

The stone floor had ended Kemp Carver's life and his screams, and a silence again descended upon the prison barracks.

"Damn," Captain Brandt said as he pushed himself up. Fallon watched the lethal stick disappear above him. "That's a shame."

Fallon closed his eyes, hoping that when he opened them, he would see . . . anything . . . Rachel . . . Renee . . . Judge Parker . . . even the cell he had been tossed into at Joliet. Anything. But when they opened, all he saw was the mangled, crushed, bloodied body of Kemp Carver.

"What did you two see?" Captain Brandt was asking.

Fallon felt nauseated, but he could not throw up. He wasn't even sure he could breathe. The words meant nothing to Fallon, but a moment later, what had been said hit him like a thunderbolt. He tensed.

"I saw," said the guard who had been holding Fallon's collar. "I saw the captain try to help pull the prisoner up to the bridge here."

"And you?" Brandt's tone was icy, cold, and calculated.

The guard straddling Fallon's legs answered: "I couldn't see all that happened, sir, as I was up here. But I saw the captain trying to save the prisoner."

"That's right," Brandt said. "The poor bastard just slipped. Another couple of feet and we could have had him. Isn't that right, Milton?"

Milton, the guard on Fallon's legs, said, "Yes, Captain."

"Anything else to add, King?"

The guard who had released Fallon's shirt by now said in a low whisper. "Just that . . ." He swallowed. "All of us tried hard to save that man's life. He just lost his hold."

"Yeah," Brandt said. "A pity. A damned shame."

Fallon felt the weight coming off him, and he wondered if Captain Brandt would kick him over, send him down, down, down to land beside the crushed remains of what had once been Kemp Carver. Instead, Brandt said in a casual voice. "Haul him up."

One grabbed Fallon's left arm. Another pulled him from his waist, and Fallon came up, ragged, bruised, and bleeding again. He was likely still stunned by what he had just witnessed. He sat on the catwalk, wet his lips, and glanced up at Captain Brandt, who was casually sliding the line stick back into its place on his belt.

"Get up, Fallon," the leader of the guards said.

The two others, Milton and King, were standing now

themselves, and not offering to help. Fallon tested his legs, and slowly came to stand in front of Captain Brandt.

"And what did you see, fish?" The captain's voice had a calm deadliness to it.

Fallon wet his lips. He knew what he saw. And he knew what he felt. Just minutes earlier he had told Captain Brandt that he had never killed a prison guard. But, damn, how he would like to do that very thing right now.

He did not get a chance to answer. The guards, King and Milton, had seen what had happened, but they knew they could never tell anyone the truth—not and stay alive. They knew they had just witnessed a cold, heartless, foul murder.

So did the prisoners across the way. And they wanted to let the whole world know.

"Murderer! Murderer! Murderer!"

"You cold-hearted bastard. You killed him."

"We saw it. Murder. Foul murder. Murder!"

Warden Underwood heard those shouts, too, and out of the corner of his eye, Fallon saw the warden ordering more men to rush upstairs. The only prisoners out of their cells, at least in A-Hall, were those across the way. Maybe fifteen. No more than twenty. But back in Joliet, the horrible riot that had gotten Fallon out of that hellish nightmare, had started, at first, with just three men.

"They'll kill us all! They'll kill us all!"

"UNLESS WE KILL THOSE BUTCHERS FIRST!!!!"

"Hell." Captain Brandt sounded so casual about this, it made Fallon's stomach turn again. "You two get over there. Get those convicts back in their cells. Now."

It appeared that guards Milton and King would

rather face rioting prisoners than Captain Brandt. They turned and hurried, but not too fast, across the catwalk.

"Let's go, fish." Brandt nodded.

Fallon swallowed down the bile in his throat and stepped past the big, brutal, cold-blooded killer in a black uniform. He walked what seemed like a thousand miles down the rickety path. His legs hurt. Most of his body ached. His calf muscles were starting to stiffen, and he had to grip the railing for support. At any moment, he expected Captain Brandt to either knock him across his skull with that studded, ugly line stick, or just shove him over the railing and watch him drop.

The roars of the inmates reached deafening proportions. Whistles screeched. Fallon's head began to ring. He wasn't sure he could breathe, even when he stepped gingerly off the catwalk and onto the flooring that led to this side of the cells.

Numbly, Fallon turned, and walked to where Ford Wagner lay on the cold floor. One of the guards knelt beside him, and Fallon stopped there. The dark, cold, hard doors to the locked cells pounded from inmates kicking or throwing whatever they had inside against the door. The young guard attending Wagner glanced up, and Fallon read the terror in the boy's eyes. He was almost as pale as Ford Wagner.

"Unconscious?" Fallon asked.

The guard only nodded.

Fallon watched Captain Brandt walk past him and stop before a circle of terrified guards. He began bellowing orders. Fallon looked across the building to the other side, where more guards were driving their bodies against the dozen or so inmates, trying to push the rioting prisoners into their cells. He could see the line sticks rising, falling, clubbing and clubbing and clubbing. All the while, on every floor, from every cell, the screams of men continued.

Could The Mole hear this from his cell in the basement? Fallon wondered, but then he looked back at the rail-thin person that was Ford Wagner.

"How long has he been out?" he asked the petrified young man in black beside him.

The guard tried to swallow. "A long time."

"He didn't see . . . ?" Fallon did not need to finish the question.

The guard's head shook. "No. He was out long before . . . that . . . incident."

Incident. Now there was a hell of a word for cold-blooded, senseless murder.

Fallon glanced at the one cell with an open door. The cell where he had been sent to room with Ford Wagner. Had Harold Underwood sent Fallon here, knowing that Wagner would do his damnedest to kill him? Or had he been sent here, as the prison's brass had alleged, so no one could think that the supervisors of the state pen were giving Harry Fallon preferential treatment.

Fallon looked up and down the path without moving his head. He nodded at the young guard, said, "Excuse me," and moved into his cell. It still stank. It remained empty. Fallon picked up his clothes and pushed them into a corner. He found the homemade knife the old geezer down on the first floor had given him, and he slipped that into the sock, down into his boot. He grabbed his jacket and put it on, and then he did the same for the hat that had been knocked off his head when the ruckus first started.

Finally, he stepped out of the cell and returned to the unconscious form of Wagner.

The noise continued. Fallon saw another guard rushing down the path, screaming as he ran, "Captain Brandt! Captain Brandt!"

The murdering captain of the guards stepped toward the charging guard. "What is it?" he snapped.

"Warden Underwood, sir," the kid said, his chest heaving. "He needs you and ten men to move to the shoe factory."

"What in God's name for?"

"They're starting something there, too. The prisoners."

"Like hell . . ."

This had to be Brandt's first riot. He didn't know how fast these things could spread. Like a grassfire on a windy day in August.

"Damn it all to hell." Brandt turned, saw Fallon and the young guard, and must have known they would be no good.

"Get that carcass out of here, Ryan!" the captain shouted at the guard beside Wagner.

"But . . . sir . . . he ain't dead."

"Hell." Captain Brandt turned around and ordered the men he had been bossing to fall in. Finally, he turned to the kid, Ryan, and said, "Take the fresh fish with you and get that lunger to Gripewater. Now. And stay there, Ryan, till we send for you. Make sure none of the damned patients in the hospital try to burn this whole damned place to the ground."

Fallon held his breath. This was unbelievable. He watched Captain Brandt and the handful of men race toward the far stairs. He saw other guards crossing the catwalks to the side to help the guards push those outside into their cells. A handful remained here just in case, somehow, the prisoners pounding inside their cells managed to break down their doors.

How old was this cellblock? Fallon thought. Didn't The Mole tell him it had been built back in '68? The doors, though, looked mighty solid.

Fallon took Kemp's shoulders and let Ryan grab the thin man's feet. Fallon also backed up, until he realized the senselessness, the slowness, of it, and managed to turn around. They brought the man dying of tuberculosis to the stairs, down the stairs, and to the bottom floor. They were heading toward the door when Harold Underwood ran toward them.

Chapter Thirty-two

"Just a damned minute!" Underwood shouted above the deafening din. "Where in hell do you think you're going?"

Ryan stopped, and stuttered, "Captain Brandt told us to get him to the hospital."

"He's still alive?"

As if in reply, Ford Wagner turned his head and coughed up bloody flux, but did not open his eyes. He just moaned and let out a hoarse, ragged breath.

"Jesus, Joseph, and Mary," the warden said and backed away from the consumptive. "All right, take him. But just you. Fallon stays . . ."

"But, warden," Ryan said. "Look at his leg."

The warden's gaze went down, but Fallon just stared out the open door, at the daylight that shined into this dark, noisy hell. Fallon didn't need to look at his leg. He could feel the blood sticking to his pants and leaking into his sock and boot. He could feel the pain.

"Damn it all to hell," Underwood said. Someone else called his name from the third floor. The warden spun around and shouted up. Neither man could hear the other, so the warden hurried closer to the far wall. Ryan took that to mean that he was cleared to take Wagner to the hospital. Fallon put up no argument. They left the chaos and stepped out into the clean, refreshing air.

Yet as they walked, away from A-Hall, Fallon heard shouts and curses across the compound. He saw more men in black uniforms running this way and that. He saw guards in their towers aiming shotguns down into the prison yards. He saw prisoners on their knees, hands locked behind their heads, with line sticks pressing against the tops of their heads. He saw a few prisoners, and at least one guard, lying unconscious. He even saw the damned black cat, sitting on a box, contentedly watching the hell all around it. The cat's tail waved.

Fallon and Ryan carried the dying lunger through all of this, out of hell, and into the prison hospital.

Thaddeus Gripewater dropped the jar when Fallon and Ryan brought Ford Wagner into the prison hospital. He cut loose with a string of curse words as the glass shattered on the floor at his feet. If he noticed the sick inmate the two were carrying, he did not appear to care. All he cared about was spreading across the floor.

"Do you damned fools know how much good gin costs?" he roared.

"You don't, either," said a big-boned woman with her hair in a bun. "That's your own remedy, and it will likely leave you blind."

Now, the doctor turned his rage onto the woman. "If I'm blind, I won't have to look at your wretched face, you miserable ol' biddy." He pointed at the remnants of the jar. "Put yourself to use, woman. Clean up that mess."

"Clean it up yourself."

"The hell I will. I got a patient to tend to." He moved from one table, and nodded to another, and when Fallon and Ryan just stood there, the doctor snapped: "If you want to hold that piece of dead meat while I examine him, fine. But you might find it more comfortable, and I probably can do a job just a wee bit more thorough if you put him on that table over yonder."

Thaddeus Gripewater looked to be about sixty years old, and from his disheveled gunmetal gray hair that looked like an owl's nest that had been rattled by a hurricane, the week's growth of beard on his face, and the bloodshot of his eyes, he might be coming off a roaring ten-day drunk. Seeing how he had just dropped a glass of homemade brew, he was still drinking. He had big ears, long arms, thin lips, and dark brown eyes. His long coat might have once been white, but it now was smeared with stains of myriad colors. Likewise, the black string tie was undone, hanging down a dirty blue shirt, the buttons missing, revealing a dingy, equally filthy linen undershirt. For all of that, though, the man's hands with the long, long fingers and even his fingernails were spotlessly clean.

The woman with him frowned. She was taller than Fallon, and probably would be a match for most of the prisoners in Jefferson City. She glared at the doctor but found both broom and mop leaning against the wall and went to work.

The young guard and Fallon carefully laid Wagner on the narrow table. Fallon even lifted the consumptive's head and pushed a small pillow under the man's head.

"You mean to tell me this old boy isn't dead yet?" Gripewater said, and he found his stethoscope.

The doctor came to the table and nodded at Fallon. When Fallon just stared, the doctor turned his head, spit on the floor, and gave Fallon a hard glare when his head came back to its original position.

"Unbutton his shirt, jackass."

Fallon worked the buttons and watched as the doctor put the stethoscope over Wagner's heart, then his lungs. The doctor frowned. He shook his head. He said in a hoarse whisper, probably to himself, "That gin was better than anything I could get at one of the saloons in this town."

Frowning, the doctor removed his stethoscope and saw Wagner's broken wrist. "What the hell happened to him?" he asked, turning to the young guard. "You boys beat the hell out of him again?"

Ryan nodded at Fallon. "He tried to kill this fresh fish."

Gripewater looked at Fallon. "So you decided to kill him. Beating a lunger half to death. I reckon you deserve to be in this hell on earth."

"No, Doc," Ryan said. "He actually saved Wagner's life." The doctor was looking at the lunger's broken wrist. "He helped pull him up after he almost fell from the third floor. And he even tried to save what's his name, you know, this convict's brother or cousin or something like that. The man with one arm."

Gripewater snorted. "You mean Carver?"

"Yeah, Doc."

"You said almost?"

"Yeah. Ummm. Carver . . . well . . . he's dead."

"Is that what's the cause of all the hell that's breaking loose?"

"Yes . . ." Ryan's voice was just audible. "Sir."

"Well, you best get back to the show, sonny. Don't want to miss your chance to be a hero, get your name written up in the papers, or get killed, and then be a dead hero and get your name written up."

Ryan frowned but turned toward the door. Fallon started to follow him, but Gripewater said, "Not you, sonny boy."

Both the guard and Fallon stopped. The old sawbones pointed at Fallon's leg. "I don't think you want to bleed to death. Hop up on that bed. I'll get to you directly." The doctor glanced at Ryan, said, "Git," and focused on Wagner's injuries.

Fallon moved down the room to a bed against a wall. He pulled himself up, but just sat there, legs hanging down. Gripewater did not look up but said, "You're bleeding on my floor, sonny boy. Get your legs on that bed and elevated on those pillows and blankets at the edge. That might keep you from bleeding to death." Fallon obeyed.

"Hey!" Gripewater yelled, without raising his head from where he was setting the broken bone or bones in Ford Wagner's wrist. "If you're going to stay here, you can at least get some work done, sweetheart. Get this new man's leg cleaned and see that he don't die before it's his time."

The doctor went back to his work on Wagner, and Fallon watched the big woman, who was sweeping up the glass into a dustpan. She appeared to have no intention of cleaning Fallon's calf.

He felt the shadow and turned his head to the right. A young woman with brown hair and hazel eyes came from behind a curtain. Fallon saw that she was a small woman, quite attractive, and wearing a striped dress that had to be three sizes too big. She made only the briefest of eye contact with Fallon before her small hands began pulling up Fallon's britches.

He felt her pull down his sock and was glad that he had put his knife in his other boot. She loosed the makeshift bandage and stopped. She looked at Fallon.

"Who stitched this?" she asked.

Fallon said, "A friend."

"What did he use?"

Fallon shrugged.

The conversation drew the attention of Thaddeus Gripewater, who left Ford Wagner, still unconscious, and moved to the far table. Gripewater put his stethoscope on Fallon's chest, though not bothering to remove the jacket or shirt, and glanced at the wound in the leg. He moved closer, and pressed his clean hands on the leg, thumbing over what was left of the stitches.

"Human hair," Gripewater marveled. "Braided together." He glanced at Fallon. "Not your hair." Now his eyes bore into Fallon. The man rubbed the stubble on his chin, snorted, and asked, "How long have you been in this prison . . . I'm sorry. What's your name again?"

"Fallon. Harry Fallon. My friends call me Hank."

"I'm not your friend."

"I didn't say you could call me Hank."

The doctor grinned. "How long?"

Fallon let out a slight laugh. "To tell you the truth, Doctor, I'm not altogether certain."

"Usually, a prisoner is examined by me when they first come here."

"They gave me special treatment," Fallon said.

"I can see that. I don't believe that our walking cadaver over on that bunk put those bruises and cuts on you."

"He's tougher than he looks."

"I'd say the same about you, Fallon. And you look mighty tough."

The doctor turned to the nurse in the prison uniform. "Clean that up. And I mean a thorough cleaning. When it's ready, I'll put some stitches in it, and we bandage it thoroughly." His eyes turned back to Fallon. "And I won't use my hair, but real sutures, shipped all the way from a medical outfit in Ann Arbor, Michigan."

Fallon smiled. To his surprise, Thaddeus Gripewater smiled, too. The old sawbones looked at the nurse who was pouring alcohol and some other mixture. "Are you feeling all right, Jess?"

Fallon turned his attention to the woman, Jessica Harper. Jessica Benton Harper, who had left her parents' home in Ray County and was married to, or at least was living in sin with, Linc Harper. She was smaller than Fallon had imagined. But the ill-fitting dress had been a good disguise. It also hid the fact that this woman, still in her teens, was pregnant with Harper's baby.

He had done it. Fallon had made it into Thaddeus Gripewater's hospital, where Jess Harper was at this very minute. And Fallon had needed neither gin nor cherry pie to make it here—just several days of darkness, pain, pure hell, and a lot of his own blood.

As Gripewater moved back to his patient and began a muffled conversation with the other woman, Fallon tried to think of his best move. Jess Harper turned to him and said, "You best lean back on that pillow, mister. And brace yourself something good. Because this will hurt . . . a lot."

A few second later, when Fallon had stopped sucking air in deeply, blowing it out harshly, and wondering if the young woman had just sawed off his leg below the knee, he managed to say, "You're weren't kidding."

Jess Harper laughed. Her laugh was musical but something sad. It reminded him of his dead wife's laugh.

Chapter Thirty-three

He did not say much to Jess Harper, just let her bandage what needed to be bandaged. She brought him water in a ladle, and he pushed himself up and drank it deeply. As he handed the ladle to her he said softly, "Thank you, ma'am."

"You don't have to thank me. You don't have to ma'am me, neither."

"Yes," Fallon said, "I do."

Their eyes met, and he smiled gently, but that was enough for now, he said. A woman like this . . . no, a *girl* like this . . . was likely used to men eyeing her long, hard, and lecherous. Besides, Doc Gripewater was coming back over, with the big matron behind him, and she was carrying a silver tray, and Gripewater was holding his hands, now reeking of alcohol and dripping wet, above his waist. Eyeglasses had been placed on his nose, and his dark eyes looked like those of some monster behind the lenses. Fallon lay back down.

"You did a real nice job, Jess," Gripewater said. "You best go lie down."

"What's going on outside, Doctor?" the girl asked.

"Don't worry your precious head over that. Our fearless warden will put out those little fires. Go on, honey. You need to get off your feet."

"You ready for this, Fallon?" the doctor asked once Jess Harper had retired behind a curtain at the end of the hospital room.

Fallon smiled, "No."

Again, the doctor returned the grin. The big matron, whose name Fallon had learned was Eve Martin, grunted and rolled her eyes.

"You want a scar or not?" Gripewater asked as he brought up the needle with the long suture dangling from the threading hole.

"I have plenty of scars," Fallon said, "already."

"And likely will get plenty more."

For all his gruff appearance and temperament, Thaddeus Gripewater had a soft touch. Fallon could feel the needle and the suture, but it did not hurt.

"What happened to Wagner's cousin, Carver?" The doctor did not look away from his hands and fingers, and Fallon kept his focus on the ceiling, trying to keep his mind off what Gripewater was doing.

"There was a fight. On the catwalk. He fell."

"And you didn't."

Fallon wet his lips. "No."

"So, first you get into a fight with Wagner over there. Then you get into a fight with Carver. Is that what happened?"

"You could say so."

This time, Fallon gasped as the doctor's fingers, the needle and the suture turned into something awful, burning, painful.

"Sonny," Gripewater said a few seconds later. "We

can do this two ways. You can try to tell me a lot of malarkey. Or you can tell me the truth. And I can show you just how good a doctor I can be. Or I can show you what you're likely used to."

Fallon leaned deeper into the pillow, but he no longer looked at the ceiling. His eyes found Doctor Gripewater, who nodded, and returned to the suture job. But his hands and fingers became gentle again.

"So, no embellishments, and no rambling. This isn't that big or bad of a cut. But you know that already. So it shouldn't take me much longer to get you patched up. What happened?"

"They put me in a cell with Wagner," Fallon said. "He came out with a knife—a big knife . . ."

"Not like the one in your other boot."

Fallon nodded. You couldn't get anything past Gripewater.

"Go on," the doctor commanded.

"It wasn't much of a fight."

"I would think not. How Wagner's still with us I don't have a clue."

For a man who wanted to hear a story quickly, the good doctor sure made a lot of interruptions.

"He almost went over the edge. We were on the third tier. I stopped that from happening. That's when Kemp Carver recognized me. They were bringing him in with other prisoners from wherever he had been working."

"Saddle-tree factory." The doctor had interrupted again, but that corrected Fallon's previous thought that Carver had been making furniture.

"He was on the other side of A-Hall. He came down the catwalk. I went out to meet him."

The doctor stopped his stitches and studied Fallon

long and hard. He even called the matron, Eve Martin, to push up his spectacles so he could see better.

"You fought Carver on the catwalk?"

Eve Martin reminded him: "The fool had only one arm, Thaddeus."

"I know that. And I've also seen what that hard case can do with that one arm, Matron Martin!"

When that bit of nonsense had ended, Fallon said, "It seemed like the thing to do." He wet his lips and explained, "I didn't want the guards near me."

"That, I understand. So you threw Carver over to his death."

"No."

"That's right. Young Ryan said you tried to save his life, too."

"That's right," Fallon said.

"But you didn't."

"No." Fallon felt the bitterness on his tongue. "I didn't."

Gripewater focused on the stitches. "What happened? . . . He pulled the sutures tighter and shook his head. "No. You can't answer that one. Truthfully, I mean. You'll just tell me that Carver slipped and fell to his death."

"Something like that," Fallon said in a dead voice.

"And the guards, those who saw it, will say the same thing."

"Most likely."

"But just for my own edification, let me ask and you tell me when to stop. Fowlson?"

Fallon just breathed in and out.

"I didn't think so. Underwood?"

Fallon pushed his head back deeper into the pillow.

"Of course not. He's a gutless wonder."

"Ryan?"

Fallon laughed slightly.

"Yeah. I just wanted you to see how I can brighten a room with my levity." He began tying off the stitching. "Brandt." There was no question to this one.

"I think we're done, Doctor," Fallon said.

"As soon as I tie this in a knot," Gripewater said.

Gripewater tossed a newspaper atop the table where he and Fallon sat in the far corner of the hospital.

"I recall reading in this . . . not this particular edition, but this paper . . . that a certain convict, bound for this level of Dante's Inferno, had helped stop a train robbery attempt led by . . ." He glanced over his shoulder and whispered Linc Harper's name before turning back to stare at Fallon. "That was a few days ago. I thought the newspaper got it wrong, that maybe the hero was going to the city jail or off to some other fine Missouri burg to await his trial. Yet here you are."

Fallon lifted his cup of coffee in a toast. Grinning, Thaddeus Gripewater raised his glass of clear liquor and tapped the cup.

"That slice I stitched up is older than a few hours, even older than a day. Did you get that when you were playing hero?"

"I wasn't playing hero, Doctor." Fallon sipped his coffee before he added: "I was just trying to stay alive."

"You're pretty good," Gripewater said.

Fallon looked at him. "At what?"

"Staying alive. I've seen what that man, sick as he is and dying of the lung illness, and what his cousin, with just one good arm, can do. Underwood put you in the basement at A-Hall?"

Fallon nodded.

"Figures. For how long?"

Fallon started to answer, but stopped, shrugged and shook his head. "I can't say exactly. But I think four days. No, five. Or . . ." He shrugged.

"Gowd a'mighty. So who stitched up that leg?"

"The Mole," Fallon answered.

Gripewater's head shook again. He killed the rest of the liquor, about four fingers of raw gin, and set the cup on the edge of the table. After which, he wiped his mouth with the sleeve of his dirty coat.

"The Mole. That can't be."

Fallon slid his cup of coffee away. He let out a soft chuckle that held no humor. "Maybe it can't. I did not have complete control of my faculties. I'm pretty certain of that. I can't be sure of anything else."

"A ghost?"

"Can a ghost sew up a cut with his own hair that he has braided together?"

"No," Gripewater said, "but only because I don't believe in ghosts."

"Then The Mole is still in one of those dark cells."

Gripewater slid his chair from the table and rose. "The Mole died sixteen years ago," he said.

Fallon never felt chills running up and down his spine, but he did at that very moment. He felt the color leaving his face, too.

"Six months after I took over the thankless job of becoming the prison's doctor." He pointed in some vague direction. "The cemetery's over there, and . . ." He stopped and shook his head, then barked an order at Eve Martin to refill his cup of gin. Once she had done that, Gripewater looked up at her and said, "Pour yourself a snort, too, darling."

"I have perfect eyesight, Doctor," the big woman said. "I'd like to keep it that way."

"Then the hell with you, darling, but answer a question for me as my memory isn't very good. I was going to tell this young whippersnapper that he can find The Mole's grave in the cemetery. But that's not right, is it?"

"The Mole?"

"Yeah," Gripewater said. "Coleman Cain."

That caused Fallon to sit up straight. "Cain?" he asked. "You mean Killer Cain."

"None other."

Fallon had to shake his head at the very thought.

"You've heard of him?" the matron asked, and she decided that Gripewater's gin might not blind her, so she drew up a chair and sat between the doctor and Fallon.

Fallon nodded. "Every boy who grew up in Missouri has heard of Killer Cain."

Eve Martin grinned. "I bet your mama and papa told you that if you weren't a good boy, Killer Cain would come see you. Take care of you."

"Like he took care of twenty-seven men," Gripewater said.

Fallon said, "I heard that more times than I could count. He never came to me, though. I heard that he hanged, though. Back when I was just a button."

"You hear everything about Killer Cain," Gripewater said. "That he hanged. That he was shot dead by posses in every corner of the state. That he rode with Bloody Bill Anderson. That he killed Bloody Bill and chopped off his head. That he rode with ol' John Brown. That he rode against ol' John Brown. That he was a pirate on the Missouri River. That he . . ."

As Gripewater talked, Fallon remembered. For all the legends and lies about Coleman Cain, Fallon remembered seeing a wanted poster tacked to the train station at Gads Hill when he was just a young boy. He was the first hired gunman that Fallon could recall. No, you couldn't limit a killer like Coleman Cain to just guns. He killed with knives, with machetes, with bombs, wagon wheels, his large fists. He killed judges. He killed bankers. Even preachers. Farmers. Ranchers. Colonels. Congressmen. He killed at least one dance-hall girl. He murdered a madam of one of the most respected cathouses in St. Louis. He killed twenty-seven people. He killed for one reason. Money.

He was a killer for hire. Pay him money—the fee would be negotiated—and he would see the job done. Always.

At least, that's what the newspapers and magazines all reported. That's how the three or four dime novels written about him had read. Killer Cain. Few men were more dedicated to their job than this man with the blood and instincts of a rattlesnake.

"I haven't heard that name since I was in my teens," Fallon said.

Gripewater nodded. "He was captured in 1871, if my memory's correct. One of the biggest and most sensational murder trials in Missouri. Reporters came from New York, Boston, Chicago, San Francisco, even London and Paris. But the prosecutor could not make a murder charge stick. That's how good Cain was. But they gave him a life sentence for kidnapping. So here he was when I joined the prison. And here he died."

Now, Thaddeus Gripewater looked at Eve Martin.

So did Fallon.

"He drowned swimming across the Missouri," the matron said. "His body was never found."

Gripewater's head bobbed slightly. "Oh yes. Now I remember. A boot and a jacket were found, washed up ten miles downstream. But the coonhounds never found any sign. Nor did the Osage scouts the Army and the district marshal brought in. And if a hound dog or one of those tall, thorough Indians could not find a trace or even a sign left by the man, he was declared dead. Dead and good riddance. Dead. Drowned and feeding the fish in the bottom of the Big Muddy."

CHAPTER THIRTY-FOUR

"And he was The Mole?" Fallon asked.

Gripewater sipped his gin. "Yes. He tried to escape a number of times. More than anyone in the history of this pen. And each time, he was put into solitary. But as you know, solitary is not just being alone in the Missouri State Penitentiary. It is alone in utter, total, and terrifying darkness."

The doctor sighed, and the matron picked up the story.

"The first time was six days. The next was a month. Then two months. I don't know how many times, or if he ever was sentenced to longer stays than sixty days. By the time he finally got out, the last time, he could barely see. And no one thought that Cain ever learned how to swim. So he tried. And he drowned."

"Was Underwood the warden then?"

"Assistant warden," the matron replied. "Or deputy warden or whatever they called it."

"The warden before Underwood was killed, too,"

Gripewater said. He shook his head. "Murdered. His head smashed to bits with a hammer."

"They say," Eve Martin said, "that Killer Cain committed that crime, too."

Fallon decided that he could use more coffee, so he found his cup and took a healthy swallow. "So if The Mole is dead," he began, "who was it in that cell with me?"

"Nobody," Eve Martin answered. "It was your imagination."

Fallon stretched his leg out so that the doctor and matron could see it.

"And who patched that up?" he asked.

"You did," Doctor Gripewater told him.

Fallon studied them, and slowly shook his head. "Ma'am, Doctor, my imagination isn't that good. And my skills as a seamstress or surgeon are even worse than my imagination."

"Doctor."

The soft, easy voice startled the three. Fallon was the one who rose, though, and nodded respectfully at Jess Harper. She stood over the table upon which Ford Wagner lay.

"He's awake," she said.

"Good," Gripewater said, finished his gin, and rose from his chair. "Come have a seat, Jess." He started toward the sick man.

"Doc," Fallon whispered, and when Gripewater looked over his shoulder, continued: "He doesn't know about Kemp Carver."

"And he won't learn it from me. Missus Martin." His crazy-haired head turned to the matron. "Would you be so kind as to go find a couple of guards and have them escort our guests, Fallon and Wagner, back to their cells."

The big woman looked horrified. "Doctor. What about all that's going on outside?"

Gripewater gave her a dismissive wave. "Darling, there hasn't been a peep outside for more than an hour and a half. Looks like old Underwood has put down another potential firestorm. And that's a damned shame."

The matron was gone. Jess Harper sat in the good doctor's vacated chair. Fallon stood at the table, gently helping Ford Wagner into an upright position. Gripewater again listened to the thin man's breathing, his heartbeat, and stuck a thermometer in his mouth.

Wagner's eyes looked tired, but every few blinks would lock hard on Fallon.

"What do you know about consumption?" Gripewater asked. He kept one hand on Wagner's pulse and held a stem-wind pocket watch in his other hand.

Fallon shrugged.

"I've seen enough of it," Fallon said, "but not enough to know that much about it."

"Any family of yours?"

"No, sir."

"Nor mine."

Wagner turned his head and coughed, but this time there was no blood, but an ugly, thick phlegm of a sickly white color.

"And how would you treat it?"

"I don't think there is any treatment. There was a man down home in Gads Hill. The doctor there always bled him. But back then, they bled everyone."

"And killed most of them," Gripewater said. He lowered his watch and released the wrist of Wagner that Fallon had not broken.

"Aren't there sanatoriums now?" Fallon asked.

Gripewater's eyes brightened. "Indeed. In my day, I have seen the preferred method move from bleeding, or purging, to resting, to sending folks to the dry desert country. Indeed, that seemed to help a little. People once thought this was something you inherited. A hell of an inheritance, if you ask me. But a Frenchman many years back proved that this came not from your blood, your ancestors, your ma and pa, but was contagious. And in the past decade, a German discovered *Mycobacterium tuberculosis.* If someone with this lung illness happened to cough on you, even sneeze on you, that could send hundreds and hundreds of these bacteria into you. And then you, my good, healthy young man, could soon look like this wastrel. So now we have sanatoriums. To send these untouchable creatures off to die. Although, I should point out, that some of these sanatoriums are not death houses. This"—He waved around him, meaning, Fallon thought, the entire prison and not just the prison hospital—"This is a death house."

Gripewater snorted and looked at Wagner. "Can you put on your socks and shoes? They'll be here to take you back to your cell in a few minutes."

The prisoner answered in a hoarse breath. "I . . . guess . . . so . . ." And he let Fallon help him off the table and onto a low couch.

The door opened a few minutes later, and Fallon was surprised at the escorts who entered the hospital. Harold Underwood followed Eve Martin. Fowlson and Captain Brandt came in behind.

"Doctor," the warden said.

"I'm surprised," Gripewater said, "that I have had no other patients today."

The warden shook his head. "You may have some in the morning, Doctor. If and when the cell doors are opened."

"You could try to treat these men decent," Gripewater said.

"They don't know the meaning of the word, Doctor, and they shall get no mercy from me. Are these two men ready to go?"

"Yes." Gripewater pointed at Ford Wagner. "This man, though, should be isolated . . . and I don't mean in the basement of A-Hall."

"No one is in the basement of A-Hall, Gripewater," Underwood said, but he kept his eyes on Fallon when he spoke those words. "Not in years. But your recommendation is sound, Doctor. Isn't it, Captain?"

"I'll see it done," Brandt said. "He'll be alone. But not in one of our basement cells."

"I'd bring him back here tomorrow after breakfast," Gripewater said.

"As you wish," Underwood said. The warden nodded, and Brandt tapped his line stick against the base of Fallon's neck.

"Up," the captain said. "Up you stinking piece of fresh fish. Up and at attention before I get mad."

"We don't get mad here, Captain," Gripewater said.

"Captain . . ." The warden used his most placating voice. "There are ladies present."

Fallon was standing though, waiting for that studded stick to crash against his skull, his shoulders, his back.

"Let's go," the warden said.

But before they reached the door, Thaddeus Gripewater said, "Aren't you forgetting something, Mr. Underwood?"

The men stopped, with Mr. Fowlson's hand on the knob to the door, and all turned except Fallon and Wagner.

"What?" Underwood was tired of trying to pretend that he had a heart, that he gave a damn.

"It's customary," Gripewater said, "and mandated by law, that all dead prisoners be examined. A certificate of death is to be filed, you remember. Things have changed since . . . oh . . . the days of Coleman Cain."

Fallon would have loved to see the expression on the faces of Underwood, Fowlson, and Brandt.

"Yes." The warden's voice had turned to ice. "But no one died today, Doctor."

"That's good to know," Gripewater said. "Because I'm being visited by a handsome young reporter from some newspaper in Kansas City. Kansas. Not Missouri. And she's accompanying me the day after tomorrow to examine the prisoners. Cell by cell."

"I don't believe I granted permission for such an interview."

"You didn't," the doctor said. "The governor did. It's an election year, you know. And he prides himself as a candidate for reform."

"He's an ignorant fool."

The warden regained his composure and painted a false smile on his face. "I am sure you will have a delightful interview, and that your reporter friend will give our prison glowing praise. Mr. Fowlson? Would you take Wagner to his cell? A cell he will have to himself tonight."

"Yes, sir." Fowlson was happy to open the door. Wagner stepped out. Fallon started to follow.

"No," the warden said. "Leave Fallon here. Captain Brandt will take him to his cell."

"Very good, sir." The door closed.

And once the footsteps of the deputy warden and the dying consumptive faded, Harold Underwood raised a finger and jammed it underneath the doctor's nose.

"You'd be smart to consider retiring, Doctor Gripewater, after your remarkable service to our fine state and this superb institution of rehabilitation."

The doctor shoved his hands in his coat pocket. "Just make sure Kemp Carver's body is brought here so I can examine the poor, dead man, Harold. I'm sure all the witnesses will swear that his death was an accident."

"Yes," Underwood said. "Both guards and even a convict—Fallon here—tried to save the man's life. Tsk, tsk." The warden's tone turned bitterly cold, though, as he continued. "Wagner doesn't know his relation is dead, does he?"

"Of course, not," Gripewater said. "I do my best to keep my patients alive. You should try that."

"You should try to keep your big mouth shut."

The doctor's head shook. "A lost cause."

"Isn't it, though?" Underwood nodded, the door opened, and Fallon, Brandt, and Underwood stepped into the prison air. But before the captain of the guards could close the door, Doctor Gripewater called out. "And, by the way, Warden. Please make sure Fallon is brought back here the day after tomorrow. I'd like to check on his stitches. I'm just not sure my sutures hold up as well by the braided hairs of a man with really, really long hair. That pretty reporter is in our fine city for a few days. If I don't see Fallon day after tomorrow, if I don't see Fallon *alive*, I mean, well, then I might have to tell that fine journalist."

Brandt answered. "Fallon will be here, Doctor." The guard chuckled and pressed the top of his line stick into the small of Fallon's back.

They walked in silence, with Fallon, knowing his place—especially with that hardcase Brandt right behind him—and keeping his head down. He could still see, of course, and he took in the inside of the prison compound. Nothing seemed out of order.

That was even the case when they stepped back inside A-Hall, although Fallon spotted a handful of guards overseeing two prisoners as they mopped the floor at the spot where Kemp Carver hit the floor.

Mr. Fowlson was coming down the stairs. He stopped, out of breath, and saluted the warden.

"Is Wagner alone?" the warden asked.

"Yes, sir."

"Is he all right?"

"I think so."

"Thinking doesn't get things done, Fowlson."

"He says he's good."

"Very well, find a place for Fallon. Then meet me in my office. This place is about to burn like hell, and we need to put out a few fires."

Chapter Thirty-five

He lay on his bed in the cell next to the one he had originally been given. Twelve-by-eight feet, crammed with four men, including Fallon. There was a chamber pot to be shared. The bed was mattress filled with straw, but there wasn't enough straw inside the ticking fabric to say it was filled. Few people could claim they felt any difference between lying on the bed and lying directly on the hard, dirty floor.

"You need anything, Fallon?"

At this time of night, the cell was pitch black. Fallon lay with his head propped up against the wall near the door. Bone tired he might be, but he kept remembering several scenes from this day over and over again. Things that did not make a lick of sense. Well, that's what he kept trying to figure out, but one of his three cellmates kept jabbering.

"It can get hard on a man, his first time in the cell. Mighty hard. I've heard men scream and scream and scream. So I'm just here to help you. Anything you need, Fallon, you just ask me. But don't wait too long. I'm getting out of this rock pile in three days."

The convict's name was Charley Muldoon. He had been born in a log cabin a few miles outside of Neeleyville, down south in Missouri not far from the Arkansas state line. The cabin had burned down when Muldoon was fourteen. Muldoon had gotten a hell of a whipping for playing with matches and almost burning alive his ma, pa, dog, and twin sisters. The next year, the St. Louis, Iron Mountain and Southern Railway depot in town burned down. No one ever figure out how that happened . . . until the schoolmaster's rented house went up in smoke just before school was set to start. That's when Charley Muldoon had hightailed it out of Neeleyville, but not before he torched the livery stable.

And thus Charley Muldoon had left a trail that was easy to follow because of the ashes, embers, and charred ruins. A four-seat outhouse behind the hotel in Poplar Bluff. A dog house in Piedmont. A summer kitchen in Ironton. The undertaker's office in Leadwood. The Methodist meeting house in De Soto. The lumberyard in Cedar Hill. And a riverboat in St. Charles. That's when Charley Muldoon had learned that some men would actually pay Charley Muldoon to do something he loved more than life himself: Lighting things on fire.

In St. Louis, Troy, Hannibal . . . across the river in Quincy, Illinois . . . up toward the Iowa line in Unionville . . . down to Trenton . . . and the opera house in Gallatin. What had landed Muldoon in the Jefferson City pen was an abandoned shack in Arrow Rock, for which he had done to satisfy himself and not for pay. Which was probably the only reason Charley Muldoon would be finishing his sentence in three days and be free to buy a box of matches and go back to getting his thrills.

"You scared?" Muldoon asked. "Is that on account you can't sleep?"

"He can't sleep, Muldoon, because you don't know how to keep your damned trap shut." That would be Frenchy Brodeur, just starting his eighth year of a fifteen-year sentence. Brodeur spoke without a trace of French accent. The other prisoner, Tom Worsnop—Fallon knew the name and the man's crimes—snored contentedly.

Worsnop was back in the Missouri State Penitentiary for his second round, which told Fallon that he, Worsnop was not a very good counterfeiter. Or maybe he was. He just wasn't good at staying out of prison. But word was that if a prisoner needed anything, Tom Worsnop, better known as Tom What You Need Get It in a Snap—maybe the lamest handle Fallon had heard—would get it to him. For a good markup, but credit was available for fresh fish. Tom Worsnop could get contraband from one cell to another, one building to another, right under the eyes of the stupid guards. Because Tom Worsnop had the perfect partner.

Which Fallon figured to be one of the prison guards.

Maybe that's why Tom Worsnop slept so peacefully.

Still, Fallon could think of no reason he would need Worsnop or Muldoon.

At least, Brodeur's reprimand had made Muldoon lower his voice. "What about it, Fallon? What do you need? Like I said, the first time . . ."

"Charley," Fallon said, "this isn't my first time behind the iron." Wasn't that the damned truth! He had not forgotten—and never would forget—his time spent with The Mole down in the basement of A-Hall. "And it's not my first time in prison."

"Oh."

A cold silence filled the room.

"Thank God," Frenchy said, and rolled over on his makeshift bed, adjusted his razor-thin mattress. When that was over, the silence lengthened, except for the snores of Worsnop and the heavy breathing of Charley Muldoon.

Fallon welcomed the relative silence. He put his mind back to what he had heard.

He pictured the terror in Kemp Carver's face as he hung on for dear life from the catwalk's support beam.

I swear to God, Fallon! I didn't have a damn thing to do with it. I swear to God. It wasn't me. It wasn't me.

Fallon sighed. Didn't have a damn thing to do with . . . what? What on earth could the one-armed man have meant? It wasn't me. It wasn't me. What did Carver think Fallon knew? What had Carver done? For that matter, why had Ford Wagner, sick as he was, immediately attacked Fallon when he first saw him? Because of what had happened all those years ago, the death of Daniel Huntington? No, Fallon just didn't think that to be the reason. Both Wagner and Carver had attacked Fallon, but not for revenge. It seemed to Fallon that they had attacked because of . . . could it be . . . ?

Fear?

I'll tell you everything, Fallon! Everything! Fallon could still hear the desperation in Carver's voice. And later, repeating: *It wasn't me, Fallon! I swear it wasn't me.* And finally: *But I know . . .*

Which is when Captain Brandt had come into view.

And that was when the true fear registered in Kemp Carver's face.

But Fallon could not make anything out of that. Kemp Carver was scared to death of Captain Brandt. Well, that likely would not put Carver in the minority. Fallon realized that if he wanted to make Charley Muldoon keep quiet, all he likely needed to do was mention Brandt's name.

Still, none of this made a lick of sense, at least for the time being. Fallon tucked the final words of Kemp Carver, and how the convict had died, into the recesses of his mind, and tried to make sense of all that Doctor Thaddeus Gripewater had told him. About The Mole. And Coleman Cain. Gripewater could be a valuable source for Fallon, not to mention a friend and colleague that Fallon desperately needed. Fallon twisted his leg just to feel the stitches and the bandage. There was no ghost in that basement cell. And Fallon did not believe he had dreamed up or hallucinated The Mole. The wound in his calf had been stitched with braided human hair. How someone could do that amazed Fallon. And that someone might have done that in a blackness darker than the ace of spades was even more . . . amazing? Preposterous? Insane?

He made himself think of Jess Harper. After all, that was why he was here. To help out Sean and Daniel MacGregor and the American Detective Agency. She was pretty, too gentle to have been hooked up with Linc Harper. Of course, many citizens of Fort Smith and Van Buren would have said the same about Fallon's wife. Which Jess Harper reminded him of. He made himself black out that memory. He focused on his job, on the young woman with child. He had taken a small step today. And he would be back in the doctor's office in a couple of days, thanks to Thaddeus Gripewater.

Charley Muldoon sucked in a deep breath, held it, and slowly let it out in an easy silence. Tom Worsnop ceased his snores. The cell became as quiet as it was dark, and Fallon heard the noise beyond the cell, too. He kept his breathing steady and quiet. He did not move.

As thick as the iron doors were, and as solid as the walls, hearing the tiptoes of men on the third floor proved frustratingly hard. Yet cellblocks at night were eerily quiet. Fallon let one finger come out of his fist. One man. A half-minute later, the second finger extended. Two. Fallon kept listening, but, as far as he could tell, there were only two men outside.

The footsteps stopped right past the door to Fallon's cell. He tensed and considered removing the knife from his boot. Sending men in the middle of the night to beat Fallon half to death, or maybe even kill him, was not the kind of thing to cause Harold Underwood, Mr. Fowlson, or Captain Brandt to lose any sleep.

In the thick blackness, Fallon looked down at his legs, seeing nothing, but knowing exactly where that knife in his boot was. He thought about reaching for it, slipping it from its leather sheath, but he had too much experience to make that kind of mistake. If he could hear the men outside, even just barely, they most likely would hear him.

He strained to hear. Metal. Just slight and then a loud creak that caused Fallon to turn his head to his left. A key in the lock of the door. Only . . . not this door. It had to be the cell next to theirs. The cell that housed, for the time being, only Ford Wagner.

There was no mistaking the next noise, and no matter how deftly the men outside worked, it was an impossible task to silently pull open an iron door on iron hinges that kept the worst men Missouri had to offer from committing more outrages.

"Wagner." The voice was muffled, barely audible, through the thick limestone walls.

Something touched the floor. A grunt.

Someone whispered. An even fainter reply came. Fallon did not think he could have heard whatever was said even had he been standing outside the door to Ford Wagner's cell.

"Here. Take it." That Fallon heard, but he could not put a name to the voice. He tried to listen harder, but if anything else was said, Fallon had not managed to grasp even a syllable.

Now, Fallon began to recall the conversation between the warden and Mr. Fowlson earlier this day when Fallon was being led to his cell.

Underwood: Is Wagner alone?

Fowlson: Yes, sir.

And then something about Wagner saying that he felt good. No. Not felt. Wagner's voice rolled across Fallon's memories. *He says he's good.* Not that Wagner felt or was feeling good, but that he was good. And despite Doctor Thaddeus Gripewater's earlier conversation about isolating those people cursed with consumption, Fallon knew that Underwood was not considering turning a cell into a sanatorium when he had asked if Wagner were alone.

There was something else going on here at the Missouri state pen.

The door closed again, the lock was set, and the footsteps led away, toward the rear of A-Hall instead of the way the two men had come. Fallon put his ear against the wall, listening for anything that would tell him that Ford Wagner was still in his cell. No footsteps. No snores. No coughs of the hard sound of a man coughing up his lungs. Just silence. Nothing.

They were gone now. Fallon heard nothing. Worsnop began snoring again. Frenchy swore and rolled over.

And Charley Muldoon gave the fresh fish named Fallon another piece of advice. But this time, the arsonist was not talking just to hear himself talk or to let Fallon know all the rules for survival in The Walls. Although what Muldoon said was likely the first rule to keep yourself alive.

"You didn't hear a thing, Fallon. There wasn't anything to hear. You best remember that. You was like Frenchy and Tom and especially me. You slept like a baby. Didn't hear a damned thing."

Frenchy added: "Because there wasn't nothing to hear."

CHAPTER THIRTY-SIX

The thickness of the walls and the iron door did nothing to diminish the blaring of the whistles, the ringing of the bells, and the cursing of the guards.

"All right, you manure-eatin' swine, time to work, time to work! So yer goin' to wash, yer goin' to eat, and yer goin' to work your arses off!

Doors began being pulled open. Guards shouted. The prisoners remained silent.

"Keep your head down," Worsnop whispered. "And your mouth shut."

"Yeah," said Muldoon. "You'll likely come with us. Ever made a broom before, Fallon?"

"Shut the hell up," Frenchy whispered.

The door opened. A burly guard Fallon had never noticed stood before them, with a heavier and longer line stick in his meaty right hand. "All right, you miserable turds. Out. Out and be damned quick."

Fallon pulled his cap on, lowered his head until it felt damned uncomfortable, and ducked to step out of the cramped cell and into the walkway.

Immediately, he went down, seeing orange and

dots and flashes and symbols in ten other colors as well, feeling a pounding in his head. His cap fell off. That movement stopped another line stick from slamming into his head or side or neck. He rolled over, squeezing his eyes shut to block out the pain, bending his knees, and drawing up his legs. He kept his mouth closed. He did not open his eyes. And he sure knew better than to yell or cry out in pain.

"I said to keep your damned eyes on the ground, you piece of garbage!" The burly man spit, but Fallon knew he was not the one who had tried to tear his head off. Fallon also knew that he had not looked anywhere but at the floor.

A boot kicked his foot. "Get up," another guard said. "Come on, fish, unless you want to miss your breakfast."

Fallon opened his eyes. He saw his cellmates standing against the wall, their heads down. The door to the cell remained open. Frenchy, Muldoon, and Worsnop said nothing.

"Get him off his arse." The burly guard poked Muldoon and Worsnop with his long stick, and the prisoners hurried to Fallon. They said nothing, and Fallon knew to hold his tongue, but he let them lift him to his feet. Muldoon picked up the cap and held it toward Fallon. His vision was blurred, and the whole cellblock seemed to be spinning out of control. It took him two tries before he grabbed the hat, which he kept holding, tighter and tighter and tighter, trying to block out the pain.

"Breakfast," the burly guard said. "After the bathhouse. And show this fish how to make a broom. And that broom had better be good enough to sweep out my kitchen so that my mother can eat off the damned floor."

Fallon blinked back the tears from the pain. He wanted to check on one thing, and he saw it clearly, if just briefly. All of the doors on this side of the third floor of A-Hall were open as prisoners filed out to be escorted by the guards, all except one.

The door to Ford Wagner's cell remained closed and locked.

Breakfast was boiled potatoes, mush, and coffee. The coffee was cold, and likely two or three days old. You had to make yourself eat that garbage and drink that filth, but it was food. It didn't fill the stomach, and it tasted awful, but it might give you enough strength to get through the day.

"Everybody remain seated until you are called!" barked the guard in charge. Those were the first words uttered in the mess hall since Fallon had walked in with the other prisoners. "Table One, shoe factory!"

Fallon waited till they called out his table. "Broom factory!" Charley Muldoon nodded, and pushed himself to his feet, along with the others sitting there. Fallon made himself stand. There was no dizziness, but his head hurt like hell.

Head down, he followed his cellmates through the opening, down the path, and all the way to the broom factory. The foreman of the factory grunted as the prisoners walked in and held out his hand to stop Fallon.

"You're new," he said.

"Yes, sir," Fallon answered.

"All right. Let's see how good you are at unloading broomcorn."

So Fallon and a dozen others went outside and began emptying boxes upon boxes of broomcorn, which smelled like some type of sorghum. Others took what would serve as the working part of the broom inside the plant, to be pressed. Across from Fallon and those working with the corn, other men pulled handles upon handles, some medium length, some short, some more for whisks, and some very long, and hauled those inside the factory.

A surly convict with a bald head walked up and down the row where men sorted the sorghum, or whatever it was, reminding them to separate the straw—which was exactly what this was—by grades. "You don't want a slave's broom to go to some rich ol' biddy with a mansion overlookin' the Missouri, now do you?"

"What the hell's the difference?" said a man a few feet from Fallon. "The same slave'll be working for the rich ol' biddy."

The surly foreman chuckled.

Fallon watched as he worked, seeing how the various grades of broomcorn were grouped together and laid in piles.

Hours later, with his hands itching from handling the sorghum without any break, or water, Fallon was ordered to begin carrying the broomcorn inside. It was no cooler inside, Fallon quickly learned.

Men like Worsnop and Frenchy worked inside, sitting at small workplaces and sweating as much as Fallon, as they wrapped a wire to secure the broomcorn to a dowel. When that reached their satisfaction, they began shaping the broom.

Well, Fallon thought, when this job is done, when

you're finally finished with Sean MacGregor and the American Detective Agency, you'll have a job you can fall back on. Wouldn't his mother be proud! He should be able to make a damned good broom.

They worked through the day. Fallon figured he could use a long shower, but someone mentioned that they wouldn't get a bath until Friday. Friday? When was that? What day was it? It didn't matter. The way the man had said it, Friday might be a month away.

A few water breaks had been allowed, and once the shift had ended, new guards escorted them to the exercise yard. That's exactly what this crew needed, Fallon figured. After working, sweating all day sorting sorghum or wiring brooms together, these men needed to burn off all that fat.

Fallon found what passed for shade and leaned against the wall. He found himself looking up at the walls, counting the guard towers, seeing what kinds of weapons they had, who was looking intently at the wall, and which guards were lazy. He sought out blind spots, where a man could be hard to see. The heel of his work boot tugged at the sand at his feet, to get a feel about how a man might go about digging a tunnel.

Which finally caused Fallon to laugh.

"What's the joke, Fallon?"

Fallon shook his head and sighed at the sight of Charley Muldoon leaning one shoulder against the wall, his legs crossed at the ankles, grinning while cracking his knuckles.

"I was figuring out how to escape," Fallon told him. He watched the arsonist quickly come straight up, away from the wall, his fingers now clasped as in prayer.

"Fallon," the little man said urgently. "Don't be joshing. And if you ain't joshing, don't say nothing to me about that. I want to get out of here. I'm getting out of here. In two days. And don't need you to get me another year tacked on. I got things to do."

"Yeah," Fallon said. "Places to see. Buildings to burn."

That caused Muldoon to laugh.

Fallon had found something more interesting than guard towers. He saw that black cat he had seen everywhere in the prison, only this time it was walking toward Worsnop, who knelt on the edge of the sand, cooing, and flexing his fingers. The cat looked as though it could care less, but it did make its way toward the convict, although it did so at its own deliberate pace.

The cat came to Worsnop and began rubbing its fur against the man's striped trousers. No one paid any attention to the prisoner or the prison's cat. Not the guards. Not the inmates. Nobody except Harry Fallon.

So it was Fallon, and only Fallon, who saw Worsnop pull something out of the makeshift collar and slide that into a pants pocket. While that was happening, the slight man was bringing his other hand out of the other pocket and tucking whatever it was inside the collar. He returned to scratching the cat, rubbing the cat, and whispering to the cat until the cat had had enough. It turned and began walking back across the prison yard.

Fallon let his eyes follow the cat, and then turned to Worsnop, who stood, stretched his back, and began walking toward a group of prisoners who were tossing a ball.

"What's the deal with Worsnop and the cat?" Fallon asked.

"Jeez, Fallon," Charley Muldoon said. "You're going to get me six months tacked on if you don't shut up. You got something to ask Worsnop, take it up with Worsnop."

"All right," Fallon said. "All right. I'll do that." So Fallon moved toward the men throwing the ball, and he came right up beside Worsnop.

"Nice cat," he said. One of the men threw the ball to Fallon. Even with his hands aching and sticking and smelling like broomcorn, Fallon managed to catch the ball, and he pitched it underhanded to Worsnop, who snagged it, nodded at another inmate, and did some crazy old pitcher's windup and threw the ball underhanded.

"Nothin' but a cat."

"How much can a cat like that carry?"

Worsnop turned and studied Fallon long and hard. "It's a small cat."

"I've seen smaller."

"You've seen a lot of things for a fresh fish."

"Because I pay attention."

"It's not good to see too much."

"Like Kemp Carver falling to his death."

"I didn't see that." He caught the ball, tossed it to Fallon, who threw a bit wild toward a dark-skinned man who made a good snag. Fallon tipped his cap and gave the convict a nod.

"What do you want, Fallon?"

"If I needed something, could I get a special delivery?"

"Do you like cats?"

"Not especially."

Worsnop relaxed. "I hate the sidewinders."

"Bitches are dogs."

Now the inmate laughed harder. "Small things. Cigarettes mostly, rolled already. No guns. No knives. Nothing that'll get me in trouble. Some of the guards let this go on, because I give them a little payment."

"Does Underwood know?"

"Hell, no. I'd be down in the caverns or in the morgue."

Fallon caught a ball, tossed it to Worsnop, who threw a hard shot to a big man in the far corner.

"Nice arm," Fallon said.

"So what is it that you'd like delivered, Fallon?" Worsnop asked.

"A key," Fallon said.

Worsnop stared at Fallon in complete disbelief.

"Fallon!" He looked up and found the prison guard, the one named Ryan, at the far side of the exercise yard. "Over here, Fallon. Pronto."

Leaving Worsnop still staring with wide eyes, Harry Fallon shoved his hands in his pockets and made his way toward the timid guard. He recognized the woman standing next to Ryan. Fallon even remembered the woman standing next to the prison's doctor. It wasn't the matron, Eve Martin. It wasn't Jess Harper, either.

Chapter Thirty-seven

The plain brown dress was gone, replaced by a long, pleated skirt of light gray, a wide belt of black leather around her waist, and a light blue blouse with a high-standing collar. She wore a short black jacket, unbuttoned, and a flat-crowned, flat-brimmed straw hat with a large black band topped her head. Her blonde hair was rather short, and she had an angular face, round chin, and rosy lips. She still had her notebook, of course, and the pencil in her right hand was holding it ready.

The little guard named Ryan stepped away from the woman and toward Fallon, and said, "Fallon, this . . . umm . . ." He frowned and looked back at the striking woman. "I'm sorry, ma'am, but I've forgotten . . ."

Fallon cut him off. "Julie Jernigan," he said. "Of the *Kansas City Enterprise*. Kansas. Not Missouri."

She smiled widely and gave a slight bow. "You have an excellent memory, Mister . . . ?"

"I am sure you know that already."

She laughed. "You have dealt with the press before."

"What do you need, Missus Jernigan?"

"It's *Miss* Jernigan. Or Julie."

Fallon waited. He had never been one to trust newspaper reporters, but on the other hand he had never met one as fetching as Julie Jernigan, though she had to be a good ten years Fallon's junior. He could not help but notice her hands, or, rather, her fingers. No band on any of them. In fact, she wore no jewelry at all. Which meant nothing. Only an idiot would come into a prison, even under the escort and protection of a guard, wearing valuable jewelry.

"Doctor Gripewater said you would be a good source for my article," the reporter said. "Mr. Getty here was nice enough to lead me to you."

Ryan Getty shuffled his feet.

"You want me to tell you about . . . being here?"

"That's the general idea."

Fallon shook his head and laughed slightly. "I haven't been here long enough to form an opinion," he lied.

"Well . . ." Julie Jernigan glanced at the young, naïve guard. "Excuse me, Ryan . . . you don't mind if I call you, Ryan, do you? Could you let me speak to Mr. Fallon here privately?"

"I can't leave you alone, ma'am. It's for your own protection."

"Which I certainly do appreciate. But I'm not asking you to leave me alone. Just give me, say, ten or twelve feet. Surely nothing can happen to me before you could swing into action with your baseball bat."

"It's a line stick, ma'am."

"Yes. Of course." She wrote that on a blank page. "Ten feet. Please. If Mr. Fallon does anything threatening, I'll scream. It won't be longer than ten or fifteen minutes, I promise." She batted her eyes, and Ryan Getty slowly backed away.

When Getty stopped, Julie Jernigan came closer.

"What are you doing here, Mr. Fallon?" she asked, with her pencil at the ready.

"Four years," Fallon said.

"Off the record," she said. She did not write down Fallon's answer. "For my own edification. You arrived here with an operative for the American Detective Agency."

"What did MacGregor tell you?" Fallon asked.

"Nothing. He didn't even meet me, although he promised. But, well, that's not the first time a member of law enforcement has failed to honor my request for an interview."

Actually, that surprised Fallon. He figured Dan MacGregor, young and handsome as he was, would have eagerly met with anyone who looked like Julie Jernigan.

"Please, Mr. Fallon. Doctor Gripewater has told me a lot, but Mr. Getty, although he's very sweet and I even think he's honest, has not shown me much. I have several stories, uncorroborated, and I need some more background, some first-hand accounts, before I can take this and convince my editor that I have a great story."

"Why," Fallon began, "would the *Kansas City Enterprise*—in *Kansas*—have any special interest in the *Missouri* State Penitentiary? Shouldn't you be writing about Leavenworth? Or the state pen in Lansing?"

"I am a reporter for the *Enterprise*. I also am a correspondent for the *New-York Tribune*."

Fallon straightened. "The paper Horace Greeley started?"

"God rest his amazing soul," Julie Jernigan said.

"We're a long way from New York state," Fallon said.

"But I'm real close to a newspaper article that would rock Jefferson City, Missouri, the entire West, and maybe even all of the United States. I am out to reform the way prisons are run."

"Muckraker?" Fallon asked.

"Revealer of truth," she said.

Fallon sighed. "Your readers, and your editor, wouldn't believe anything I had to say. A prisoner's word doesn't count for much, ma'am."

"But a detective's word does . . ."

His head shook. "I'm no detective."

"But you were once a deputy for Judge Parker over in Arkansas and the Indian Territory."

Fallon stepped back and reassessed the beautiful young woman next to him. She most certainly was a newspaper reporter.

"How'd you find that out?"

"It's not that hard, you know. Once you have a man's name, and a lot of time to dig through old newspapers or ask officials in state government or the U.S. marshal in town, things sometimes—though certainly not always—fall into place."

"Then you know . . ."

She cut him off. "About what happened in the Nations? Yes. Joliet? Of course. And even your wife and daughter." She began to write. Fallon realized he had just clenched both fists.

He exhaled. "I've only been here a few days," he said.

"Is that how they treat you? A bruise a day?"

Fallon shook his head. "I got a lot of bruises on

the train ride coming into Jeff City, ma'am. You must remember that."

"I do." She stopped writing. "But Doctor Gripewater told me about The Mole. The basement cells. And, again, he said you were not the average prisoner in Jefferson City. And Doctor Gripewater has been here for a long, long time."

He still was not one to trust newspaper scribblers, no matter how good looking they were. He also had just learned that Thaddeus Gripewater had a big mouth.

"Ma'am," he said, "if I'm here, then you know that the American Detective Agency has a reason for me being here. And I'd like to get out of here alive. Talking to you . . ." He let the sentence fade into the afternoon heat, and his heart stopped pounding when he saw the reaction on the young woman's face.

"Oh, my goodness," she said, and dropped her pencil. "I didn't think . . ."

Fallon knelt to pick up the pencil. He frowned when he looked past the light gray skirt to see Warden Harold Underwood charging in this direction.

"Getty!" the warden boomed.

Julie Jernigan spun around, sending her skirt spreading like a balloon that slapped Fallon's head. He rose, saw the pencil, felt its point, and slipped it into his pocket.

Ryan Getty hurried toward the warden, about twenty yards away, but abruptly stopped when he remembered his job, and he looked back at Fallon and the *Enterprise* reporter.

"I do not recall giving permission for Miss Jernigan

to speak to any prisoner," the warden said when he stopped. His face was red. So were his ears.

"Doctor Gripewater . . ." the young guard said.

"Is a drunken lout, a pathetic surgeon, and most certainly is *not* the man in charge of this prison!" The warden extended his hand toward the woman. "I'll have your notes, Miss Jernigan."

Smiling, she showed him her page.

The warden frowned.

"Obviously," Jernigan said, "Mr. Fallon was not the most cooperative interview." She turned the pad around and read, "Makes fist." Next, she flipped back a page and revealed other pages. "The rest came from Doctor Gripewater. Now, may I have the chance to talk to you, sir?" She did not try to bat her eyes.

Pivoting so that he could glare intensely at Ryan Getty, Underwood said, "You were ordered to keep a close eye on her."

"I was, sir. I only wanted to give them some privacy."

"Privacy?" About fifteen seconds of foul oaths spat out of the warden's mouth. "This is the Missouri State Penitentiary, Getty. Inmates get no privacy. Certainly not among reporters."

"Yes, sir."

"About that interview?" Julie Jernigan said sweetly.

"I have a full day," Underwood said. "I am a very busy man. Prisons do not run themselves."

"That's a shame," the woman said. "I really hoped to talk to you before I met with the governor and the attorney general for the state."

Underwood stared at the woman for a long time. His chose his words carefully. "You are writing this for a Kansas newspaper?"

She laughed a forced but sweet laugh. "We are neighbors, Mister Director, or is it superintendent? You see. I really need to talk to you, to get all my facts straight."

"Yes. And I remember, before you were born, Miss, just how neighborly we could be in the days of Old John Brown, William Quantrill, and Jesse James."

"Well . . ." the reporter tried.

"Where are you staying?" the warden interrupted.

"The Hotel Missouri on Jackson Street."

"What time are your meetings with the governor and General Waterston?"

"Oh." She shrugged. "Not until three-thirty tomorrow."

"All right." Underwood wet his lips. "I will send word to your hotel. You'll be back tomorrow, I'm sure. For your article. Am I correct?"

"Of course."

"And, most likely, your night is filled."

"With supper and sleep."

The warden smiled.

"I will make room on my schedule for us to meet tomorrow morning. How long do you need? An hour? Two?"

"That would be most welcome, sir. Perhaps Mr. Fowlson and Captain Brandt can join us."

The smile vacated the warden's face. "I shall ask them to be there."

"And how about The Mole?"

The warden glared. "The Mole is just a myth, Miss Jernigan. We can talk about all the lies and far-fetched stories one hears from prisoners. Regular tales of blood and thunder more suitable for a dime novel than a solid newspaper like the *Enterprise*."

Miss Jernigan bowed. Fallon figured that she knew, as well as he knew, that Harold Underwood had never even heard of the Kansas City *Enterprise*.

"Mr. Getty," the warden said. "Please escort Miss Jernigan to the gate." Underwood bowed slightly. "I look forward to seeing you tomorrow morning, ma'am."

As the young guard went to the young woman, warden Harold Underwood went straight to Fallon.

"What did that prying little weasel ask you?" he said.

Fallon shrugged. "Nothing much," he said.

"Maybe you'd like to go see The Mole again."

Fallon smiled. "Well, Warden, sir, seeing as how The Mole's just a myth, some far-fetched story of blood and thunder that belongs in a dime novel, I doubt if that's possible, sir."

"Anything's possible in prison, Fallon. Remember Just ask Kemp Carver."

Fallon stared.

"Did she ask about Carver?"

Fallon's head shook.

"Well, that doesn't matter. Gripewater signed the death certificate. I even sent statements to the *Jefferson City Herald* and the *Evening Star*, so word will be out about Carver's misfortune and accidental death."

The warden snapped his fingers, and two big men stopped tapping their line sticks on their thighs and came over.

"The prisoners have had enough exercise for the day," Underwood told them. "Round them up and get them to the mess hall for supper. Then get them to their cells for the night. And if you see him talking to anyone who is not a guard, I expect you to tear his head off with your line sticks." He turned away to return to his office, but stopped, and looked over his shoulder.

His smile was like a serpent's.

"That would be an accident, too, Fallon. You might not believe this, but most deaths in prison are accidents."

Yeah, Fallon thought as the two guards came up to his side. Fallon did not believe that.

Chapter Thirty-eight

Lights out. Back in the cell with Worsnop, Muldoon, and Frenchy, Fallon waited. His muscles ached, and he swore he could still smell broomcorn on his hands. His jacket stank of sorghum, too, and that smell was more pronounced since Fallon had rolled it up and stuck in under his head to serve as a pillow.

Fallon put his ear against the wall and tried to hear inside Ford Wagner's cell. Nothing. A man suffering from consumption, living in a dark, dank dungeon, would likely be hacking up his lungs, and that kind of noise Fallon could at least detect.

He had been listening for what felt like an hour and heard nothing. That left him wondering if Ford Wagner was dead. Would Underwood leave the man in there to rot as he had left The Mole—Killer Coleman Cain—in the basement dungeon?

"Fallon."

He tensed, and twisted his head, looking in the darkness.

"Yeah?" Fallon whispered back.

"What kind of key?"

He grinned then. Worsnop was a scrounger, and unlike Charley Muldoon, he was willing to take risks. Then again, Worsnop, unlike the weak little arsonist, wasn't due to be released from The Walls anytime soon. Fallon slid up, using the cold, hard wall like the back of the chair. He had given up on hearing anything next door. Ford Wagner was either a corpse or . . . where could the guards have taken him? And why? The hospital.

"Not one to the front gate," Fallon said, "if that eases your mind. But it's one that could get you in trouble with the guards." He quickly turned toward the bunk of the arsonist. "Charley."

Muldoon did not reply.

"You're not asleep, Charley."

"And I'm not hearing a thing," the little man said.

"You went to the hospital today."

"Yeah. The old sawbones said he had to make sure I wasn't sick before they send me out. And I thought they'd let me out tomorrow, but, no, no, that hard case Fowlson said they won't let me out till the weekend's over. He told me that today, while I was at Doc Gripewater's office. Laughed when he said it, too, just sucked the breath out of me. Ain't right. No. That ain't right. Sentence ends tomorrow, and those bastards are keeping me in here till Monday. Ain't right. Ain't right at all. But at least I'll be out of here . . . providing you boys don't get another six months tacked on to the sentence that fool judge give me."

"You'll be back," Worsnop said. "Your bed won't even be cold."

"Like hell."

"Hey," Fallon said. "Before you get into a fight, I just have one question for you, Charley. Was Ford Wagner in the hospital?"

"Wagner?" Charley Muldoon scratched the beard stubble on his chin. "No. No, he wasn't. He . . ."

"Let it be, Charley," Worsnop said. "If you really want to get out of here."

Fallon felt the tension settling over the dark, cramped cell. Frenchy rolled over on his bunk, mumbled something, and fell silent again. He might be asleep, Fallon thought, or he might be listening. Fallon guessed it to be the latter. No one slept that soundly in prison.

All right, Fallon told himself. There was no need to bring up Ford Wagner. He wasn't in the hospital. Most likely he wasn't in the cell next door. The guards had taken him away in the dead of night for some reason, and the men in this cell knew that reason, but they were not about to tell a fresh fish. Especially a fresh fish who had been a federal lawman. Fallon had no reason to believe that little fact remained a secret. Secrets were as hard to keep in a prison like a good night's sleep was hard to get.

"About that key, Fallon." Worsnop was changing the subject, and Fallon was fine with that.

"To the basement cells," Fallon said.

"That's a big key," Worsnop said.

"Your pal is a big cat."

Muldoon pulled up his blanket. "I had a calico cat once. Do you know that practically all calico cats are girlie cats? You hardly ever see a boy calico cat. I don't know why. But it's a fact. My calico cat was named

Johnnie. But that was spelled with an *ie* on account she was a girl."

"Did you burn her, too?" Frenchy said. So he was awake.

"No. Of course not. I never burned no animals. At least, not on purpose."

Fallon waited for the banter to cease. When it did, he listened again, but A-Hall remained quiet. His cellmates listened, too, and once Worsnop had convinced himself that no guard was lurking around the third tier of the building, he cleared his throat and whispered, "What do you need a key to the basement dungeons for?"

"I think I left something in there," Fallon answered.

The room fell quiet again, until Frenchy broke out laughing. "You're all right, Fallon," he said and coughed a little laugh again. "Left something in there. That's funny."

"Only thing anyone ever left in solitary," Worsnop said, "is about ten years off his life."

"Can you get one?" Fallon asked.

"That's a tad harder than cigarettes . . . and smokes ain't easy because all the guards think we'd burn the damned place down."

"Which we would," Frenchy whispered.

"Pills is what mostly I get. Snuff, tiny bottles of hair tonic, needles, soap that won't take the skin off a man's body. Seidlitz powders. Plug tobaccy. And, well, money."

"I don't dip snuff," Fallon said. "And hair tonic won't get me inside the basement cells."

"But hair tonic will give you a little kick," Muldoon said. "Closest thing to liquor a man can get here."

"A key," Fallon said.

"A key, like you said, would get me in trouble with the guards," Worsnop said. "I'd have to bribe them good. And I mean *real good.*"

"Which cell do you want?" Frenchy asked.

"The locks are all the same," Worsnop told him, or maybe he was just thinking out loud. "A key would unlock all the cells, I think, in this here prison. At least A-Hall."

"But not the front door," Frenchy said. "I've been here long enough to see how those locks work. One key to the doors coming in or out this dungeon. Another one for the doors to the cells. But the ones down in the basement here. I think that's a different key."

"I ain't hearing none of this," Charley Muldoon whined again.

"I don't want a key to the front door," Fallon said. "Just one to the basement cells."

"It'll cost you," Worsnop said.

"I figured. How much?"

Worsnop started thinking. "Ain't you going back to the doctor in the morning?"

"Gripewater said I was to come back. That doesn't mean Brandt, Fowlson, or Underwood will let me go back."

"Yeah. That's a fact. But, well, the doc has a lot of gin. A bottle of his hooch. And ten dollars. The dollars need to be script money. One-dollar bills. Those are easier for Edmond Dantès to carry."

Fallon laughed out loud. In prison, that had to be the perfect name for the cat. Worsnop surprised Fallon. The prisoner was well-read, but then Harry Fallon had to guess that any convict, who knew his letters, would enjoy reading *The Count of Monte Cristo* by Alexandre Dumas. Fallon had read it at least three times while he was serving his sentence at the Illinois State Penitentiary in Joliet.

"What about the gin?" Frenchy asked.

"The bottle of hooch stays here," Worsnop said. "I'll share it with you boys, though, just a little. A buck a snort."

Another silence filled the dark cell. Fallon guessed that his cellmates were imagining savoring the swill Doc Gripewater called gin.

"What about it Fallon?" Worsnop said.

"You drive a hard bargain," Fallon said, "but that's a deal."

"I'll need the money in advance," Worsnop said.

"I'll pay you tomorrow night," Fallon said. He had to guess that he could get some money from Doctor Gripewater, and if the sawbones wouldn't come up with the cash, Fallon had heard that newspaper reporters sometimes, if desperate enough, would pay their sources a few bucks for a good story. And Julie Jernigan seemed desperate enough.

That morning, when the cell door was dragged open and the guards started their bellowing and cursing, Fallon braced himself for that line stick to crack his skull open. It didn't happen, though, and he turned to stand next to the railing, head down, eyes on his boots, Muldoon in front of him and Worsnop and Frenchy behind him. He did manage to sneak a look at Ford Wagner's cell. That door still remained closed and locked.

"Bathhouse, then mess hall," the lead guard barked.

And so Fallon's morning went. A quick scrubbing of hands and face, drying off with a towel that felt like a brick, and then into the dining hall for another wretched meal of boiled potatoes and cold, repugnant coffee. They did serve biscuits this time, which if you dipped into the coffee for a few minutes did not break your teeth. And there was a smidgen of ham, or something that looked kind of like ham, with the potatoes.

After breakfast, he marched with the others to the broom factory, while other groups went off to make saddle trees, or shoes, or furniture; some went to the exercise yard; more than a few went to break rocks; and others were returned to their cells. No one was sent to the hospital. And Ford Wagner remained nowhere to be seen.

At the broom factory, Fallon was ordered to the makeshift barn in the corner, where he and other inmates whose names he did not know found the bins of sorghum, tons and tons of broomcorn, sorted out by grades in quality.

He set to it, scooping up an armful of the dried, tan crop and moved in a line from the barn to the factory, always with his head down, always in an orderly fashion, and once he was inside the rank-smelling factory, he followed his instructions. He deposited the corn in the basin where another inmate would put a broom together. Then Fallon was heading back to the barn to gather more sorghum.

It was work. Like the jobs he had been given in Joliet, mostly where he had worked in the laundry. It was work. Yes, sir. And Fallon thought about the men who had to do this to put food on the table for their wives and kids. He understood how he had been blessed with the jobs he had held. Driving cattle, sitting on a horse, free as the day is long. It wasn't easy work. Not by a damned sight, but it had seemed so wonderful all those years ago. Those jobs weren't the same anymore, though. The railroads had ended the long drives. So had barbed wire. And working as a deputy marshal had always seemed like being free, too. Dangerous. Even deadlier than punching cattle. But he was good at it. And, deep down, he knew how much he loved it. Not the killing. Not the gunfights. Not the pressure of not knowing who might be waiting behind the door you were about to kick open. But he was free.

Always free.

The whistle blew at last. Again, Fallon's clothes and hands and fingers smelled like the straw, the broomcorn, the working end of hundreds of brooms, that he had been handling all day. He stank of his own sweat. His legs and arms and back were sore. He filed into a line and waited to be marched back to the bathhouse and maybe over to the exercise room. It looked like he would not be visiting Doctor Thaddeus Gripewater this day. Maybe never.

"Fallon!"

Eyes down, Fallon stepped out of line. "Yes, sir!" he answered.

A brute of a guard came to him. "Step in front of me, fish," the guard said. "You're to report to the hospital. Ready. March!"

Chapter Thirty-nine

Thaddeus Gripewater was drunk.

That much was obvious to Fallon, and to the big guard, who had announced, "Prisoner here as ordered, Doctor," as soon as they had stepped inside the hospital.

The old man sat at a table, his eyes red, his face without much color, a glass, almost empty, in his hand, and two bottles before him. One was empty. The other was uncorked and the contents down to the label.

"Doctor?" the guard called out again.

Gripewater lifted his head and stared, but his dead eyes did not appear to realize who stood before him. Slowly, with trembling hands, he brought the glass to his lips and slurped down the rest of the contents. Just as slowly, the glass was lowered. It rested on the table, and Gripewater brought the hand back up to wipe his mouth with the back of his hand.

His hand, Fallon noticed, usually spick-and-span, appeared filthy.

"Oh," Gripewater said. He reached his shaky hand

and picked up the bottle, tilted it, and filled the glass. The bottle returned, and Gripewater stared at the glass.

"Oh," he said again.

The big matron, Eve Martin, stepped around a corner, followed by four female prisoners. One of those was Jess Harper. Fallon did not know the others.

"Well," the guard standing behind Fallon said in a voice that made one of the girl's shudder. "I didn't know you were up here, Bedbug. You're lookin' fine, darlin', real, real fine."

The smallest of the women, the girl who had to be Bedbug, shivered. Like all of the prisoners, she kept her eyes on the floor, refusing to look up. No, that wasn't quite the case. Jess Harper stared directly at the guard, and her eyes burned with fury. So did the matron's.

"Get out," the matron ordered.

The guard cleared his throat. "Now, ladies, this here is a desperate criminal."

"Out!" Eve Martin put her hands on her hips. She might have outweighed the guard. She certainly was two inches taller.

"It's all right," Doctor Gripewater said, slurring his words. He gestured. "There's no place for him to go. There's no place for anyone here to go. Except . . . to . . . hell."

The matron now turned her hot glare to the drunken sawbones, but only briefly. An instant later, she was moving to an examining table, barking orders at Gripewater, Fallon, the guard, and the women convicts.

"I'll examine him, Thaddeus. Just the stitches in his legs. Harper, fetch some alcohol from the counter.

Claire, get some bandages off the shelves. Liza, take that bottle away from Thaddeus before he throws up all over the floor you just mopped. Fallon, hang your jacket on the rack by the window. And take that hat off. Where were you raised, in a barn? And you . . . are you deaf or something? I said get out. Get out, Malachi, right now before I throw you out. Wait by the door, you big galoot. I'll have Fallon out of here before you can whistle *Yankee Doodle Dandy.* No, that'll take longer. God, Fallon, I can smell you from here. Off with the shirt, too, and go wash your arms and hands good and thoroughly in the basin on the table over there. Bedbug, get some towels. Move, Fallon. Move before you miss your supper. And I'll tell you just one more time, you giant, stick-wielding sadist, get out of here before I toss you out. Thaddeus, do us all a favor and go lay down or just drop dead."

Fallon hung up his jacket, stripped off his shirt, and found a stool to sit on while he unlaced his work boots.

"Socks, too, honey," said Bedbug, a thin, brown-haired girl with scars on her face and a nose that had been busted more times than Fallon's. Fallon wet his lips and moved toward his wool socks.

The girl whispered. "Don't worry, hon. Malachi ain't lookin' inside, and I won't tell nobody about the blade you're hidin'." She giggled. "Hell's fire, sonny, ever' man in stir has got hisself a pig-sticker of some kind."

Fallon shoved his socks, and his knife and sheath, into the boots, and stood, feeling awkward about being shirtless and in his bare feet in a room filled with four women. No, five women. He had to remind himself that Eve Martin was of the fairer sex.

Bedbug wet her lips. "All right, hon, now let's go get yerself cleaned up a mite before Miz Eve starts curin' all that ails ya."

He sat on the table, clean as he could be, and watched Jess Harper clean the stitches over his wound. The other women prisoners stood before him, while the big-boned woman of a matron ran her rough fingers through Fallon's hair.

"No lice," she announced.

The raven-haired girl, Claire, snorted: "He ain't been here that long, Miz Martin."

Martin's fingers stopped on the lump on Fallon's head. "Does that hurt?" she asked.

"Not as much as when it got put there."

"Today?"

"Yesterday."

Her fingers left his head, and she moved down the table, where Jess Harper gently rubbed alcohol over the stitches in his calf. Unlike the matron, the young, expectant mother had a gentle touch. Fallon could not imagine what his cellmates would say if they heard about his examination in the hospital. Four young women doted on him. Of course, then there was Eve Martin, too, who doted on no one—especially Doctor Thaddeus Gripewater.

Martin stopped beside Jess. Her giant right hand reached up, and Jess Harper froze, lifted her head, and closed her eyes as the matron placed the back of her hand against Jess's forehead.

"How do you feel?" the matron asked in a soft voice that made Fallon think the big, surly woman actually had a heart. She lowered her hand and waited for the answer.

"I'm all right," Jess said faintly.

"Go lie down," the matron ordered.

"But . . ." Jess stopped herself, nodded politely, and left Fallon. He watched her go behind the curtains. Bedbug went with her. Claire took over the cleaning of Fallon's leg, and Liza wrapped the bandage over the wound.

The matron stuck a thermometer in Fallon's mouth. "Hold that under your tongue, Fallon," she said. "I'll be back in a moment." She glared again at the doctor, who still sat at the table, a newspaper before him, but the bottles of alcohol long removed. Fallon watched Martin disappear behind the curtain, too, where he figured she was checking on Jess Harper and Bedbug.

"Whatchya in fer?" Liza asked.

Fallon turned his attention to the two other prisoners. "Hell if I know," he replied.

Both of the girls laughed.

"He's funny," Claire said.

"Cute, too," Liza said.

"Ain't they all?" Claire said.

"I'm a pickpocket," Liza said.

"She's good at it, too," Claire said.

"Not good enough," Liza said. "Or I wouldn't be here."

Claire batted her eyes. "I'm in for manslaughter. He didn't treat me right. I got two more years to go, but that's fine with me. It wasn't manslaughter. I murdered the bastard."

Fallon nodded. He couldn't figure out what else he could do.

Liza walked away, to chat with Doctor Gripewater, who just stared off through the window, looking at nothing, comprehending nothing. The pickpocket lifted the newspaper, and her eyes widened.

"Claire!" she called out, and the woman swore under her breath and walked across the room to the table.

Pointing at a headline, Liza said, "Ain't this the fella . . . ?"

Claire said, "Liza, you dumb hussy. You know I can't read."

Liza read the name, "Mr. R. R. Ness, attorney at law, forty-two years of age."

Claire stepped back. "Oh, my word . . ." she said.

But then the matron was back. She jerked the thermometer from Fallon's mouth, tossed it into a bowl with hardly a glance, and told Fallon: "Get dressed, get out. You're the healthiest man in The Walls." Her hard eyes turned toward the doctor sitting in his chair. "Prisoner or free person," she added.

Standing by the window, Fallon pulled on his shirt. He watched the big guard—Malachi, that was what Eve Martin had called him—standing a few feet away from the hospital, carving his quid of tobacco with a pocketknife. Fallon looked at the keys hanging from his belt. He heard himself whisper, "Pickpocket," but quickly dismissed that thought, and sat down to pull on his socks and shoes, discreetly returning the sheathed knife into his left boot.

"Thank you, ladies," he said as he took his hat. He glanced at Gripewater, but realized the doctor was in no condition to be asked to loan a prisoner ten dollars in paper currency, one-dollar notes. He sighed. He was pretty certain Eve Martin would not loan him a penny.

Hat on, he pulled on his jacket, and reached for the doorknob.

"Fallon," Gripewater said hoarsely.

Turning, Fallon saw the old man beckoning him. He did not look back at the guard, who had been keeping his attention on the prison yard. Fallon came up to the doctor, who just sighed and tapped the newspaper that Liza had been reading.

It was not much of a story, with a small headline, but Fallon picked up the paper and read.

NO MOTIVE, SUSPECTS
IN MURDER OF
SLAIN ATTORNEY

Governor, Police Chief
Plead for Any Witnesses
To Come Forward—
Demand Justice

LOCAL BUSINESSMAN MIRED IN DISPUTE
WITH DECEASED HAS ALIBI, TELLS REPORTER,
"I WOULDN'T NEED A KNIFE TO KILL THAT SWINE"

R. R. Ness to be Buried
In Family Cemetery

The headline was longer than the article, which ran on the bottom of the right-hand corner next to some advertisements and a few quotations from the Bible the editor had used to fill white space. The paper was the *Citizen's Evening Call*. Fallon read:

Mr. Toby Q. Harrelson, Jefferson City's chief of police, said no witnesses have come forward after the brutal murder of Mr. R. R. Ness, attorney at law, 42 years of age.

Mr. Ness, whose ancestors date to when Missouri was a territory, was found in an alley next to his office. He had been stabbed repeatedly, and his throat was cut. Police officers believe that the foul crime was committed sometime after 8 p.m. Wednesday night after Mr. Ness had dined with clients and friends at Delaney's Fried Fish.

Mr. Jonah McNabb, a longtime associate of Mr. Ness, said the attorney was in fine spirits after taking supper and said that he was returning to his office to finish a brief that he intended to file with the court on Monday morning.

It was been well reported that Mr. Ness was preparing a case against Mr. Luther Scott, of Scott & Associates Enterprises of Missouri. The two men have been feuding for months, and Scott, Mr. Ness has alleged, even threatened the life of Mr. Ness.

Reached in his office this morning, Mr. Scott denied the allegation and also said that he was eating in the same restaurant on the night of the murder and was still dining until the restaurant closed. Dominique Delaney, owner of the popular eatery on the waterfront, confirmed that to this *Evening Call* reporter.

Governor Horatio Boone, who was a solicitor with Mr. Ness a decade earlier,

> pleaded for anyone who might know something of the crime, or saw anything suspicious, to contact the city police as soon as possible.
>
> "This outrage must be righted with a quick and just trial," Governor Boone said.
>
> Mr. Ness is to be buried at the Ness Family Cemetery tomorrow immediately after his funeral at the Lutheran Church of Jefferson City.

Fallon laid the paper back on the table. He wondered if the man named Scott had actually told a reporter what the headline claimed but the story never mentioned. None of the names mentioned, none of the places, and nothing in the article meant a thing to Fallon, who stared at the doctor and waited for the drunk's eyes to focus.

"Now look at page four." This time, Thaddeus Gripewater did not slur his words. "Above the fold, in the first column, halfway down."

CHAPTER FORTY

Fallon read:

BODY FOUND IN HOTEL ROOM

Second Brutal Murder in Days Shocks Our Beautiful City

The body of a woman visiting Jefferson City was found in her room at the Hotel Missouri this morning. She had been stabbed repeatedly, and the brutal nature of the bloody act left Mr. Toby Q. Harrelson, Jefferson City's chief of police, asking if Jack the Ripper has arrived in the capital city of Missouri.

Jack the Ripper is the name given to the scoundrel who murdered several women a few years back in London.

The murder is the second in as many days in Jefferson City, following the brutal slaying of Mr. R.R. Ness, a prominent attorney. Mr. Ness was also knifed repeatedly and his throat cut from ear to ear.

> This time, however, the killer left behind the weapon. Policeman George White described the knife used as a hunting knife with a handle made from a deer's foot. The blade was seven inches long and razor sharp.
>
> The woman murdered was Julie Jernigan, a reporter for the *Kansas City Enterprise.* She has been registered at the hotel for five days and was writing a feature article on the state penitentiary in town.
>
> Harold Underwood, superintendent of the prison, expressed his sadness over the slaying. Jernigan was a fine reporter, Underwood said, adding that he regretted her story about the fine job being done in the prison would never get to be read.

Fallon now knew why Thaddeus Gripewater had been drinking. He felt like taking a shot of the doctor's rotgut gin right about now.

And now Harry Fallon had a pretty good guess about what was going on inside The Walls. He remembered that knife. He knew that weapon all too well. It was the knife Ford Wagner had brandished, had tried to plunge into Fallon's heart.

Dazed, stunned, disgusted, and saddened, Fallon stepped away from the doctor, uncertain of what to do next. He moved toward the door but felt that pressure rushing to his head, and now he turned and strode back to the doctor. His first instincts were to jerk the drunken sop to his feet, slap him senseless, shake the old man till he spilled out everything that he knew. That, however, would just send Malachi in with his line stick. And Fallon would be back in the basement of A-Hall.

Fallon sat back in the chair. If the guard outside looked through the window, it would appear that Gripewater was still examining, or at least talking to, Fallon.

"The man who killed her," Fallon said, barely recognizing his own voice. "Was the same man who killed that lawyer."

Gripewater only blinked.

"Ford Wagner," Fallon said. "They let him out to kill the attorney. Right?"

No response.

"And then they had him kill the girl, because they feared what she knew?"

The doctor wet his lips.

"But how did they get Wagner out?" The question trailed off. He remembered the conversation with The Mole. Killer Coleman Cain had talked about being let out to do jobs. Jobs he did not like. Then, after he refused to do any more of those . . . hired assassinations, that was the only thing to call those murders. After that, Underwood and the others left The Mole in the dungeon but brought other men to kill people. That's why they had thrown Fallon in with The Mole. They hoped the crazy old man would have killed Fallon.

"Why kill the lawyer?" Fallon asked, not expecting a reply and getting none. "Was that Ness fellow putting together something against the warden? Did he know? Was he working with Jernigan?"

The doctor sighed. "Ness was killed . . . for money."

Fallon blinked. Murder for hire. They had started

with Killer Cain, who was a hired assassin. Now they used anyone they could.

"For fifteen years?" Fallon asked. "Longer? They've been sending out convicts to commit murder. They got paid to do this?"

"That's what Miss Jernigan had learned. I don't know how."

Fallon wanted to vomit. "How long have you known?"

The doctor shook his head. "I guessed. But I didn't know. Not until I read . . ." His finger pointed to the afternoon newspaper.

Fallon leaned back in the chair. He had been sent to The Walls to find out the location of money stolen during a bank robbery. He had stumbled upon something much bigger, horrible, unthinkable. Fallon had lived through hell in Joliet, even in Yuma. But nothing that he had witnessed in those prisons compared to what he had just learned was going on here. The prisoners weren't all to blame, either. Those who had masterminded this . . . this . . . Murderers Incorporated . . . were those men in charge.

Dumbly, Fallon rose. He crossed the room, trying to think of what he needed to do. He was at the door before he realized it, staring at the prison yard. It struck him that he had been inside the hospital for maybe forty minutes. He felt fifty years older.

Fallon blinked and swore. He stepped out of the door, and Malachi, his escort, leaped around, startled, almost dropping the line stick. Somehow, Fallon managed to smile as he pulled his cap onto his head.

"I'm done," he said. "Doc Gripewater says I need to stretch my legs some. Back to the exercise yard, I guess."

Malachi blinked, shrugged, and stepped back. The

line stick was firm in his hands. "You first, fish. Lead the way. You got fifteen minutes left before you get off to supper and back to your home. So stretch those legs out good, 'cause you ain't got no longer than that."

"Yes, sir." Fallon lowered his head, kept his eyes down, and started walking.

The guard left Fallon alone and wandered to a corner to talk to other guards. Fallon made himself blend in with the inmates. He moved casually, but with a purpose. He checked the guards in the towers along the wall. He stopped to tie his work boot and slipped the knife out of his sheath and into the pocket of his jacket. He let a prisoner walk past him, and then Fallon came up and put his right hand on that inmate's back.

Fallon pressed the blade of the little knife against the man's back. The point cut through the wool and pricked the skin. The man tensed and stopped.

"It's not what you used on that lawyer in town, or that young girl in her hotel room, and it's not what you tried to use on me," Fallon said in a whisper. "But it'll get the job done sure as hell."

"Fallon," Ford Wagner whispered.

"Keep walking," Fallon told him. "Smile. We're old friends. We knew each other back in the Indian Territory. Right?"

They moved into a crowd. It would be harder for the guards to see what was going on, and inmates in the bloodiest forty-seven acres in America knew to mind their own business.

"The first part's easy," Fallon said. "I ask the questions. You nod or shake your head. Do you understand?"

Ford Wagner's head nodded.

"You killed the lawyer?"

Another nod.

"And the woman reporter?"

"Yes."

The knife cut deeper, but not deep enough for blood to start showing on the soiled striped shirt and jacket. "Nod. Remember?"

Wagner nodded.

"They pay you?"

This time, Wagner shook his head.

"Threaten you?"

That answer was more of a shrug.

"Were these your first killings? In prison, I mean."

This answer surprised Fallon, too. Wagner's head moved up and down.

Fallon considered this. They moved from that gathering to another. "Your cousin," Fallon said. "Kemp Carver. Did he do any of these . . . jobs?" He hated using that word.

Wagner nodded.

"Someone had to tell you who to kill. Was it Brandt?"

The head bobbed.

"Brandt got you out of our cell the other night. Right?"

The head nodded.

"You'll answer this one. Quietly. Who was with Brandt?"

"Fowlson," came the answer.

"Nod or shake again. Did Underwood know about all of this?"

The head nodded.

"Did Underwood order the murder of the girl?"

Wagner shrugged.

"All right. Was Brandt outside with you? Did he get you to the lawyer's office? I know you didn't do this alone. Brandt?"

The head shook.

"Fowlson?"

Another shake.

He hated this one. "Gripewater?"

The head shook, and Fallon sighed with relief. Who? One of the guards? He took a long shot. "Underwood?"

The head bobbed. Fallon couldn't believe it.

"And the woman?"

"Brandt," Wagner answered. He coughed.

They moved away from the crowd. "I'll ask questions. You'll answer. Quietly. How did they sneak you out of The Walls?"

"The Mole," Wagner said.

Fallon blinked and shook his head. "The Mole guided you out?"

"No. We used his cell."

That would explain it. "A tunnel?" he asked.

Wagner nodded.

"All right. They didn't pay you for this. They threatened you. How?"

Wagner had to cough again, and Fallon let him wipe the white phlegm with his sleeve. "They said they'd leave Kemp in a solitary till he died. Kemp was supposed to do the job. The lawyer. I didn't know about the woman till later."

"Kemp?"

"Yeah. He killed the congressman five months ago. And the banker a year or more back."

Fallon stopped walking. Wagner stopped, too.

Running everything he had heard through his

head, Fallon figured out what had likely happened. Kemp Carver was the assassin. But Carver was dead, and Captain Brandt had let the murderer die. Why?

"Of course," Fallon said aloud. Hanging from the support of the catwalk, Carver had said he would tell Fallon everything he knew. Brandt couldn't let that happen, so he had sent the killer plunging three stories to his own death. And since Ford Wagner was unconscious, he had not witnessed the cold-blooded murder of his cousin. They simply used him.

"Ness was killed for profit," Fallon whispered. "Jernigan was killed to shut her up."

"I don't know," Wagner whispered. "They just told me that the only way they'd let Kemp out of the dungeon was if I did what they told me to."

"So you carved up a lawyer? And a woman?"

"He's my cousin, Fallon. I ain't got long to live anyhow. And it's not like God would ever welcome me through the Pearly Gates."

Fallon lowered the blade from the consumptive's back and discreetly slipped it inside his jacket pocket.

"You're going to break into a coughing fit when we reach that guard straight ahead," Fallon said. "I'll say we have to get you to Doc Gripewater. Make it look good. Because those ruthless devils used you and your cousin good. And you're going to make everything right and get revenge. Walk."

They moved toward Malachi and Ryan, maybe the only two guards of lesser rank whose names Fallon actually knew or at least remembered. "Now," Fallon whispered, and Wagner began coughing harshly. Fallon did not know how much of this was acting and how much of it came from what was left of the dying man's lungs. Malachi and Ryan turned, and Fallon wrapped an arm around Wagner's waist.

"Hey," Fallon called out. "He's real sick here. Need to get him up to the hospital."

Wagner spit out blood. That wasn't acting.

Malachi and Ryan stared at Wagner—Ryan even took a slight step back—and quickly glanced at each other.

Grumbling, the bigger of the guards spit, sighed, and said, "You take him, fish. We ain't touchin' him."

Apparently, the guards at the pen had been educated that consumption was passed on through germs, and not something that you were born with or God just decided you needed. With a nod, Fallon helped Wagner away from the exercise yard and to the doctor's office.

"But we're right behind you, fish," Malachi said. "So don't try nothin'."

This might just work, Fallon thought.

The biggest hurdle was getting the guards to let him take Wagner to Gripewater's office, and that's what was happening now. Fallon hoped the frail man could make it to the doctor's office, write out a confession, and then maybe Doc Gripewater or Eve Martin could take that to the governor, the district attorney, or one of Jefferson City's newspapers.

But that wasn't going to happen.

The gates of hell were about to open.

CHAPTER FORTY-ONE

"Fowlson!" a voice thundered across the prison compound. "Fowlson!"

Fallon hurried his step. The voice, even at that distance, Fallon recognized as Warden Harold Underwood's.

"What the hell . . ." Ryan Getty said.

"Stop him!" Underwood shouted. "Stop them both!"

Fallon looked. Underwood and Captain Brandt were running past A-Hall. The black cat scurried out of their way. Underwood was pointing in the direction of Fallon, Wagner, and the two guards. The warden had to mean Fallon and Wagner, but why would he yell for Fowlson, whom Fallon could not see anywhere, and not Malachi or Ryan? It didn't make sense.

"Kill them! Shoot them, Fowlson. Shoot them now!"

The prison yard, always hushed, quieted into an unnerving silence.

"They're escaping!" Underwood yelled.

Fallon let out a breath. Then the warden couldn't mean Fallon and Wagner, for they had reached the steps to the doctor's office.

That's when Fallon heard the buzz of a bullet and heard the sickening impact as a heavy slug tore through Ford Wagner's chest and exited through his back, the impact knocking Wagner to his knees and pulling Fallon down with the consumptive prisoner.

"Hell's fire!" Ryan Getty was screaming, and the second shot whined off the rock wall above Fallon's head.

Fallon rolled, as a third shot dug into the dirt where he had been lying a second earlier. He saw Wagner lying faceup, eyes open, his shirtfront covered with blood. Most likely he was dead, but if he still held any life, that left him an instant later when a bullet blew off the top of his head.

"Hell's fire!" Ryan Getty shrieked again.

Fallon saw Malachi, too. The guard lay behind Wagner. He wasn't moving either, and Fallon realized that the bullet that had gone through Wagner's body had slammed into the big prison guard.

A bullet zipped over Fallon's head, but that one had come from another direction. Fallon looked, saw Captain Brandt spreading his feet. The brute had stopped running and had pulled a pistol. Brandt had to be a good shot to cover that kind of range with a handgun.

"Hell's fire!"

Fallon was growing mighty tired of the little guard.

Brandt leveled his big gun but stopped. Warden Underwood had stopped running, as well, and had fallen silent. Because the prisoners—those in the exercise yard, those being marched to the washhouse, those being marched from the various plants at the rear of the prison—maybe every one of them had taken up various cries.

"They're murdering us!"

"Butchers! Killers!"

Guards began pulling their line sticks. Others merely turned and ran. Fallon felt a bullet fired from above tear through the collar of his jacket. That's when he saw Mr. Fowlson. The deputy warden stood on the edge of a guard tower, working the lever of a repeating rifle. He brought the stock to his shoulder, aimed again, but quickly stopped. Fallon just saw the flash. Over the din of noise from prisoners, he could not hear the sound as the line stick hit the deputy warden in the side. Fowlson slipped, and stumbled, and cartwheeled over the edge. The lever-action rifle hit the ground first.

And the prisoners were all over him.

"Fallon!"

He turned, saw Charley Muldoon racing across the yard, carrying the black cat in his arms. Ryan Getty was running. Other guards weren't so lucky. The rifle spoke, but this time it was held by one of the inmates. The guard in the tower staggered back, dropped another rifle into the yard, and slumped against the outer wall of the watch post.

Line sticks crunched sickeningly against the skulls and backs and ribs of guards who had been overpowered by inmates.

"Fallon!" Charley Muldoon was almost to Fallon. Others hugged the wall, trying to make it to the front gate. Underwood made a beeline for A-Hall. Captain Brandt started toward Fowlson, which was a stupid thing to do, and he realized it—but too late. A mob swallowed him.

That gave the prisoners three weapons, Fallon figured, not counting the line sticks or the knives every inmate likely had on his person. Maybe more guns, too, if some of the unfortunate guards they had caught had been carrying hideaway weapons.

"Inside!" Fallon stood before Muldoon reached him and pointed to the front door—the only door—to the hospital.

The door was being opened. Fallon saw the frightened face of Eve Martin as she took in the scene across the prison yard.

Fallon started after Muldoon and the cat, but stopped, and he quickly ran back to Malachi's body. He grabbed the belt, unbuckled it, all the while placing a finger on the guard's throat, hoping to find a pulse, but feeling none. He had the keys, and the line stick, and that was all he had time to get.

Rioting prisoners, Fallon knew from experience, did not always try to beat the hell out of guards and prison officials. They'd hit, kick, slice, bash, burn, and rip apart prisoners they didn't like, trusties and friends, and, definitely, former federal lawmen.

Seeing Charley Muldoon, the big matron started to slam the door shut, but Ryan Getty was right behind Muldoon. The fear in both men's eyes, or maybe just because it was a prison guard, stopped her, and she widened the door and let both men stumble inside. Fallon ran, too, holding the dangling belt and the line stick. The matron didn't shut the door until Fallon was inside, dropping the belt and the stick onto the floor, and looking around.

The door shut. The lock was bolted. A bar was

placed in the wooden holders—none of which would keep the prisoners out if they remembered that women were in here. Charley Muldoon huddled in the corner, clutching the cat, which looked more frightened than the arsonist.

"Damn!" Fallon was up, running past Bedbug and Claire, and sliding to the floor, where he stopped beside the prostrate body of Jess Harper.

Whistles began shrieking. Horns blared. Rifles fired.

Fallon grabbed the girl's wrist. He felt the heartbeat, but it was far faster than normal, and he saw the sweat dampening her face, hair, and clothes. Jess Harper moaned. Fallon made himself look between her legs. He saw no blood.

Eve Martin was beside him. She looked calm. The matron had a hell of a lot better nerves than Harry Fallon.

"Help me lift her," Martin said. "We'll get her to the table. Gently. Gently."

Gentle as they tried, the girl, maybe conscious, maybe out of it, yelled in pain as they lifted her off the floor.

Bedbug, Liza, and Claire were pulling back blankets on a table.

"Hot water!" the matron shouted, and Claire took off to the stove.

Fallon set Jess Harper's head on a pillow. Eve Martin frowned.

"Honey," the matron said in a soft voice. "You're going to be fine. And your baby's going to be fine."

"She's not . . ." Fallon started.

"She is," Eve Martin said.

"But it's too early."

"Yes," the matron said. "But not all babies follow a calendar."

Liza started praying. Fallon moved to the chair and knocked the bottle out of Thaddeus Gripewater's hand before the gin reached his mouth. Then he slapped the doctor's face.

"Listen to me, you drunken sot. You're getting out of this chair and you're doing what you get paid to do. Now!"

He found a bottle on a table and tossed the contents in Gripewater's face.

Claire was back with the water. Bedbug was helping Eve Martin undress Jess Harper. Fallon jerked Gripewater to his feet but had to let go as soon as the doctor's boots dropped back to the door.

Somebody had just kicked in the front door.

Fallon turned, saw two men in striped uniforms coming inside. He scooped up the belt by the buckle, and swung it, the keys slamming hard into a wild-eyed bald man's head, knocking him to the floor, where he slid into Muldoon. The cat leaped out of the little man's hands and landed on the bald convict's face.

Fallon ducked underneath the punch thrown by the man who came in with the bald man. Bringing his head up quickly, Fallon felt his skull catch the wiry man's jaw, and he threw a left into the man's side, stepped back, and slammed a right into the man's nose. Cartilage gave way, blood poured out, and Fallon brought his knee into the man's groin. As the man doubled over, Fallon grabbed his close-cropped hair and slammed the man's head down while he raised his knee again. The man slumped onto the floor, rolled over, and lay still. By now Liza and Claire were pounding the bald man with chairs. The cat had screeched its way toward the rear of the building, and two more men were coming inside.

Desperately, Fallon grabbed the bottle of gin at his feet. He broke it against the corner of a cabinet, but he knew he wouldn't be able to take them all. Two more men had come in through the door. Fallon brought his elbow back, preparing to thrust the jagged end of the bottle into the closest prisoner's gut. But the man was pulled back just in the nick of time.

Fallon's weapon punched nothing but air. And Fallon blinked. The two prisoners who came in last were kicking and pounding the other two convicts. Dully, Fallon recognized two of the men. Worsnop grabbed one man's head and slammed it against the head of the inmate Frenchy was holding.

Fallon's cellmates let the convicts drop into a heap on the floor.

"Can we get that door shut?" Claire asked, dropping what was left of a chair onto the battered, bloody body of the bald man.

Worsnop glanced at the door and shook his head.

Tossing the busted bottle to the floor, Fallon grabbed Malachi's belt. Rising, chest heaving, Fallon looked around the hospital. *Think, man,* he told himself. *Think!*

"Those are just the first." Frenchy had stepped to the door, too, and looked through the window. "Look at them. I've seen riots in my time, but nothing like this."

Worsnop's head bobbed in agreement. "We came here to hide. Guess Charley Muldoon's worn off on us. But when others realize they can't get out—or inside the women's prison, over that wall, past those guards with the Winchesters, they'll remember the women up here."

Fallon spun. Doctor Gripewater appeared to be passably sober as he held out his hands and let Bedbug empty a bottle of alcohol over his hands.

"Can she be moved, Doc?" he asked.

"She'll have to be. If she wants her and that baby to live. If we all want to live. But not far."

"A-Hall?" Fallon asked.

"A-Hall!" Worsnop snapped. "Are you daft, man? A bunch of the worst lot are in A-Hall now. Freeing the scum of the prison. And killing those who ain't."

"Yeah," Fallon said. "But there's the basement."

"It's risky," Frenchy said. "We get trapped down there, there's no way out."

"Maybe," Fallon held the keys in his hand. "But there's certainly no way out from here."

Outside came curses, shrieks, gunshots, the sounds of dying men, and the sounds of a whirlwind of chaos.

Chapter Forty-two

While Doc Gripewater kept track of Jess Harper's signs and Fallon bathed her forehead with a wet rag, Eve Martin, Bedbug, Claire, and Liza hurriedly stripped and put on the clothing of the unconscious or dead inmates lying on the hospital floor. Likewise, Ryan Getty shed his guard uniform and put on Charley Muldoon's uniform.

Muldoon was adamant about staying put.

"If they see me outside, they'll kill me. Or they'll say I was rioting. I'm getting out of here Monday morning, guys. I can't go. I can't risk it."

"They catch you in here, they might just kill you," Fallon told the man wearing nothing but prison underwear and holding a frightened black cat.

"I'll hide."

"Don't burn the place down," Worsnop said. Maybe he was joking. Fallon wasn't sure.

"There's likely room for you in the cabinet over there." Fallon's head bobbed. "Just keep the cat quiet."

The women were dressed. Fallon stepped away from the table. "You women will have to carry Jess

Harper. Doc will be right by you. The rest of us will flank you. With us blocking the view, and the fact that the sun's getting low, and those uniforms, maybe no one will realize you're women." He frowned. "That said, there's no guarantee one of the guards won't shoot you dead from a tower. You can stay here, hide with Muldoon in one of the cabinets."

Bedbug snorted. "We ain't leavin' Jess."

"All right. Let's go."

They stepped over the dead. Fallon lowered his head as they moved toward the walkway. A bullet whined off a rock somewhere, and Fallon saw a half-dozen men racing toward them. He clutched the key in his right hand. It would be a painful weapon for whoever he hit . . . just before the others cut him to pieces.

If the key didn't work in the basement cells. No. It had to. Fallon remembered that Malachi had been one of the guards who had taken him to see The Mole that first time.

The charging men rushed right past them, barely noticing them. Fallon did not ease his grip on the key. He moved around a moaning guard.

"They're going into the hospital," Getty said.

"Don't look back," Fallon told him.

Glass shattered. Men roared. Fallon shivered and heard the matron muttering a prayer, asking God to protect—not them—but that tiny arsonist hiding in a bottom cabinet with a black cat.

Another prisoner rushed toward them. Bare-chested, wearing the black cap of a guard, and holding a line stick in his blood-smeared right hand, he stopped and grinned.

"What's in the box, Frenchy?" the man said, and he came up to Frenchy and glanced in the box.

"Candles?" The man shook his head and walked along side Frenchy as the procession turned a corner. "Candles?"

"We're going to burn down A-Hall, Festus," Frenchy told him. "Want to join us?"

"A-Hall." The man shook his head and looked at the women carrying Jess Harper.

"Who's that?" the man named Festus asked.

"Muldoon," Frenchy said. "The arsonist." He laughed. "We're gonna burn him, too."

A rapid firing stared on the northwest corner.

"Gatling gun," Fallon said.

Festus said, "I'm going to find me one more guard to kill before they gun me down." And Festus raced off, but not toward the northwest corner.

Several men raced out of A-Hall's front door, screaming, charging, while waving anything they could find as weapons. Yet one, a black man with a patch over his left eye, stopped and, oddly enough, held the door open as Frenchy and Fallon led the way.

"Thank you, sir." Fallon nodded politely at the tall, bald man.

"Don't mention it," the black man said. When Worsnop and Getty came through, the door closed.

Bodies of the dead littered the floor. Above, the marauders had reached the fourth floor. Men above them dumped slop buckets over the railings. They ripped their mattresses and let the straw fall with the urine and the excrement and the buckets and blankets.

Fallon moved past the cell that held the supplies.

They had to make it all the way to the back of the building and down the steps. The place stank of filth. A man screamed as he was flung off the fourth tier but somehow landed on the catwalk that connected the two sides of cells on the third floor.

Angered at the man's poor throwing ability, men grabbed the prisoner who had tossed the first one over the railing.

"Nooooo!" the man cried, but the prisoners threw him over, too, and he did not land on the third-floor catwalk.

"It's a madhouse," Claire whispered.

"It's always been a madhouse," Ryan Getty told her.

They walked around a dead body, through puddles of blood and urine, and came to the steps.

"Careful," Fallon called and took the first step down.

"How's she doing, Doc?" Fallon asked as he shoved in the key and twisted it, hearing the grating noise as the bolt slid.

"It won't be long," Gripewater said.

Fallon pulled on the door and heard the groan.

"Mole," he called out. "It's Fallon. Just close your eyes."

He saw the hulking, hunched wild figure of Coleman Cain, whose head was turned toward the wall and covered with the rags he wore on his arms.

"Get the candles lighted," Fallon ordered, pushed the door shut, and hurried to the wall, where he knelt beside The Mole.

"Cain," he whispered, and saw the man tremble. "Listen, I've brought some friends down for safety. There's a riot going on. The worst I've ever seen. One of the people here is a woman prisoner, and she's going to have a baby. So there's going to be light. Just candles, but we need light to see. You understand."

"It huuuurts my eyeeesssss."

"I know. But we can put you somewhere safe." Fallon pressed his lips together. "But you have to show me where it is."

"What?"

"The tunnel that leads out."

"But the key . . ."

"I have the key." He thought: *If the damn thing works . . .*

The Mole's finger pointed. "The funny man keeps his eyes on the door." Fallon moved.

The flickering candles held by Getty and the others provided enough light for Fallon, though he wasn't certain how well Doc Gripewater could see.

He saw the skull of the "funny man" who had been left with The Mole, forgotten, so The Mole had been forced to eat him. Fallon saw the holes where the man's eyes had once been, and he walked to the wall and began fingering the stones. One was loose. The Mole might have been able to move the stone, but Fallon would need help. He looked at the men, though, and frowned. Doc Gripewater needed all the light he could get, so Fallon tried to wiggle the rock. He found places where he could slip his hands inside. That had to be how this was done, but that stretched his arms so wide, he couldn't get any leverage.

Then, the light diminished, and Fallon heard The Mole's breath on his back.

"You'll never get that done," The Mole said, "and the candles hurt my eyes."

Fallon withdrew his hands from the holes, and let The Mole do his work.

Iron bars blocked the hole, but Fallon saw the lock. He crawled into the little cubbyhole and prayed, prayed as hard as he ever had, that the key would work to this door, too. The iron-barred door swung open. "God," Fallon said, "you're . . ." He paused. They weren't out of this yet. "Just keep the women safe, Lord. Please. Just keep them safe."

He couldn't see much more than a few feet into the tunnel, but he could see clothes, hats, what looked like walking canes, canteens, torches to be lighted, and even a lantern. The lantern would help, so Fallon crawled through the opening, and breathed in the damp but clean air of the cave.

He picked up the lantern, and turned as The Mole climbed through the opening, and sat on a rock in the corner.

"How far?" he asked The Mole. "And where does it come out?"

"Two hundred yards," The Mole said. "By the river."

He set the lantern inside the hole. "So after you stopped, they used other men. They'd leave them in the cell, and . . ."

"I had to let them out," The Mole said. "Otherwise, they would not feed me. And there was little left of the funny man to eat."

Fallon frowned, considering this. A man like Ford Wagner would slip out at night, dress into something that wasn't a prison uniform, commit the crime, and return at night—possibly the very same night—and return to the solitary confinement cell. How many people had been murdered . . . murdered by people in prison with nothing to lose?

As The Mole rubbed his eyes, Fallon climbed into the hole.

"You know," Fallon said as he slid back inside the cell, "no one would try to stop you if you just walked down this tunnel and kept walking."

Back inside, Fallon brought the lantern toward Getty, who used the candle to light the wick as Fallon turned up the coal oil.

"Thanks," Doc Gripewater said. "Now hold her hand, Fallon!"

"What?"

"You've been a father, boy," the drunken lout said. "Nobody else has. Talk to her. Like you did to your wife when she was giving you a son, damn you."

Fallon dropped onto the floor and reached for Jess Harper's tiny hand.

"It was a girl," he said, but nobody heard.

"It's all right, Jess," he whispered. "You're doing great. Now when the doc says to push, you just push." He slipped his left hand around her other hand. "And you just squeeze my hand and dig your fingernails into it and yell as loud as you want. It'll wake up your baby."

She squeezed, and her nails dug into his palms. Fallon smiled.

"You have the toughest job of anyone. But all this pain. It'll be worth it. Trust me. Once they put that bundle of joy in your arms. It was . . ." He had to stop whatever it was rising up his throat. "The happiest day . . . of . . . my . . . life."

That's when the door to the cell ground against the floor and creaked about a quarter of the way open. Fallon turned around, and watched the figure come in, yelling, "Mole. Easy, Mole. It's me. Now . . ."

When the warden, Harold Underwood, turned around, he gasped. But he only panicked for a second before bringing the Schofield revolver up. The big .45 was already cocked, and there was plenty of light now, thanks to the lantern, for him to see.

"What the hell . . ." He stopped, seeing that the stone had been pulled down, and that the barred door was open. "Where's The Mole?" He pointed the revolver at Eve Martin.

"We let him out," she said. "Do you mind? Thanks to you we've had to turn this into a maternity ward!"

"A what?" Underwood stepped aside. "If anyone tries to stop me, I'll shoot you all dead."

"Go on," Ryan Getty said. "Good riddance."

"I mean it!" The man's eyes were wide with fright. Fallon didn't think the warden even recognized him. He backed along the cold walls, licking his lips and blinking frantically.

Fallon just held Jess Harper's hands. He didn't care about Harold Underwood. He didn't care about a damned thing except this young girl who was about to have a baby. That was his world. That was Harry Fallon's entire world.

CHAPTER FORTY-THREE

Warden Harold Underwood was out of Fallon's line of vision. Fallon could hear the warden's panicked cries, then he heard the man's frightened gasp. "Mole!"

"You," said The Mole, who must have been climbing through the opening, out of the tunnel and back into the cramped cell. "I've been waiting for you a long, long time."

"I've been hiding," Underwood said. "I mean. I mean . . . just now. Had to hide. Till I could make it down here. Come on, Cain. You and me. I've got more money than you've ever seen. You and me. We'll get the hell out of here. Mexico. Bolivia. Hell, France maybe."

"You are a bad, bad man," The Mole said.

"PUSH!" Doc Gripewater yelled, and Fallon echoed the doctor's command, and let the woman's fingers dig deeper into his palms.

Suddenly the gun roared, and the echoes were deafening in the cramped cells. The Schofield barked again and again and again.

"Push!" Fallon yelled at Jess Harper, but he doubted if she could hear.

There was another gunshot, and then Harold Underwood was back in view. He lifted the smoking .45 at Doc Gripewater's head and yelled at Worsnop and Getty. "Get that man out of the hole. Move his body. Move him now. I've got to get out of here."

The echoes faded. "Move The Mole. Now!" His finger tightened against the trigger. "Move, damn you. I've got one shot left and I'll splatter Gripewater's brains over these walls."

Gripewater smiled down at Jess Harper. "You're doing fine. I see some dark hair. A couple more pushes . . ."

"Move, damn you!"

Suddenly, the warden grinned, and the barrel of the Schofield tilted down at Jess Harper's belly.

"I don't think this bitch or her bastard kid would survive a bullet in her belly. Do you, Doc?"

Fallon felt that pressure building now, and he saw Doc Gripewater step away from the woman. Getty and Claire stepped back. Bedbug began praying. The warden laughed, but that stopped abruptly, and his eyes widened. "What the hell, Doc?"

Fallon looked up. He just couldn't let go of Jess Harper's hands. He saw the Remington over-and-under derringer in Doc Gripewater's right hand, and the twin barrels were pointed at warden Harold Underwood.

"I'll kill her, Doc," the warden said. "So help me God, I'll kill them first. The girl and her baby."

But the Schofield's barrel was being pulled away.

"You're doing fine," Fallon whispered to Jess. "It's almost over. It's almost all over."

"Doc . . ." Underwood managed to swallow. "You took that oath. You can't kill me, Doc. The Hippocratic oath. Remember. You have to save lives."

The Schofield was coming back up, toward the doctor, when Thaddeus Gripewater sent two .41-caliber slugs into Harold Underwood's forehead.

"Saving lives . . ." The doctor dropped the empty derringer on the hard floor and moved back to Jess Harper. "That's what I'm doing." He smiled. "Push, Jess."

Harry Fallon did not glance at the bloody, dead body of Harold Underwood. He just looked at Jess Harper's eyes. He echoed the doctor's encouragement.

And when he heard the baby cry, he smiled and felt a joy he had thought he had lost so many years ago.

"Fallon," Ryan Getty whispered. "He's still alive."

Fallon stared into Jess Harper's excited eyes. "He's a good-looking boy, ma'am," he said. He rubbed the wounds in his palms and pushed himself off the floor. It didn't take him long to cross over to where Getty and Frenchy stood over The Mole. The big man sat on the stone that had been pulled out of the wall, blood pooling all underneath him, as he blocked the entrance into the tunnel that led to the Missouri River.

Fallon took Coleman Cain's right hand in his own.

"Cain," he whispered. "We can't thank you enough. And . . . well . . . I'm sorry."

"The light," The Mole whispered.

"I know," Fallon said. "I know it hurts. I'm sorry for that, too."

"No." The Mole smiled. "It's . . . the moon . . . the

light from the moon. The moon's . . . rising . . . and . . . it's . . . so . . . beautiful . . ."

Then, Coleman Cain was dead.

It was probably not the scene the militia commander or his men, or even his escort—Charley Muldoon, still clutching his black cat—expected to see when they pulled open the cell door.

"What in the Sam Hill . . ." the major whispered, as he lowered the hammer on his revolver and stepped inside.

"Hey!" Frenchy yelled. "It's the little arsonist. He ain't dead!"

As Frenchy and Worsnop greeted their cellmate, the major walked numbly to Doctor Gripewater, glanced at the baby, the pale but smiling mother, and Harry Fallon.

Two other soldiers walked and stared at the body of The Mole, still sitting on the stone, and his back blocking the hole in the wall. Another one picked up the Schofield that Warden Underwood had dropped.

"What in the Sam Hill . . ." The major tried again.

"How are things outside?" Eve Martin asked.

The major started to answer, then realized that the matron was a woman. Slowly, he recognized the sexes of Claire, Liza, and Bedbug.

"What in the Sam Hill . . ."

"Outside?" Doc Gripewater reminded the commander.

"It's . . . slowly . . . It's . . ."

"The bloodiest forty-seven acres in our country," Gripewater said.

"Ain't that the God's own truth," muttered one of the militiamen.

"I'd like to get this woman and her son to the city hospital," Gripewater said.

"Well . . . yes, sir, Doctor, ummm, of course."

"And these prisoners . . . well, no . . . that one there. The puny one. He's a guard. Don't look at me like that, Major. I've had a hell of a day and a long, long night. These prisoners are to be treated with the utmost of care. They are heroes. And the whole world is going to know about them. All except . . ." He pointed at Fallon. "This one."

A few rifles were now trained on Fallon, but he didn't care. He was staring at the little baby, wrapped in his undershirt.

"No." This time it was Eve Martin who spoke. "Don't touch that body. Isn't that right, Doctor?"

Gripewater blinked. "Yes. Absolutely. Leave the bodies where they are. It'll come in handy for the investigators. Mister . . ." Gripewater glared at Fallon. "If you touch one of these bodies before we come to fetch you, there will be bitter hell to pay. Do you understand?"

Fallon nodded.

"Major," Gripewater said, "if your men could shoulder their rifles and give us a hand, I'd really like to get this young woman out of there and to the city hospital. And then I'd damn sure like to get drunk."

Fallon leaned over to Jess Harper and whispered. "You did a great job, ma'am. And your boy's going to love you forever and ever."

"I'll love him, too," she said softly.

"I know you will. It comes with the job."

Still smiling, Fallon moved toward the skull of the

funny man, and watched the soldiers as they started to lift the blanket. But his eyes fell back on the bodies of The Mole, and the warden, and then he saw himself staring at Charley Muldoon and the cat.

Gripewater looked at the soldiers. "I don't suppose," he said, "that one of you soldier boys would happen to have a snort of gin, would you?"

Chapter Forty-four

So here sat Harry Fallon, back on the other side of a giant chair in a dark brown office in a flatiron building in Chicago, Illinois, across from a little man in a brown suit who puffed on a repugnant cigar.

"How'd you get out?" Sean MacGregor asked.

"I walked to the depot," Fallon said. "Took the train."

"I see." MacGregor flicked ash into the tray. "Where's Holderman?"

Fallon shrugged. "For all I know, he's still in Jefferson City. Waiting for me to get out."

Fallon looked around. "Where's Dan?"

"If I were him, I'd be hiding. Maybe trying to catch the next stagecoach to Canada."

Fallon kept quiet. MacGregor laid the cigar in the tray, spit out some flakes, wiped his mouth, and leaned back in the chair.

"What about the woman? And the money from Linc Harper's bank robbery?"

Fallon shook his head. "She didn't know anything

about it. A smart man like Linc Harper. He wouldn't trust anyone, especially a woman, with that tidbit. I'm afraid the money's lost."

If that wasn't the truth, well, a young woman with a little baby would have need of money.

To Fallon's surprise, the detective agency president nodded in agreement. "Which is what I told Dan when he came up with the confounded idea."

Fallon waited an eternity in silence. At length, Sean MacGregor reached over, lifted the Chicago newspaper off the desk's top and tossed it across the big hunk of mahogany. Fallon somehow managed to catch the paper.

"I don't suppose you know anything of this, do you, Hank?"

So he was Hank now? Fallon unfolded the paper and read the headline. He didn't have to read it aloud, but he did.

"Pinkertons End Linc Harper's Reign of Terror. Outlaw's Body Discovered After Lightning Strike Burns Down Ice Factory in Small Missouri Town. Detectives . . ."

"Enough with the headlines, damn you!"

Fallon dropped the paper to his side, but he shook his head and could not resist. "Do you really think it was lightning?"

"I don't know." Sean MacGregor sounded a hell of a lot older, and very, very tired.

"But if it was an icehouse, how could they identify the body?"

MacGregor was relighting his cigar. "It says the ice melted. The body was soaked. There's a woodcut of the body in another newspaper. Yeah, it was Linc

Harper all right. No question. At least my damned fool son kills him. And that cheap bastard across town gets all the glory. I'll nail Dan's hide to the barn." He puffed on the cigar for a moment but brought it out of his mouth and blew smoke toward the ceiling. "Yours, too, perhaps."

"Listen," Fallon said. "You don't get Harper. You don't get the reward for the missing money. But you get something better."

"What?" The man waved the cigar in a dismissive gesture.

"You know exactly what. You can point out the hired murders going on, right out of the Missouri State Penitentiary."

"Yeah. And with Underwood, Fowlson, and even Brandt dead, finding proof will be hard. Nothing but speculation. I bring that up, I'll be hounded for defaming the character of the dead."

Fallon leaned back, drew in a deep breath, and let it out. "So it's true."

"You knew it was true," Sean MacGregor said.

"But I wasn't sure you knew."

The room turned frigid.

"The Mole," Fallon said. "Coleman Cain. He killed Renee. He killed Rachel. Didn't he?" He felt his fingers clench into tight balls.

The cigar dropped again into the ashtray. This time, Sean MacGregor sighed. "We don't know for sure. We thought so. Dan thought so. Well, you must've thought the same thing. Isn't that why you killed him?"

"I didn't kill him," Fallon said.

The room fell silent for a long, long time.

"Well, now you know." MacGregor shook his head.

"That had to have been a costly job. Underwood must've been well paid for that one."

"They were living in Columbia," Fallon said. "With her mother. Short trip, more or less, from Jefferson City."

"I'm sure," MacGregor said, "that Underwood and his predecessors had people murdered even further away."

"Maybe." His voice sounded as frigid as the room.

"Well. Now you know. Or as close to knowing as we can."

Fallon knew. Maybe he couldn't prove it to a judge or a jury or a newspaper reporter, even one like the late Julie Jernigan, but he knew. It made sense. Coleman Cain had been released for a few days to kill Renee and Rachel. And that's what had likely snapped The Mole's grasp on reason. The hired killer who had put preachers and saloon girls and politicians in their graves had gone insane. After murdering the only people in the world that mattered to Harry Fallon, Coleman Cain couldn't kill anyone else—except a funny man who had been dumped into the cell with him and forgotten. And maybe a few others who told The Mole what they planned on doing, who they had been told to kill.

Fallon tried to get his feelings back under control. If he didn't, he might wind up killing Sean MacGregor, today, this very minute.

"That's why I got put in the cell with The Mole," Fallon said. "Underwood recognized my name. He thought either I would kill The Mole or The Mole would kill me. And The Mole recognized my name. But . . . well . . . But what I can't understand is why

Underwood and the others kept him alive all those years."

"My guess," MacGregor said, "is that they wanted him to suffer. Or they wanted him to come back to their fold. Face it, Fallon. Nobody in Missouri killed better than Killer Cain."

"Yeah." Fallon wanted to spit the bitterness out of his face.

"So . . . now you know. I told you I'd help you, Fallon. You've gotten your revenge."

"No," Fallon said. "Coleman Cain might have murdered my family, but the man in that basement cell wasn't Coleman Cain. He was The Mole. And he saved my life."

"All right." MacGregor had spoken merely to fill the dead space.

"I want the man who paid for it."

Sean MacGregor nodded. "I know you do."

"And when I first was brought to this office, you said three jobs."

"Or four."

"So . . ." Fallon swallowed down the gall. "What's next?"

Sean MacGregor sank deeper into his chair. "Let's talk about it, Fallon. Have you ever been to . . . ?"

Chapter One

Dewey McKenzie spun away from the bar, the finger of whiskey in his shot glass sloshing as he avoided a body flying through the air. He winced as a gun discharged not five feet away from his head. He hastily knocked back what remained of his drink, tossed the glass over his shoulder to land with a clatter on the bar, and reached for the Smith & Wesson Model 3 he carried thrust into his belt.

A heavy hand gripped his shoulder with painful intensity. The bartender rasped, "Don't go pullin' that smoke wagon, boy. You do and things will get rough."

Mac tried to shrug off the grip and couldn't. Powerful fingers crushed into his shoulder so hard that his right arm began to go numb. He looked across the barroom and wondered why the hell he had ever come to Fort Worth, much less venturing into Hell's Half Acre where anything, no matter how immoral or unhealthy, could be bought for two bits or a lying promise.

Two different fights were going on in this saloon, and they threatened to involve more than just the drunken cowboys swapping wild blows. The man with the six-gun in his hand continued to ventilate the ceiling with one bullet after another.

Blood spattered Mac's boots as one of the fistfights came tumbling in his direction. He lifted his left foot to keep it from getting stomped on by the brawlers. A steer had already done that a month earlier when he had been chuckwagon cook on a cattle drive from Waco up to Abilene.

He had taken his revenge on the annoying mountain of meat, singling it out for a week of meals for the Rolling J crew. Not only had the steer been clumsy where it stepped, it had been tough, and more than one cowboy had complained. Try as he might to tenderize the steaks, by beating, by marinating, by cursing, Mac had failed.

That hadn't been the only steer he had come to curse. The entire drive had been fraught with danger and more than one of the crew had died.

"That's why," he said out loud.

"What's that?" The barkeep eased his grip and let Mac turn from the fight.

"After the drive, after the cattle got sold off and sent on their way to Chicago from the Abilene railroad yards, I decided to come back to Texas to pay tribute to a friend who died."

The bartender's expression said it all. He was in no mood to hear maudlin stories any more than he was to break up the fights or prevent a disgruntled cowboy from plugging a gambler he thought was cheating him at stud poker.

"Then you need another drink, in his memory." When Mac didn't argue the point, the barkeep poured an inch of rye in a new glass and made the two-bit coin Mac put down vanish. A nickel in change rolled across the bar.

"This is for you, Flagg. I just hope it's not too hot wherever you are." Mac lifted the glass and looked past it to the dirty mirror behind the bar. A medium-sized hombre with longish dark hair and a deeply tanned face gazed back at him. The man he saw reflected wasn't the boy who had been hired as a cook by a crusty old trail boss. He had Patrick Flagg to thank for making him grow up.

A quick toss emptied the glass.

The fiery liquor burned a path to his belly and kindled a blaze there. He belched and knew he had reached his limit. Mac had no idea why he had come to this particular gin mill, other than he was footloose and drifting after being paid off for the trail drive. The money burned a hole in his pocket, but Dewey McKenzie had never been much of a spendthrift. Growing up on a farm in Missouri hadn't given him the chance to have two nickels to rub together, much less important money to waste.

With deft instinct, he stepped to the side as two brawling men crashed into the bar beside him, lost their footing, and sprawled on the sawdust-littered floor. Mac looked down at them, then let out a growl. He reached out and grabbed the man on top by the back of his coat. A hard heave lifted the fighter into the air until the fabric began to tear. Mac swung the man around, deposited him on his feet, and looked him squarely in the eye.

"What mess have you gotten yourself into now, Rattler?"

"Hey, as I live and breathe!" the cowboy exclaimed.

"Howdy, Mac. Never thought our paths would cross again after Abilene."

Rattler ducked as his opponent surged to his feet and launched a wild swing. Mac leaned to one side, the bony fist passing harmlessly past his head. He batted the arm down to the bar and pounced on it, pinning the man.

"Whatever quarrel you've got with my friend, consider it settled," Mac told the man sternly.

"Ain't got a quarrel. I got a bone to pick!" The drunk wrenched free, reared back, and lost his balance, sitting hard amid the sawdust and vomit on the barroom floor.

"Come on, Rattler. Let's find somewhere else to do some drinking." Mac grabbed the front of the wiry man's vest and pulled him along into the street.

Mayhem filled Hell's Half Acre tonight. In either direction along Calhoun Street, saloons belched customers out to continue the battles that had begun inside. Others, done with their recreation outside, crowded to get back in for more liquor.

Mac brushed dirt off his threadbare clothes. Spending some of his pay on a new coat made sense. He whipped off his black, broad-brimmed hat and smacked it a couple times against his leg. Dust clouds rose. His hair had been plastered back by sweat. The lack of any wind down the Fort Worth street kept it glued down as if he had used bear grease. He wiped tears from his cat-green eyes and knew he had to get away from the dust and filth of the city. It was dangerous on the trail, tending a herd of cattle, but it was cleaner on the wide-open prairie. He might get stomped on by a steer but never had to worry about being shot in the back.

He knew better than to ask Rattler what the fight had been over. Likely, it had started for no reason other than to blow off steam.

"I thought you were going to find a gunsmith and get some work there," Mac said to his companion. "You're a better tinkerer than most of them in this town."

Mac touched the Model 3 in his belt. Rattler had worked on it from Waco to Abilene during the drive and had turned his pappy's old sidearm into a deadly weapon that shot straight and true every time the trigger was pulled. For that, Mac thanked Rattler.

For teaching him how to draw fast and aim straight he gave another silent nod to Patrick Flagg. More than teaching him how to draw faster than just about anyone, Flagg had also taught him when not to draw at all.

Rattler said, "And I thought you was headin' back to New Orleans to woo that filly of yours. What was her name? Evie?"

"Evangeline," Mac said.

"Yeah, you went on and on, even callin' out her name in your sleep. With enough money, you shoulda been able to win her over."

Mac knew better. He loved Evangeline Holdstock, and she had loved him until Pierre Leclerc had set his cap for her. Leclerc's plans included taking over Evie's father's bank after marrying her—probably inheriting it when he murdered Micah Holdstock.

Being framed for Micah's murder had been enough to convince Mac to leave New Orleans. Worse, the frame had also convinced Evie to have nothing to do with him other than to scratch out his eyes if he got close enough to the only woman he had ever loved.

His only hope of ever winning her back was to prove Leclerc had murdered Holdstock. Somehow, his determination to do that faded after Leclerc had sent killers after him to Waco.

He smiled ruefully. If he hadn't been dodging them, he never would have signed on with the Rolling J crew and found he had a knack for cooking and cattle herding. The smile melted away when he realized Evie was lost forever to him, and returning to New Orleans meant his death, either from Leclerc's killers or at the end of a hangman's rope.

"There's other fish in the sea. Thass what they say," Rattler went on, slurring his morsel of advice. He braced himself against a hitching post to point at a three-story hotel across the street. "The House of Love, they call it. They got gals fer ever' man's taste there. Or so I been told. Less go find ourselves fillies and spend the night, Mac. We owe it to ourselves after all we been through."

"That's a mighty attractive idea, Rattler, but I want to dip my beak in some more whiskey. You can go and dip your, uh, other beak. Don't let me hold you back."

"They got plenny of ladies there. Soiled doves." Rattler laughed. "They got plenny of them to last the livelong night, but I worry this town's gonna run outta popskull."

With an expansive sweep of his arm, he indicated the dozen saloons within sight along Calhoun Street. It was past midnight and the drinking was beginning in earnest now. Every cowboy in Texas seemed to have crowded in with a powerful thirst demanding to be slaked by gallons of bad liquor and bitter beer.

"Which watering hole appeals to you, Rattler?" Mac saw each had a different attraction. Some dance halls had half-naked women willing to share a dance, rubbing up close, for a dime or until the piano player keeled over, too drunk to keep going. Others featured exotic animals or claimed imported food and booze from exotic corners of the world.

Mac had become cynical enough to believe the whiskey and brandy they served came from bottles filled like all the others, from kegs and tanks brought into Hell's Half Acre just after sunrise, when most customers were passed out or too blind drunk to know the fancy French cognac they paid ten dollars a glass for was no different from the ten-cent tumbler filled with the same liquor at the drinking emporium next door and called poor man's whiskey.

"Don't much matter. That one's close enough so I don't stagger too much gettin' to it." The man put his arm around Mac's shoulders for support, turned on unsteady feet, and took a step. He stopped short and looked up to a tall, dark man dressed in black. "'Scuse us, mister. We got some mighty hard drinkin' to do, and you're blockin' the way."

"Dewey McKenzie," the man said in a hoarse whisper almost drowned out by raucous music pouring from inside the saloon.

"Yeah, he's my friend," Rattler said, pulling away from Mac and stumbling to the side.

When he did so, he got in the way of the dark man's shot. Mac had never seen a man move faster.

The Peacemaker cleared leather so swiftly the move was a blur. Fanning the hammer sent three slugs ripping out in a deadly rain that tore into Rattler's body. He threw up his arms, a look of surprise on his face as he collapsed backward into Mac's arms.

He died without saying another word.

"Damn it," the gunman growled, stepping to the side to get a better shot at Mac.

Shock disappeared as Mac realized he had to move or die. With a heave he lifted his dead friend up and tossed him into the shooter. The corpse knocked the gunman's aim off so his fourth bullet tore past Mac and sailed down Calhoun Street. Almost as an afterthought, someone farther away let out a yelp when the bullet found an unexpected target.

Mac had practiced for hours during the long cattle drive. His hand grabbed the wooden handles on the S&W. The pistol pulled free of his belt. He wasn't even aware of all he did, drawing back the hammer as he aimed, the pressure of the trigger against his finger, the recoil as the revolver barked out its single deadly reply.

The gunman caught the bullet smack in the middle of his chest. It staggered him. Propped against a hitching post, he looked down at a tiny red spot spreading on his gray-striped vest. His eyes came up and locked with Mac's.

"You shot me," he gasped. He used both hands to raise his six-gun. The barrel wobbled back and forth.

"Why'd you kill Rattler?" Mac held his gun in a curiously steady hand. The sights were lined on the gunman's heart.

He never got an answer. The man's pistol blasted

another round, but this one tore into the ground between them. He let out a tiny gurgling sound and toppled straight forward, like an army private at attention all the way down. A single twitch once he hit the ground was the only evidence of life fleeing.

"That's him!" a man shouted. "That's McKenzie. He gunned down Jimmy!"

Another man said, "Willie's not gonna take kindly to this."

Mac looked up to see a pair of men pushing hurriedly through the saloon's batwing doors. It didn't take a genius to recognize the dead gunman's family. They might have been chiseled out of the same stone, broad shoulders, square heads, height within an inch of each other—and the way they dressed. Their coats were of the same fabric and color, and the Peacemakers slung at their hips might have been bought on the same day from the same gunsmith.

Even as they took in how the dead man had found the quarry Leclerc had put a bounty on, their hands went for their guns. Neither man was too quick on the draw, taking time to push away the long tails of their coats. This gave Mac the chance to swing his own gun around and get off a couple of shots.

Flying lead whined past both men and into the saloon they had just exited. Glass broke inside and men shouted angrily. Then all hell broke loose as the patrons became justifiably angry at being targeted. Several of them boiled out of the saloon with guns flashing and fists flying.

The two gunmen dodged Mac's slugs, but the rush of men from inside bowled them over, sending them stumbling out into the dusty street. Mac considered trying to dispatch them, then knew he had a tidal wave to hold back with only a couple of rounds.

"Sorry, Rattler," he said, taking a second to touch the brim of his hat in tribute to his trail companion. They had never been friends but had been friendly. That counted for something during a cattle drive.

He vaulted over Rattler's body, grabbed for the reins of a black stallion tethered to the side of the saloon and jumped hard, landing in the saddle with a thud. The spirited animal tried to buck him off. Mac had learned how to handle even the proddiest cayuse in any remuda. He bent low, grabbed the horse around the neck, and hung on for dear life as the horse bolted into the street.

A new threat posed itself then—or one that had been delayed, anyway. Both of the dead gunman's partners—or brothers or whatever they were—opened fire on him. Mac stayed low, using the horse as a shield.

"Horse thief!" The strident cry came from one of the gunmen. This brought out cowboys from a half dozen more saloons. Getting beaten to a bloody pulp or even shot full of holes meant nothing to these men. But having a horse thief among them was a hanging offense.

"There he is!" Mac yelled as he sat up in the saddle and pointed down the street. "The thieving bastard just rounded the corner. After him!"

The misdirection worked long enough for him to send the mob off on a wild goose chase, but that still left two men intent on avenging their partner. Mac put his head down again, jerked the horse's reins, and let the horse gallop into a barroom, scattering the customers inside.

He looked around as he tried to control the horse in the middle of the sudden chaos he had created. Going back the way he came wouldn't be too smart. A quick glance in the mirror behind the bar showed both of the black-clad men crowding through the batwings and waving their guns around.

A savage roar caught his attention. In a corner crouched a black panther, snarling to reveal fierce fangs capable of ripping a man apart. No wonder the black stallion was going loco. He had to be able to smell the big cat.

The huge creature strained at a chain designed to hold a riverboat anchor. The clamor rose as the bartender shouted at Mac to get his horse out of the saloon. The apron-clad man reached under the bar and pulled out a sawed-off shotgun.

"Out, damn your eyes!" the bartender bellowed as he leveled the weapon.

Mac whirled around and began firing not at the panther but at the wall holding the chain. The chain itself was too strong for a couple of bullets to break.

The wood splintered as Mac's revolver came up empty. When the panther lunged again, it pulled the chain staple free and dragged it into the room. The customer nearest the cat screeched as heavy claws raked at him.

Then the bartender fired his shotgun and Mac yelped as rock salt burned his face and arm. Worse, the rock salt spooked the horse even more than the attacking panther.

The stallion exploded like a Fourth of July rocket. Mac had all he could do to hang on as the horse leaped through a plate-glass window. Glittering shards flew in all directions, but he was out of the saloon and once more in the street.

The sense of triumph faded fast when both gunmen who'd been pursuing him boiled out through the window he had just destroyed.

"That's him, Willie. Him's the one what killed Jimmy!"

Mac looked back at death stalking him. A tall, broad man with a square head and the same dark coat pushed back the tails to reveal a double-gun rig. Peacemakers holstered at either hip quickly jumped into the man's grip. Using both hands, the man started firing. And he was a damned good shot.

Chapter Two

Dewey McKenzie jerked to the side and almost fell from the horse as a bullet tore a chunk from the brim of his hat. He glanced up and got a quick look at the moon through the hole. The bullets sailing around him motivated him to put his heels to the horse's flanks.

Again the horse bolted through the open door of another saloon. This one's crowd stared at a half-naked woman on stage gyrating to bad piano music. They were too preoccupied to be aware of the havoc being unleashed outside. Even a man riding through the back of the crowd hardly pulled their attention away from the lurid display.

Mac slid from the saddle and tugged on the reins to get the horse out of the saloon. He had to shoulder men aside, which drew a few curses and surly looks, but people tended to get out of the way of a horse.

Finally he worked his way through the press of men who smelled of sweat and lust and beer. He emerged into the alley behind the gin mill. Walking slowly, forcing himself to regain his composure, he left the Tivoli Saloon behind and went south on Throckmorton Street.

The city's layout was something of a mystery to him, but he remembered the Wagon Yard was between Main and Rusk, only a few streets over. He resisted the urge to mount and ride out of town. If he did that, the gang of cutthroats would be after him before dawn. His best chance of getting away was to fade into the woodwork and let the furor die down. Shooting his way out of Fort Worth was as unlikely to be successful as was him galloping off.

Where would he go? He had a few dollars left in his pocket from his trail drive pay, but he knew no one, had no friends, no place to go to ground for a week or two. Mac decided being footloose was a benefit. Wherever he went would be fine, with the gunmen unable to track him because he sought friends' help. He had no friends in Fort Worth.

"Not going to get anybody else killed," he said bitterly, sorry for Rattler catching the lead intended for him.

He tugged on the stallion's reins and worked his way farther south along Rusk until he reached the Texas Wagon Yard. He patted the horse's neck. It was a strong animal, one he would have loved to ride. But it was distinctive enough to draw attention he didn't need.

"Come on, partner," Mac told the stallion quietly. The horse neighed, tried to nuzzle him, and then trotted along into the wagon yard. A distant corral filled with a dozen horses began to come awake. By the time he reached the office, the hostler was pulling up his suspenders and rubbing sleep from his eyes. He was a scarecrow of a man with a bald head and prominent Adam's apple.

"You're up early, mister," the man said. "Been on

the trail? Need a place to stable your horse while you're whooping it up?"

"I'm real down on my luck, sir," Mac said sincerely. "What would you give me for the horse?"

"This one?" The liveryman came over and began examining the horse. He rested his hand on the saddle and looked hard at Mac. "The tack, too?"

"Why not? I need some money, but I also need another horse and gear. Swap this one for a less spirited horse, maybe? And a simple saddle?"

"This is mighty fine workmanship." The man ran his fingers over the curlicues cut into the saddle. "Looks to be fine Mexican leatherwork. That goes for top dollar in these parts."

"The horse, too. That's the best horse I ever did ride, but I got expenses . . ." Mac let the sentence trail off. The liveryman would come to his own conclusions. Whatever they might be would throw the gunmen off Mac's trail, if they bothered to even come to the Texas Wagon Yard.

He reckoned they would figure out which was his horse staked out back of the first saloon he had entered and wait for him to return for both the horse and his gear. Losing the few belongings he had rankled like a burr under his saddle, but he had tangled before with bounty hunters Pierre Leclerc had set on his trail. The man didn't hire stupid killers. Mac's best—his only—way to keep breathing was to leave Fort Worth fast and cut all ties with both people and belongings.

A deep sigh escaped his lips. Rattler was likely the only one he knew in town. That hurt seeing the man cut down the way he had been, but somehow, leaving behind his mare, saddle, and the rest of his tack tormented him even more.

"I know a gent who'd be willing to pay top dollar for such a fine horse, but you got to sell the saddle, too. It's mighty fine. The work that went into it shows a master leathersmith at his peak, yes, sir." The liveryman cocked his head to one side and studied Mac as if he were a bug crawling up the wall.

"Give me a few bucks, another horse and saddle, and I'll be on my way."

"Can't rightly do that 'til I see if I can sell the stallion. I'm runnin' a bit shy on cash. You wait here, let me take the horse and see if the price is right. I might get you as much as a hundred dollars."

"That much?" Mac felt his hackles rise. "That and another horse and tack?"

"Don't see horses this spirited come along too often. And that saddle?" The man shook his head. "Once in a lifetime."

"Do tell. So what's to keep you from taking the horse and riding away?"

"I own the yard. I got a reputation to uphold for honesty. Ask around. You go find yourself some breakfast. Might be, I can get you as much as a hundred-fifty dollars."

"And that's after you take your cut?"

"Right after," the man assured him.

Mac knew he lied through his teeth.

"Is there a good restaurant around here? Not that it matters since I don't have money for even a fried egg and a cup of water." He waited to see what the man offered. The response assured him he was right.

"Here, take five dollars. An advance against what I'll make selling the horse. That means I'll take it out of your share."

"Thanks," Mac said, taking the five crumpled greenbacks. He stuffed them into his vest pocket. "How long do you think you'll be?"

"Not long. Not more 'n a half hour. That'll give you plenty of time to chow down and drink a second cup of coffee. Maggie over at the Bendix House boils up a right fine cup."

"Bendix House? That's it over there? Much obliged." Mac touched the brim of his hat, making sure not to show the hole shot through and through. He let the man lead the horse away, then started for the restaurant.

Only when the liveryman was out of sight did he spin around and run back to the yard. A quick vault over the fence took him to the barn. Rooting around, he found a serviceable saddle, threadbare blanket, bridle, and saddlebags. He pressed his hand against them. Empty. Right now, he didn't have time to search for food or anything more to put in them. He needed a slicker and a change of clothing.

Most of all he needed to leave. Now.

Picking a decent-looking mare from the corral took only a few seconds. The one who trotted over to him was the one he stole. Less than a minute later, saddle and bridle hastily put on, he rode out.

As he came out on Rusk Street, he caught sight of a small posse galloping in his direction. He couldn't make out the riders' faces, but they all wore black coats that might as well have been a uniform. Putting his heels to his horse's flanks, he galloped away, cut behind the Texas Wagon Yard's buildings, and then faced a dilemma. Going south took him past the railroad and onto the prairie.

The flat, barren prairie where he could be seen riding for miles.

Mac rode back past Houston Street and immediately dismounted, leading his horse to the side of the Comique Saloon. He had to vanish, and losing himself among the late night, or early morning now, imbibers was the best way to do it. The wagon yard owner would be hard-pressed to identify which horse was missing from a corral with a couple dozen animals in it. Mac cursed himself for not leaving the gate open so all the horses escaped.

"Confusion to my enemies," he muttered. Two quick turns of the bridle through an iron ring secured his mount. He circled the building and started to go into the saloon.

"Door's locked," came the warning from a man sitting in a chair on the far side of the door, rocked back on the chair's hind legs. He had his hat pulled down to shield his eyes from the rising sun.

"Do tell." Mac nervously looked around, expecting to see the posse on his trail closing in. He took the chair next to the man, duplicated his pose, and pulled his hat down, more to hide his face than to keep the sunlight from blinding him. "When do they open?"

"John Leer's got quite a place here. But he don't keep real hours. It's open when it's needed most. Otherwise, he closes up."

"Catches some shut-eye?"

The man laughed.

"Hardly. He's got a half dozen floozies in as many bawdy houses, or so the rumor goes. Servicing all of them takes up his spare time."

"You figuring on waiting long for him to get back?"

The man pushed his hat back and looked over at

Mac. He spat on the boardwalk, repositioned himself precariously in the chair, and crossed his arms over his chest before answering.

"Depends. I'm hunting for cowboys. The boss man sends me out to recruit for a drive. I come here to find who's drunkest. They're usually the most likely to agree to the lousy wages and a trip long enough to guarantee saddle sores on your butt."

"You might come here and make such an appealing pitch, but I suspect you offer top dollar." Mac tensed when a rider galloped past. The man wore a plaid shirt and jeans. He relaxed. Not a bounty hunter.

"You're the type I'm looking for. Real smart fellow, you are. My trail boss wouldn't want a drunk working for him, and the boss man was a teetotaler. His wife's one of them temperance women. More 'n that, she's one of them suffer-ay-jets, they call 'em. Can't say I cotton much to going without a snort now and then, and giving women the vote like up in Wyoming's just wrong but—"

"But out on the trail nobody drinks. The cook keeps the whiskey, for medicinal purposes only."

"You been on a drive?"

"Along the Shawnee Trail." Mac's mind raced. Losing himself among a new crew driving cattle would solve most of his problems.

"That's not the way the Circle Arrow herd's headed. We're pushing west along the Goodnight-Loving Trail."

"Don't know it," Mac admitted.

"Don't matter. Mister Flowers has been along it enough times that he can ride it blindfolded."

"Flowers?"

"Hiram Flowers, the best damned trail boss in Texas. Or so I'm told, since I've only worked for a half dozen in my day." The man rocked forward and thrust out his hand. "My name's Cletus Grant. I do the chores Mister Flowers don't like."

"Finding trail hands is one of them?" Mac asked as he clasped the man's hand.

"He doesn't stray far from the Circle Arrow."

"What's that mean?" Mac shifted so his hand rested on his gun when another rider came down the street. He went cold inside when he remembered he hadn't reloaded. Truth to tell, all his spare ammunition was in his saddlebags, on his horse left somewhere behind another saloon in Hell's Half Acre.

When the rider rode on after seeing the Comique was shuttered, Mac tried to mask his move by shifting in the chair. He almost toppled over.

He covered by asking, "You said the Circle Arrow owner was a teetotaler. He fall off the wagon?"

"His missus wouldn't ever allow that, no, sir. He upped and died six months back, in spite of his missus telling him not to catch that fever. Old Zeke Sullivan should have listened that time. About the only time he didn't do as she told him." Cletus spat again, wiped his mouth, and asked, "You looking for a job?"

"I'm a piss-poor cowboy, but there's no better chuckwagon cook in all of Texas. Or so I'm told, since I've only worked for the Rolling J in my day."

Cletus Grant's expression turned blank for a moment, then he laughed.

"You got a sharp wit about you, son. I don't know that Mister Flowers is looking for a cook, but he does need trail hands. Why don't me and you mosey on out to the Circle Arrow and palaver a mite about the chance you'd ride with us to Santa Fe?"

"That where the herd's destined?"

"Might be all the way to Denver. It depends on what the market's like over in New Mexico Territory."

"That's fair enough. I might be willing to go all the way to Denver since I've never been there but heard good things about the town."

Cletus spat and shook his head sadly.

"Too damn many miners there looking to get rich by pulling skull-sized gold nuggets out the hills. The real money comes in selling them picks, shovels . . . and beeves."

"Which is what the Circle Arrow intends," Mac said. "That suits me." He thrust out his hand for another shake to seal the deal, but Cletus held back this time.

"I can't hire you. Mister Flowers is the one what has to do that." The man looked up and down the street, then rocked forward so all four legs hit the boardwalk. One was an inch shy of keeping the chair level. When Cletus stood, his limp matched the uneven chair. He leaned heavily on his right leg. "Let's get on out to the ranch so's he can talk with you. I don't see much in the way of promising recruits."

Mac mounted and trotted alongside Cletus. The man's horse was a fine-looking gelding, well kept and eager to run. From the way the horse under him responded, Mac thought it would die within a mile, trying to keep pace.

"Yup," Cletus said, noticing Mac's interest. "The Circle Arrow has the best damned horses. Mister Flowers says it pays off in the long run having the best. We don't lose as many cattle—or drovers."

"That's good counsel. There're too many ways of dying on the trail without worrying about your horse dying under you." Mac thought a moment, then asked, "What's the trail like? The Goodnight-Loving?"

"The parts that don't kill you will make you wish you were dead. Drought and desert, Injuns and horse thieves, disease and despair."

"But the pay's good," Mac said, knowing the man tested him. "And if I'm cooking, the food will be even better."

"You got a wit about you, son. Let's hope it's not just half a one." Cletus picked up the gait, forcing Mac to bring his horse to a canter.

As he did so, he looked behind and saw two of the black-coated riders slowly making their way down the street. One pointed in Mac's direction but the other shook his head and sent them down a cross street. Being with Cletus Grant might just have saved him. The bounty hunters thought he was alone. That had to be the answer to them not coming to question them about one of their gang getting shot down.

The thought made Mac touch his S&W again. Empty. He kept reminding himself of that. The saddle sheath lacked a rifle, too. If they caught up and a fight ensued, and he couldn't bite them, he was out of luck.

"You got a curious grin on your face," Cletus said. "What's so funny?"

"Drought and desert, Indians and—"

"I get the drift. And I wasn't joking about them. The trail's decent enough, but the dangers are real."

"Nothing like what I'm leaving behind," Mac said. That got a frown from Cletus, but he didn't press the matter. That suited Mac. He didn't want to lie to the man.

Not yet. Not unless it became necessary to escape the killers Pierre Leclerc had set on his trail.